"YOU TANTALIZE ME," he said, very low, only sheer willpower keeping him from gathering her into his arms. "Do I frighten you?"

Unnerved by her exposed feelings, unsettled by the novelty of her sensual vulnerability, Elizabeth didn't answer—and another small silence fell in the candlelit tower room.

"Talk to me," he murmured, afraid of the violence of his feelings.

"You don't frighten me ... I frighten myself," she finally whispered, reaching out for a chair back to steady her trembling. She no longer questioned the extent of his allure, for no man had ever made her tremble merely at the sight of him.

And she should know, after the dozens of candidates her father had paraded before her.

She never trembled. Never.

And her heart never pounded like this.

And the heat warming her face matched another heat, a pulsing ache, deep in the pit of her stomach.

Johnnie Carre was the cause of that heat. Maybe he was the answer to her need. . . .

BANTAM BOOKS BY SUSAN JOHNSON

BRAZEN
LOVE STORM
PURE SIN
SEIZED BY LOVE
BLAZE
SILVER FLAME
FORBIDDEN
SINFUL
OUTLAW
SWEET LOVE, SURVIVE
TABOO
A TOUCH OF SIN

OUTLAW

Susan Johnson

BANTAM BOOKS

NEW YORK TORONTO LONDON SYDNEY AUCKLAND

OUTLAW

A Bantam Book / November 1993

ISBN 0-553-29955-7

Published simultaneously in the United States and Canada

Bantam Books are published by Bantam Books, a division of Random House,
Inc. Its trademark, consisting of the words "Bantam Books" and the portrayal of
a rooster, is Registered in U.S. Patent and Trademark Office and in other
countries. Marca Registrada. Bantam Books, 1540 Broadway, New York, New
York 10036.

CHAPTER 1

Goldiehouse, Ravensby, Scotland
March 1704

"Are you sleeping?"

"Ummmm ..." Johnnie Carre surfaced from a light doze, the soft sound of the woman's voice secondary to the carnal pleasure he was suddenly feeling. It took a moment more to definitively focus his senses: A warm tongue was leaving a cool path. . . .

He shifted his powerful body slightly, the sensation exquisite. A faint smile lifted the corners of his mouth in pleasurable remembrance of the woman's special skills, and a second later his vivid blue eyes opened. Reaching down, his fingers lazily slid through honey-colored silken curls, and he murmured, his deep voice still drowsy, "Don't you ever sleep?"

He'd met Mary Holm two days ago in Kelso at a country inn where her acrobatic troupe was staying. She'd caught his eyes deliberately and then came up to him where he stood watching his men throwing dice.

"I'm Mary," she'd said, looking up at the tall, dark-haired Border Lord with an open invitation in her eyes.

And after a long afternoon of sampling Wat Harden's special reserve French brandy, he let his gaze drift downward briefly to the luscious swell of her bosom before returning to her sweetly smiling face, and he'd simply said, "I'm on my way home. Are you hungry?"

They'd hardly been out of bed since Tuesday.

"Now, if we weren't leaving for Berwick on Friday, darling Johnnie," the pretty young woman replied, lifting her head to smile at the Laird of Ravensby with cheerful impudence, "I might be inclined to sleep. But who knows when I'll have such a bonny stud to entertain me again?"

He was fully awake now, and his own grin matched hers. "In that case I'll try to last till Friday."

"You're doing gracious fine," she purred, and with a wink, resumed her pleasuring.

On the muddy forest road south of Goldiehouse that evening, an exhausted rider whipped his lathered horse to more speed, every minute of delay terrible in its consequences. Like all Borderers, he knew the countryside even at night with the moon behind more threatening rain clouds. Now if his mount would just hold out. . . . He swore under his breath as the black stallion faltered in the rough going and, taking pity on his Laird's best bloodstock, eased the pace. But even as he drew the horse to a trot, he debated whether his chieftain would rather he ride the black barb to death, so urgent was his message.

"Come sit on me," Johnnie softly said, touching Mary's chin with a finger. "I like the feel of you. . . ."

Rising in a lithe movement, her slender body, supple, feline, she stroked his splendid arousal and answered, "And I adore the feel of you, my darling Laird."

She grinned as she moved over him. "How pleasant to discover all the stories are true."

"You're testing my stamina, pet," Johnnie murmured, aware of the stories but disinclined to discuss his reputation as stud to the Middle Marches. "But I'm not complaining," he added with a small smile, gently placing his palms on her hips as she slid down his erection, his eyes closing against the delicious friction. "God, you're tight. . . ."

Mary's own blue eyes were half-closed, as profligate sensation flooded her mind. "And you're enormous. . . ." she whispered into the firelit room, feeling his hard, rigid length stretch her. Her back arched against the delirium. "You're my lovely rutting stallion," she breathed, the exquisite feel of Johnnie Carre filling her.

The bedchamber was utterly silent for a time, the small sounds of the crackling fire distinct in the hushed, charged atmosphere. She moved down, he arched up. And they both caught their breath for that moment of indelible glory. Then she'd glide upward again with riveting slowness. And they'd both breathe again.

It was a languorous rhythm, not impatient after two wanton days in bed but feverishly acute after forty-eight hours of sexual excess. Extravagant, luxurious feeling reigned. No distractions tempered the irrepressible passion.

And then, overzealous once, Johnnie penetrated too deeply, and she cried out. Instantly remorseful, he touched her rosy cheek, his fingers as gentle as his voice. "I'm sorry," he whispered. "Am I hurting you?"

It took her a shuddering moment to open her eyes and a moment more to answer. "It's fine," she ambiguously replied, her words uttered with a soft, breathy sigh.

He understood what she meant; he was an experienced man. But he cautioned himself to more control. She was small and fragile, and it was possible to do damage.

The fatigued horseman spurred the black stallion up the last incline to Goldiehouse, no longer concerned with his mount's failing strength. Only a few hundred yards remained of his breakneck ride. Galloping through the courtyard gate, he shouted to rouse the household, the lantern-lit court empty. Throwing himself off the winded barb, he collapsed on the courtyard flags, damp and puddle-strewn from days of rain, just as the studded door to the old keep burst open. With drawn swords three clansmen bolted through the massive doorway, their jackboots like mallets on the cobblestones. Spread-eagle like a dead man on the wet ground, the messenger spoke, breathless, panting.

And they stopped cold when they heard his words.

Johnnie was unaware of the tumult, his private quarters of the last few days distant by his choice from the daily bustle. His attention at the moment was totally absorbed, his climax imminent.

Mary Holm's arms were laced tightly around his neck, her breasts warm and soft against his chest, her sleek rhythm increasing in intensity. Her body was damp with sweat; his own temperature feverish; he could feel the heat of his arousal as if a tropical sun had invaded the massive stone walls and raftered ceiling of the room. Her agitated breathing warmed his neck; his strong fingers possessively captured her narrow waist, exerting a minute pressure at times that caused small, breath-held pauses while they both gathered new air into their lungs.

"I'm dying," she breathed.

He shook his head, a small movement of negation, all he was capable of at the moment. Never, he thought, and if he'd had the capacity, he'd have smiled.

Reaching up suddenly, she twisted her fingers into his unruly black hair, jerked his face downward, and kissed him, devoured him, frantically ate at his mouth, greedy for the feel and taste of him everywhere.

He felt her begin to quiver, his own release racing downward.

•   •   •

Two Carre clansmen raced through the first-floor corridors, took the wide, shallow steps three at a time to the second floor, and ran full out to the narrow staircase at the back of the west wing, taking the corners in flying swoops. They sprinted up the narrow circular stairwell of the original tower[1], their hearts beating a frantic tattoo. Johnnie had left orders that he not be disturbed, but neither questioned the need to disobey. In the medieval portion of Goldiehouse the ceilings were low, the hallways narrow, built for defense centuries ago. Only one man could comfortably navigate the corridors. One racing after the other, they dashed toward the small room at the end of the passage.

Lord, she was hot . . . on fire, Johnnie reflected as he exploded in orgasm, agonizing bliss convulsing his senses, the world diminished for brief seconds to one small woman in his arms and incredible sensation.

She was amazing.

Which exact thought was passing through Mary Holm's mind as she lay overcome, panting, Johnnie Carre living up to his amorous fame. He was truly amazing . . . again.

She licked him like a contented cat, her warm tongue tracing a slow path across his muscled shoulder. She felt him tense minutely. His head lifted suddenly, and a second later he shifted her in his arms, unconsciously readying himself.

And then he heard it clearly. The faint pattern of running feet. When he'd made it clear his privacy was sacrosanct.

He lifted her from him in a flash of movement, set her against the pillows with a curious tenderness considering his blurring speed, and gallantly threw the embroidered sheet over her just as the door burst open.

He'd only half turned from her, his peripheral vision searching out the intruders, when the brutal exclamation struck him like a blow.

"They've taken Robbie!"

There was no need to define who "they" were. The same enemy had confronted the Roxburgh Carres for a thousand years.

He leaped from the bed, reaching for his weapons left conveniently on the bedpost. The Borders had been Scotland's battleground since the dim dawn of history; a man's dirk and sword never left his side.

His men swiftly related the facts of his brother's abduction as Johnnie gathered his clothes, the woman forgotten. His questions were harsh staccato queries, his dark brows drawn together in a scowl at the answers. His leather breeches were on in seconds, his boots jerked on next, his shirt thrown over his shoulders followed by his leather jack. Handing his sword belt to a clansman to carry, he strode from the room, closing his shirt, tucking it into his leather breeches with rough thrusts.

Halfway down the second-floor corridor he remembered Mary Holm. "See that the girl is sent back to Kelso with an escort," he curtly said, buckling his jack shut, reaching out for his sword baldric. Taking the belt from his lieutenant, he slipped it over his shoulder. "Give her a purse and my thanks. Are the horses saddled?"

At a nod he adjusted the dirk at his waist, pulled his sword slightly out of its scabbard to test its feel, jammed it back in, and, in a voice harsh with hatred, growled, "Damned Godfrey! Damned English! They're fucking vermin."

Descending the broad balustraded stairway in long, racing leaps, he broke into a run immediately he reached the main floor. "How long ago was it?" he asked again of the man keeping pace with him.

His muttered curse at the unpalatable reply reflected everyone's unease.

CHAPTER 2

Five hours later, shaking his wet head to check the water dripping into his eyes, Johnnie Carre walked into his weapons room. Weary and frustrated, he unslung his sword belt, hung it on the wall rack, and began pacing.

His rain-soaked lieutenants followed him in, disposed of their weapons, and sank exhausted onto the heavy wooden benches and chairs. No one spoke, their chieftain's exasperation echoing in their own minds. Five hours in the saddle, riding hard in despicable weather, and they'd been too late to overtake the English who'd abducted the Laird of Ravensby's young brother. Riding two hours behind, they knew their chances had been slim at best—only the bad weather was in their favor. But the English troop had reached Harbottle ahead of them, and in all likelihood Robbie Carre was prisoner now in Harbottle Castle.

"If Godfrey harms a hair on Robbie's head, I'll see him on his way to hell," Johnnie Carre muttered, the low sound of his voice clear and distinct in the utter silence of the castle arsenal room, the small metallic jingle of his spurs counterpoint to his threat.

Reaching the limits of the large room, the tall, powerful warlord of striking presence swung around to retrace his stalking passage across the flagstone floor, a shimmering trajectory of water droplets from his drenched leather jack and plaid spraying out behind him. "Bloody damned English!" Rage and disgust pervaded his tone. "They're looking for an excuse to take a Scotsman!" Last year's Scottish Parliament had been rabidly anti-English, and with the war on the Continent and the controversy over Succession, for the first time in a century Scotland's demand for independence had the hope of success.[2] Tempers were flaring on both sides of the border.

The flames of the candles in the heavy silver branches on the tables trembled before his swift movement. The light danced fitfully, illuminating in flickering chiaroscuro the harsh modeling of his face, the arresting beauty of his stark features.

"Can we get Robbie out?" Underlaid with weariness, the voice of one of his young clansmen uttered everyone's concern. Harbottle Castle, England's defensive fort on the Middle Marches, was heavily garrisoned; recently England had scrambled to defend her northern border against Scotland's volatile bid for independence.

His mind on the frustration of a pursuit begun too late . . . on the worrisome plight of his young brother, John Carre didn't answer. And for a moment it seemed as though he hadn't heard. But when the clansman resting his head against the carved chair back bearing the coat of arms of the Earls of Graden began to repeat his question, the Laird of Ravensby softly said, "No, not if he's in Harbottle."

And then, as if the unpalatable thought had reined him in, the young Laird stopped before one of the neoclassic windows his father had added to the fortified castle when he'd returned from Ferrara with the Douglas in '79.

A sudden hush descended on the room at his response. The weapons hung on the wall racks, the targes, basket-hilted swords, the muskets and pistols, seemed to gleam in contradiction, as if mocking his assertion.

Slashing rain beat at the windows, pelted by violent winds driving down from the north, the wail and howl like Valkyrie cries. Outside the night was pitch-black, wet as Neptune's kingdom, cold, stormy, fog-shrouded, impossible for accurate tracking.

Just as Harbottle Castle was impossible to infiltrate, the Laird of Ravensby pragmatically acknowledged. With the hostilities over and the Act of Security threatening to bring England and Scotland to war, the English had recently increased the castle garrison by an extra company of dragoons. Which meant the means to Robbie's freedom would have to take some form other than a frontal assault.

John Carre, Laird of Ravensby, chief of the Roxburgh Carres, Eleventh Earl of Graden, slowly turned to face his friends and kinsmen, his movement restrained like his voice once again, his temper held in check, his mind already sorting through the available options.

"How many horses did we lose?" At word of Robbie's abduction they'd immediately set out in pursuit, despite a week of rain, despite the late hour, despite the burns in flood-tide.

"Eight."

"Permanently?"

"Red Rowan should know by morning. The Neapolitan barb may be one of the badly crippled ones."

"In that case we'll have to get something more, then ... in addition to Robbie in exchange," the Earl said, his tone businesslike, direct. "Assess the damage in the morning and give me an accounting." The word "exchange" set him thinking, and a series of speculative possibilities began to unfold in his mind.

"And what, Johnnie, would you be thinking to exchange of sufficient interest to bring Lord Godfrey to the bargaining table?" The trooper asking the question had one brow lifted in whimsical inquiry.

"It may not come to that," the young chieftain of the Roxburgh Carres answered with the smallest hint of drollery in his voice. The age-old border-raiding was part

game, part business, part drama—at least for the Scots
Borderers; the English regarded everything in life with
more seriousness—but *always* stimulating. "First we'll
send the Queen's illustrious Warden a polite request for
Robbie's release." He was anticipating the necessary
steps already, a new assurance in his mood.

"And when that doesn't bring your brother his
freedom . . ." one of his lieutenants sardonically drawled.

"*Then,*" the dark-haired Laird of Ravensby softly
answered, looking tranquil, untroubled, his abstract sup-
positions having crystallized into a plan, "we'll offer him
something he prizes."

"Which is?" Adam Carre spoke for all of them. Every man's eyes were trained on their tall, rangy Laird
dressed like a freebooter: the shoulder armor on his
leather jack gleaming in the candlelight; two pistols still
shoved under his wide leather belt; an ivory-handled dirk
swinging from a scabbard at his hip; his long black hair
wet because he refused to wear headgear; his green-and-
brown hunting plaid—the color of concealment—draped
over one shoulder; his leather breeches and spurred riding boots dull earth brown like the landscape.

Bred up to combat on the Borders, where one
didn't travel abroad without an escort, where protection
money—forbearance money—had been a tradition in the
past, where the powerful clans could still muster two
thousand horse in a matter of hours, where a glorious,
rash, and hazardous young man could do anything . . .
Johnnie Carre pleasantly said, "I hear the English Warden holds his daughter in high regard now that she's nabob wealthy. With old Hotchane Graham dead and
Godfrey's daughter a widow, a very *rich* young widow . . .
gossip has it Lord Godfrey's planning on making another
fine match for her." A faint smile spread across Johnnie
Carre's finely sculpted mouth.

"She's heavily guarded," several of his men instantly replied, their shock and astonishment vivid, like
the striking platinum of Elizabeth Godfrey's hair. Everyone on the Borders knew how rough Harbottle was when
the Redesdale men came to town, how Harold Godfrey,
the Earl of Brusisson, protected his marketable daughter.

No longer young at twenty-four, she would still bring a spectacular dowry as prize to a second marriage. And even if she were barren, which possibility existed, since her marriage of eight years had resulted in no children, her lavish fortune would serve to mitigate that serious failing.

"Guarded she may be, but not flung into a dungeon in Harbottle Castle, garrisoned with two companies of dragoons," the young Laird replied, beginning to strip off his sodden green leather gloves, his mood lightened now that a reasonable means for his brother's release had come to him. "So I think," he said with a dazzling smile, "we can begin to plan Robbie's coming-home party."

"Send the letter first," his practical cousin Kinmont said, understanding that flaring light of excitement in Johnnie's eyes. "Time enough for your notions of fun later."

"Of course." The young Earl's expression took on an angelic cast; his voice purred like velvet. "We'll write something charming and nice to the faithless rogue ... with not a mention Robbie was unlawfully taken."

Over the decades since England and Scotland had been joined in 1603, the semblance of peace in the Borders had been accomplished in the early years by mass deportations of renegade clans and septs, by wholesale slaughter and massacre by superior English forces. Later more civilized methods had maintained the peace; English peerages and government pensions were popular methods of control, or, those failing, the occasional stay in the Tower of London or the Tolbooth in Edinburgh was effective. Or banishment, exile, or beheading for those most recalcitrant. But certainly in Robbie's case, regardless of the war fever, there were no legitimate grounds for his capture.

"Considering the nature of the man serving the English Queen," John Carre softly went on, "and the particular style of Godfrey's sense of honor, *and* old Hotchane's fondness for his wife, estimated to be in the neighborhood of sixty thousand English pounds"—the Laird of Ravensby's mouth twitched into a grin—"I personally feel having Elizabeth Godfrey Graham for a short visit would not only be a fair quid pro quo in terms of Robbie's abduction, but perhaps a financially sound proposition as well. Any questions?"

"When do we leave?" a hotspur young clansman cheerfully inquired.

"First Kinmont will send a courteous request for Robbie's release. Godfrey should have that by tomorrow afternoon. A day or two for his reply—three days at the outside for delaying procedures ... which I anticipate." The Earl slapped his gloves against his palm with a smile, as if he were recounting nothing more untoward than a list of kitchen victuals. "Then two or three more days to reconnoiter the *Dowager*"—he emphasized the unsuitable word—"Lady Graham's daily schedule." Throwing the beautifully embroidered green gloves on a nearby table, he reached for the pistols at his waist. Pulling them free, he balanced them for a moment in his hands, as if gauging the perfect timing of the Lady's coming abduction, then carefully set them down next to his gloves. "In the meantime," he cheerfully said, "I'll have the East Tower room fit up for the darling Elizabeth. . . ."

His lieutenants were smiling now, too, even Kinmont, who was Johnnie's voice of reason. "You'll make a shekel or two on Lord Godfrey's arrogance," said Kinmont Carre, a businessman at heart, like so many of the Borderers. Raiding was an enterprise for profit, although its danger and daring offered excitement along with the gains.

"Would you like to negotiate that for me?" Johnnie mildly said, aware of his cousin's special joy in acquisition. "Beginning with the obliging letter to that scoundrel Godfrey?"

"With pleasure."

"In that case the rest of us are free to sample the new Rhenish wines delivered from Berwick yesterday."

But despite the casualness with which the Earl of Graden overtly dealt with his brother's abduction, a very real apprehension gripped him. Harold Godfrey was a blackguard and a knave, and the dungeons of Harbottle Castle had been the cause of many a Scots death. Time was at a premium; he wouldn't have Robbie lying in that hellhole more than a week.

So while he joined his men in their drinking revels that evening, he found himself remarkably sober as he entered his bedchamber. And further sobered at the sight of Janet Lindsay in his bed. As Laird of Ravensby and Earl of Graden, he attracted women with his title alone, but had he been dispossessed of a title, his bonny looks would have served him equally well.

"Is Jamie gone south again?" he casually remarked, softly closing the door behind him. His neighbor's wife was one of several local women who entertained him. And while he never sought them out, he didn't refuse them either. But tonight, with Robbie sleeping in a dungeon pit under Harbottle Castle, he found he didn't have the stomach for pleasure.

"He's gone for a fortnight, darling," replied Janet Lindsay, a Countess by birth and marriage and very used to doing as she pleased.

"You heard they took Robbie today. From our side, too . . . and with no provocation." He hadn't moved from the door.

She nodded, her hair black as midnight, shining in the candlelight. "It's the war fever. I thought you might be in need of . . . consolation."

He refused her gently, politely, standing very still . . . far away from the bed.

But she hadn't ridden four miles through the storm to be turned away. Raised in a wealthy, privileged household, unfamiliar with refusals, she ignored Johnnie's words as though they'd been directed at someone else. Pushing the green coverlet aside, she rose from the bed in all the fulsome bloom of her womanly beauty and slowly walked nude, rose-petal pink and luscious, across the large, firelit bedchamber to encourage her suit at close range.

Johnnie Carre found his appetites disinclined to fine nuances of principle at close range, and he drew in a steadying breath.

"Robbie would never turn me away," Janet purred, reaching up to brush a kiss over the dark stubble shadowing Johnnie's jaw, pressing her opulent breasts into the leather jack he still wore, leaning her weight into him so he was softly forced back against the door.

She was right, he knew, which didn't help his battle with principle. At eighteen Robbie was unbridled, freely dispensing his handsome favors on the female populace north and south of the border.

"I'm tired," the Laird of Ravensby said in honesty, two days of little sleep and five hours in the saddle exhausting even his vitality. Perhaps sincere fatigue might be excuse enough, since Robbie's plight had failed to impede her interest.

"You needn't move at all, darling," the Countess murmured, tracing a finger lightly over the roughness of his unshaven face. "Simply lie there, and I'll ride *you*."

He tried not to respond, but his body reacted automatically to her husky suggestion; she was warm and inviting, her words instant trigger to his senses, her small hand drifting down the smooth leather of his jack, over the ornate silver buckle of his belt, then lower to rest provocatively on the sleek leather over his growing erection.

"See . . ." she murmured, rising on tiptoes to nibble at his bottom lip, "you're not *too* tired. . . ."

The scent of her drifted into his nostrils, the heady fragrance of exotic jasmine familiar, insinuating, reminiscent of other nights with his neighbor's wife.

"I adore you in your raiding garb." Her whisper warmed his face as she clung to his tall, leather-clad body, the metal plate on his jack leaving marks on her pliant flesh. "Johnnie Carre as war chieftain . . ."

He shook his head faintly in denial of her melodramatic image. A practical man at heart, he did what he had to do—what his father and grandfather and forebears before him had done to maintain their possessions.

"Did you kill any English tonight?" Janet Lindsay breathed, her wet pink tongue licking a leisurely path up his tanned corded neck, his damp clothing cool to her heated body. Johnnie Carre's exploits in border-raiding were an aphrodisiac . . . like his large, muscled body and haunting dark beauty. Like his stamina and teasing playfulness in bed.

"Jesus, Janet." And he started pulling away.

"You can't say no." Her arms tightened on his broad shoulders. "I won't let you." Her tongue reached his chin. "And Robbie won't mind . . . so kiss me, and I promise you won't regret it. . . ."

Pulling his head down, she kissed him instead. But he found he didn't mind. Or not enough to be discourteous. And in the end he didn't regret it, either, for she was a woman of remarkable virtuosity.

But sometime later when his neighbor's wife fell asleep, he left her, his thoughts consumed with his brother's plight. In the throes of passion one could forget for those brief seconds when nothing mattered but release. And after, out of politesse, he stayed with Janet because where he slept wouldn't change Robbie's status or bring him out tonight.

Throwing on a quilted robe he'd bought in Macao, a Japanese silk that was warmer than fur, he left his bedchamber and moved down the dimly lit corridor to his map room, where he spent the next hours assessing the best routes between Ravensby and Harbottle. Looking for those least populated on the English side—with the most gentle ascent into the hills and the widest pass over the Cheviots.

Taking into account every possibility of pursuit on the homeward journey.

CHAPTER 3

The next morning, under a flag of truce, the letter of courtesy and restraint was delivered to Lord Godfrey.

Kinmont politely pointed out that by seizing Robbie Carre, Lord Godfrey had acted unlawfully, and asked that the young brother of the Earl of Graden be immediately returned in redress of the wrong.

Lord Godfrey by his answer excused himself and referred the matter to the Queen's Deputy Chancellor, Lord Scroope, who was at the time unavailable at his house in the country.

Lord Scroope was duly written to. Kinmont's second letter suggested the prisoner Robbie Carre be set at liberty without condition or bond, seeing as he had been unlawfully taken.

Lord Scroope answered he could do nothing without the consent of Queen Anne and her council.

Understanding these replies were no more than delaying tactics, the Laird of Ravensby had already set his plans *en train*.

On the day the first letter was delivered to Lord

Godfrey, seven Ravensby men entered Harbottle as scouts. A day later a cryptic message made its way to Robbie via an inn servant and prison guard—both fifty pounds richer for their mission.

A trade in progress ...

was all it said, but those few words brought a smile to the face of the Laird's young brother and made his *durance vile*—his imprisonment—more bearable.

Four days passed, with messengers riding out for the Laird of Ravensby as far south as Durham, where Lord Scroope was enjoying his daffodils at his country home, Bishopgate.

Four days passed during which Ravensby scouts gathered the necessary information on Elizabeth Graham's daily schedule.

Four days passed in a flurry of preparation for the abduction of Robbie Carre's reciprocal exchange.

And on an unseasonably warm Friday in March, Johnnie Carre entered Harbottle in the guise of an itinerant preacher, flanked by two clerical minions, all three men bristling with weapons beneath the concealing volume of their long black robes.

They rode slowly through the village toward the castle, stopping at Peartree's Inn to stable their mounts and bespeak a sleeping room. By noon they'd eaten dinner in their private parlor, drunk two bottles of Mr. Peartree's best hock, and set out with the proprietor's excellent directions to call on Dame Rosbery, who dispensed culture and learning to the genteel young ladies of the community.

Dame Rosbery, at one time governess to Lady Graham, had been subsidized sufficiently by her former charge to allow her to establish her own school in Harbottle. And the Dowager Lady Graham, the Ravensby scouts discovered, paid a call on Miss Rosbery at two o'clock each afternoon.

"I'm *going*, Father, with or without a guard," Elizabeth Graham insisted, exasperation in her voice, "and if you don't muster an escort posthaste, I'll leave without one. Although why a guard is required in a burgh of this size with two companies of troops garrisoned in the castle is beyond me. Have I ever been harmed or even *accosted*? Good *God*, Father, everyone knows who I am—everyone knows you're Warden here," she finished in a breathless rush, her temper up at her father's unwanted restraints. After eight years of marriage to a man who, despite his myriad faults, at least had allowed her a modicum of freedom, she wasn't about to re-establish herself as a submissive daughter.

"Why do you have to go to Rosbery's every day?" her father hotly inquired, his own temper barely leashed, finding his daughter since her return to Harbottle impossibly arrogant.

"Why not, pray tell? Is there something profoundly important keeping me in this dank, dull, boring castle? Another suitor, perhaps, you plan on parading before me at dinner?"

With every intention of ultimately controlling her fortune if not her person, Lord Godfrey snapped, "You should be married again."

"We disagree," his daughter acerbically replied. "And unless the men you gather to your table have more to recommend them than land grants in Northumbria adjacent to yours, I won't change my mind."

"Perhaps I could make you change your mind," her father suggested unkindly, familiar with absolute power, but unfamiliar with his newly returned daughter, who was no longer a docile sixteen-year-old.

"Not on God's green earth, Father," Elizabeth Godfrey Graham said, each word emphatically pronounced, as if she were practicing an exercise in diction. "Is that plain enough?" Her brows rose over green eyes hot with temper. "My funds are liquid, Father, which means your control over them doesn't exist. The Graham curate keeps my money, and he's guarded by a band of Redesdale men. That should stop even you—which I think was Hotchane's intent." She half turned away from his desk, where she'd been confronting her father, then turned back to add in a voice less combative, "I'm here to visit Rosie and help at her school for a time." She disliked this continuing argument; she disliked having to constantly fight for authority over her life. "Kindly resist your urge to interfere."

And with a scowl drawing his beetled brows together over his chill grey eyes, Lord Godfrey, an Earl, an English Warden, and a man of consequence and power watched as his daughter turned her back on him and left his office.

"Wharton!" His shout could be heard out in the courtyard. "Get me a guard!"

So a short time later, ignoring her guard, Elizabeth Graham left the castle gate and, carefully descending the steep cobbled incline down to the village, reached the bustling highway serving as Harbottle's main thoroughfare.

Her progress was interrupted often by greetings from shopkeepers and villagers; she'd grown up in Harbottle and knew everyone. Stopping for a moment before the church, she admired the stained-glass window depicting Saint George and the Dragon, a favorite of hers since childhood. The small medieval structure perched on the north side of the road, where the hillside continued to fall away to the valley below, had the unpretentious air of a private chapel. It was Romanesque in style, unornamented save for the small cross over the doorway and the colored windows, and she'd often wondered if the original baron who'd raised both the castle on the hill and this diminutive church had subscribed to the premise that God helped those who helped themselves. The brilliant windows depicted scenes of a distinctly military nature; the golden-haired Saint George, the most romantic figure in the scenes of battle, had been her first hero.

After eight years of marriage to Hotchane, she no longer believed in heroes, although she still enjoyed the vivid beauty of the composition. And she smiled at the maiden being rescued. "Good luck," she murmured under her breath. "He probably sleeps with his boots on."

Continuing her journey toward Rosie's, she shook away the melancholy memory of her marriage. Despite her father's continuing pressure to remarry, she was free now, in charge of her own wealth; the past could be left behind. Taking delight in the spring air fresh with the scent of new green grass, her own life facing a new spring, a new beginning, she thrust aside her niggling unease.

As always, she looked forward with pleasure to visiting with Rosie and her charges. Each afternoon she helped the younger students with their reading, played the harpsichord while the girls sang, and afterward enjoyed a cozy chat with her beloved governess over tea.

Her guards were left at the front door, and Rosie, buxom, huggable, and welcoming, greeted her with a kiss.

"Would you like tea first today?" her old governess inquired, immediately recognizing her former student's suppressed disquiet.

"How can you tell, Rosie?" Elizabeth marveled, her mood considerably lightened since her confrontation with her father.

"He won't give up, you know." Agnes Rosbery had watched with horror when Elizabeth had been married at sixteen to the seventy-year-old Hotchane Graham.

"He'll have to."

"He could find an amiable judge to rule in his favor," Dame Rosbery quietly said, leading Elizabeth down the narrow hallway to the back parlor.

"But my money's hidden."

"And well guarded, I hope," Rosbery cautioned, opening the door into the small room off the garden.

"Moderately," Elizabeth replied, not certain even a troop of lawless Redesdale men would be proof against two companies of dragoons.

"Come sit down," her old governess said in the comforting tone so familiar from her childhood, "and I'll go and have Tattie put on tea for us." Handing her a small volume from a table near the door, she added, "See what you think of Defoe's newest work."

Elizabeth couldn't read, though; her thoughts were too much in disarray, her resistance to her father's plans for her remarriage an ongoing struggle she found upsetting. So when the man stepped through the glass-paneled door half-open to the garden, she was still standing in the middle of the room, exactly where Rosie had left her.

His black robe was stark contrast to the scene outside, where blooming crocuses brightened the small walled garden, but his smile was warm, mitigating the cold black of his attire and his abrupt appearance.

"Good afternoon, Lady Graham," Johnnie said, pale sunshine gleaming off his sleek dark hair, his cultivated bow too much the courtier's for a minister of the church.

"Do I know you?" Perhaps she should have shown fear, but his smile charmed, as did his eyes, and she wondered at such seductive allure in a man of God.

"We haven't met before, I'm sorry to say." His pale blue eyes, cool in color like North Sea ice, seemed somehow incongruously to exude a delicious heat. "And rumor doesn't do you justice, Lady Graham." The Laird of Ravensby moved two paces nearer to better judge the jewel-like quality of Elizabeth Godfrey's brilliant green eyes. "Cat's eyes," he murmured, his voice like velvet, its resonance curling around her like lyrical poetry. And then he grinned.

Sunshine seemed to fill the room, bathing her in warmth, and she wondered briefly if she were having a religious experience, if her tumultuous thoughts had somehow conjured up this glorious image. "Are you a Covenanter?" she quickly asked to steady herself, "a Presbyterian ... a Reformist?" He was dressed in a severe long frock she didn't recognize.

"I am actually ..." he softly said.

And for a moment she thought he was going to name himself one of God's archangels—so radiant and beautiful was his countenance.

". . . the Laird of Ravensby," he quietly finished.

And Elizabeth reflexively sucked in an inhalation of fear. No archangel here, come unbidden to her mind, but the Devil himself, the most celebrated rogue on the Border, where a certain degree of lawlessness was a way of life and personal armies bespoke a man's power.

"We must go," he added while she still reeled at his disclosure. "Come," he said, putting out his hand as if he were asking mildly for a dance.

"No . . ." she whispered, backing away, all the wild and sinister stories of the Black Laird flooding her mind.

"I'm sorry," he apologized, his courtesy astonishing considering his purpose.

And suddenly her will reasserted itself, her momentary shock and paralyzing terror evaporating before the force of her nature. She opened her mouth to scream, but Johnnie Carre was faster, no tyro to reprisal raids, no novice on abductions for negotiated settlements. His hand came up in a flash, stopping her cry.

He had no intention of hurting her.

Even the hand on her mouth was lenient, almost gentle.

Elizabeth Godfrey Graham was only the negotiating hostage necessary for Robbie's release. Beyond that, he had no designs on her. It was moot whether her father prized her person as his daughter's, but there was no doubt in anyone's mind that he valued her fortune.

He would want her back.

Two men materialized when Johnnie issued a soft command, and her hands were swiftly bound, her mouth muffled by a gag. And when the Laird of Ravensby tossed her over his shoulder, her ankles were tied as well.

The small party exited the back parlor and then the garden through a gate in the redbrick wall, at which point she was placed in a burrow readied for her in a small covered cart piled high with hay. All three men discarded their black robes, becoming instantly ragged sheepherders.

Crawling into the narrow cart, Johnnie Carre compressed his large frame into the space available, murmuring as his body touched hers, "I won't hurt you."

Despite his words, she attempted to move away, the extent of her danger ominously real.

"Because of the hay," he said next, placing a fine silk shawl over her face, and after that she could no longer see, although she felt the solidness of his body against hers. And she smelled the sweet scent of clover, timothy, and rye grass above her as the contents of the cart were piled over them in concealment.

Adam and Kinmont led the horse-drawn cart through the village as swiftly as they could without drawing notice. And once they were a suitable distance away, the cart was discarded in a copse of alder near a stream where a small band of men leading horses awaited them.

Elizabeth rode then as they galloped north, settled across the Laird's muscular thighs, the saddle pommel brushing her hip, her hands and feet still tied, her gag still in place.

Johnnie Carre could see the fire in her eyes and, a man of experience, he preferred not listening to her outrage.

An escort of two hundred Carre men fell in with them short miles away, at the dale below Allenton, and from that point every man's countenance was wreathed in smiles. Two hundred Carres could fight their way through anything they met, take on any troop in pursuit. They were in high spirits.

"My brother's in Harbottle Castle dungeon," Johnnie said to Elizabeth shortly after they entered the ascending pass through the Cheviot Hills, no pursuers yet visible. Scotland lay on the other side; they would shortly be safe, and he wanted her to know the price of her freedom. "If you won't blister my ears, I'll free your mouth."

She nodded, and he untied the white linen handkerchief.

"Well, Johnnie Carre," she said, businesslike and cool, understanding now why she'd been taken, her fear allayed by her knowledge of the machinations of border politics, "I expect your brother will be home in Ravensby soon. My father wants my money."

"I know." He grinned, his eyes slowly traveling down her body before returning to her face. "And a shame, too, Robbie's caught, for I wouldn't mind keeping you myself."

His smile infectious, she grinned back, recalling the stories beyond the Laird of Ravensby's border raids, the ones detailing his amorous exploits.

"Perhaps I'm rich enough to afford you both." She surveyed him as slowly as he had her. "Although I'm not at the moment in the market for someone to . . . keep me. Remember that," she added in an altogether different tone, a warning that he duly noted. "But if I were," she went on, the warmth returned to her voice, her green eyes amused, "I'd *certainly* consider you."

It stopped him for a moment, the fact that she showed no fear, the additional fact that she propositioned as a man might. And Godfrey's daughter took on an instant fascination. While he'd previously harbored no designs on her except for her value in Robbie's release, he found himself suddenly aware of the soft warmth of her bottom bouncing gently on his thighs as they rode hard for the border.

As instantly, he reminded himself Robbie's cause came first, and he forcefully set his thoughts into more prudent channels. He couldn't afford to jeopardize the negotiations; Elizabeth Graham was not to be touched.

He had all the women he needed, in any event.

Although his wicked voice of unreason noted, "But none so pale and blond and green-eyed . . ."

He abruptly called for a halt then and had her put on her own horse. Never prudent or cautious, in fact self-indulgent and profligate, he didn't trust his libido against two hours more of Elizabeth Graham's sweet bottom bouncing on his lap.

She looked at him with a curious smile a few moments later, when he had her brought alongside his mount and he handed over her reins—as though she knew what he was thinking.

"You'll be more comfortable," he said, his voice dispassionate, courteous.

"And you, too, I expect." She wasn't flirtatious by

nature; she was merely stating a fact, although she couldn't help but smile a bit at the Laird of Ravensby's devilish dilemma. From all reports he was a man whose dalliances with women were legion. And now he was forced to curb his carnal instincts, or his brother might be put in jeopardy.

"You shouldn't be at Ravensby long." His hair lay like dark silk on the embossed silver of his shoulder armor.

"No, I won't." They were both practical people at base; they understood what was at stake. Her father would never chance losing her fortune for one man in his dungeons, however illustrious his family.

"We'll send a message to your father from Uswayford." His horse, recognizing his restless unease, curveted beneath him, held in place only by Johnnie's firm grip on the reins.

"Two days, then, at the most," Elizabeth casually remarked, "need I impose on your hospitality." Her voice was as polite as his, as though they were discussing a country holiday.

"No more than two, I agree," Johnnie said, holding his horse in check.

He had beautiful hands, Elizabeth noted, large, tanned, his fingers graceful, strong. "Maybe even less," she added, his physical presence suddenly disturbing her.

He didn't answer, only nodded.

Not much time, his wicked voice of unreason whispered.

Abruptly loosening his grip on the reins, he straightened as the black barb he favored leaped forward, leaving the beautiful, pale-haired Elizabeth Graham behind.

Safely behind.

And he didn't speak to her again until they reached Ravensby.

CHAPTER 4

Goldiehouse, a fortified castle much altered over the years into the embellished baronial style, offered a flamboyant display of European architectural fashion from the Gothic to the neoclassic. Dramatically situated in a parkland by the River Tweed, the structure had evolved into a full quadrangular complex and was, Elizabeth thought, the most princely home she had ever seen.

The local stone of its walls glowed golden in the setting sun, splendid against the dark pine and new-leafed beeches of the parkland, while its windows glittered like jewels.

No rough Border chieftain resided here, she thought as the troop clattered into the large paved courtyard, more like a Renaissance prince, from the magnificence of his establishment.

Scores of retainers poured out into the courtyard to assist the returning company, and Elizabeth found herself helped from her horse by no fewer than four servants. In the bustle and commotion of troopers dismounting she looked for sight of Ravensby's Laird but caught no glimpse of him. Threading her way through the crowd of men and horses, Elizabeth was led inside through a heavy studded door, originally constructed in the days when the keep needed to be defended. A large entrance hall rose around her like a treasure cave, the walls hung with rich tapestries, its ribbed Gothic ceiling of arched wood forty spectacular feet above her, a fireplace dominating one wall, a blazing fire taking the chill from the room.

Across the hall a woman stood on a small rise of flagstone stairs leading from the room, her presence conspicuous in the emptiness of the enormous space. Dark-haired, fair-skinned, slender, and beautiful, gowned in sapphire cashmere, she gave the appearance of the castle chatelaine.

"You won't be here long, I expect," the woman said, her cold voice carrying in the silence.

Elizabeth hadn't anticipated heartfelt welcome in the home of her father's enemies, but neither had she contemplated such hostility. The Laird of Ravensby had treated her with courtesy. Who was this woman? "I hope to be released very soon," she replied as she approached the stairs. Sensing an air of disquietude in the small, middle-aged man escorting her, she quickly glanced at his face and found he was blushing beneath the weathered bronze of his skin.

"Has he touched you?"

There was no mistaking the umbrage in the woman's tone or the identity of the man referred to, but before Elizabeth could answer, the familiar voice of her captor spoke from behind her.

"Good evening, Janet." John Carre's voice from the direction of the doorway was without inflection or emotion, mild, infinitely courteous. "Let me introduce you to Lady Graham," he said, his long stride bringing him swiftly near, "although I see you've informally met. Lady Graham, Countess Lindsay, a neighbor of mine." A small courtly bow made the women known to each other. "Your father has had some official Border transactions with Countess Lindsay's husband, the Earl of Midlothian," he said to Elizabeth, the scent of his cologne close, momentarily diverting her attention. "Now if you'll excuse us, Janet, I'll see Lady Graham to her quarters. The ride has tired us all." An experienced man with women, he was never impolite, but beneath his temperate voice was a distinct authority.

"I'll wait dinner for you." Janet Lindsay's directness was intentional. She knew Johnnie well enough to know he'd decline making a scene in public.

His hesitation was minute, and then he quietly said, "Give me ten minutes to wash away the mud from the ride."

Ravensby's Laird seemed engrossed on their journey through the labyrinthine corridors of the castle, unresponsive enough that the steward had to twice repeat his questions concerning Lady Graham's luggage or lack of it.

"Have Mrs. Reid find her some clothing," Johnnie answered at last, clearly not entirely focused on the present. Even his pace was slightly too fast for Elizabeth and the steward. "Do you need anything?" His query to Elizabeth reflected his remoteness as well, the nature of his words no more than a formality.

"No . . . nothing, except perhaps something to read. The wait could be dull." She didn't expect an answer with his detachment so obvious, but at least the steward would be aware of her request.

Something in her words must have caught his attention, for he seemed to notice her for the first time since their journey began up the stairways and through the corridors of Goldiehouse, although he didn't slow his gait. "You needn't be locked up, Lady Graham. If you give me your parole, you'll have your freedom of the castle and grounds." It was a normal procedure with hostages; the Borderers were ever gallant to their political guests. But she would be housed in the tower room against the possibility of an attack from Godfrey.

"In that case, naturally, you have my word." Approaching the third level of stairs, Elizabeth took a fortifying breath.

His breathing unhurried, fitness a requirement for border-raiding, John Carre smiled at her, disarming and conciliatory. "I hope you'll find your sojourn at Goldiehouse pleasant. Dankeil Willie will see to your wishes. Ask him for anything. A maid should be waiting for you in your chambers. The cooks are capable of most delicacies; simply put in your requests. Have I forgotten anything, Willie?"

"The wines, Johnnie." Kinship of various degrees related everyone under the Laird of Ravensby, and he was addressed with familiarity.

Johnnie smiled back at Willie, who was following them at a comfortable trot, his wiry body perhaps the result of the castle's miles of stairways. Regardless that England was at war with France, the Scottish Parliament had chosen to remove the restrictions on trade in French wines.[3] "We have French wines, while the English have to smuggle them in," Johnnie explained to Elizabeth as they reached the top of the stairs, "so feel free to ask for your favorites. Our supply of hock is excellent, too, since the English and Dutch secured the Rhine last fall. Willie prides himself on his palate, so let him guide you if you're uncertain."

Willie's beaming expression offered his expertise with sincere warmth, and Elizabeth allowed herself to be tempted. "I put myself completely in your hands, Willie."

"Very good, my Lady." Clearly he was pleased.

When they reached the tower room a few moments later, Elizabeth found a large chamber providing all the luxurious comforts as well as a magnificent view. Windows overlooked three vistas; the ceiling was exquisitely plastered, the walls colorfully painted by Italian artists lured to Ravensby by a former Laird; the floor, piled with layers of Turkey carpets to keep away the cold from the stone beneath, fairly invited bare feet; and the furniture, quaintly carved in a curious amalgam of classical and medieval motifs, brought to mind the time of the abbeys.

"Have the fairies had a hand in this?" Elizabeth softly inquired, momentarily awestruck at the rich drama of the room. And when she turned to express her delight to Johnnie, she found his eyes regarding her with unmistakable attention.

Instantly shuttered, his expression reverted to that

of congenial host, and he said with dry good humor, "If I had the fairies on my side, you could have stayed in Harbottle, and I'd have had the wee people bring Robbie out of the dungeons. I think my mother is to blame for this room. She painted up here."

"Oh," Elizabeth said in a small exhalation, not certain how inquisitive she could be about his mother and his family, or how much she wished to know about a man who studied her with such a predatory gaze. Or how much she dared learn about a man she found increasingly attractive.

Johnnie found he wished to respond to her obvious uncertainty by kissing her perplexity away, by soothing her bewilderment in a mutually pleasurable way. Married to a man four times her age, either she had taken lovers or was badly in need of one—which thought almost broke the hard grip he was maintaining on his willpower. No—he almost said it aloud. Maybe later, he thought in an attempt to distract the fierce need he was feeling. . . . *After Robbie's free.*

"Good night, Lady Graham," he said, turning away abruptly. And without explanation, he walked away.

Embarrassed, Willie uncomfortably ran his hand through his spiky hair, making the short red tufts even more disheveled, and then began talking into the sudden silence, as though his rush of words might mitigate the lingering aftereffects of his Laird's obvious carnal interest. "Let me introduce you to Helen, your lady's maid, and then you can tell me what you wish to eat. Helen will bring you a robe and warm water; I'll find you some reading matter too. Helen, come here and meet Lady Graham. . . ."

CHAPTER 5

Johnnie entered his private dining room a short time later, his riding clothes discarded for informal dinner attire. His hair, still damp from a swift washing, was tied back, his green velvet coat left open, the beauty of his white brocade waistcoat stylish foil to his rugged masculinity. The loose steinkirk knot at his throat was casually held in place with a small diamond pin. And the fine wools of his trews and stockings were patterned in plum and moss green. He looked the young warrior prince at home: rough-hewn, powerful, the renegade Border Lord volatile in velvet and diamonds, his size infinitely more striking with lace at his throat and wrists.

"Darling, I missed you. . . ." Janet cooed, her lounging pose artfully composed to accent the extreme décolletage of her silver tissue dressing gown. The merest suggestion of lace-trimmed corset peeked out from the deep vee of her gown, the rising swell of her breasts deliberate invitation.

"*Do* make yourself at home," Johnnie sardonically murmured, his temper held tautly in check at this command performance for dinner. As he moved across the carpeted floor, he surveyed the table for two set cozily by the fire, the lack of servants, his best hock on a silver salver at Janet's elbow, and his moody resentment at her uninvited presence in his household increased measurably.

Dropping into a chair close to his wine, he reached for a bottle and a glass. Gazing across the small distance to the tapestry settee where Countess Lindsay reposed, he curtly said, "Don't *ever* give me directions." His pale blue eyes were chill as Greenland's ice cap. "I prefer making my own plans for dinner."

"Now don't be surly, sweetheart," the lovely Countess retorted, her sapphire eyes cloudless despite Johnnie's sharp, glowering look. Familiar with cajoling men, more familiar with Johnnie's indulgence, she said, "I had your kitchen staff make *all* your favorite dishes. Your special reserve aqua vitae is waiting near the fire, and I gave strict orders not to be disturbed. . . ." She gracefully shifted her shoulder on the settee arm so her dressing gown fell open another fraction, further exposing her voluptuous breasts, pressing lushly above the crimson silk corset. And she smiled, an intimate, familiar smile.

"I'm not your middle-aged husband, Janet," Johnnie said with one arched brow and a shuttered glance. "I see a lot of plump young breasts." And pouring himself a drink, he raised the spiral-stemmed hock glass to his mouth and emptied it.

"I can see I'm going to have to exert myself tonight," the dark-haired beauty purred, undeterred by his temper, skilled at coaxing men. "To bring you out of your sullen mood."

"My sullen mood," the Laird of Ravensby brusquely retorted, reaching for the decanter again, "is the result of your damnable presumption." Although, had he been totally honest with himself, Janet's presumption was of long custom in his household. And had he been more punctilious at dissecting his feelings, he would have recognized that Janet Lindsay's possessive display before Elizabeth Graham figured prominently in his ill temper.

"I'll make amends, darling," the sleek and radiant Countess gently soothed, "for claiming your company at dinner. I'll wait on you, humor you, be *ever* so attentive." She smiled prettily, as a young girl would asking for a favor. "Perhaps"—she winked at him flirtatiously—"I could be your personal maidservant tonight. Would you like that? I could serve you your dinner and feed you a morsel at a time. . . ." Warming to the potential of the role, she murmured in a suggestive tone, "I could wash your fingers after dinner and see that you're comfortable and relaxed. I could be abjectly submissive and obedient," she dulcetly went on, "like a young girl. When you want your aqua vitae, I'd pour it for you and bring it to you in your chair near the fire and sit at your feet. . . ." Her eyes held his for a moment before her gaze drifted downward to gauge his interest in submissive women. "You could reprimand me if my service failed to please you," she softly offered, a small smile noting Johnnie's unmistakable arousal, "and take out all your churlishness on me. You could be autocratic . . ." Her voice was seductive, her dark eyes sultry. "And difficult . . . and demanding. . . ."

Johnnie gazed at her over the rim of his newly filled glass. "Keep it up, darling," he murmured, a hint of amusement in his eyes, "and you won't *need* me for your orgasm." A sudden grin lifted the corners of his mouth, the liquor warming his stomach and mood. The Countess's costly gown and stylish beauty were the antithesis of any serving maid in memory.

"But I *do* need you, Johnnie," she whispered, ignoring his mockery, her mind taking license with the role, the prospect of Johnnie Carre forcing her to submit to his authority sending a spiraling heat downward, like molten pleasure. "Let me be your servant girl . . . I really want to . . . *please*, Johnnie. You'll find me excessively . . . obedient."

He could see her nipples harden beneath the fine silk of her gown and felt an answering heat strike his senses. But his faint ironic smile and lazy drawl took issue with her breathy declaration. "I doubt you understand the word 'obedient,' puss. . . ."

"Try me, Johnnie." And she drew the gold-embroidered silver tissue of her skirt aside to offer him a tantalizing view of her crimson silk stockings, her pale thighs, her dark, silken curls. "I'll do anything. . . ." she breathed.

Perhaps a monk could have resisted. Perhaps not. But Johnnie Carre had no religious bent at all and a vigorous, well-exercised sexual appetite. His erection swelled. She was splendidly female, and her offer of sexual carte blanche had a predictable effect on him. But it didn't completely obliterate his grievance against her proprietary airs. He disliked possessive women; he disliked any sense of constraint from the females in his life, and this distinction took precedence even over lust. "One small warning," he said, his voice absolute.

"Anything." The throbbing between the Countess's legs quickened her unconditional response.

His look was guarded for a moment as he set his glass aside. "This isn't part of the game."

Janet took a small breath, forcing herself to meet his eyes with a degree of composure. "I understand."

"If you ever dictate to me in my own home again, I'll humiliate you, regardless of the company." Although his voice was infinitely soft, the undisguised menace in it struck her like a stinging slap.

"Yes, my Lord," she whispered, intimidated for the first time in her life, reality and game-playing coalescing, sending a thrilling heat trembling through her.

"You understand then." A small remnant of annoyance prompted him to press his authority, and something more perhaps—an exasperated obsession, a restless, headstrong desire to plunder Elizabeth Graham's provocative innocence. She was like forbidden fruit, and he found himself craving a taste of her.

"Unequivocally, Your Grace," his neighbor's wife submissively replied, a blush shading her luxurious breasts, her slender neck, infusing her porcelain complexion with a rosy glow. Her dark lashes half lowered over her eyes. "I humbly defer to your wishes."

"You needn't feel *obliged* to play games, darling,"

Johnnie said with a lazy insolence, recognizing the actress in her demure pose. "I'll fuck you anyway."

The Countess hesitated a moment, not because of his ungallant phrasing, but rather to debate the possibility of immediate gratification against the promise of lascivious delay. Her decision made, the lacy fringe of her lashes lifted, and her gaze met her lover's eyes with smoldering anticipation. "But I want to play," she said.

"And if I don't?" But his voice was teasing now, and his pale blue eyes, taking in her magnificent courtesan's body, had lost their coolness.

"I'll change your mind. . . ." Pure unadulterated sorcery as old as Eve whispered through her words . . . and an uninhibited assurance based on their past history together.

"You're a randy tart, sweetheart," he said lightly. "You should have married someone younger."

"*You* suggesting faithfulness to my husband?" Her query was offered with a wide-eyed feigned innocence.

Johnnie sighed, reminded of the stark reality of aristocratic marriages and his own lenient view of morals. "Forgive my momentary lapse into naïveté," he murmured.

"The *ultimate* naïveté, darling," the Countess softly replied, "coming from you." She arched one perfect dark brow. "Surely, after having pleasured most of the beautiful ladies in the Borders, married or otherwise, you'd be disabused of the notion of fidelity in marriage."

"Point taken," he quietly said, not about to discuss faithfulness *or* marriage with Janet Lindsay. But a small impetuous afterthought questioned whether the young Elizabeth Graham *might* have been faithful to her aged husband. And if so, he wondered, how would she respond to a man in his prime? He felt himself quicken at the possibilities. How would she respond to his touch? Would her skin be cool? Would *she* be cool . . . or flame-hot after years of sexual deprivation?

"*Well* . . . would you?"

Distracted by intemperate visions of Elizabeth Graham in his bed, he'd missed the entirety of Janet's query. Forcing the delicious Lady Graham from his thoughts, he smiled his apology and said with a small sigh, "It's been a long day."

"I was just wondering," Countess Lindsay said in her best rendition of a servant girl's tone, "would you like more wine, my Lord?"

He paused for a moment, digesting her words and the sharp contrast between Janet Lindsay's overt vice and the coolly composed Elizabeth Graham. But Lady Graham was beyond his reach at the moment, and the very delectable hot-blooded Janet was only inches away. He smiled a slow, lazy smile. "Why not?"

"Why not indeed, you incorruptible prude," Janet facetiously retorted. "I thought for a moment I might have to tie you up and strip your clothes from you against your protests."

His smile widened. "Maybe later . . ."

"You're not tired?" It was her only truly concerned query of the evening, although her impulse was purely selfish.

"And if I were, after riding to Harbottle and back today?" he impudently reminded her.

"You're never tired, Johnnie," she declared like a child who believed in certainties.

And he wasn't. Actually, now that the question of his independence had been sufficiently clarified with the Countess, he was in extreme good humor. With his hostage snug at Goldiehouse, the bargaining for Robbie's release could begin in the morning; his brother should be home within the week.

"All right then," he said with a grin, "if you insist—I'm not tired, but I *am* damnably hungry. Also," he softly added, "you have altogether too many clothes on, puss, if you want to be my personal maid tonight." And rising from his chair, he moved over to the table near the fire without a glance for the Countess.

He stood for a moment at the table as if waiting for something, and then very quietly said, "My chair, Janet. I need my chair pulled out."

Unfamiliar with orders, unaccustomed to responding to that particular tone in a man's voice, Janet took a brief lapse of time to acknowledge his command. But presently he heard the soft rustle of silk and the sound of her slippers on the carpet. Coming up to him, she stood very close, so her breasts brushed his arm, and, lifting her face to him said, seductively and assuredly, "Kiss me."

He didn't turn to look at her, nor did he give evidence he'd heard her. Instead, he quietly repeated, "Pull my chair out so I can be seated."

She could smell the clover-scented dampness of his hair, feel the heat of his body. "Kiss me first," she whispered, rubbing the length of her body against his. Since her adolescence no man had refused her.

"The chair," he said, his voice sending tiny shivers down her spine, his cool indifference aphrodisiac.

She reached up, her palm resting on his shoulder, the solid feel of his muscles beneath her hand further igniting her passion. "Please ..." she whispered.

His strong fingers curled around her hand, removed it from his shoulder, and, half turning to face her, placed it at her side. "You don't understand," he calmly said, releasing his grip on her fingers. "I give the orders. You obey them."

She reached for the chair.

He made her adjust his position several times until he was sufficiently comfortable with his distance from the table, saying simply, "Closer."

"No, back a bit."

"To the left now."

"There."

Until she'd worked herself into a small temper and a light sweat. And then, like the titled Earl he was, he motioned with a small gesture for his wineglass to be filled.

"Should I take my gown off first?" the Countess inquired, wishing to equalize the dynamics, her sexual allure always a potent force.

"No," he said, leaning back in his chair, "pour my wine first."

The siren in her took staggering pause. Was she suddenly as inconspicuous as a servant? Unobtrusive as the furniture? Petulance drew her dark brows together, and her bottom lip turned sulky. But then the Laird of Ravensby uncrossed his legs, and the soft wool of his trews, raised conspicuously over his arousal, gave her heady pause.

She poured the wine, leaning over with courtesan expertise so her bounteous breasts, quivering above her tightly laced stays, offered an enticing display. A natural coquette, she understood the finer points of seduction.

"Kindly keep your breasts out of my face," Johnnie told her. "I prefer more discretion from my servants."

"You're rude," she pouted, dropping the decanter on the table with a thud.

"Servants' opinions are of no interest to me," Ravensby's Laird curtly said. "Unless you're asked a direct question, remain silent." Leaning back in his chair, he held the Rhenish wine up to the light of the candelabra and studied its golden hue for a contemplative moment as though he were alone in the room.

"You're hateful." But her voice held a trembling huskiness; his nonchalance was sensual, challenging. And she stood suddenly quiet before him, like a reprimanded servant.

"Whether I'm hateful or not," he murmured, looking at her finally, his gaze insolently raking her body, "or autocratic and demanding—I think those were the words you suggested," he softly went on, "is of no significance to your . . ."—he paused—"*position*." His blue eyes held hers for a significant second, the exact nature of that position blatantly clear. "And if I decide I wish to fuck you later, after you've fed me, you have the choice of submitting or losing your post in my household. Is that clear?"

"Yes, Your Grace," the Countess whispered, her body on fire, her hand deferentially covering her deep décolletage in recognition of her employer's wish for less display.

Moving her hand aside, he lightly brushed his fingertips over the swell of her breasts. "I didn't say I didn't *like* your breasts," he said, sliding his hand inside her gown to touch the hard tip of her nipple through the sheer silk of her corset. "I just don't care for them in my food." His hand fell away as he settled back in his chair, and his voice when he spoke held a distinct remoteness.

"Now kindly disrobe, and I'll assess my interest in you for purposes other than serving my meal."

Nerveless, inaccessible, he gazed at her like a stranger.

A small shiver of excitement raced down her spine, and her hands trembled as she reached for the hooks on her gown. She found it difficult to concentrate with desire flaring like wildfire through her blood, but she managed finally to unfasten the small silk-covered hooks, and the silver tissue fell in a whisper to the carpet. Like an expensive harlot, she stood before her master in red silk stockings, flowered garters, violet velvet slippers, and a crimson corset laced so tightly, her breasts rose above her compressed waist like silken globes.

"A shame you're so large-breasted," the Laird, sprawled at his ease, lazily drawled. "I prefer smaller women. Perhaps I should send you away."

"No! Please, my Lord!" Panic swelled her voice. She was peaking already, her blood pulsing in her ears and deep inside her, the rhythm of her heart counterpoint to the steady hard throbbing between her legs. "I'm sorry," she abjectly apologized, pressing her hand against her breasts in an effort to hide their abundance. "I could wear a chemise, Your Grace, and not offend your eyes."

He seemed to consider for a moment, lounging like an Eastern potentate, his finger tracing the base of his wineglass in idle half-circles. He glanced at the tall case clock in the corner briefly, as if contemplating his options against time. "It *is* late," he said at last, "you're conveniently at hand, and regardless you have those enormous breasts, I do have need of a servant." He sighed. "You might as well stay." A touch of reluctance graced his voice, and then his tone flattened as he added, "I wish to be served without conversation. Take off your corset. Leave on your slippers and stockings. I like red silk stockings." With that same lack of inflection one might say, "I like sugar with my tea."

At the present state of her desire she would have

agreed to anything, her hunger for him desperate, ravenous. So she struggled with the laces at the back of her corset while he leisurely drank his wine. Normally, a lady's maid or a helpful lover was on hand for such occasions; she had never undone a corset.

Long, frustrating minutes later she was at last free of it, flushed and heated, her hair tumbled about her face, her need for sexual release flagrant.

"You may feed me," he said then as she stood before him, lushly nude except for her violet slippers and red stockings. And he pointed at a small plate of fruit scones.

"Later," she said, as dismissive as he, no longer concerned with obedience or compliance, the aristocrat born and bred in her disposed to immediate gratification. "Make love to me now," she demanded. Aflame with desire, she moved very close, the sight of him fully clothed in contrast to her nakedness intoxicating; his composure, his careless detachment, tantalized like a favorite dessert almost within reach, like ungentle surcease to the fire within her.

"But I don't want to eat later," he replied, a distinct edge to his voice. "I want to eat now."

"Lord, Johnnie," she whispered, her breathing unsteady, trembling on the brink. "I can't . . ."

He looked up at her. "Do it," he simply said.

Taking a deep breath to steady herself, she reached toward the plate and broke off a crumbly piece of scone.

"Come closer." His voice was very low.

She moved forward, closing her eyes for a moment against the heady friction walking induced, so near was she to climax. She felt his hand drift up her thigh. "Are you hungry?" he conversationally inquired as if he were suddenly a courteous host, and his hand, inches from the damp heat of her desire, was no more than a commonplace gallantry.

She shook her head, too overcome to speak.

"Open your eyes," he softly ordered. And when she did, gazing down at him, aglow with heated passion, he said in a low, level voice, "Open your legs." She yielded instantly, humbled by her need, and the warmth of his palm slid upward until his fingers touched the damp evidence of her carnal hunger. She moved against the light caress, urging him to enter her.

"Stand still," he quietly commanded.

She whimpered but meekly obeyed.

"Excellent," he murmured, his fingertips delicately stroking her swollen labia as if testing her readiness, the softly uttered word ambiguous comment on her compliance or the state of her receptivity. He seemed satisfied on either count apparently, for he slipped a finger inside her.

"Now feed me that," he murmured, as though he didn't hold her prisoner at his side, a nod of his head indicating the bit of scone in her hand.

His stroking fingers continued their arousal, the slow, luscious invasion, the widening penetration echoed in her soft sighs.

"Feed me," he softly repeated when she hadn't immediately responded, sliding two more fingers inside her, driving in so deeply, she caught her breath. "You must mind me," he calmly murmured, "or I'll send you from the room."

It was unthinkable in her current state, and wrenching her mind back from voluptuary sensation, she obeyed, unable to keep her hand from trembling as she carried the small portion of food to his mouth.

He spoke while she stood with her arm extended, forcing her to wait a moment more. "I want you to watch me eat. Keep your eyes open. When I'm finished, I'll want more." He opened his mouth then, allowing her to feed him, and he slowly chewed the delicate flaky morsel as if time had no meaning, his fingers buried inside her, her bare hip against the velvet of his shoulder. His touch was exquisite, skilled. Accomplished.

She had great difficulty properly focusing her attention.

Enormous difficulty keeping her eyes open.

But his warning impelled her.

And her peaking orgasmic state.

"So obedient," he murmured a short time later, her breathing erratic, her entire body above the red silk of her stockings flushed a delectable pink. "Feed me some of that apple cake over there, look, I want you to look . . . that's a good girl. Here, take the knife and cut me a piece. If you follow my instructions completely, I'll make love to you all night. . . . Have you ever been with a man who made love to you all night?"

She had. They had. Memories of excess flooded her mind, and she climaxed with a small smothered cry.

Bending his head, he leaned over and gently suckled her rigid nipples, intensifying the slow-ebbing pleasure. Then, satisfied her orgasm was complete, he gently withdrew his fingers, relaxed in his chair, and, reaching for an appliquéd linen napkin, slowly wiped his hand.

Only the sound of the Countess's ungentle respiration broke the silence of the small paneled chamber until, some time later, her feverish breathing abated and her sensibilities returned to a degree of normalcy. Her dark lashes lifted; she drew in a deep breath and glared at Johnnie. "Damn your smug competence. I hate you!" And swiveling her arm back, she swung at him.

He caught her vicious blow easily, his reflexes honed to a fine pitch. "Really," he said with a grin, holding her wrist with a gentle strength. "And it looked like you were enjoying yourself."

"Are you saving that erection for someone else?" she hissed, shaking his hand away, flouncing down in the chair opposite him, her pout and glowering look stormy.

The thought of a *particular* someone else had crossed his mind, of course, several times since he'd met the pale and lovely Lady Graham. But with Robbie's life at issue . . . "Not tonight," he said, his grin still in place, his insolent blue eyes offering unbridled pleasure. "Are you available?"

"I should make you wait," she muttered, sulky still.

"If you had the patience, you might," he softly goaded.

"*You* apparently have enough for both of us."

"How fortunate, then. Are we through with your game? Or do you want me to continue playing the dominant male?"

"A role to which you're eminently suited," she spat,

her frustration still explosive. "I hate those elusive orgasms."

"You're greedy, pet. They can't all be consummate sensation."

She gazed at him from under half-lowered lashes, her glance still gimlet-eyed.

The blue of his eyes, in contrast, was pure angelic sunshine. "I see. . . ." he said with a small repressed smile, a perceptive man when it came to interpreting female glances. "Apparently, some improvement is required here. Why don't you tell me what kind you like, and I'll see what I can do." The teasing in his voice was familiar and warm and not at all the sovereign Lord.

"Oh damn you," she said with a sigh. "As if you don't know. . . ." Leaning back in the upholstered chair, the burgundy damask handsome foil to her ivory skin, she stretched like an indolent cat, her resentment fading. Johnnie Carre was always capable of amusing her in the best possible way. "With that cock at attention," she added with an answering grin, "how can I stay angry?"

"How indeed?" he immodestly replied, but his smile was boyish and charming and exclusively hers that night in his private dining room at Goldiehouse.

But before she left in the morning, with grace and care and utmost diplomacy, he made her understand she must stay away until Robbie was home safe. He wouldn't take any chances the negotiations might go awry, he told her. He needed his full concentration on Robbie's release. He couldn't afford to be distracted by seductive ladies no matter how lovely, he declared. He convinced her finally with a persuasion backed by a noteworthy stamina. And when he finally fell asleep toward morning, he was pleasantly content; in a few hours Lady Graham would be alone in his home.

CHAPTER 6

Elizabeth rose the next morning after a dreamless sleep, Willie's French wine no doubt accounting for her untroubled slumber. After a breakfast that would do justice to a hardworking farmer, with Helen's assistance she dressed in an exquisite tartan gown of silk in shades of green and red. Consciously ignoring thoughts of the gown's previous owner, Elizabeth retraced her journey of the previous night through the descending corridors of the castle and found her way to the courtyard.

She intended to spend the morning exploring the grounds.

A lady's horse, saddled and held ready by a stable boy, stood at the front door. Janet must have stayed the night. Highborn slut.

Chastising herself a moment later for responding to that notion with a flaring resentment, Elizabeth briskly traversed the broad courtyard as if she could leave behind her annoyance at the palace door. Passing through the old castle gates, she stood on a gentle rise near the grassy moat surveying the sweep of green landscape falling away toward the river, wanting to forget Janet Lindsay and all the women in Johnnie Carre's love life.

He was a libertine by reputation, the evidence of which she'd witnessed herself. He made no distinction about whom he slept with, and she would do well to put him from her mind.

In the following days she saw little of the castle's Lord. Johnnie Carre wanted no untoward problems arising over Robbie's release, and Elizabeth Graham's simple presence posed a threat. He had no practice in temperance with women. It was best he didn't see her.

His subconscious, however, responded less well to the logic of restraint, and his dreams were frequented by constant, combustible images of Elizabeth Graham in his bed.

Elizabeth spent long hours in the library at Goldiehouse, fascinated by the Carre collection of architectural books and carefully maintained models of the various additions to the family seat. The love of building had apparently been passed down the generations, each heir taking on a project to further beautify Goldiehouse. The newest working model was grand in scale, designed in the classical style; the foundations for a new wing were being laid facing west. More intimate, more human in scale, it looked as though the latest Earl of Graden intended to live in a less feudal environment.

She became friends with Munro, the young architect only recently returned from Vicenza, where he'd gone to study Palladio's country villas. She visited him often in his office, listened while he spoke glowingly of Palladio's vision of making his homes one with their natural setting. And she asked serious questions as he showed her drawings by the master and pointed out Palladio's elements of number, measure, and proportion as the means of making architectural space conform to natural principles. Her interest in design and workmanship was more than that of a dilettante, for her own plans included the construction of a home. With Hotchane's inheritance she intended at last to live independently, and to that purpose she had a land agent searching for property in Northumbria at a suitable distance from her father's meddling.

She ate her meals in her tower room or in the kitchen with the large, friendly staff. She spent cozy hours over tea in Mrs. Reid's parlor, too, listening to the housekeeper's stories of the Carre family. She wasn't invited to dine with Johnnie and his men—a deliberate decision on Johnnie's part. Knowing the fragile state of his resistance to her, he chose the safe ground of complete avoidance. Particularly in light of the drinking customary at dinner with his men. After the brandy or claret had made several rounds of the table, he knew he couldn't trust his restraint.

They met in the formal garden one afternoon though, very much by accident. Saving time, Johnnie had cut through the garden after having met with his architect, Munro, down by the river. They had discussed the projected height of the dome over the small orangery attached by a covered walkway to what would be Johnnie's suite of rooms in the new wing under construction. It was a question of proportion from a distance, and both men had agreed on a lesser height after observing the site from several vantage points. Particularly from the riverbank, the planned elevation would have disturbed the harmony of the skyline.

Late for a meeting with Kinmont to determine their reply to the newest terms delivered that morning from Godfrey, he rapidly strode through the symmetrical parterres, vaulting over the orderly floral borders as he came to them, leaping across the small reflecting pool at the entrance to the garden rather than waste time circling it. Sweeping around the box hedge separating the pool from the gravel walk leading up to the house in a flying turn, he hurtled into a body.

Automatically, his hands came up to steady Elizabeth as she stumbled backward with a small cry. And the books and papers she was carrying tumbled from her arms.

Her eyes flared wide in apprehension. Whether his

touch had alarmed her or the suddenness of his appearance was the cause, perversely he found himself stirred by that apprehension. As if he were the hunter and she his prey. An inherent emotion, perhaps, in a man trained to the chase; he didn't question what it meant. But he was acutely aware of his response, and his fingers reflexively closed more firmly on the soft flesh of her upper arm. How can it hurt? a part of him insisted; a hostage isn't sacrosanct. Certainly in the history of the Borders women had been violated; it was the norm rather than the exception. She knew it. He knew it.

His feelings showed in his eyes.

She should be more fearful, she thought, with this powerful man towering over her, holding her captive, the message in his luminous blue eyes unselfconsciously direct. "I'm sorry," she said instead, as if *she* had abruptly collided with him, and only politesse was on her mind. Or, perhaps unconsciously, she was apologizing for her sudden response to his candid look.

He hesitated for a moment. Her softly uttered phrase struck him oddly. Had he misinterpreted her apprehension? Could she simply be offering a mundane courtesy? Or had he indeed heard an enticing sensuality beneath the simple words? But then the literal meaning of the phrase became clear, and regret of another kind forcibly struck his consciousness. Negotiations were well along for Robbie's release. His brother would soon be out of Harbottle prison, so acting on carnal impulse at the moment seemed foolhardy. Even if she were willing.

"I'm sorry too," he said, more bluntly than she, his voice harsh with the logic of restraint. "Let me help with your scattered books." And so saying, he released her and stooped to gather her books and papers from the raked gravel path.

Her slippered feet were mere inches from his hands as he stacked the few books and brought the papers into order. Her legs were as close. He smelled the fragrance of Mrs. Reid's clover-scented soap, and he couldn't forestall the spontaneous image of Elizabeth Graham lounging in her bath, a hand-milled ball of soap in her palm, steam rising around her, her breasts half-submerged in the heated water, her hand leisurely rubbing Mrs. Reid's soap over the swelling mounds. . . . A spiking lust flashed through him at his lascivious imagination, and he ground his teeth in resentful frustration.

The width of his shoulders beneath the utilitarian buff wool startled Elizabeth at close range. She'd not seen his athletic body so vividly before, at her feet, as it were. How would those brawny shoulders feel beneath her hands, how intoxicating the stir and shift of hard muscle, the lithe grace and power? Suddenly captivated by the irresistible virility of the Laird of Ravensby, she clenched her hands against the impulse to brush her hand over those powerful shoulders.

He came upright with a graceful energy before her control weakened.

"Here," he said, handing her the books, the papers stuffed hodgepodge between them.

"Thank you," she replied on a small caught breath, feeling as though she'd only narrowly escaped disaster.

And they stood for a moment like uncertain adolescents, unable to converse when raw sensation overwhelmed them.

Johnnie spoke first because he was more accomplished at social banter. Years of pursuing women had polished his graces. "You're interested in architecture," he said, noting the books she'd dropped.

"I'm planning on building a house," she quietly said.

"You intend to live alone?" He shouldn't have said "alone" with that particular emphasis. He should have better masked his feelings.

"Yes," she said. His insinuation had been plain, palpably sexual. "I *wish* to live alone," she added, as if further definition would shield her from his potent sensuality.

It was suddenly too much, Johnnie abruptly decided, after days of avoiding her and thinking of her, days of denial and restraint. Never a man of indecision, he struggled as a clear choice offered itself. Elizabeth Graham stood inches away, breathtaking even in a plain dove-gray linen gown made for a slightly larger woman.

She looked more fragile, more delicate, the green of her eyes intensely vivid in contrast to the pale gown. The word "unguarded" came powerfully to mind, sharp-cut as a whip on his back.

He could take her now on the clipped green lawn in full view of the house, or damn his pride and call retreat. He could pick her up and carry her, struggling or not, to his rooms and not let her out until Godfrey's minions came with his brother. Or he could turn away.

He debated momentarily under the warm spring sun in a parterred garden shaped by the concept of restraint. And those few seconds seemed a lifetime to a man much motivated by instinct, a successful commander who understood that indecision often meant the difference between life and death.

It salved his conscience in the end that he was decamping for Robbie.

"I wish you luck then," he softly said, "living alone." An easy sensuality lay beneath the casualness of his words, as if he knew intrinsically women always wanted him.

He bowed then in a swift, graceful leave-taking.

And she felt for a moment when he'd gone as though she'd won. But the small insolence in his parting words lingered in her mind. He knew how women responded to him. And she was intelligent enough to realize that victory had been granted her.

They met each other once more, the following morning when Johnnie walked into Munro's office and found Elizabeth there. He stopped on the threshold when she turned at the sound of the door opening, the sight of her breathtaking in the plain, unadorned room. Her light coloring, the lemon-yellow gown she wore, were the only source of brilliance in an atmosphere of unmitigated browns. The paneled walls, plank floor, the woodwork and doors, Munro's desk and drawing table, all contrived to frame her fair beauty.

"Come in, Johnnie," Munro welcomed him. "Add

your expertise to the topic. Lady Graham and I were analyzing the merits of garden architecture."

"Why don't I come back later?" A dazzling light seemed to emanate from the lady seated before Munro's desk, as if she absorbed the rays of the sun shining through the bank of windows behind Munro. As if she absorbed their heat too. She always struck him gut-hard; he preferred lesser feelings toward women. "We can go over the matter of the archway between the main house and the new wing this afternoon."

"Look now," Munro urged, immune to his employer's discomfort. "I've redrawn the plans. Why come back when you're already here?" He was pawing through the stack of prints on his desk. "I think you'll find all your suggestions appropriately incorporated. Elizabeth has already given them her approval," he finished, looking up with a grin.

Momentarily startled at the obvious informality between his architect and hostage houseguest, Johnnie's gaze quickly regauged their proximity. And his next reflection, decidedly possessive in nature, questioned the exact measure of that friendship with a jaundiced glance. "Really," he said, "in that case you must show me them." And he strode into the room with the grudging resentment of a guardian protecting his personal property.

Ignorant to Johnnie's misjudged suspicions as he surveyed the array of new designs, Elizabeth and Munro jointly annotated the redesigned drawings. "Actually, Elizabeth helped draw these cross sections," Munro noted when they came to the detail drawings.

"He let me handle the unimportant details," Elizabeth interjected with a grin.

"Never say the foundation is unimportant," Munro gallantly protested.

"Well, just boring then," she cheerfully pointed out. "You did all the beautiful relief arabesques—and most wonderfully, I might add." The smile that passed between Elizabeth and Munro was duly noted by the Laird of Ravensby.

"Although tomorrow," Elizabeth went on, "you *must* let me try my hand on the cartouche."

And Johnnie was shocked to see her stick her tongue out at Munro as a child would at play.

"Or will you pout?" Munro teased.

"I most certainly will."

"In that case I have no choice."

"How insightful. You see," she playfully said, turning to Johnnie in her good spirits as though he were a part of their banter, "how accommodating he is?"

"Indeed." And the single quiet word wiped the smile from her face, so sharp its query.

"Acquit me, Ravensby," she snapped, "from the multitude of your sins." She'd changed completely in that flashing second from a lighthearted maid to an imperious female, her expression one of disdain.

"Johnnie, you're out of bounds," Munro said quickly. "Apologize."

They were friends, the two men, cousins raised in the same household, but Johnnie's eyes when they swiveled to Munro held no friendship. "As Laird," the chief Lord in Roxburgh said to his cousin, "I have no bounds."

"She's not like your other women, Johnnie." Unintimidated, often in disagreement with Johnnie over the years, Munro pugnaciously repeated, "Apologize to Lady Graham."

"And if I don't?" While he'd been uncommonly circumspect in his desires, when he'd been denying himself like a chaste knight, Elizabeth Graham and his cousin had been enjoying a flirtation.

"That's enough!" Elizabeth sharply exclaimed, rising from her chair, the anger in her voice distinct. "You're mistaken, Lord Graden, in your presumptions. Although with your reputation it's understandable. Kindly excuse me from this unsavory discussion. Hotchane would have had you both thrown into the river to cool off."

"He could have tried," Johnnie darkly muttered, still heated from an unrecognizable jealousy.

"Hotchane survived seventy-eight years, my Lord, because he enforced his will with his Redesdale army."

"But he's dead now, my Lady," Johnnie murmured. "And the Redesdale army is across the border."

"Are you threatening me?"

"Of course not." His voice had further hushed.

"Kindly recall I'm a hostage. There are certain rules."

"And kindly recall *I* make the rules here."

She paused for the space of a heartbeat. "I see." Drawing a small breath, she sarcastically went on, "In that case I no doubt require your permission to leave."

"Leave?" The tone of his voice required more definition from her.

"This room."

He hesitated just long enough for discourtesy, an implied lesson on the extent of his power in the Borders.

He nodded his head finally in dismissal.

She refused to verbally acknowledge his authority but simply turned in a swish of silk and walked from the room.

"So . . ." Munro murmured, "that's the way of it. . . ." He was shocked at the tangible heat he'd just witnessed between his cousin and Elizabeth Graham—an explanation for Johnnie's unjustified jealousy. "And you've managed to keep your hands off her?"

"Just barely," Johnnie said with a sigh. "My apologies if I gave offense."

"You *should* apologize to her."

Johnnie shrugged. "She'll be gone soon."

"The negotiations are going well?"

"We're down to the small details."

"Ah . . . and it's getting harder."

Johnnie's eyes met his cousin's, amusement rife in their smiling blue depths at the unintended double entendre. "You might say that."

"And this is all new for you—this abstinence."

Johnnie's sigh this time was an exhalation of strained resignation. "Totally."

"Do you feel the inspiration of this new and noble temperance infusing your soul with virtue?" Munro teasingly mocked.

"Actually, I'm at the point of hitting the next person I speak to out of frustration alone."

"Perhaps you *do* need to be thrown into the river as the lady suggested, to cool your ardor."

"Perhaps *she* needs to be thrown into my bed to cool my ardor."

"Hmmm," Munro replied.

"Exactly," Johnnie muttered. "A damnable quandary for a godless renegade like me."

CHAPTER 7

Late in the evening of the sixth day of Elizabeth's detention, a final messenger arrived from Lord Godfrey with
his agreement on a compatible time and appropriate
place for the exchange of prisoners.

After seeing that his men were alerted to the morning rendezvous, Johnnie arranged to see Elizabeth and
inform her of her imminent release.

He sent a footman up first, cautious of intruding
into her chamber so late in the evening, wanting the lady
to have time to dress, allowing himself every prudence.
Then, waiting a circumspect half hour, he mounted the
numerous stairways to the tower room.

At his knock, the lady's maid, Helen, opened the
door to him, her young face smiling, her bobbing curtsy
deferential.

The candles were all aglow, he noticed, a maximum
of light illuminating the low-ceilinged room, relegating
the velvety shadows to remote corners. The crimson and
indigo silk carpets gleamed under the flickering light,
and the plaster relief on the ceiling took on a three-

dimensional quality, the acanthus wreaths and fruited garlands hanging short inches from his head.

Elizabeth Graham had chosen to greet him standing, her pale hair loose on her shoulders, undressed as it was in sleep. He noted the bed, quickly made, bore evidence of her recent occupancy, with the pillows in disarray. The mild disorder shouldn't have prompted such a powerful response in him, but he felt himself quicken at the thought of her lying there.

He shifted his stance, restless under the pressure of his feelings, wanting to speak quickly and leave, wanting also paradoxically to render the minutiae of the room with infinite clarity into his brain, in memory of his rare, compelling need.

A shimmering green robe covered her night rail, the white lace of her sleeping gown evident beneath the rich brocade, fur-trimmed against the spring night. The room was cool in March despite the fire in the grate and the multitude of candles.

Or at least it was cool for her.

He felt on fire.

What did he want? Elizabeth wondered, her gaze mesmerized by his powerful image, the ceiling no more than a foot above his head, his height dwarfing the proportions of the room, the breadth of his shoulders enormous beneath his tartan coat, his muscular build vivid reminder of his strenuous physical life. The blue velvet of his coat collar, in contrast, was soft like his heavy downy brows.

What would it feel like, she thought, to trace their dark arc? How would he respond to her fingertips drifting over his face? In some unknown, secret part of her being, she wanted to be able to *make* him respond; she wanted, inexplicably, in some feminine, enigmatic way, to touch him intimately.

He offered himself openly to women. A natural posture for him. As natural, she didn't doubt, as it was for him to accept what they gave him in return.

And he was offering her a degree of that freedom now . . . however unspoken the invitation.

But she quelled her unspoken wishes and undefined feelings because she didn't wish to be like Janet Lindsay—conveniently available for a night. With Johnnie Carre she'd be too easily forgotten, and her pride deterred her.

He was too beautiful and charming and overtly sensual to have to petition.

He was simply there for the asking.

And she wouldn't ask.

At the price of eight years of her young life, she had a fortune now, and she intended to prudently use her hardwon wealth to create a protected garden of Eden for herself in Northumbria. Johnnie Carre, arch pragmatist and worldly sensual man, wouldn't fit into her planned paradise.

So her voice was temperate and calm when she spoke, her expression schooled to betray nothing.

"You have a message?" she said.

"Yes, your father has agreed to a time and place." He kept his voice as neutral as hers. "We ride for Roundtree in the morning to make the exchange. I thought I'd give you warning tonight."

"So your brother will soon be home."

"Yes." He smiled, his happiness a tangible thing.

"Let me thank you now, then, for your hospitality. The morning will be frantic, no doubt."

"No doubt." He smiled again.

She was remarkable, he reflected. Cool and collected, without subterfuge, a woman genuinely composed. Was that coolness attributable to a marriage without passion, or had she always been so self-controlled? How would it be, he wondered, at sixteen, to lie with a seventy-year-old man, or at eighteen or twenty-four?

He wished to make her feel the difference, he suddenly thought, although an instant later he contemplated how presumptuous his arrogance was. Perhaps she was abundantly familiar with young lovers.

"Have you had lovers?" he asked, unreasoning, without contemplation, the plain question like thunder in the quiet room.

Like thunder in her heart. But Elizabeth subdued her tremulous reaction, considering instead the consequences when apparently he did not, and said, very coolly, "I beg your pardon."

With most men that chill disclaimer would have been enough.

"Tell me," he said.

She drew herself up very straight, as if her physical stance would act as barrier or still her racing heart. "I don't have to tell you. And might I remind you . . . we're not alone."

He glanced quickly at Helen, as though he'd forgotten her presence, and when she appeared quite lucidly in his field of vision, he told her, "Go."

"Stay," Elizabeth commanded.

He was surprised to be countermanded. No one had dared since he'd come home from Paris at his father's death eight years ago to become Laird. He hesitated a brief moment before he gestured toward the door with the merest nod of his head.

Helen gazed at Elizabeth for a heartbeat, apology in her look, and then left the tower room.

"Will you force me?" Elizabeth inquired as the door clicked shut, sarcastic in her anger. Like Johnnie, she'd been seldom thwarted in the last few years, save for the occasionally oppressive bonds of matrimony imposed by Hotchane.

"Of course not." The thought was incomprehensible. "Answer my question."

"About my lovers, you mean." Haughty, she demonstrated the arrogance commensurate with her rank of heiress.

"Of course," he said again, but his voice was softer now. In control again, familiar with seduction, he relaxed. "Have you?"

"Why does it matter?"

"I don't know. It shouldn't."

"Then I won't answer."

"Why so defensive?" he mildly retorted. "I'm not judging you. Far from it."

"I may not wish to discuss my private life with you."

And at the phrase "private life," Johnnie saw her again lying on the bed, the image so intense and vivid, he half reached out to lift her in his arms.

But he restrained himself. Walking over to a cushioned chair, he sat down. "I'm twenty-five," he said.

She knew what he meant as though he'd written a lengthy essay on his feelings, but she was still fighting her own chaotic emotions. "Then I'm too old for you."

"Really? Why?"

"Men like young women."

He laughed. "How very sheltered you've been."

"Maybe I'm just realistic."

"Maybe you're just wrong." Janet Lindsay was older than he, as were several of the women who'd entertained him over the years. "You're very beautiful, and I expect all the marriage applicants your father's bringing round aren't exclusively interested in your wealth."

"Are you proposing?" she inquired, her voice oversweet.

"No. I don't need your money—or a wife."

"You steal what you need—is that right?"

"I'm a businessman," he softly said.

"You're in the business of raiding other people's property."

"I take back only what's stolen from me and protect my family and land. My business is in trade: cattle, sheep, wool"—he grinned—"and wine. I've a fleet of merchant ships currently trying to evade the English fleet. But the profits are enormous on the Continent right now after two years of war."

He looked very beautiful lounging in the oddly carved chair in her bedchamber, the soft blue plaid of his coat[4] invitation to touch, his long legs sprawled out before him, their powerful muscles visible beneath the fine wool of his breeches. He wore diamond buckles on his shoes, and she believed him when he said he had no need of her money.

His clear blue eyes held hers for a moment before he softly said, "I think I know the answer to my question. Come sit with me."

"No." Her voice was no more than a whisper. "I don't want to."

"Yes, you do."

He knew. How could he know? And she took a step backward as though that small extra distance would stop him, the silken swish of her robe overloud in the sudden silence.

He rose then, but didn't move further, not wishing to frighten her more. "I've tried to avoid you," he said very quietly. "I've never done that with a woman." He paused, trying to arrange his emotions into some order when what he wanted was to hold her beyond all rational thought. "But Robbie's more important to me, so I stayed away. I intended to do the same tonight. I sent the servant up to give you warning ... and also as a conscious obstruction to myself." Restlessly, he raked both hands through his hair, forgetting he'd tied it back in a queue. "Oh, hell," he exclaimed, referring both to his disturbed hair and his tumultuous desires. "You tantalize me," he said, very low, only sheer willpower keeping him from gathering her into his arms. "Do I frighten you?"

Unnerved by her exposed feelings, unsettled by the novelty of her sensual vulnerability, she didn't answer, and another small silence fell in the candlelit tower room.

"Talk to me," he murmured, afraid of the violence of his emotions.

"You don't frighten me ... I frighten myself," she finally whispered, reaching out for a chair back to steady her trembling. She no longer questioned the extent of his allure, for no man had ever made her tremble merely at the sight of him.

And she should know after the dozens of candidates her father had paraded before her.

She never trembled. Never.

And her heart never pounded like this.

And the heat warming her face matched another heat, a pulsing ache, deep in the pit of her stomach.

Johnnie Carre was the cause of that heat.

His gaze dwelt for a moment on her small hands gripping the carving of the chair before he raised his eyes to her face.

"Let me hold you," he said, his deep voice hushed. And he held out his hand.

No man had ever said that to her before. She'd never been offered tenderness and comfort by a man. Like so many other young women, she'd been sold to the highest bidder—although marriage settlements couched the transaction in more palatable euphemisms.

"I won't hurt you," Johnnie murmured, walking over and gently loosening her fingers from the saints' heads bordering the chair rail.

She believed him, despite the fact that his hand dwarfed hers when he enclosed it in his palm. He towered over her—a Border chieftain of renown, a freebooter in diamond buckles and courtly attire.

"I'm not afraid of being hurt," she quietly replied, her face lifted to his, the warmth of his hand surrounding hers. She smiled then, her green cat's eyes gazing up at him from under a drift of lacy lashes. "I'm afraid of being forgotten."

He grinned, boyish and sweet, his ruffled dark hair framing his aquiline face, a small gold earring visible for the first time on his left ear as he brushed his hair back in an unconscious gesture. "I never forget." He said it very plainly, the way a boy would assure his mother of some act of faith.

She liked the simplicity of his reply. It reassured her . . . although she wondered for a cynical moment whether in her current state of desire she would have accepted any suave disclaimer.

"You're very gallant," she said, and touched her free hand to the downy black silk of one brow. "I've been wanting to do that," she remarked, as direct as he and as simply.

"It's a start," he noted, his grin widening so his fine white teeth showed in the dark bronze of his face. "What I've been wanting to do," he went on, his voice a low murmur, his hand tightening on hers, "is see you lying on that bed."

Without pretense or coyness she said, "You have to stay the night then." Imperious, she was setting the guidelines.

Unknowingly, Elizabeth Graham was offering him paradise, but he controlled his exultation. Pulling her close in a fierce rush of pleasure, he whispered as his mouth touched hers, "My pleasure . . ."

She tasted sweet as he'd imagined.

His mouth, she thought with shameless joy, was resolutely twenty-five . . . and wonderful. He tasted deliciously of Rhenish wine, and when she told him so, he offered to pour her some.

She refused, drunk already with uncontrollable desire.

A fact he'd noted with a connoisseur's eye for detail. She hadn't had lovers, he could tell. And that knowledge brought his own urgent passion to the flash point.

They didn't wait the first time for languorous kisses and drawn-out foreplay. He had, in fact, to rush, for she said, breathless with passion, "I can't wait," while he was unclasping the closure at the neck of her fur-collared robe. Momentarily startled, he quickly improvised and, slipping his hands under her knees, lifted her into his arms.

She clung to him as he carried her to the bed, covering his face with kisses, beside herself with desire, not caring if he thought her shameless. She'd never experienced the sheer physical splendor of youthful muscled strength, and the feel of him, powerful and hard against her body, intoxicated her, made her dizzy with longing.

Reaching the bed in three lithe strides, Johnnie laid her on the crewel-worked coverlet and lace-trimmed pillows, following her down when she wouldn't release her arms from his neck, kissing her while he gently extricated himself from her grasp.

"I'm not going anywhere," he murmured as she whimpered, frantic at her loss. "I'm here," he soothed, "I'm staying. . . ." And he wondered at the degree of her deprivation during the years of her marriage.

"Help me," she whispered, flagrant in her need, beyond pride, humbled by her desire for this man who wouldn't remember her next week. No longer caring, with her aching need overwhelming all else . . . she only wanted to feel him inside her.

"We'll help each other," he breathed, his face very close to hers as he traced the curve of her mouth with a fingertip. "A few seconds more . . ." And he brushed aside the hem of her robe, beginning to push it upward to free her body from the encumbrance of the voluminous garments. When his fingertips brushed her thigh, she climaxed with a muted groan.

Incompletely, imperfectly. And tears filled her eyes.

"Don't cry," Johnnie softly said. "You'll feel better next time. . . ."

Her lashes fluttered open at his words, a small inkling of recognition flaring in the green of her eyes.

"There *is* a next time, darling child," Johnnie murmured, feeling eons older than the untried woman who apparently didn't know there could be. He stroked her warm thigh, a light upward drifting of his fingertips, a gentle motion, incidental to his words.

Overcome by a flaring heat spiking upward from his touch, she moaned, an indistinct sound muffled by her notions of nicety. Conscious of her repression, Johnnie moved his hand closer to the seat of her desire. "No one's here . . . except you and me. There aren't any rules. . . ." His soft voice mollified and absolved her, his warm palm resting firmly on her mons made her forget all a young woman was taught about purity and licentiousness, about temptation and excess.

"You never have rules, though," she murmured, her huge eyes half-drowsy already with new-felt passion. "I haven't had as much practice."

If he'd been less polite, he would have mentioned

she'd had no practice at all, but in a strange way that circumstance roused him more acutely than a dozen proficient Janet Lindsays.

"Well, then," he whispered, lifting up the brocade robe and night rail so her pale white flesh was exposed from the swell of her breasts to her toes, "we'll have to apply ourselves to remedy that situation."

"I won't be biddable." Her voice had a small edge to it, and he wondered how often in her past she'd been admonished to conform.

"Tell me no whenever you wish. I'm not overly selfish ... although," he added with a teasing grin, "if you don't mind, my darling Elizabeth, we'll slow the pace just a fraction this time."

"Am I supposed to apologize?" She was half-teasing now, the transient seriousness banished from her gaze.

"Never apologize in bed—rule number one, and that's the only rule recognized, although if you don't mind," he added, the fair hair between her legs gleaming like innocence, "we'll slow the pace *next* time." His own need for release—albeit more controllable than hers—was fierce; he'd been wanting to lie with her since Uswayford.

He reached for the buttons on his breeches.

And found her small hands ready to help.

Unskilled and clumsy, she was allowed to unfasten two of the gold buttons before he placed her hands on his shoulders with a smile and swiftly finished the task. If he didn't hurry, he'd embarrass himself like a schoolboy, and after six days of resisting Elizabeth Graham's allure, he wasn't about to relinquish the pleasure of climaxing inside her sweetness. He quickly lowered himself between her warm thighs and guided himself into her warmth.

She fit around him with perfection, and when she lifted her hips to draw him in more completely, enchantment streaked up his spine and exploded inside his head like corporeal pleasure. Gratified, more, obsessed with sensation, he glided into her slick, hot passage, penetrating deeply in compliance with the lady's strong, insistent hands on his lower back. His withdrawal was leisurely, the continuing, languid rhythm of withdrawal and penetration a tantalizing dance of passion enchanting for them both. And when he could no longer wait, he moved that small obliging distance more, so he touched her where sensation exquisitely peaked, and he heard her climax break in a high, keening cry.

A step behind the impetuous Lady Graham, he was able to please her again almost immediately as she followed him a third orgasmic time in conjunction with his own explosive release.

Reaching up, she rained kisses on his face and neck and chest in grateful, blissful content as he rested above her, her soft, breathy words of gratitude and awe punctuation to her trail of kisses.

His own sense of satisfaction throbbed in his head and toes and fingers and in his erection rampant still. He liked her kisses, he liked the feel of her surrounding him, he liked her hands stroking his spine, and he considered with satisfaction the number of hours until dawn.

"Is it possible . . ." she said into the bewitching afterglow that bathed the room in resplendent gold quite separate from the candlelight, "I don't know . . . and I don't wish to appear greedy, but with . . . your experience—well—you *should* know . . . I mean—do you think—"

"I can keep you up all night, darling," he replied, amusement rich in his voice, "if that's what you're trying to ask."

Her eyes opened wide, eloquent with surprise and astonishment. "All night?" she breathed, clearly amazed.

"All night, darling Bitsy," he gently answered, the image of a child in a candy shop coming emphatically to mind, "unless you think you're too old."

She stuck her tongue out at him, prompting him to cheerfully reconsider her maturity on several counts. "You're absolutely perfect," he assured her, "not too young, not too old, faultless in every respect," he facetiously went on, "except . . ."

"Except?" Uncertainty and a kind of newfound arrogance simultaneously infused her tone, a sense of wonder and accomplishment blissfully existing in concert.

"You've too many clothes on," he said in the direct way men approaching problems do.

"Oh . . . is that all? I was afraid I'd made some terrible sexual faux pas. Um, can women ask for things—I mean—" At his seductive grin she knowingly acknowledged, "With you . . . they can ask for anything, can't they?"

"I'm always willing to learn," he teased.

"So modest . . ." Elizabeth purred.

"One of my many virtues." Johnnie Carre could almost make her believe he had virtues with the radiance of his smile.

"But not one I'm currently interested in." Her own smile was pure seduction.

"A wanton woman. How nice." His pale blue eyes glittered down at her, alive with merriment.

"Yes, isn't it?" she honestly murmured, enjoying all this night offered her, her life too long bereft of pleasure. "And now, if you'll just give me a minute," she went on, tumbling him off her and rolling from the bed, "we'll see how you respond to some suggestions. . . ."

Lying on his back in an abandoned sprawl, he laughed out loud, the sound one of roguish pleasure. Turning on his side, he propped his head on his hand and, surveying her with a faint smile as she unfastened the closures on her robe, mildly said, "I look forward to the education. Was Hotchane a good teacher?"

"None of your damn business," she sweetly replied. "Are men always territorial?"

Lifting his brows and the palm of the hand not currently supporting his head, he shrugged and said, "Certainly not me."

"Good." Too long under the dominance of a father or husband, touchy and thin-skinned regarding control, she wished to make her position clear. And slipping her arms free of the night rail and robe, she let the garments slip to the floor. Gloriously nude, slender and long-legged and feeling unreservedly free, she pointed out to Johnnie with coquettish innuendo, "Now *you're* overdressed."

He readily obliged her, divesting himself of his clothing with a prompt readiness. Lying on the bed some moments later, bronzed and powerful, a pagan god, half rogue, half sublime splendor, he opened his arms to her and caught her effortlessly in midair when she leaped at him in gamboling frolic. Tumbling over on the wide bed made in the days when families slept together, he rolled her under him and, amid giggles and laughter, kissed her while she wiggled and squirmed like a puppy and kissed him back.

She was by turns playful and serious that night, deeply moved at times by her new awareness of the pleasure two people could give each other.

"May I?" she'd asked once early in the night, her eyes on the object of all her pleasure. At his smiling accession she'd touched the thrusting tip lightly with her fingertip as though it were dangerous. It wasn't, she discovered as she experimented with a growing assertiveness. Such tentative sensuality brought back long-forgotten memories to Johnnie Carre, and his smile was like the one enjoyed by the young Duchesse D'Artois during his schooldays in Paris.

"More, more . . . more, more . . ." Elizabeth joyfully demanded, long hours later, voluptuous and genial, sweet as marzipan kisses. And Johnnie Carre, young and captivated and willing, obliged.

Johnnie found himself curiously touched by her utter abandon and ingenuous appreciation, by the simple charm of her delight in him. Long after midnight, when the candles were burning low and the fire had almost died out, when she was once again momentarily sated and she lay in his arms, curled close to the warmth of his body, she told him, "I never thought I'd experience such pleasure. My measure of contentment was paltry in comparison. Thank you, Johnnie." Reaching up, she kissed him gently.

With such unsophisticated candor, childlike in its naïveté, he found himself momentarily questioning all the casual entanglements in his past. And more than his usual self-indulgence affected his senses that night. He found his heart touched by the unreserved depth of her need.

"I never knew . . ." she murmured just before she

fell asleep. Smiling contentedly, she snuggled closer, her pale, fragrant hair draped over his arm, the warmth of her breath on his chest. "And now I do," she finished with a sigh.

She reached up in her sleep later to touch his face.

"I'm here," he whispered in reassurance, taking her hand and gently kissing her palm.

She smiled in her sleep, content.

When she'd had enough of all he could give her and she no longer woke, he discovered he couldn't sleep.

Uncharacteristically for a man who could snatch a nap on horseback, sleep eluded him.

He didn't know why, or, more precisely, he didn't want to know why.

But he watched the sun rise before he kissed Elizabeth Graham awake, and when he made love to her before leaving, he experienced a poignant sense of sorrow.

A first for Johnnie Carre.

They said good-bye in the morning, because political factions didn't realign and age-old enemies reconcile in recognition of two people sharing a night of pleasure.

In any event, a world of differences separated them.

Nations separated them.

Cause and motive and protocol separated them.

They understood.

"I'd like to cordially thank you," she said at the end, when they'd both politely bid adieu to each other as if they weren't lying nude in each other's arms. As if they were parting instead at some obligatory afternoon soiree. "For a very enjoyable night."

He looked down at her quickly from under his

lashes, gauging the exactitude of her words. He'd never been precisely thanked before.

She smiled up at him, her cheek resting against his chest as she lay in the curve of his arm. "You aren't usually thanked, I presume, from the look on your face."

A sudden smile lifted the corners of his mouth. "You're the first, actually. But you're very welcome. And if the borders separating us weren't so vast, I'd say, Come and see me anytime. . . ."

"And if some international incident weren't likely to occur because of my visit, I might be tempted."

And he was tempted, too, if he didn't hold her father in such loathing. "The discretion could be handled easily enough. We cross the border with great frequency. It's the rest. . . ."

"My father, you mean." She spoke of him with a sudden coolness in her voice.

"He and his keepers both. The Sassenach are looking for provocation since last year's Parliament. I don't intend to be their victim."

"Will Scotland really seek independence?" She recalled that in November, when the first Scottish Parliament to sit since 1689 had adjourned, several acts hostile to England had been sent south to London. With the succession in question after a hundred years of a common monarch and Continental courts once again interested in Scottish affairs for their own private ends, Scotland's opportunity for leverage against England had arrived.

Johnnie exhaled softly, reluctant to reveal any significant political intelligence; regardless of their intimacy, she was the daughter of his enemy. "There're many who feel that way," he neutrally replied.

"Do you?"

"Would I tell a Sassenach that?" he said with a grin, touching the tip of her nose lightly with his finger. "Even if she's more fascinating than Circe herself."

"Am I really?" Her voice was filled with a girl's curiosity.

"Surely, other men have told you that."

She paused for a moment, as if considering. "Never," she said then, very simply.

Shocked at her answer, for her green-eyed, golden beauty was incomparable, he said, "Did Hotchane lock you away?"

"No, but I was his property."

"And no one cared to die over a compliment."

"Something like that." Her voice had gone very quiet suddenly. But only seconds later her chin came up, a small pugnacious gesture. "It won't happen to me again."

"You say that with some conviction," Johnnie said, his voice teasing.

"I've had eight years to become convinced of the merits of independence," she softly replied.

"I wish you much luck then." He knew the limits of female independence in the culture of his time and chose not to reply with complete frankness.

"You don't need luck with an inheritance like mine."

"Perhaps not as much," he ambiguously said, in no position after a single night in her company to presume to direct her life. But women alone were prey to coercion of many kinds; he'd seen his share of females used as pawns by families with fewer scruples than avarice.

"Hotchane's Redesdale men are an additional aid to my independence."

"Of course," he said. But they wouldn't follow her; they required a man who'd proved himself their leader, who added to their coffers with occasional lucrative raids. He expected several members of Hotchane's family were already jockeying for that powerful position. "Do you have a personal guard?" he inquired, debating how much he owed her for the pleasure she'd given him.

"A small one."

"How many?" Trained to border-raiding, he was already calculating the number required for her safety.

"Sixty."

Not a small force in anyone's estimation; clearly she understood her peril. "Are they trustworthy?"

"Infinitely."

Sliding up on the pillows stacked behind him into a sitting position, he shifted her onto his lap in a swift, graceful movement that belied the enormous strength required to lift her weight so effortlessly. "You sound very certain," he said. "How do you know they're completely loyal to you?" Hotchane's bloodthirsty relatives occasioned in him a genuine concern for her safety. The extent of her wealth made her excessively vulnerable.

"They've been my personal bodyguard for eight years; I trust them implicitly."

Sixty lawless Redesdale men should prove sufficient, he decided, relieved at her certainty. "You know Hotchane's sons will be after your money," he cautioned.

"The list of persons anxious to relieve me of my money is extensive, beginning with my father. Are you sure you don't want any?" she facetiously inquired, comfortable in his arms, strangely secure even knowing she was theoretically his enemy.

"I don't take money from women," he quietly said, "even if I needed it—which I don't."

"A wealthy Scotsman? Surely, you're a rarity." She was teasing still, feeling curiously happy.

"There *are* a few of us, despite England's disadvantageous trading terms for Scotland," he dryly replied.

"I'm sorry," she instantly returned, aware of England's prejudicial policies and her recent uncharitable reaction to the Darien colony that had further beggared Scotland.[5] "Forgive my tactlessness."

"Forgiven," he said with a smile. "And now, if you don't mind . . . With a beautiful woman in my arms, I prefer a less political conversation." His mouth softly brushed the curve of her cheek. "We don't have to leave," he murmured, his breath warm on her skin, "for another ten minutes. . . ."

"How nice," she whispered, lacing her arms around his broad shoulders, reaching up to nibble on his bottom lip. "But then," she murmured against his mouth, her words a delicate vibration on his lips, "I don't really care if Father waits for me. . . ."

CHAPTER 8

Harold Godfrey didn't wait, as it turned out, because Johnnie Carre had a young brother to ransom, and he wasn't taking any chances. But the Laird of Ravensby's houseguest had no complaints, and the Carre troop arrived at the designated rendezvous point precisely as agreed.

Waiting for the English to appear, they sat their horses side by side in the open field at Roundtree, a chill breeze from the north promising rain. Swirling remnants of fog covered the low ground, twisted between the horses' legs on fitful gusts, mist from the nearby loch drifting by in wispy fingers. The sun, hidden behind lowering clouds, tipped the uppermost reaches of the overcast, as if silvery lace edged the vast canopy of sky.

Separated by a dozen yards from the Carre horsemen, Elizabeth and Johnnie waited in silence, the little they could say to each other of farewell having been said in bed that morning. Both were experiencing a novel sense of loss, unusual for two people who had long ago learned to hide their emotions. Both were paradoxically wishing for the Harbottle troop to appear more swiftly or not at all. Both were acutely aware of each other's presence

Johnnie shifted his gaze from the southern horizon over which Godfrey's horsemen would appear and turned to Elizabeth. He found himself drawn to her as though minutes were ticking away in some internal timepiece that would break forever when they parted. Framed by the softly draped lavender wool of a hooded cape, her exquisite face was pinked from the breeze; pale wisps of her hair, loosened by the wind, blew across her cheeks. She had faint blue shadows under her eyes, he noted, her fair skin bruised by fatigue.

"Forgive me for keeping you up all night," Johnnie murmured, reaching out to gently touch her gloved hand where it rested on the saddle pommel, the embroidered violet leather a vibrant touch of color in the misty landscape. "You must be tired."

Her smile when she turned to him held that particular winsome innocence he found so captivating, and he almost said, "I'm keeping you," the impulse instant, powerful. He could have, too ... and taken his chances at overcoming Godfrey's troopers guarding Robbie. But he didn't confess his transient urge to possess her, nor did Elizabeth express the tumult of her emotions. "I'm *pleasantly* tired," she simply replied, "and there's no need to apologize."

She could have been assuring him the hospitality of his dinner table had been adequate, so temperate was her tone.

Her words strengthened his brief lapse from practicality. "In that case," he said with a charming nonchalance she immediately suspected came effortlessly to a man reputed to be accessible to all the beautiful women pursuing him, "I'll save my small reserves of gallantry for the coming confrontation with your father. I'll need whatever politesse was beaten into me by my tutors to keep from strangling him." His grin mitigated the threat of his words.

Her own grin was equally casual. He had the capacity to inspire cheer no matter how dismal the circumstances. It was his lighthearted smile, she decided. "Never fear, your brother's safe," she assured him. "Father is intent on having my inheritance."

"Will you be all right?" Genuine concern colored his words; he knew the ruthless character of Harold Godfrey.

"My money's hidden; Hotchane understood my father well."

"After hammering out the marriage settlement, no doubt," Johnnie dryly noted.

"Exactly."

"You're sure you're safe then?" His need for assurance surprised him. Women rarely interested him beyond the immediacy of lovemaking.

"I'm not sixteen anymore," she whispered.

One dark brow rose wolfishly. And his voice, too, was hushed. "No argument there."

"You project an outrageous sexuality, my Lord," she murmured, as a tingling heat raced through her senses. Dressed in a black leather jack, worn chamois breeches, and riding boots, his sleek, dark hair lying free on his shoulders, he exuded an intense virility, his lean, athletic body relaxed, graceful in the saddle.

"But no match, Lady Graham," he quietly whispered, his dark brows rising in gentle emphasis, "for yours. . . ."

"Is that a compliment?" she flirtatiously replied, wanting to dispel the melancholy of their leave-taking, taking her cue from Johnnie's easy smile. "Do well-bred ladies respond to such personal comments?"

"It's definitely a compliment, my dear Bitsy." His eyes, the color of summer skies that morning, leisurely perused her. "As for well-bred ladies . . ." he went on, his gaze returned to her face. And as he debated what to tell her, a cheer erupted behind them. The English troopers had ridden over the horizon. And issues of good breeding were instantly displaced by more pertinent issues of politics.

"Pardon me," he said, his voice suddenly changed, chill, businesslike, and he gathered her reins into one of his large gloved hands. "A precaution only . . ." he added, no smile on his face this time, his glance dismissive as he raised his free hand briefly to bring his men up.

She watched him become Laird of Ravensby before her eyes, a sudden transformation from the warmhearted, teasing man she'd spent the night with, whom she had only seconds before regarded with pleasure. Grim-faced now, commanding, he directed his lieutenants with brisk orders, his gaze sweeping the ranks of English troopers, searching for his brother. And moments later, when he caught sight of Robbie in the midst of a strong English guard, he murmured, "Thank God," in a gruff, relieved utterance. His eyes intent on the advancing English, he twisted Elizabeth's reins another turn tighter around his hand and pulled her mount closer. Swiveling away from her in his saddle, he turned enough so his voice reached all of his men. "Now watch the bastard Godfrey," he said. "Watch his eyes and his hands and his deceitful face. Pay attention to the men in the farthest ranks, take note of any unusual hand signals. You can't trust a Sassenach," he softly finished, "to keep his word."

It was as though she no longer existed, Elizabeth thought, the past week forgotten, last night not even a memory. The animosity between English and Scots ran too deep, centuries of hatred a powerful deterrent to personal feelings. She could as well have been a herd of cattle being traded back or a prized mare stolen in a midnight raid.

"Robbie looks well," someone remarked.

"He'd better," Johnnie replied, curt, decisive.

"The lad's carrying a lady's scarf tied round his arm," another clansman noted, surprise in his voice.

"And a smile on his bonny face," a voice from the back jovially declared.

A ripple of laughter ran through the ranks of armed men.

"Sassenach hospitality's improved," Adam Carre said.

"Or Hamilton's letter eased his stay," Johnnie quietly added. The Duke of Hamilton, suspected by many of closer relations with the English than he admitted, had been persuaded to write to Godfrey on Robbie's behalf.

"Like you eased Hamilton's debts."

"We were fortunate he always has need of money."

Then Robbie waved, an ebullient, unrestrained gesture, the lady's favor tied round his arm fluttering in the breeze, and a wide smile instantly altered the gravity of Johnnie's expression.

There was no resemblance at all, Elizabeth swiftly observed, as Robbie Carre came more closely into view, between the brothers. No younger version of the huge, dark man at her side rode at her father's flank. Instead, Robbie Carre had brilliant rust-red hair favoring curls, the whipcord-lean body of youth, a restless, unrestrained energy even visible from a distance, and the face of a troubadour. Refined rather than starkly modeled like his older brother, with enormous dark eyes, his features reminded her of a Renaissance prince. All subtlety and elegance.

Then he smiled.

And Johnnie's smile shone on his face . . . exactly.

"Are you ready?" Johnnie said, not to her but to his lieutenants.

"The muskets are behind the tree line. We're at your back." Kinmont's voice was no more than a murmur.

And with a minute nod of acknowledgment Johnnie urged his black forward, drawing Elizabeth's mount along with a sudden jerk of her reins, their legs suddenly brushing as he pulled her closely to his side.

He seemed not to notice; Elizabeth felt the hard strength of his booted leg and thought instantly of the muscled feel of his body. He was warm, her errant mind reminisced, so hot-blooded and heated, her hands felt cool on his skin. And he moved with infinite grace, she recalled, his muscles rippling and coiling beneath her palms with tensile strength. The night she'd spent in his arms would stay forever in her memory—his pas-

sion, his power, his teasing smile and eyes, the pleasure
he gave so generously. She glanced at him as if to preserve a final image in her mind.

And was struck by his splendid, stark beauty: the
gleam of his long black hair, his perfect profile etched
against the ashen sky, his potent power evident in the
width of his broad shoulders, the bulging muscles of his
thigh, his strapping arm beneath the fine burgundy wool
of his shirt, the sheer brawn of his wrist visible between
his cuff and the rolled edge of his glove—an overwhelming display of brute force.

But she was struck as well by his utter remoteness.
He had displaced her already from his life.

As previously arranged in the weeklong negotiations,
Godfrey and Johnnie rode forward alone with the hostages.

The English Warden of Harbottle Castle, a large,
fair-complexioned, handsome man, now past fifty, was remarkably fit for his age. Thanks in part to London's best
armorer, the corpulence of thirty years' dissipation was
partially concealed beneath the well-cut leather and elegant bossing of his silver-studded jack. Although a man
of commanding presence, he had a mean and selfish soul,
completely without honesty or resolution. False and
cruel, covetous and imperious, altogether destitute of the
sacred ties of honor, loyalty, justice, and gratitude, for
three decades he had functioned perfectly as an agent of
the Court.

Unarmed, as they all were, without jack or helmet,
Robbie sat his mount with a casual indolence, easily
keeping pace with Godfrey's Yorkshire-bred chestnut, his
youthful good spirits in marked contrast to the Earl of
Brusisson's lowering scowl.

Rarely bested in a long life of ruthless acquisition
and cunning maneuvering for advantage, Harold Godfrey
had been forced to acknowledge the rash success of the
Carre chieftain at thwarting him. Not only had he lost
the opportunity for an enormous ransom, but his daugh-

ter had been snatched from under the very shadow of Harbottle Castle, a galling embarrassment for which he intended future redress.

"Don't think you'll get away with this, Ravensby," he curtly said as they pulled their horses to a halt on the windswept field, his hand reaching for his missing sword in an automatic gesture of animosity.

"But I already have, Godfrey," Johnnie said, his voice bland. "Consider your current position."

"A temporary necessity, no more," Elizabeth's father bluntly retorted. "Short-lived as your Parliament's naive rush of patriotism."

"At least we still have the capacity for naïveté, my Lord," Johnnie said with an impudent civility. "England is bereft of all but deceit. And now, sir," he went on, not interested in trading insults with an old enemy, "your daughter is returned to you." He wished only to have Robbie back and be done with Harold Godfrey.

Taking note finally of his daughter, Godfrey scrutinized Elizabeth's pale face and, goaded by Johnnie's insolence, demanded sharp as a whiplash, "Did he mistreat you?"

His tone struck Elizabeth harshly like a blow. And for the briefest moment she was vulnerable to her past. But she had vowed at Hotchane's death to sustain her independence, and in a fleeting moment more, her composure returned. "No," she quietly answered, thinking the words so wrong for what Johnnie had given her. "I was dealt with honorably."

Something in her voice caught her father's attention, for he paused a moment, his gaze insolently traveling down her caped form. "Will you be bringing a Carre bastard into the world sometime soon, then?"

"Mind your manners," Johnnie brusquely challenged.

"I'll speak to my daughter as I please," the Earl of Brusisson snapped. "Did you fuck her, Ravensby, like you fuck all the women?"

"You insult her," Johnnie said, his voice utterly without expression, the possible consequences of a Carre bastard entirely his responsibility, not hers. Elizabeth's innocence had been no match for him. "Retract your words, Godfrey," he went on with a forced politesse, "and apologize or pay for your rudeness."

"And you'll make me pay, you arrogant pup?" Harold Godfrey's reputation as a swordsman hadn't diminished with age.

"I will," Johnnie quietly said, "and I'll kill you this time." He'd trained on the Continent and at his father's side, and his skill was celebrated.

"Ah . . ." the English Warden drawled, unintimidated, confident experience would always prevail over youth. "A gallant knight to defend your honor, my virtuous daughter. Remind me to keep you locked up for a few months, and we'll see if there are more personal reasons for his chivalrous defense."

Johnnie had had no intention of challenging the Earl of Brusisson; he had in fact intended to politely exchange Elizabeth Graham for his brother with a minimum of conversation, no display of emotion, and expeditious speed. But Godfrey was more of a Sassenach pig today than he'd expected. "I'm surprised you recognize gallantry, Godfrey," he said in a lazy drawl. "But since you apparently do"— and his voice changed suddenly to an icy chill—"kindly name your weapons."

"That's absolutely enough!" Elizabeth furiously exploded. "If you two would *kindly*," she sarcastically emphasized, "forget your utterly useless, masculine sense of outrage for a moment, we could expedite this exchange. And, Father," she went on, glaring at the man who had sold her unwillingself into eight years of conjugal servitude, "if you so much as put a finger on me, I'll see that you never come within a mile of my money. In addition," she said, her voice as unyielding as her rigid spine, "I'll have you skinned alive—literally. My bodyguard, Redmond, has long-standing orders from Hotchane to do just that should you harm me."

"I'd definitely listen to the lady, Johnnie," Robbie cheerfully interposed, amiable and good-humored, detached from the dramatic emotion. "She appears to have the situation under control without your accomplished sword arm."

"This Redmond is competent?" Johnnie inquired, his voice silky.

"Don't toy with me, Ravensby."

He'd not heard that uncompromising tone of voice before in the week of her detention, and he knew at that moment how she'd survived eight years of marriage to Hotchane Graham—a man not known for his benevolence.

"As you wish, Lady Graham," he replied, all fine breeding and deference. "Your servant, ma'am." He bowed gracefully from his saddle. "And with your assent," he mockingly said to Godfrey, whose violent disposition had been summarily tempered by the graphic threat of Hotchane's posthumous orders, "my brother and I will take our leave."

With cheeky boldness Robbie unwound his reins from Godfrey's saddle pommel, looked at his brother for sanction, and at an infinitesimal nod from Johnnie swung his mount away from his Harbottle warder.

A fraction of a second later, waiting only long enough to see his brother free, without a word to Godfrey or Elizabeth, Johnnie nudged his black into a turn, kicked his horse into a canter, and the brothers Carre began their journey home.

The exchange was over.

The brief acquaintance of Elizabeth Graham and the Laird of Ravensby was over.

In that moment the sun broke through the threatening clouds in shafts of glorious golden light, like glittering fingers from heaven, bestowing blessing on the consummated trade.

CHAPTER 9

The celebration of Robbie's return lasted three festive, sleepless, roisterous days, and would have continued longer had it not been interrupted by a messenger from Berwick with news of their long-overdue ship from Macao. The *Raven* was currently anchored off Berwick, waiting to be offloaded with luxuries from the East.

"Your homecoming brought us luck," Johnnie cheerfully declared, raising himself into a more upright position from his indolent sprawl in a heavily carved armchair at the head of the long dining table, the polished cherry wood littered with glasses and half-emptied bottles. He lifted his tumbler in theatrical salute to his brother and, waving a footman forward with a fresh bottle, said to their messenger of good cheer, "Sit down, Jervis, have a drink and fill us in. Robbie is back in the fold, which is why we're all celebrating," he went on in a lazy drawl, sweeping his arms expansively around the table to include all the Carre clansmen. "That ass Godfrey is licking his tarnished reputation in Harbottle Castle. England is currently being royally fucked over the funds for the army, and now that the *Raven* has returned after we thought you lost these three months past, all is infinitely right with the world."

"I'll drink to that," a rather drunken voice from the far end of the table remarked.

"Hear, hear, and to the Carre sword arm," another celebrant vigorously added.

A dozen men stood, a dozen voices thundered as one, glasses were emptied, chairs reclaimed, and Johnnie's smile of contentment re-echoed on each man's face.

"But then I've always brought you luck," Robbie facetiously noted, his grin evidence not only to the good news from Berwick but to three days of imbibing the best wines from Goldiehouses's cellars.

"For once I'm a believer," Johnnie replied, pouring Jervis another drink. "Some of your other escapades haven't been as profitable. This last one could have been a financial disaster."

"Godfrey's men were over the border, Johnnie, by five miles or more. It's God's truth. I'd not ride alone into Sassenach land."

"Even for Emily Lancaster?"

"Not since last Parliament session—my word on it."

They'd gone over the minutiae of Robbie's capture a dozen times since his return. The English troopers had been illegally in Roxburgh, it appeared; for what purpose was still unclear.

"Send some spies to Harbottle to ken their intent," Kinmont suggested.

"And find out what happened to the fair Elizabeth," a young lieutenant in a mellow frame of mind declared. "I wouldn't mind abducting her again, Johnnie. What say we ride south tonight?"

"She's returned to Redesdale," Johnnie said.

And even inebriated, every man understood what that simple sentence implied.

"So tell us, Johnnie, my fine stud," Munro dramatically murmured, his brows rising into his hairline, "how exactly you have possession of that information?"

And a dozen pair of eyes, in various degrees of

drunken languor, all consumed with curiosity, trained themselves on their young chieftain.

"A paid informer brought me the information."

"You paid someone to follow Elizabeth Graham." Munro seemed flabbergasted.

"I felt some responsibility for her."

"But not for any other woman." Munro was pressing slightly, his glass set aside, his tone interrogative.

"Her father's dangerous."

"Did you hear, then, if Redmond met her in Harbottle?" Robbie roguishly inquired. "The one with the skinning knife," he said as reminder to the table at large, the story of Elizabeth's threat a source of fascinated conversation after the exchange at Roundtree.

"As a matter of fact, he did." Johnnie appeared more sober suddenly, or perhaps simply less jovial. And those not completely in their cups noted a new edge to his voice. "And regardless of everyone's avid interest," he lazily drawled, his steady glance sweeping around the table, "I have nothing more to say about Lady Graham."

Despite his indolent tone, despite his quiet delivery, the coolness in his eyes prompted each man to understand the subject was closed.

"So tell us, Jervis," Adam Carre diplomatically inquired into the sudden silence, "do the ladies of Macao still favor those interesting positions?"

The return of the *Raven* set into motion a busy spring of trading, for two more of the Carre ships cleared the roads at Leith in the following weeks. Both brothers made individual trips to their warehouses in Rotterdam and Veere, to Bordeaux and Ostend, with portions of their Eastern goods. Tea from Canton, spices from the East Indies, Japanese silk out of Macao, Chinese porcelains—the sale of luxury goods was always exceedingly profitable, while the war on the Continent made all items more dear. Their return cargoes were primarily French wines; London merchants came to Edinburgh to buy the finest vintages.

One day at their warehouse in Leith, after having gone over their accounts with their factor, Johnnie said to his brother, "If this war runs on another two or three years, we'll be indecently wealthy. You can set yourself up as a bloody nabob at your property in East Lothian."

"Well, don't tell anyone. There're enough simpering misses with panting mamas chasing me already. I prefer being simply the Master of Graden with a modest living."

"It's easy enough to avoid those pursuing mamas," Johnnie said with a grin.

"Easy for you because you take pleasure in saying shocking things to prudish matrons. But admit, it only deters a minimum of determined mamas. The rest are still measuring you for the marriage bed despite your disreputable ways. The Carre fortune overrides even *your* propensity for scandal."

Johnnie cast his brother a speculative look. "Atholl's wife withdrew her daughter from the running."

"Only because that daughter was about to jump into bed with you without a marriage ring. They trundled her off to one of their remoter estates until she finds you less alluring."

"Really."

"You didn't notice, of course."

"Was she the tall brunette with the improved version of the Murray nose?"

"No, that's Talbot's daughter. Fortunately for the pretty chit, Atholl's daughter doesn't resemble anyone in her family. So with the exception of your unattainable hand, they'll be able to find her a husband easy enough, although with her heated desires, she might find one herself up in the Highlands."

Johnnie had lost his air of concentration several sentences ago, and at the smallest pause in Robbie's discussion of local courting rituals, he unceremoniously said, "I dislike this subject intensely. Enough of eligible young women; they're all a dull lot. Have you heard Hatton's plans? Is he coming up to Parliament early?"

"He, Dunston, and Fenshaw will all be in a fortnight beforehand. Are you expecting Munro to come for the excitement?"

"He tells me yes, although with the expected fight on seating, I don't know if he'll be allowed in. Tweedale has orders from London to seat no one save the members." Johnnie stretched comfortably in his chair. "I'm pleased for Hatton; his fiery brand of English baiting appeals to my irrepressible dislike of London's iron fist. And I'm anticipating Munro will probably come back with me. With the walls up on the new addition, I've orders to appear at Goldiehouse to give my approval. I don't suppose you're interested in joining me."

"Maybe next time."

"Maybe after Mrs. Barrett returns to her husband in Inverness?" Johnnie smoothly inquired.

Robbie grinned, his tanned skin touched with a pink flush. "Yes, after that would be much better for me," he said, consideration of his newest paramour prompting a smile of satisfaction.

"I don't suppose I need lecture you on discretion," Johnnie remarked. "Barrett may be old, but not senile."

"A lecture on discretion from you would be fascinating. What would you suggest?" Robbie inquired. "Not bedding the Chancellor's wife on High Street at noon?"

"I was thinking more seriously," Johnnie said in a temperate tone, "of keeping your sword close at hand, or at least your boot dirk. It's small enough to slip under a pillow. Barrett doesn't fight his own battles anymore, and the men he hires to settle his accounts aren't known for their honor."

"I'll be careful," Robbie replied with the nonchalance of youth.

"Why not take a few men with you to your nightly rendezvous with Mrs. Barrett?"

Robbie's amusement altered to a mild scrutiny. "You're serious."

"You weren't here last year when your inamorata was entertaining herself with one of the Glendale Armstrongs. He was savagely attacked leaving her house."

"Wat Armstrong?"

"Yes, and he'll never use his right arm again. He hovered near death for weeks." Johnnie closed the account book in front of him, leaned back in his chair, and gazed at his brother sitting across from him with a rare earnestness. "I'm not saying *Mrs. Barrett's* dangerous, but don't discount her husband's sense of insult."

The window behind Johnnie overlooked the busy harbor of Leith, their trading house conveniently located on the shore of the Firth of Forth. Gazing past his older brother at some distant point, Robbie said very softly, "Do you think that's part of the excitement?" For a moment Robbie's dark eyes seemed unfocused on the maritime scene, and then suddenly his gaze returned to Johnnie. "The possibility of violence . . ." he speculatively murmured. "Do you ever experience that intense arousal when a forbidden lady's sighing and trembling under you, and your exposed back is to the door?"

Johnnie smiled faintly but said, "No," to his young brother, who didn't need further encouragement in vice. "Never."

"Right. And that's why you've fought six duels in the last few years."

Johnnie shifted uncomfortably in his chair, awkward in his position of protector. "Well, I'm not recommending it, regardless. So take a guard with you. Please." His deep voice diminished in volume. "For me."

Robbie hesitated for a moment, youthful indiscretion struggling with moderation. Then he nodded.

His brother visibly relaxed. "Good," he said, gratified. "And now you'll live longer to enjoy the bountiful charms of Mrs. Barrett. I'll leave half the men with you when I ride to Goldiehouse in the morning."

"She spent a year at Versailles," Robbie said, recalling Mrs. Barrett's charms. "Did you know that?"

Johnnie knew; he also knew some of her particular excesses that year. But his brows rose in polite inquiry, and he softly repeated, "Versailles, you say." His voice took on an amused intonation. "*That* accounts, no doubt, for your acute interest. The Court of Versailles is unrivaled in superlative vice. How nice of Mr. Barrett to occasionally share his wife with the world."

"How nice for me," Robbie pleasantly agreed. "Why don't you join us for dinner tonight? She speaks French with a delightful small lisp."

"Thank you," Johnnie courteously replied, "but I'm already engaged." The possibility he and Mrs. Barrett could meet in friendship was remote after their last conversation, when she'd flounced away in a sulky pet. He'd simply pointed out to her one day last week, in the sumptuous privacy of her apartment subsidized by Robbie's generosity, that he had no problem with her cajoling expensive gifts from his young brother, but Robbie hadn't the experience of a Versailles courtier, who considered honesty a personal failing. And if she tried to blackmail Robbie as she had young Tallier, he would see that she spent the rest of her life in Inverness with her aged, bad-tempered husband.

"Are you seeing Roxie tonight?"

Johnnie nodded. "She has a gift for conversation."

"Among other things."

"Yes, of course," Johnnie acknowledged with a roguish smile, "among other things." Roxie was Edinburgh's reigning belle, and while he was enchanted by her beauty, he also enjoyed her cosmopolitan intellect. She kept him amused with all the latest gossip, scandal, and news from the Continent. And as a wealthy, twice-widowed young matron with a large brood of children and a penchant for independence, she wasn't in the market for a third husband. It was a decided factor in their long friendship.

"So I'll see you next when Parliament sits."

"Or two weeks earlier, if I have my way and Goldiehouse affairs allow." Raising an admonishing finger, Johnnie jabbed it once at his brother. "Remember the guards now. I don't usually press you on your style of living, but on this I will." A niggling unease still lingered.

"My word on it," Robbie soothed. "Rest easy. I'd just as soon keep the use of my sword arm intact. And now, if you don't have any more advice for me," he said, rising and picking up his riding gloves from the table spread with sailing charts and account ledgers, "I'll begin my evening of dissipation."

"Enjoy yourself," Johnnie said, looking up at his fair young brother. "I'm completely out of advice."

"And if we don't run into you at one of the evening soirees, give Roxie a kiss for me."

Johnnie grinned. "I'll give her two. She thinks you're sweet."

Robbie groaned.

"*Au contraire,*" Johnnie contradicted. "Her tone of voice definitely implied a compliment. Actually, if I recall," he went on with a smile, "she also said, 'I have a penchant for young men with red hair.' "

Robbie's expression brightened.

"So you see, when you lose interest in your Mrs. Barrett, consider the exquisite Roxie. . . ."

A flare of excitement touched Robbie's eyes. "Would you mind?"

"Why would I mind?" Johnnie calmly responded.

"Well . . . I just thought . . . that is . . . you've been seeing her for so long. . . ." Robbie shrugged. "Oh, hell . . ." he muttered, thwarted by the casual scope of his brother's reply, "I'll see you in two weeks." And on that confusion of half-formed thoughts and baffled frustration, he waved and left.

CHAPTER 10

In the meantime, while the Carre brothers were adding to their fortunes, Elizabeth Graham had diminished her hidden gold by a third. But willingly.

Since her return to Harbottle last March, she'd reached an uneasy truce with her father—for a price. With the understanding that he would discontinue harassing her about marriage to any and all men who might possibly be advantageous to his advancement at Court or his finances, she'd agreed to turn over to him one third of her cash inheritance. Twenty thousand pounds had been sufficiently tempting to Godfrey. So her attorney had immediately drawn up the necessary papers to protect her in court from his machinations. By law, she already had legal right to control the money left to her by Hotchane, but the added security of her father's signature on their agreement was well worth twenty thousand pounds.

Although she'd never trust him completely, and her bodyguard was ever alert to her security, she'd not heard

from her father since Harbottle. This offered her a modicum of comfort.

Returning to Three Kings in Redesdale almost immediately after leaving Goldiehouse, her spring had been
consumed by construction plans. With Munro's consent,
she'd continued to ask his advice, and they'd exchanged
letters on a regular basis.[6] She'd taken a hand in many of
the construction drawings herself, and was proud of her
newfound skill. While she'd hired a local master to help
her and oversee the building, she'd often think of some
new question to ask Munro. By June he'd begun teasing
her that they were single-handedly supporting the local
postal system, for he often sent along architecture books
with his letters. And Mrs. Reid, who always referred to
Elizabeth as "that sweet Lady Graham," had taken to
sending along fresh produce or new-baked pies or other
household items she thought Elizabeth would enjoy. Recently, the parcels had reached such proportions, two
Ravensby men had begun driving them to Redesdale.

And while none of this was deliberately concealed
from the Laird of Ravensby, since he'd not been in residence at Goldiehouse except briefly since the exchange
at Roundtree, he only became aware of the interchange
when he returned from Edinburgh in early June.

Returning from the stables after an early morning
ride, the fragrance of Mrs. Reid's strawberry tarts had
drawn him to the kitchen entrance, where he'd found her
carefully packing the pastries into cushioned wooden
crates.

"Now drive careful like—watch the potholes and
no sudden stops," she admonished the two men helping
her arrange the confections in the heavily ladened cart.
"I dinna want tha' pies to be al' mush for the sweet Lady
Graham."

At the sound of Elizabeth's name Johnnie literally
stopped in his tracks and stood for a moment on the
gravel drive, thinking he must have misunderstood.

"An when ye ken the Lady Graham, tell her the
new peas are fresh this morn so eat them right soon. And
the tatties are from the hothouse, not last season's. And

we'll have fresh strawberries for two weeks more, so I'll
be sendin some along next time too."

Elizabeth's name shouldn't have struck him so profoundly. He'd considered Roxie's company sufficient to
reduce memories of Elizabeth Graham to the far reaches
of his mind. But this commerce between their homes
brought her intimately into his life again. As though they
shared a residence again—or at least a housekeeper, he
wryly thought. And he struggled with his composure, for
he instantly visualized her again as she'd been that last
morning in bed. It seemed as though he could smell
her. . . .

Until he realized Mrs. Reid's clover soap was trig-
gering the sensations. Its fragrance was so vividly reminiscent of Elizabeth's skin, he'd refused to use it since
her departure.

"You're up early, Johnnie," Mrs. Reid said, noticing
him when she turned around from her ministrations in
the cart. "Are ye hungry after your ride?"

He ignored her question and mildly inquired,
"What do we have here?" He wanted to know how long
the exchanges between his home and Elizabeth's had
been taking place.

"We have goodies for Lady Graham I'm adding to
all them books Munro's always sending. Do ye have a
message yerself ye'd be liking to send her? Jed's memory
is perfect."

Not a message, Johnnie thought, that could be conveyed verbally by Jed. Although some comments came to
mind. . . . Instead, he courteously suggested, "Why don't
you send her some of the new wines? Although," he
added, almost immediately, "they probably won't travel
well."

"They travel just fine," Mrs. Reid cheerfully retorted. "I already sent her two cases of champagne, since
fine ladies do like that specially."

He found himself smiling, not only at his lack of
control in his household but at the charming picture of
Elizabeth enjoying his champagne. Or did she not drink?
he wondered. That night in the tower room, she'd refused his offer of wine.

How little he knew of her, he reflected, considering how she'd insinuated herself so powerfully into his thoughts the past months. In Edinburgh Roxie had helped of course to displace the remembrance, as had the busy incoming trade on their ships and his trips to the Continent. But whether he was drinking or sober, awake or sleeping, busy or at leisure, Lady Graham had figured prominently in his thoughts.

"Where's Munro?" he asked. He found he suddenly wished to know if Munro knew if Elizabeth drank champagne. As if the contentment and rhythm of his day turned on such a triviality.

And when he found his cousin minutes later in the library per Mrs. Reid's directions, he sank into a chair opposite him and bluntly said, "Does she drink champagne?"

"Are you referring to any 'she' in particular?" Munro facetiously replied, looking up owlishly from a rare copy of Vitruvius' *De Architectura*, wondering why it had taken Johnnie so long to come to him for enlightenment. He'd been home for two days.

"Yes, one in particular, and you have two seconds to give me the right answer," he said in a sulky drawl, "or I'll have those new walls taken down by sunset."

"She enjoyed it very much," Munro primly replied, "but when people are rude to me," he added with soft emphasis, "I find I forget so many things—"

"Bastard."

"And I thought you didn't care about women," Munro succinctly retorted.

"I don't care about women, plural. One in particular is driving me insane, as you well know."

"And the beautiful Roxie isn't extinguishing the flame?"

"Only transiently. Tell me now, before I strangle you."

"I accept your apology," Munro said with a grin. "What do you want to know?"

"What she's doing, how she looks, is she seeing anyone, mostly is she seeing anyone?"

And Munro commenced to tell Johnnie what he knew.

Numerous questions later, satisfied he'd heard all Munro could tell him, Johnnie thanked his cousin. "She seems content," he went on, "and her father's keeping his distance. Good." And then, as if none of their conversation had taken place, Johnnie said, "Can you be ready to leave with me by the fifteenth?"

"For?"

"The sessions in Edinburgh, of course. Where else?"

"I thought you might be visiting Lady Graham, after your keen curiosity in her life."

"I may be interested, but I'm not completely witless," he said with a smile. "Elizabeth Graham represents a veritable Pandora's box of political and personal repercussions that could raise havoc with my purely *selfish* life," he added in a lazy drawl. "*No* woman is worth that sacrifice," he said with finality. "Now if you don't need me today, after breakfast I'm riding over to the Blackwood estate to check the state of the timber for cutting." He stood quickly, impatient to be off.

At Munro's wave of dismissal he smiled and left.

But despite his bland denial about the degree of his interest in Elizabeth, he found it increasingly difficult to dislodge her image from his mind.

And when his estate manager, Gibson, sat down to dinner with Mrs. Reid and the majordomo that evening in Mrs. Reid's parlor, he said, "The Laird seemed preoccupied at Blackwood today. I had to ask every question twice, and he still didn't always respond. Do you think the possible war with England's on his mind?"

"Umph," Mrs. Reid pronounced. "As if a little war would make him daft. It's that woman he locked up here for a week. That sweet Lady Graham. If you ask me, he should take himself down to Three Kings and get her off his mind one way or another."

"But she's English," Gibson said, a degree of shock in his voice.

"As if our own Scottish kings haven't married an

English on occasion," Mrs. Reid returned with vigor. "And many a magnate has gone south for a wife."

"But England's garrisoning the Border castles," the majordomo reminded her.

"It don't mean ordinary folk can't go about their business."

"But the Laird dinna be ordinary folk," Gibson noted.

"Aye," Mrs. Reid said with a sigh, "and I suppose that's the rub."

CHAPTER 11

Johnnie had been in Edinburgh for a fortnight before
Parliament reconvened on July sixth. For two weeks, talk
had been volatile and contentious, days and nights spent
at Patrick Steil's planning tactics. Perhaps a more important battle than any military one, this summer's session
could well determine the future of Scotland's independence movement.

"Do you think Tweedale will recognize you on the
floor today?" Johnnie asked Andrew Fletcher as they
walked to Parliament on the first day.

"If not today, tomorrow," the older man replied.

As it turned out, it was a week later before the
Laird from Saltoun had his turn to speak. The opening
was delayed to allow nobles from outlying areas to arrive;
then challenges to seating had to be resolved, and a day
was required to read the letter from Queen Anne. The
missive was couched in terms of urgency, if not desperation, after the Parliament of 1703 had failed to approve
the Court's two main objectives: a vote of supply to pay

the armed forces and the approval of the Hanoverian Succession to the throne.

Andrew Fletcher, the natural leader of the Country party, was a man of ideals who appealed to all those weary of the selfish machinations of the Court and its co-horts. He spoke of Scotland's need for independence in terms of the classical government of Greece; and while many held less visionary opinions than he, most Scots-men wanted what he wanted.

For the next two weeks, through four sittings of sessions and fourteen days of behind-the-scenes tactical maneuvering by the Court and the opposition, during heated debate where passions ran high, fundamental is-sues about Scotland's future were emphatically debated.

Johnnie spoke eloquently against the Navigation Acts that had effectively shut out Scotland from most of the world's markets unless one's fleet was equipped with fast cruisers to outrun the British navy. He also spoke twice in defense of the volatile issue of refusing a vote of supply for England's army, literally putting his life on the line in sessions where hands often rested on swords and the possibility of duels was a daily occurrence. He be-lieved passionately in the issues of independence, and many nights he went without sleep in order to devise new strategies to check an unexpected maneuver of the Court.

The two weeks of trying to pull together frag-mented factions in order to pass the necessary resolves culminated on July twenty-fifth, when a new overture was offered on the vote of supply. Essentially Roxburgh suggested that if there was no independence for Scot-land, there must be no money for England's armies. Rox-burgh's overture carried by an overwhelming majority.

Tweedale, the Queen's Commissioner, immediately adjourned the sessions for ten days, giving him time to parley with London.

Talk ran high that night in Edinburgh and the ad-jacent countryside of their having won their way clear of England at last, of London being forced to approve the Act of Security or lose the desperately needed funds for the army. Marlborough was even now planning his march to Blenheim, so military uncertainty was a powerful reason for England to avoid provocation of Scotland. The mood at Roxane's dinner party the evening of the twenty-fifth was jubilant. A multitude of toasts were proposed to all who had worked so hard to resist the pressures of the Court.

"And may Queensberry burn in hell with his tainted money," Hatton declared in defiance, raising his glass to the table at large, vilifying the man.

"After he answers for his liability first here on earth," Johnnie cheerfully noted, his glass, newly refilled, lifted high.

"We'll pass the resolve on accounts after the adjournment," Lord Rothes said, his voice raspy after two weeks of shouting in the sessions. "Damned if we won't. And then Queensberry can pay up the forty-two thousand pounds he used for bribery."

"Or sell his daughter to you, Lanarck . . . to raise the money," Roxane suggested, a faint smile on her lovely face. "So what do all of you plan for the adjournment?" Roxane inquired into the hum of conversation. "Could I interest anyone in a sailing excursion between your councils of war at Patrick Steil's club?"

And a tentative time and place was settled on for two days hence. Afterward, she smiled down the long table at Johnnie, seated opposite her, playing host tonight to her assembled guests. "Did I mention we're using your yacht, my dear?" she said.

"No, but since you generally arrange my life without prior notice," he replied with a grin, "I assumed as much."

"You flatter me, Ravensby," she playfully said, his friend as much as his lover. "As if you'd let any woman order your life."

"Or you, Roxie, let any man dictate to you," her best friend, Elene, interposed.

"Which, no doubt, is why we get along so well . . ." Johnnie drawled, lifting his glass to her in salute, genuinely fond of the beautiful flame-haired woman.

"And if you wish to continue such harmonious accord," Roxane said to Johnnie, rising from her chair, a teasing light in her violet eyes, "you have thirty minutes to pass the decanter around after we women leave, and then I'll expect you to bring your political discussion into the drawing room." Her smile took in the full array of her male guests. "We'll have spirits for you there."

It was still early when Johnnie took his leave of Roxane, excusing himself from the play they were all attending, restless after several hours of drinking, a common occurrence for him since March. A drink or two now brought with it unwanted memories of the tower room at Goldiehouse, more vivid with the alcohol, never far from his consciousness even when he was sober. He hadn't seen her for four months . . . slightly more—and he couldn't remember a day he hadn't thought of Elizabeth Graham. Tonight he wasn't in the mood to trade pleasantries or amuse . . . or be amused.

Even his jubilation over the victory in the House today was tempered. Although he couldn't blame Elizabeth Graham exclusively for his moderated joy. She was a factor, of course, in his disquietude, his fickle mood, but his volatile thoughts of her had nothing to do with politics. In terms of Scotland's independence, he was more cynical than most, but then he was actively engaged in trade, and he was familiar with the Court of St. James's. He knew England's Parliament had no intention of allowing Scotland freedom in any arena: political, economic, or religious.

He desperately hoped he was wrong.

Too restless to sleep, too moody to partake of the camaraderie in the clubs, Johnnie stopped by Munro's apartment in Ravensby House to pass the time when he arrived home. Munro was in the process of packing.

"You're taking advantage of the adjournment, I see," Johnnie said, dropping into a cushioned chair near the door. "Checking on the state of the new addition at

Goldiehouse? Do me a favor and look in on my new colt. Adam writes he's grown enormously since I left. I haven't seen him in"—he mentally counted for a moment— "Lord, it's been over a month."

"I'm not going to Goldiehouse." Munro looked up briefly from the folding of a waistcoat. "I'm on my way to Teviotdale."

"You're mangling that waistcoat, Cuz. Why don't you have a servant do that for you? And where are you going in Teviotdale?"

"I told you. Hawick."

"Was I sober? I don't recall Hawick coming up in conversation." Leaning over to reach for a decanter and a glass set on a silver tray on a nearby table, he poured himself a measure of cognac, replaced the decanter, took a sip of the liquor, registered satisfaction in his expression, and, settling back in his chair, answered his own question. "I must have been drunk. Who in Hawick, where in Hawick?"

"Giles Lockhardt and the church in Hawick. It's his wedding."

"And who is poor trapped Giles marrying?" Johnnie mournfully queried.

"Angela Graham."

"Of the English Grahams?" Johnnie's voice had lost its leisured indifference. He knew Grahams lived on both sides of the border; he knew they were all related; he knew how short the distance between Three Kings and Hawick.

"No, the Scottish branch. And yes, to that penetrating look, Elizabeth is attending the wedding."

"How do you know? For certain."

"Because we're going over the final plans for her house. Her site is ready now for construction."

And the room was filled with a charged silence for several moments while Munro continued packing and Johnnie contemplated the liquor in his glass.

"I'll keep you company," Johnnie abruptly said, his voice no more than a murmur in the stillness.

Gazing across his bedchamber at his cousin, the large red damask chair framing Johnnie's dark hair, the brilliant green of his evening clothes, Munro said by way of discouragement, "You don't like weddings."

"I'm at loose ends for a few days," Johnnie calmly replied, stretching his legs out and contemplating the toes of his black kid shoes. "Hawick is pleasant in July. Unlike the stench of this city.[7] I'll ride along."

"I don't think she wants to see you."

Johnnie didn't pretend to misunderstand what he meant. "I have no evil designs on her person," he said.

"She might disagree with you," Munro sharply retorted, tossing a pair of socks into his bag with unnecessary force.

"I don't think she will." Struck by Munro's obvious affront, Johnnie quickly added, "Has she said so?"

"We speak of construction only."

"Then you're speculating."

"She's too genuine for you to dally with, Johnnie. She's only now living for the first time in her life." Munro continued throwing items into his luggage with obvious exasperation. "Don't ruin her contentment."

"Are you in love with her?" It startled him, the sudden revelation, Munro's resistance to his journey. "You *are* in love with her. Is that it?" He found himself inexplicably apprehensive.

"It wouldn't do me any good if I were," Munro said, turning toward Johnnie and sitting down heavily on his bed. "She's not in love with me."

"She told you so?"

"No."

"Then you can't be certain."

Munro's artistic fingers briefly traced the gold-filigree work on the corner of his small leather trunk. "Lord, Johnnie," he said, restlessly running his fingers through his sandy-colored hair, "I'm not a novice with women. I know when a lady's interested."

Johnnie found he'd been holding his breath. He exhaled slowly. "I see."

Munro's head came up, and his eyes met his cousin's. "You'll just hurt her; you're not looking for permanence. Tumble someone else if you're bored and beset with ennui and the stench of the city."

"Will you be angry if I come with you to Teviotdale?"

"Frustrated, more like. Elizabeth Graham's not sophisticated enough to withstand your predatory skills, and I'll have to watch you lure her into your bed."

"Suppose I respect her virtue and act the gentleman. Would that satisfy your reservations?"

"You can't."

"Why can't I?"

"You never have."

Johnnie shrugged. "Maybe I can."

" 'Maybe' doesn't protect her sufficiently."

"She may not need protection."

"She does from you."

"Do I detect some newfound chivalry from my cousin the womanizer?"

"Elizabeth's different," Munro slowly said, as if selecting each word to best explain his feelings. "She's wounded like a fragile bird by a lifetime of her malicious father's greed. She needs more protection than the Janet Lindsays of the world." Munro grimaced and looked out the window at the walled garden. Then, turning back to Johnnie, he exhaled a great sigh of resignation. "I shouldn't augment your already oversized ego," he softly said, "but I think she's half in love with you already."

Johnnie found himself strangely pleased at Munro's reluctant admission. Normally, women who fancied themselves in love with him generated a sensation of unease ... not this novel feeling of satisfaction. "What makes you think so?"

"I watched her at Goldiehouse even before you seduced her that last night."

"She told you about that?"

"Lord, no. No one had to tell anyone. You both fairly glowed the next morning."

Johnnie raised one disparaging brow. "I don't glow."

Munro's shoulders moved in a negligent gesture of dismissal. "Call it what you like. And she couldn't keep her eyes from you on the ride to Roundtree, no more than you could tear your attention from her."

"She's unusually beautiful. . . ." Unbidden memories of their night together fired his blood. Lacing his fingers together around the delicate glass, Johnnie inadvertently flexed his hands in unease. Oblivious to the cognac sloshing very close to the rim of the glass, his gaze focused somewhere above Munro's head, he slowly said, "I'm not promising anything. . . ." Then his eyes swung back to Munro's face, and it was his turn to sigh. "Oh, hell, I suppose I can try. But that's all I can guarantee. Although why I'm considering gentlemanly behavior anyway is beyond my comprehension. I can go to Giles's wedding with or without your consent; I can take Elizabeth Graham to bed with or without your approval. Seduction is a game of long standing, Munro, not just to me but to everyone. Tell me why I'm even considering self-denial, because I'm at a loss to understand."

"Because Elizabeth Graham isn't one of your usual highborn tarts. She's actually virtuous."

"I don't like virtuous women."

"You don't like most virtuous women."

"Maybe she's rolling in the hay by now with any number of her Redesdale bodyguard. She's a woman of passion, no mistake."

"Would you care to wager a significant sum on that possibility?"

Leaning his head back in his chair, Johnnie contemplated Munro's smug expression from under half-lowered lashes, his mouth a grim, straight line, the glass between his palms just short of being shattered. "You're irritating the hell out of me."

"Because I'm right and you know it, no matter you wish Elizabeth Graham was as available as all the other of your aristocratic ladyfriends."

"Why this sudden moral stance, Munro? Good God, why now, why me, why this woman we both barely know?"

"You can try to evade and avoid and circumvent and talk around this; you can more aptly, perhaps, wish you'd never met her—"

"Amen in spades to that," Johnnie grumpily muttered, slumping lower in his chair, setting his glass aside as if the liquor, too, had lost its taste.

"You could simply forget her," Munro suggested, a facetious gleam in his eye.

"Not likely that. She's inside my head like a perpetual vision, whether I'm drunk, sober, bedding someone else. . . ."

"You could approach her honorably."

"Meaning?"

"Court her."

Johnnie's eyes widened in alarm. "With what intention, pray tell?"

"Marriage, of course."

"Bite your tongue, man. I'm twenty-five."

"A predicament of enormous difficulty then." Munro seemed to be enjoying Johnnie's sudden discomfort.

"Fuck . . ." The muttered expletive signified his vast frustration.

"You could avoid the Hawick wedding."

"I want to see her. Don't ask me why. If I knew why, I could talk myself out of it."

"Well, then, it should be an interesting expedition." Munro grinned. "Are we going to wager anything on your self-control?"

"It pleases me to amuse you, my dear Munro, but I wouldn't recommend betting a shilling on my self-restraint." Johnnie's grin was faintly ironic. "After all, I haven't had much practice."

"You haven't had any practice at all, which should make for a diverting experience." Munro actually chuckled.

And Johnnie suddenly laughed too. "Lord, this is going to be unnatural."

"Only for you, my friend."

"And perhaps," Johnnie softly breathed, "for the Lady Graham as well. . . ."

CHAPTER 12

The lady in question was currently climbing into her carriage for the short journey across the border to Hawick. Well supplied with construction manuals, house plans, a dozen gowns, and a cheerful disposition, Elizabeth was very much looking forward to seeing Munro. She hadn't admitted to herself that her excitement at renewing her friendship with Munro had anything to do with his rash, handsome cousin. Nor did she allow herself to question her motives for attending the wedding of a cousin by marriage she barely knew.

She needed a holiday, she consciously allowed herself to admit. She'd been working feverishly overseeing the site preparation for her new home at Three Kings the past weeks; she needed some professional help to finish her plans. And when Munro had mentioned he'd be attending Lockhardt's wedding in Hawick, she thought, What better occasion to take advantage of his expertise?

So she deserved her first holiday in twenty-four years, she told herself.

She deserved the pleasure she was feeling in anticipation of seeing Munro again.

She felt gloriously young, an altogether uncommon feeling for a woman who had never had the opportunity to experience the joys of youth.

She felt blissfully like breaking into song. She smiled instead inside her luxuriously appointed carriage. She smiled so often, her maidservant told the driver at their stop for luncheon that she wondered if the mistress had been nipping at that new French brandy sent over from Ravensby.

Hotchane's relatives were pleased to welcome Elizabeth to the festivities; the young bride greeted her with open arms. No doubt her generous wedding gift added to the warmth of her reception, but what better way to spend her money than to give a lavish present to a young couple setting up housekeeping?

Elizabeth was kept busy from the moment she arrived on Saturday until late in the evening. Dozens of Grahams renewed their acquaintance with her; she'd forgotten how extensive the Graham clan was. And by ten o'clock she'd dined and danced and gossiped while watching out of the corner of her eye for Munro to appear. He'd planned on being there by two, he'd written.

But she knew he'd come; Munro was dependable. Something must have delayed him. In any event the wedding wasn't until Monday. Even with delays, he had time to reach Hawick.

And while Elizabeth was wondering at Munro's delay, he had just ridden into Hawick, hot, tired, dusty and without his favorite horse, which had gone lame at Ashkirk. The search for someone qualified to see to the care of the horse's leg had taken most of the afternoon. To further add to his discomfort, an uneasy apprehension had followed him from Edinburgh. He was clearly worried about his traveling companion's unpredictable behavior while in close proximity to Elizabeth Graham. And if all that weren't enough to cause him serious consternation, his cousin had decided to ease the boredom of their wait by drinking away the hours at the local tavern.

As they rode down the lane to the Graham country house, Munro was debating who at the Grahams' he could call on if Johnnie required subduing. After the third bottle, he knew, his brawny cousin took offense easily.

"Now you promised to remember your manners," he warned, as the lights of the house came into view.

"Lord, Munro, you worry. I drink more than this at breakfast sometimes. Relax."

"I'll relax when you're sober tomorrow."

Johnnie's grin shone in the moonlight. "What makes you think I'll be sober tomorrow?"

Munro groaned. "You're going to be a goddamned burden."

"Don't worry about me. I'll stay out of your way," Johnnie promised.

"That's what I'm afraid of. I'll have to keep you on a leash."

"An interesting concept if I were into perversity," Johnnie lazily replied, amusement in his voice. And then his head lifted slightly as the sound of music reached them over the moonlit meadow. "Ah, we haven't missed the dancing at least," he went on, as though the subject of his unmanageability hadn't come up. "Does Elizabeth dance?"

"I don't know. Lord, Johnnie," Munro exclaimed, frustrated after their hindered journey south, "you'd think I'd been raised as her twin. You'll have to find out for yourself."

"Actually, I was planning to," the Laird of Ravensby murmured. "In very short order . . ."

A swift half hour later, bathed, dressed, and at last smelling as if they hadn't ridden all day, the two men descended the main staircase, followed the sound of music down a meandering corridor to the baronial ballroom in the east wing, and stood in the doorway surveying the colorful throng.

Only two generations removed from a time of continuous border warfare, the ballroom reflected the Grahams' martial traditions. Beneath the high-ribbed ceiling, the paneled walls held an array of weapons, enough for a small army, arranged in symmetrical patterns: swirls of swords centered by a targe; scores of pikes marching in perfect order across the wall; muskets and claymores placed in circular array or sweeping upward in series toward the ceiling. And colorfully punctuating the armorial decor, Graham family portraits repeated the distinctive Graham visage in subtle variations down through the centuries.

All of which went ignored by the Laird of Ravensby, whose interest was focused not on decorative detail but on discerning one particular lady in the crowd of dancers noisily engaged in a country dance.

His own appearance, however, didn't go ignored. The powerful and bonny chief of the Roxburgh Carres always drew attention. The women immediately took notice, his magnificence in teal silk striking, his beauty and reputation tantalizing. Men noticed too; as a prominent magnate, Ravensby was an influential voice in Scottish politics, and in the current parliamentary debates, a strong force on the side of independence. They wondered what had drawn him so far from Edinburgh during the short adjournment. And while the men speculated on his reasons for being away from the capital, the women reflected more particularly on whether they might catch his eye; which conjecture, intrigued and conversational, rose like a soft buzzing hum above the sound of the violins.

"She's not dancing. Are you sure she's come?" Without turning from his scrutiny of the ballroom, Johnnie brusquely queried his cousin.

"Elizabeth's here. The majordomo remembered her particularly. Maybe she's in the card room or outside in the garden."

"Why would she be outside in the garden?" Gruff

and curt, the blasé Earl of Graden sounded like an af-
fronted guardian.

"For God's sake, Johnnie," Munro replied in murmured remonstrance, "you don't own her. Perhaps she's
enjoying the summer night."

"Then perhaps *I'll* go outside and see with whom
she's enjoying it." Johnnie was moving away from the
doorway already, the tone of his voice provocative,
heated. Munro hurried after his cousin, uneasy warder to
a man with three bottles in him, looking to take exception.

The crowd parted before the chief of the Roxburgh
Carres, as though propelled aside by the sight of Johnnie's determined stride. He only casually acknowledged
the numerous greetings, with a smile or a swift response
or a hand raised in greeting. He stopped to speak to no
one.

Where was he going? Whom was he looking for?
He'd been drinking, for the smell of brandy drifted along
his wake. Why had Johnnie Carre come so far to a Graham wedding when it was common knowledge he never
attended weddings? The tittle-tattle of curiosity followed
him, a roomful of gazes watched his purposeful progress,
all the while wishful young ladies imagined delicious fantasies . . .

Until he suddenly stopped.

He'd found her.

Radiant in cherry-red georgette trimmed with lace
and embroidered ribbon, Elizabeth had just entered the
ballroom through the terrace door with a young man who
was smiling down at her.

At the same moment the country dance ended.

A hushed, fascinated silence fell as the Laird of
Ravensby stood motionless before Elizabeth Graham.
And everyone in the ballroom understood why Johnnie
Carre had journeyed south.

"Would you care to dance, Lady Graham?" he
softly said, self-possessed and poised, his bow courtly
perfection.

Her startled, upturned gaze rose to the man towering above her. Overcome by surprise, by the sudden ac-

celeration of her heartbeat, by an instant sensual response, she fought for composure before this stylish, dégagé Laird. He was more beautiful than she'd remembered, his potent virility heightened by the splendid brocade he wore, his shoulders broader, his hands larger, his eyes asking for more than a dance.

She glanced quickly at her escort, but he'd moved a half-step away in deference to such a powerful noble. "Perhaps later, my Lord, when the music resumes," she quietly said, wanting more time to gather her emotions. A gentleman would accept her refusal politely.

"Come dance with me now," he said. And raising his hand, he signaled for the musicians to begin. "You see," he murmured, his gaze returning to her, "we've music again."

What other man would assume all eyes were on him; what other man would understand the musicians in the gallery were concerned with his wishes? What other man indeed, she thought, but the Laird of Ravensby, who viewed the world as his personal playground. Powerfully attracted on a sheer physical level, she struggled to maintain a necessary distance. Johnnie Carre had been the only man in her young life to arouse her, and she'd wondered at times whether she was to blame or he. Lately, she'd even found herself surveying her guard on occasion, debating if bedding one of them would rid her mind of Johnnie's image, or the memory of that night.

And now he was here, elegantly handsome—and waiting for her.

Fascinated, apprehensive, attracted, she fought against succumbing to his powerful masculinity. How could he so effortlessly make her want him? He had only to smile like that. . . .

But a lifetime of wariness intervened, and her practical nature firmed her wavering resolve. She would not, she resolutely decided—after months of assiduously obliterating memories of Johnnie Carre—so quickly fall under his spell.

She *could not*, not if she valued her hard-won independence.

But his strong hands closed around her waist, and

he grinned down at her. "We mustn't disappoint all these gaping guests," he said, and swung her out onto the dance floor. She shut her eyes against a surge of lust as she clutched at him to keep her balance, the feel of his body familiar, recognizable. With her hands at the small of his back and his firmly at her ribboned waist, they twirled halfway around the ballroom alone, the object of all eyes. Breath held, the throng watched the palpable display of stunning sensuality. And for a moment the beautiful young couple seemed oblivious to their surroundings: a slender, pale woman in the arms of a dark, predatory Border chief, sexuality incarnate, shameless, compelling.

"How does he know Hotchane's widow?" a local matron asked her neighbor, both women observing the young couple from their vantage point near the door. Bolt upright in her chair as if struck rigid by the vivid, overt passion, the minister's wife held her closed fan to her mouth in shocked wonder.

"Haven't you heard of the abduction?" her less prudish companion remarked, a small smile on her face, her gaze riveted on the dance floor. "I thought all the Borders knew."

"Oh!" her friend exclaimed, her mouth formed into a round O of astonishment, her fan dropping away at the word "abduction." "How can she welcome the fiend?" she whispered in captivated horror.

"Has Ravensby ever been turned away?" One question answered the other, the reply uttered in a languid murmur, blatant appraisal in the speaker's eyes as she viewed Johnnie Carre, resplendent in well-cut teal-blue silk.

"I didn't know if you could dance," Johnnie remarked, immune to the intent scrutiny, inured after a lifetime of scandal. "Hotchane must have allowed you the diversion.

You're very good." The country dances were intricate, involved. "But then you're good at many things. . . ." he softly added, his voice no more than a whisper.

She could feel the heat race up her spine and down to the pit of her stomach, and it took a moment to find breath to respond. But she'd survived her father's indelicate upbringing and Hotchane's idea of marriage, she resolutely reminded herself, so even Johnnie Carre's potent sexuality could be managed. "Thank you," she said in the distinct enunciation of a prim spinster. "It was one of my few entertainments."

Undeterred by her fastidiousness, as aware as the Graham guests of her quivering response, he softly asked, "Have you more entertainments now, in your widowhood?" Insinuation sweet as honey flowed through his words.

And she understood in a clarifying instant why women threw themselves at him; he promised pleasure so genially. "I only work, my Lord," she carefully said. "I have no diversions at all." Her polite smile gave away none of her feelings.

"Perhaps you need a holiday then." Distinguished for his seductive charm, he could be infinitely polite.

"I don't have time."

"It wouldn't take long."

"Are we speaking of the same thing, my Lord?" She found a degree of pleasure in maintaining her sangfroid before such pointed motive.

"I believe we are."

"Such assurance, Ravensby."

His smile, enchanting and poised, was answer in itself. Although his words were modest. "I'd never presume to be assured with you, Lady Graham. You strike me as a woman of remarkable confidence and self-control."

"Keep that in mind, Johnnie."

It was a mistake to pronounce his name, for the sound of it, intimate and hushed, brought intemperate memory to the fore. They both remembered with a singular feeling of heated urgency when she'd last spoken his name in that intoxicating way. "I wonder then . . ." he murmured, his deep voice pitched low, "whether you might change your mind about the sights in Edinburgh. A few days away from your construction ... you might enjoy yourself."

"I know I'd enjoy myself," Elizabeth replied with honesty, wishing very much to throw her arms around his neck and kiss him for days despite the interested crowd. "But my life continues once you leave again, Johnnie. And selfishly, I'm unwilling to accept your habits of impermanence. So thank you for the invitation, but no."

"You're not coy, Lady Graham. Perhaps you might be induced to change your mind concerning impermanence?" He had time here in Teviotdale, and she wasn't unresponsive. . . .

"I've never acquired the fine art of coyness. I've missed the company of women in my life. And I won't change my mind, because I'd be a fool, considering your reputation for dalliance. Now wouldn't I?" She gazed up at him with a half-smile.

Disconcerted by her candor, he ruefully admitted, "You're blunt about seduction, pet. Munro must have been right."

"About?"

"About you not entertaining yourself with your guardsmen. He adamantly defended your honor."

She grinned. "I see. You stand corrected, I presume. Contrary to your assumption, my Lord, I've been quite celibate."

No explicit sexual advance, however contrived, could have equaled the power of her simple declaration, and for a feverish moment Johnnie Carre was hard-pressed to keep from carrying her off the dance floor and up the stairs to his room, public be damned.

"I would find celibacy difficult," he said on a half-suffocated breath, wondering how much his honor would be impugned if he failed to act the gentleman as promised.

"I don't doubt that, my Lord. But then, we live in a world in which men and women are judged by different standards." She had had a lifetime to be certain of that principle.

"Widows have considerably more freedom," he pointed out to her, well aware of the double standard but driven by desire to distinguish the nuances.

"But not unlimited freedoms."

"You've become prudish since Goldiehouse," he murmured, remembering a night of wildness and passion.

"More sensible, I think, with distance."

"From me."

"Yes." But her smile suddenly held a touch of playfulness.

"I can be persistent," he promptly teased, unruffled by her practical reasons, delighted by her smile, astute at recognizing subtleties in the game of *amour*.

"And I obstinate."

"About sex."

She smiled. "Were we talking about sex?"

He laughed. "No, of course not." He pulled her closer so their thighs brushed as they danced, and his hands moved up slightly on her rib cage. "I believe the discussion concerned whether you had time for a holiday."

"You're very smooth, my Lord. Does it come with practice?"

"Everything comes with practice, my darling Bitsy."

"And you should know . . . my dissolute Ravensby . . . about that. . . ."

"While you, Lady Graham, know how to play the coquette with irresistible sincerity."

"Do I really?" She seemed flattered.

"You do."

"But I shouldn't with you."

"Not if you actually mean it. My well-bred civility has its limits."

"I should take warning then."

"With anyone else I'd say no, but, yes, I think, you should."

"So blunt, my Lord."

"I'm surprised myself," he said with a grin, "at my frankness. It must be the three bottles of brandy I drank."

"You dance well after three bottles."

"It was because Munro's horse went lame; I only drank to pass the time. Do you drink?" He'd wondered earlier.

"Occasionally."

"Did you like the wines Mrs. Reid sent from Goldiehouse?"

"Yes, thank you." How could she tell him that she'd not dared drink his wines after the first bottle, when her longing for him had reached such intensity, she'd nearly saddled a horse herself and ridden to Ravensby?

"Come have a glass of wine with me and tell me of your building," he suddenly said, as if they'd not been discussing seduction, as if they were merely friends renewing an acquaintance. And he pulled her to a stop.

"I shouldn't."

"How can it hurt?"

An honest answer wouldn't do; he'd take advantage of her susceptibility. "Perhaps one," she said, because she didn't wish to leave him.

Johnnie Carre had heard those words a thousand times before ... that first small capitulation. He smiled down at her with an open, boyish grin, content with the progress of his seduction. "One it is," he said, taking her by the hand. "Rhenish or French, my lady?"

But his warder, Munro, approached them later when Johnnie signaled a footman for a refill as if he, too, were keeping track of Elizabeth's consumption of spirits.

The conversation turned more serious then, the particulars of construction taking the stage, and Munro wouldn't be dislodged as the evening progressed, taking his duties as duenna to heart. Near midnight Johnnie gave up, ordered himself a fresh bottle, and indulgently listened to Munro and Elizabeth detail each step in the building process while he emptied an exceptional bottle of claret. It was only Saturday, after all.

And when Elizabeth took her leave much later, he

tolerantly remarked to his friend, "My compliments on your staying power."

"I told you I'd keep you on leading strings."

"She's very delightful."

"You mean besides in bed."

He nodded. "She's well-read."

"If you had spent more time with her, you would have realized that before."

"I was avoiding her because of Robbie's circumstances. You had more opportunity to know her."

"Because I don't consider seducing every beautiful woman, you mean?"

"Sorry . . . force of habit."

"I don't suppose you've ever considered restraint."

Johnnie looked for a considering moment at his cousin. "Not until yesterday," he replied with a grin.

Munro groaned. "It's going to be a long three days."

Johnnie raised his wineglass to Munro in salute. "But an interesting three days, Cuz. I'm already looking forward to morning."

And the next two days of wedding festivities continued apace, with Johnnie pursuing Elizabeth, Munro playing chaperon, and all three participants experiencing a high degree of frustration. The Grahams arranged a picnic outing, boat rides on the lake, impromptu races, dances at night, and of course the wedding on Monday afternoon.

Johnnie adhered to his promise of gentlemanly behavior, but that didn't discourage him from attempting to bring Elizabeth into his bed of her own accord. But at the end of two days, he found himself depleted of compliant good humor. And evil-tempered.

Elizabeth had resisted the seductive Laird of Ravensby with all the logic of her sensible nature, but she wasn't immune to the intensity of her emotions. And she lay awake at night, fighting her susceptibility, wishing she could allow herself to give in to her carnal longings.

Munro, for his part, counted the hours while he parried the insinuations and intimations and sat up late into the night protecting Elizabeth Graham from herself. And from his cousin's skillful seduction. He was exhausted by Tuesday morning, when he felt himself being roughly jolted awake.

"She's gone." Johnnie curtly declared. Fully dressed, he stood at the bedside, Munro's shoulder in his savage grip, shaking his cousin awake with an only partially restrained violence. "She left this morning. I wonder if she actually thought she would get away." His fingers tightened.

Munro winced and grunted at the sudden twinge of pain.

Looking down, Johnnie seemed momentarily surprised. "Sorry," he said, releasing his punishing hold and spinning away. He strode to the window overlooking the drive. Gazing at the landscape falling away to the south—to England—for a brief moment, he restlessly tapped his fingers on the pane. Then, turning back to his cousin, he decisively said, "You can come or you can stay. I'm beyond caring what you think, what *anyone* thinks. . . ."

"An unusual sentiment for you," Munro sardonically murmured.

"A damnable aberration, as you well know," Johnnie snapped, testy and exasperated after days of restraint. "But I've finally slipped my leash, Munro, and I'm after her. And don't look at me like that." Raking his hands through hair in an agitated gesture, restive and mutinous, he glared at his cousin, bereft of benevolence after three days of pretense and prevarication. "Thanks to your refined notions of good breeding, I've had a perpetual erection for three days, make it four; the ride down was hell. I've been teased and tortured beyond endurance . . . holding Elizabeth in my arms on the dance floor, wanting to kiss her luscious mouth, smelling that damnable clover-scented soap of Mrs. Reid's that always reminds me of our time together at Goldiehouse, lying awake at night wondering what she's wearing in bed or if she's wearing anything or who's sharing her bed."

At which point Munro's eyebrows rose.

"All right, all right," Johnnie grudgingly agreed, his hand coming up slightly as if to ward off Munro's dissent. "So she sleeps in a damned virginal bed. Do you know," he softly queried, standing very still suddenly, "I almost climbed the tree outside her window simply to *watch* her." He grimaced in disgust. "I'm like an adolescent in heat. And in my current mood"—his teeth flashed white in a grin and one dark brow rose—"I'd even consider tumbling you, if you weren't so hairy. So I'll have her now or at least try, dammit, like a man instead of a simpering fop. And you can't stop me!"

"You're beyond stopping, I'd say," Munro acknowledged, rubbing his aching shoulder, his voice deliberate, his eyes half-lidded not in sleep but in assessment.

"At *last* we agree." An intrinsic air of command colored Johnnie's tone. "Do you ride with me? Or I can ride alone," he added, his voice conciliatory, appeasing his cousin's more decorous nature. "You needn't come if it offends you."

Tossing aside the covers with a sigh, Munro threw his legs over the side of the bed and, heaving himself into a sitting position, gazed at his cousin for a thoughtful moment. "Oh, hell . . . I'll go. I've been your keeper for three days now. What's a few more hours? At least I can bring your body back if the lady has her Redesdale guards kill you on the spot. Although," he went on with a faint smile, "you're not thinking she ran away because she finds you repulsive?"

"She ran for the same reasons I'm going after her," Johnnie bluntly said. "She can't help herself, nor can I."

"You could be wrong."

"I'll find out then, won't I?"

"Perhaps at the price of your life."

He didn't want to argue with his cousin about the style and degree and manner of Elizabeth Graham's response to him the last few days; accomplished at reading female sensibilities, Johnnie didn't question her interest. The Redesdale guard was another matter, but he doubted Elizabeth would protect her virtue so far as to allow him to be killed. "Nothing so dramatic will transpire," he replied to his cousin's concern. "She's above all a practical woman."

"In which case she'll refuse you."

"We'll see. . . ." In control of his life again now that he'd cast aside his abnormal discipline of the last few days, Johnnie's voice took on a lazy drawl. His unreserved smile appeared, fresh as a morning sunrise. "Or maybe I'll have her instead . . . if she doesn't order me skinned alive first."

Elizabeth had left very early that morning, unable to withstand another day of close proximity to Johnnie Carre without helplessly giving in to her yearnings. Restless, disquieted, stretched taut with longing after having Johnnie Carre tempt and seduce her every waking moment during her stay at Hawick, she felt her only option was escape. Or else take the scandalous Laird of Ravensby into her bed before all the watchful Graham guests, which would be tantamount to broadcasting her lust to all of Scotland.

Which consideration had ultimately prompted her to flee; last night, lying in bed unable to sleep *again*, she'd found herself considering the limited range of secluded retreats suitable for an amorous rendezvous, a site safe from prying eyes of guests and servants. And this morning she'd controlled her impulse to walk unannounced into Johnnie's room only because she didn't know its location. Panic-stricken by the intensity of her need, she decided it was time to leave. Short of embarrassing herself by exposing her unsated desire for the Laird of Ravensby before all of Hawick, she simply had no choice.

Once the environs of the Graham country house had been left behind, she'd felt less vulnerable. Instructing her driver to slow the horses to a walk as the road beyond the village narrowed, she'd found herself relaxing.

She was safe. Away from the irresistible Johnnie Carre, beyond the formidable power of his smile and charming ways, a comfortable distance from his unbridled sensuality.

Taking a deep breath, she inhaled the fresh summer air drifting in through the coach's open windows, the day cool but sunny as if the change of temperature since yesterday reflected her own more temperate decision to leave. The tranquility and quiet of the countryside further calmed her, an added degree of serenity returned to her mind, and moderation was once again restored to her life after three days under the tempestuous spell of hot-blooded desire.

She had acted properly in leaving.

The wild and headstrong Johnnie Carre would have shattered her placid domestic existence.

Familiar with every inch of the Borders, Johnnie and Munro rode overland to save precious time, forcing a headlong pace, knowing they could gain easily on a slow-moving coach. Scottish roads were rough tracks off the main routes to Edinburgh, Glasgow, and London; the carriage would travel at no more than walking speed.

A few miles north of the border, where the route passed through a small plantation laid out by a local landowner a generation ago, the sound of hard-ridden horses first caught the outriders' attention. Automatically reaching for their weapons, they stopped to listen. Shaded by tall old pines fragrant in the cool early morning air, the narrow road had an air of isolation, separated from the rural countryside by acres of towering trees. An ambush in such remote surroundings was possible; they signaled the coach to stop.

As her carriage came to rest, Elizabeth leaned out of the window, surveyed the quiet lane, and shouted to her driver, "Is there a problem?"

"The outriders, my Lady," her maid said, from her seat beside the driver, where she'd chosen to ride on the glorious morning. "They've heard something."

Scanning the landscape in both directions, Elizabeth saw nothing but trees and a ribbon of dusty road. "Do *you* hear anything?"

"Not yet, Lady Graham," her driver replied, "but Michael did, else he wouldn't have raised the alarm. Best stay inside until we know for certain."

The summer morning was too idyllic for danger, with birdsong melodic on the crisp air, the bright sunshine luminous ribbons where it gleamed through openings in the pine boughs, wildflowers splashes of color bordering the country road.

An assault seemed incongruous in such a picturesque setting.

But the sound of galloping horses suddenly reached the coach, and Elizabeth's escort shifted their mounts into a position of readiness, an armed shield against danger.

And moments later, two riders appeared in the distance, traveling fast, racing point-blank at them. As each Redesdale guard sighted his musket on the horsemen, Elizabeth stretched a fraction farther out the window, more curious than frightened. Highwaymen were rare on summer mornings in the country; nor were they generally so bold in their approach. Narrowing her gaze, she focused on the riders. They were too distant yet. Several seconds passed as everyone waited in silence, the rhythm of hoofbeats loud in the stillness of the forest. At the moment her captain ordered his men to prepare to fire, she caught a glimpse of windswept black hair, recognized the familiar powerful frame on the horseman in the lead, the colors of the plaid, and hysterically screamed, "Don't shoot!"

Redmond's head snapped around.

"It's Ravensby," she said, breathless, the drama of Johnnie's appearance stunning her. "Don't shoot him!"

"We'll see what he wants," Redmond directed his men. "Keep him in your sights."

"He's not dangerous, Redmond."

"Yes, my Lady." But no one lowered his weapon.

•   •   •

"They might shoot you before you get within speaking range," Munro pointed out as they slowed to a canter, his gaze on the firearms trained on them.

"No risk, no pleasure . . ." Johnnie amiably replied, stroking his lathered horse as he brought it to a trot. "Now don't make any sudden moves," he cheerfully instructed. And slowly opening his arms in a gesture of friendship, he showed his weaponless hands to the men guarding Elizabeth, a smile on his handsome face.

"Stop and state your business," Elizabeth's captain shouted, still cautious despite Elizabeth's recognition.

"I'd like a word with Lady Graham," Johnnie casually replied, bringing his horse to a halt.

No! was her first reaction when she heard his words . . . Lord, save me, her second. But a flutter of excitement struck her senses separate from any reasonable repudiation. And in the next moment she reminded herself she wasn't a sixteen-year-old child without the means of independent action, but a grown woman capable of dealing with adult dilemmas, with temptation, with infatuation and desire. Surely, a few words with Johnnie Carre would be possible without a complete loss of restraint. After all, she'd kept him at bay for more than two days at Hawick.

But reason and rationalization aside, she found herself drawing in a deep, steadying breath as she placed her hand on the door handle.

The instant the carriage door opened, regardless of a score of muskets pointed at him, Johnnie dismounted, swiftly sliding off his horse before Elizabeth had fully gained the ground. And ignoring the mounted troopers eyeing him suspiciously, he strode toward her.

"You left early, my Lady," he said as he reached her side, his bow polite, his gaze appreciatively taking in her slender dimity-clad form, her short cashmere cape tied under her chin with a symmetrical primness. "Did you tire of the Graham festivities?"

He could have been greeting her outside church, she thought, from his well-bred manner and tone, not standing sweaty, windswept, and casually dressed on a country road miles from home.

Less capable of the politesse that passed for feeling in the aristocratic world, she said, "You shouldn't have followed me."

"You shouldn't have left without saying good-bye." His pale blue eyes were angelic.

"I didn't realize a farewell to you was required," she stiffly replied, her voice as studiously cool as her flower-sprigged frock and leaf-green capelet. But the damp linen shirt clinging to Johnnie's muscled frame, the scent of sandalwood from his heated body, his wild dark hair curling on the muted red-and-green plaid draped over one shoulder, disastrously affected her pretense at self-possession.

"I missed you," he plainly said, as if she hadn't offered him a standoffish reply, as if she weren't surrounded by a troop of armed men, as if he rode after ladies every day of his life, when in fact he never had.

"I'm sorry," she said, but her voice was a small, hushed sound. Her eyes lifted to his; she'd never learned the duplicity of flirtation, the mummery of fashionable deceit.

And undisguised desire met his gaze.

"Come talk to me," he murmured, his voice low, intimate, "away from all these people."

"I shouldn't."

"I shouldn't be here, but I am," he countered, insistent, almost a touch of resentment in his tone. "So call off your guards. Come walk with me. . . ." He glanced quickly to where his cousin sat his horse. "Munro will stay as hostage."

Reason no longer held sway; she couldn't help herself. After the minutest pause, she gave orders to her troopers to put away their weapons, dismount, and take their ease. "And I'm not in danger," she finished, thinking even as she spoke how inaccurate her words, for she was in the ultimate peril—in danger of surrendering her heart.

CHAPTER 13

They walked together down the road a short distance until they were out of sight of the carriage, speaking of the wedding, the weather, neutral topics that could be discussed in bland conversation, avoiding the urgent reasons they were alone on an isolated country road miles from their homes. Until a few moments later Johnnie indicated a trodden grassy path with a slight gesture of his hand. "There's a small glade down this deer trail. Munro and I rode from this direction," he continued, as though an explanation were required, as though any words mattered. "We won't be disturbed."

An audacious small phrase, pregnant with suggestion.

He was offering her a choice.

"How far is it?" she asked, avoiding the more pressing questions crowding her brain.

"Not far." He smiled faintly. "Your guards can hear you if you call."

"Do you intend to be unmanageable?" she inquired with an answering smile.

"Never."

"In that case," she replied, moving past him down the grassy way, "I'm quite safe."

A relative expression, Johnnie thought, considering his intentions, but he doubted she was in the mood for such a discussion. Nor was he, with more vital issues on his mind.

They reached the silent green glade rimmed with lacy fern, the soft grass flattened in places where the deer had slept, the tall pines towering dark above them, the sun warm. And they stood facing each other across a small distance, neither finding the facile words to ease the momentary silence.

Until Johnnie spoke at last, his voice low-pitched and quiet in the sheltered glade.

"This is very awkward."

"You mean women don't usually resist you?"

She could see his grin begin and then as suddenly disappear.

"I don't think so."

His manners were impeccable, she thought, his smile now fully under control. "You don't *think* so?" The uncomfortable realization that she might be simply another of that vast horde of women impelled her resentment.

He heard the anger in her voice and debated for a moment the merits of honesty. But after playing the courtier for days at Hawick, he was beyond the falsehood and pretense of fashionable flirtation, and he answered, "Actually, no . . . they don't."

"Ah . . ." she softly exclaimed, the way a cat might pounce on a hapless mouse, "they all fall into your lap then. Is that it?"

He didn't answer that time because the very last thing he wanted to do was fight. He said instead, very slowly, as though the words expressed were not only difficult to say but difficult to understand, "I've thought of you often—when I should have been thinking of other things." He shifted his stance slightly, restive at revealing his feelings. "The business of Parliament is moving Scotland critically toward war or independence," he went on in a carefully modulated tone, "and I'm spending an unconscionable amount of time thinking of you. I shouldn't have come to Hawick. Tweedale is diligently wooing those of the Country party who need money, while I'm here playing the gallant to you."

Elizabeth moved away from him, and he watched her but didn't follow. Mildly resentful of her overpowering allure and the need for such personal disclosures, he kept his distance as she sat down on a fallen tree trunk, although he felt his heartbeat quicken at her action; she wasn't going to run, he realized, or cry for help or resist him. He should have felt more elation.

Looking up at him, Elizabeth spoke so quietly, he had to strain to hear her. "You've disrupted my thoughts, my dreams, my life," she whispered, "since Goldiehouse. . . ." Her hands clasped in her lap were clenched tightly together. "I didn't want to start all over again."

"So you ran away."

"Yes."

"I came to Hawick only for you," he said.

"And not for the young bride and groom?" she queried with a smile, warmed by his simple admission.

He shrugged and shook his head. "I avoid weddings as a rule."

"I see."

And the silence surrounded them.

He had come to see her, Elizabeth happily thought, the proud and arrogant Ravensby had come to Hawick despite the pressing needs of his party and his country. Despite his better judgment apparently, if his moodiness and aloof stance were any indication. *And* with some constraining agreement with his cousin Munro, she suspected.

"Is Munro still a restraint?" she quietly said, enormously gratified to know a mutual desire overwhelmed them both, no longer guarded with her feelings. "Is it some wager?" she added with a smile when he still hadn't answered or moved.

"No." Uneasy at being so drawn to a woman, at having exposed his feelings, he resisted as if in some paradoxical way self-denial would preserve his freedom.

"Come sit by me then." Elizabeth gently patted the rough bark beside her, as if coaxing a small child to an unpleasant task.

He should leave, he thought. He shouldn't have ridden after her, he shouldn't be panting like a dog in heat for any woman ... particularly for this woman, the daughter of Harold Godfrey, his lifelong enemy.

"Are you afraid of me?" She'd stopped running now from her desire. There was quixotic pleasure, too, in the new awareness of her power over Johnnie Carre. But perhaps paramount of the essential reasons impelling her, she was blissfully happy ... without thought or reason. It was an enormous leap of faith, a rash and venturesome sensation for a woman who'd always viewed the world with caution.

"I'm not afraid of anything," Johnnie answered, unhesitating confidence in his deep voice.

"I didn't think so," she replied. Dressed like a reiver in leather breeches, high boots, a shirt open at the throat, his hunting plaid the muted color of autumn foliage, he looked not only unafraid but menacing. The danger and attraction of scandalous sin, she thought—all dark, arrogant masculinity. "My guardsmen will wait indefinitely," she said very, very quietly, thinking with an arrogance of her own, There. That should move him.

And when he took that first step, she smiled a tantalizing female smile, artless and instinctive.

"You please me," she said, gazing up at him as he slowly drew near.

"*You* drive me mad," Johnnie said, sitting down on the fallen tree, resting his arms on his knees and contemplating the dusty toes of his boots.

"And you don't like the feeling."

"I dislike it intensely," he retorted, chafing resentment plain in his voice.

He wouldn't look at her. "Would you rather I leave?"

His head swiveled toward her then, a cynical gleam in his blue eyes. "Of course not."

An answer of sorts, she decided, but not one twined with daisy chains. "Why was it different at

Hawick?" she asked. His mood was so different now, his familiar charm suppressed.

"Because it was a fashionable game with acceptable rules at Hawick," he said, surprised at his honesty. He was rarely frank with women. But Elizabeth Graham was different from the other women. That was why he was here, discontent and thoroughly aroused, wondering how to deal with his feelings.

"And now it isn't?"

He gazed at her from under the dark fringe of his lashes, not certain himself. And after a lengthy pause he said, "I don't think so."

"And you prefer games," she said, understanding a portion of his dilemma.

"Yes."

"Hmmm," Elizabeth murmured, pursing her lips, clasping her hands together and studying her yellow kidskin slippers. "This *is* awkward," she said after a moment, amusement in her voice. Sitting up straighter, she half turned to gaze at him. "I've never seduced a man before." A smile of unalloyed innocence curved her mouth. "Could you help me? If you don't mind, my Lord," she demurely added.

A grin slowly creased his tanned cheek. "You play the ingenue well, Lady Graham," he said, sitting upright to better meet her frankly sensual gaze. His pale blue eyes had warmed, restoring a goodly measure of his charm. "Upon reflection, Bitsy, my dear," he decided, "I suddenly find I don't mind at all. . . ." It was a revelation of some consequence, considering his previous ill temper. "Actually, I'd be a damned fool to mind," he said, his grin in sharp contrast to the curious affection in his eyes.

Exhaling theatrically, Elizabeth said, "Thank you, my Lord," in a blatant parody of gratitude. "Without your assistance I despaired of properly arousing you."

He laughed, a warmhearted sound of natural pleasure. "On that count you needn't have worried. I've been in rut since I left Edinburgh to see you."

"How charming," Elizabeth said, mischievous, teasing.

"Only from your point of view, pet, I assure you," he drawled.

"Could I be of some help?" she murmured, her voice husky, enticing.

His erection grew sizably at her invitation, and he found himself attentively searching the ground for a suitable place to lie with her. "I warn you," he said very low, his mouth in a lazy grin, "I'm days past the need for seduction. I hope you don't mind the grass. My bed at Hawick would have been softer."

"But then all of Hawick would have known."

"That matters?" Genuine surprise registered in his voice.

"We can't all live undisturbed by scandal." But in contrast to her conventional words, she was feeling as though she'd be willing to endure anything for Johnnie Carre's body next to hers.

All Johnnie could think of was feeling her close around him. Society's censure was so far down his list of concerns, it didn't bear comment. Rising abruptly, he held out his hand and said, "Hawick be damned. All I can offer is this country setting. Do you mind?"

She smiled up at him as she put her hand in his. "As long as you hold me, my Lord, and as long as the grass stains don't show."

He paused for a moment with her small hand light on his palm. "You're very remarkable," he softly said. The women in his life had been careful to avoid sincerity.

"Too candid for you, my Lord?" she playfully inquired.

His long fingers closed around her hand in an act of possession, pure and simple, as if he would keep this spirited, plain-speaking woman who startled him. "Your candor excites me," he said. "Be warned," he murmured, drawing her to her feet, "I've been wanting you for three days past; I won't guarantee finesse." Releasing her hand, he held his own hands up so she could see them tremble. "Look."

"I'm shaking *inside* so violently, I may savage you first, my Lord," Elizabeth softly breathed, swaying toward him, her fragrance sweet in his nostrils, her face lifted for a kiss. "I've been waiting four months since I left Goldiehouse."

A spiking surge of lust ripped through his senses, gut-deep, searing, her celibacy a singular flamboyant ornament offered to him as if it were his duty, his obligation, to bring her pleasure. In a flashing moment his hands closed on her shoulders. Pulling her sharply close, he slid his palms down her back—then lower, swiftly cupping her bottom, dragging her into the rigid length of his erection. He moaned deep in his throat as she touched him there. His mouth dipped to hers, and he forced her mouth open, plunging his tongue deep inside.

Like a woman too long denied, Elizabeth welcomed him, pulling his head down so she could reach his mouth more easily, straining upward on tiptoe so she could feel him hard against her, tearing at the buttons on his shirt so the heat of his skin touched hers.

"Hurry, Johnnie, please . . ." she whispered into his mouth, impatient, moving her hips in age-old enticement.

As if he needed any incentive to hurry; as if he had anything on his mind but consummation. As if he didn't ache so desperately to bury himself inside her, he felt his brain burning away.

"You should take your dress off," he murmured, acting the gentleman only with extreme effort, setting her at arm's length, reaching for the bow at her neck. "For the grass stains," he muttered. Shutting his eyes briefly against the overwhelming desire engulfing him, he groaned, a suffocated sound of superhuman restraint. Then, concentrating, he drew her cape from her shoulders and reached for the buttons on her frock.

Brushing his hands aside, she whispered, "I can't wait." Her eyes already heavy-lidded with passion, she breathed, "Please . . ."

Remembering her premature release at Goldiehouse, in a rushing second he stripped his plaid from his shoulders, unbuckled his belt to release the folds of fabric, spread the soft wool on the grass at their feet, and, sweeping her up into his arms, whispered, "Wait for me."

A second later he lowered her to their makeshift bed, swiftly pushing the fullness of her skirt and petticoats upward with a practiced touch.

"Hurry," she breathed, the touch of his fingers leaving a trail of fire on her thighs, her breath caught in her throat as his fingertips stroked her mons.

"I'm almost there," he whispered, reaching for the buttons on his breeches.

"Lord, Johnnie . . ." she pleaded, her eyes shutting against the flame-hot need streaking through her body, her arms reaching for him.

Heedlessly, he wrenched the last button off, dropped between her pale legs, and, still booted and spurred, plunged inside her.

She cried out, a high, keening pleasure sound, as he filled her, her hands clutching his muscled back. And he sank hilt-deep inside her, his breath in abeyance as violent sensation pulsated through his body and brain and heated blood. She was worlds better than he'd remembered; she was perfect . . . exquisite, the fit of her tight, sublime.

With the pressure of her hands hard at the base of his spine, she suddenly lifted her hips, reminding him of her four months' celibacy, and he began moving in her, penetrating, withdrawing, sliding in and gliding out, bracing his booted feet to gain more leverage, plunging in again. . . .

She wanted this always, Elizabeth thought, almost purring with rapture, she wanted the feel of the Laird of Ravensby deep inside her, she wanted the solid weight of him under her hands and over her, she wanted this inexplicable feeling of bliss to never end.

Then she smiled at the notion, because after months of sexual deprivation, her orgasm was fast approaching, and "never" had a finite quality.

In a flashing heartbeat her breathing changed, intensified. Her hands slid lower down his back, and he matched her new rhythm, following her, until at the peaking last he drove in and held himself hard against her womb. With her arms laced around his neck she arched into the hard length of him and clung to him as if he were the indispensable center of her world. And he was, for that long, endless, feverish space of time that melted reality into oblivion. As she shuddered around him, he poured into her with a pent-up wildness, soul-stirring, tumultuous, explosive.

Trembling, shaken, moments later they gasped like swimmers rescued from drowning.

"I'm ... not used ... to this," Johnnie panted. A spontaneous utterance—his climax so pure, so relentless, he was near prostrate, a unique sensation for the suave, sophisticated Laird of Ravensby.

"Nor I ..." Elizabeth whispered.

He smiled down at her, an odd triumph in his eyes, as if he'd won a great victory. Her pale hair lay like shimmering pearl on the subdued colors of his plaid; her gleaming emerald eyes looked directly into his, a glimpse of their recent vision of paradise in their depths. She was unutterably glorious, he thought.

Elizabeth had never felt the exquisite wonder of carnal lust and utter happiness, of warm affection, and more—a kind of hot-blooded passion fused with inexpressible joy.

"How could you ... have married him?" he whispered, a kind of shock in the words. It seemed a sacrilege, although he knew how prevalent the practice of bartering young girls for family profit. But she was too perfect to be sold away to an old man of Hotchane's evilness.

If I had known you then, she wanted to say, I would have killed myself before I'd ever gone to Hotchane. "I didn't realize I had a choice," she said, her voice unconsciously touched with her newfound jubilation so his brows drew together at her seeming indifference.

Unlacing her arm from around his back, she touched the crease of his scowl in soothing gentleness. "Now I wouldn't have," she said, moved by his concern. "Now I would have rather picked turnips in the fields or begged work at the village school." She smiled then, a small exultation of the soul. "Now that I've met you." She kissed him, a butterfly kiss of sheer joy. "And I'm glad you rode after me," she confessed. "I shouldn't tell you ... but ... I've only wanted *you* since Goldiehouse. I've never felt that way before ... about a man—desperate to feel him." Her words came tumbling out in a rush of emotion, liberated after months of yearning. "I even considered inviting one of my guards to sleep with me to clarify whether it was actually you or simply some unfathomable impulse, or, well ... your—" A blush stole over her face; she drew in a swift breath and quickly said "enormous size" in a tiny voice. Lifting her lashes, she found him grinning and grinned back. "But I never did," she quickly added, plunging on as though the words had been locked away for four long months and *required* divulgence. "Sleep with my guards or George Baldwin, who's forever underfoot and pleading for a kiss, or—"

"George Baldwin?" Johnny interrupted, as if he had the right to inquire.

"A neighbor who's very kind and sweet—"

"Sweet?" The single word was a sibilant hiss.

"Are you jealous? How interesting," she added before he could deny it or even consider the astonishing possibility. "But he's *only* nice, like an amiable curate."

"He's a curate?" A curious sense of relief colored his tone.

"Well, no ..."

"Well, what is he?"

"He's not *you*, darling," she replied in her blunt way that continued to fascinate him. "Nor is any man I meet. And I *really* shouldn't tell you this, because even a tyro in dalliance should know better, but I *passionately* desire only you, and even my brawny guardsmen don't intrigue me. So much as I considered bedding them—or one of them ..." she quickly modified when his brow rose in conjecture, "I couldn't."

Inexplicably, he found her artless naïveté had a lurid effect on his psyche. And the discovery that she'd saved her delectable passion for him *alone* strangely provoking.

Arousing.

Exciting.

"So I was wondering ... since you rode so far ..."—her lashes half lowered over saucy green eyes—"to—keep me company," she delicately teased, vividly conscious of his swelling erection. "I was wondering whether I might impose on your—er—renewed interest."

He grinned. "Greedy child."

"My abstinence, no doubt," she explained, her voice altered to a throaty lushness as his arousal filled her.

The concept of abstinence stupefied him, the doctrine mystifying to a dissolute worldly man. But he had no difficulty interpreting the muted suggestion in her voice. "Could we approach this with less speed this time?" he inquired with a charming smile.

"I've all day," she replied in a languid whisper, moving her hips in a lithe, imaginative incitement.

His body instantly responded to the compelling invitation of "all day" with Elizabeth Graham, to her stirring stimulation. "In that case," he offered with a wolfish grin, "I'll set my mind to some more leisurely pleasures. Beginning," he said, touching the rumpled lace kerchief at her bosom, "with fewer clothes and more—contact."

"Ummm ... I like that."

"I like it with *you*."

"Good. I'm not too forward for your sensibilities?" He smiled and shook his head.

"I can attack you then with impunity?" She was enjoying herself like a young child practicing a new game.

"You can *always* attack me with impunity." A lazy insouciance drawled through his words; he'd been playing the game for a long time.

Always. She liked the sound of the word although even she knew better than to mention permanence to a man of Ravensby's notoriety. Bracing her feet, she experimented with a delicate form of attack, lifting her hips so the sensation of pleasure intensified, so the throbbing pulse inside her quickened, so she felt him penetrate farther.

And his hand slid behind automatically to grasp her lifted thigh, forcing it higher, forcing himself deeper.

And they both stopped breathing for a moment as stabbing ecstasy trembled anew.

"You don't understand," he whispered when he found his breath again, releasing his hold on her leg, relaxing as much as possible in his present position of arrested intercourse. "You're not having your way this time."

"But I like having my way." And she moved in a slow rhythm of arousal, the undulating friction delectable. Part teasing, partly testing her newly discovered powers of persuasion, she smiled up at him with a flaunting coquetry.

"No," he said, his voice deceptively soft. "Although," he quietly went on, his graceful smile mitigating his unrelenting authority, "if I didn't plan on making love to you all day, I might be more susceptible to your enchanting temptation."

"I shall pout," she warned, which she did with melodrama and sweet charm.

He grinned. "And I shall remain immune." His immunity was the consequence of a decade of pouting females.

"You're unkind," she declared with a credible sullenness.

"No," he gently replied, "I'm about to show you a new degree of *kindness*. Now let me go." He nudged her thighs still holding him tightly. "And I promise you," he said with a facetious lift of his brows, "your forbearance will be rewarded."

Her thighs relaxed, although her pout was more genuine now and less theatrical.

"Look at it this way, darling," Johnnie said, withdrawing from her and resting back on his heels, still booted and fully dressed except for his unbuttoned breeches. He grinned. "It's one small lesson in obedience."

She lunged upward, her fingers already closed in a fist.

And he rolled away so swiftly, she grudgingly decided he'd had frequent practice.

"I could have you skinned alive," she said, sitting in the center of his plaid, fists clenched, a spark of fire in her green eyes.

Lounging at his ease a safe distance away in the sweet-smelling grass, he looked entertained. "But then I wouldn't be much good to you."

"I hate masculine control." A long history of uncharitable men prompted her outburst.

His blue eyes held hers for a grave moment, and his voice when he spoke was utterly without badinage. "I was only teasing."

She looked at him suspiciously. "I won't be obedient to you or any man."

"It's the last thing I'd expect from you." Johnnie Carre preferred women of spirit; obedience for him was no more than a playful dare.

And while she was debating whether to believe him or not and whether her hot-blooded desire could stand on principle at all, Johnnie spoke very quietly with deference and courtesy. "You set the rules."

"Perhaps ... I overreacted," she said in a small whisper, his good-natured indulgence reminding her of the vast differences in men.

"I understand overreaction too," he commented, a slow smile drifting across his mouth. "I had Munro out of bed this morning *extremely* early."

"You're very kind."

His eyes gleamed with mischief. "It was a long ride down here."

She smiled. "Am I taking this too seriously?"

He shrugged, a well-bred ambiguity. "War is serious; national honor is serious. Famine, people dying ..." He inclined his head in a mild disclaimer. "This doesn't have to be serious."

A small silence fell between them, only the sound of birdsong conspicuous in the stillness, miles of towering pine a barricade between them and the contentious world. A man and a maid and tremulous passion ...

He didn't importune, nor had he ever in his commerce with women. But he wanted her, that was plain. And after a very short moment of reflection, she held out her hand, smiled, and said, "Come, make me happy."

He rolled back onto the plaid as deftly as he'd escaped her. The fragrance of his cologne surrounded her, his smile brought with it his own special sunshine, and his voice when he spoke was familiar in its irony. "Now that we've disposed of the profundities—"

"And very easily too," Elizabeth interjected, feeling lighthearted again.

"My specialty, madam," he said with a small dip of his head. "Ask anyone."

"I *know* what your specialty is, Ravensby," she replied with a sidelong glance.

"Ah ... well then," he murmured, shameless. "Would you mind, Lady Graham," he went on, all teasing deference and amusement, "if I undressed you now? I know we have all day, but then"—he paused in delicate emphasis—"we'll *need* all day. . . ."

Sitting cross-legged, her yellow gown rumpled around her, her platinum hair tousled, her cheeks flushed, she gazed at him playfully. "I'd be foolish to say no, wouldn't I?"

He only smiled and nodded.

"Arrogant man."

"I'm the one who chased after you, darling. Hardly an act of arrogance."

"You have a charming honesty, at least."

"And several other cultivated charms eager to be put at your disposal ..."

"Cultivated in the boudoirs of other women, no doubt."

"Developed solely with your interests in mind," he smoothly replied.

"Liar."

"I prefer the word 'diplomatic.'"

Her gaze lazily drifted over his body, taking special notice of his partially unbuttoned breeches. "And *I* prefer that gorgeous cock of yours inside me."

He looked down briefly. "Well, then," he said with

a rakish grin, "we'll have to see that you get what you want."

As it turned out, the undressing, a reciprocal process, took enormous time, each item of clothing unlaced or unbuttoned or unpinned with artistic, riveting attention. She helped him, and he helped her; they laughed and giggled and kissed, licked and stroked, and before they both climaxed again, Elizabeth Graham had discovered the very advantageous merit in delay.

"You're *very* good," she said in luxurious contentment much later as they sat together, she straddling his legs so they faced each other, joined, replete with a glorious satiation.

He rocked her gently, his arms holding her close, his body hot against her. "We're good *together*," he corrected, an expert on mutual pleasure. His skin was shades darker than hers, bronzed by the sun; her flesh was very white, and the contrast stark, stunning. The muscled power of his body was striking counterpoint to her slender, voluptuous grace. Lazily plucking a daisy from the meadow grass beyond the border of their makeshift bed, he tucked it behind her ear.

"Happy twenty-ninth July, Elizabeth Graham," he whispered, thinking he could stay content in this isolated clearing till the ice cap melted.

Leaning away from him so he had to hold her tightly to balance her, Elizabeth picked a daisy, too, and sliding it behind Johnnie's ear into the dark tangle of his unruly curls, she said hushed, low, "You bring me joy, Johnnie Carre." Contentment was too tame a word for the wonder of her feelings, for she'd discovered the existence of unalloyed pleasure, and she was drunk with the delight of it. Her smile shone suddenly warm as the tropics. "You should wear daisies more often." So did satyrs look, she thought, all flourishing powerful virility, adorned with wildflowers.

"For you I will," he said. And at that moment he meant it.

They were warm, hot from the leisurely foreplay and prolonged intercourse, from the tempestuous fever of orgasm. A droplet of sweat slid down Johnnie's temple.

"You're on fire," she whispered, touching his forehead, catching the gleaming drop on her fingertip, tasting his saltiness with a glorious sense of ownership as if he belonged to her for these rare moments.

"This could be the dead of winter," he murmured into her hair, breathing the sweet scent of her, "and I wouldn't notice." He was rigid still inside her, as though he hadn't just climaxed, as though he always had a perpetual erection with Elizabeth Graham. As though his raging hunger for her were a kind of insanity.

She kissed him back, seated atop him with his pulsing erection buried deep inside, her knees grazing his ribs, her breasts soft against his chest, her body ripe with a combustible sexual urgency that could burn down transiently only to flare again. And she said in a tiny vibration of longing that touched his lips and moved directly downward to his hardness, "Do you mind . . . I feel greedy . . . insatiable . . . inflamed. . . ."

"Do I mind what," he murmured, teasing.

"I need you again."

"Again?" His husky whisper drifted across her mouth.

"I'm sorry," she breathed, the tip of her tongue gliding over his bottom lip. "Do you think you could . . . arrange—something?"

"It's possible. . . ."

"I could reward you. . . ."

"Really." His brows rose a minute fraction. "Or I you . . ."

"Yes. Please."

He could give her what she needed. Dominant, in control but only marginally, for he was as compelled as she—as needful, as tantalized.

"*Now*," she dictated, sliding her fingers through his dark ruffled hair, leaning close again to nibble on his bottom lip.

Restless, disquieted, averse to women giving him orders, he said, "No."

And she bit him.

His shock was replaced a second later by hotspur instinct; hair-trigger impulse reacting to her barefaced challenge as if some subconscious curb was suddenly released. Or perhaps the taste of blood in his mouth impelled him—and he tumbled her onto her back so abruptly, she squealed. Following her in a graceful roll that didn't dislodge him, he heatedly whispered, his face only inches from hers, "You want it right now?"

Holding her hips firmly between his large hands, he thrust solidly into her, his muscled buttocks flexing until he heard her gasp. "Will that do?" he prompted, on a suffocated breath. "Or that ... or that?" His words, high-strung, moody, matched his deliberate, driving invasion, a form of retaliation perhaps. Or perhaps no more than his own wild obsession.

Ablaze, audacious in her own need, wanting him possibly more than he her, on the trembling brink of an ecstasy so intense, she felt momentarily as if she would shatter, she flagrantly mated with the man she'd dreamed of for four long months.

His back arched, his eyes half-shut, he drove into her, mindless, out of control, unaware of the sheer power and violence of his penetration.

Forcing her upward with each powerful surge, he followed her as she slid away, impatiently dragging her back, his hands recapturing their harsh grip on her hips, the sound of her panting cries a distant echo in his ears. Clinging to him, her fingers tangled in his hair, she met him in her own feverish need, her body as much on fire as his, their frenzied course moving them off the plaid and across several feet of meadow, the scent of crushed flowers and grasses pungent in their nostrils.

Like a battering ram, his lean, hard body drove into her, heedless of her panting whimpers, her impassioned response, like a man possessed, the pumping rhythm of his lower body, pitiless and turbulent, buffeted her, propelled her backward.

Until his orgasm overcame him, her piercing cry of release was unheard.

Until his madness was temporarily assuaged.

Until he lay quiet, his forehead resting in the grass near her shoulder, his chest heaving, his weight balanced on his elbows and knees, wondering if it were possible to exorcise this volatile, all-consuming lust for Elizabeth Graham—or whether he'd fuck himself to death first.

"Come ... with me ... to ... Three Kings," she panted, into his damp hair.

Rolling off her as if her invitation were the lethal poison of personal attachment, he sprawled on the cool grass beside her, his arms thrown over his head, his eyes closed. A second passed, then two, and ignoring the danger, he said, half-breathless, "Yes."

Later, when his mind was less dizzy with the delirium of release and his equanimity was restored, when his eyes were open again and he remembered where he was, he tranquilly said, "We could make love in a bed at Three Kings."

And when she smiled at him from her own sprawled position short feet away, he pointed out with a captivating grin, "My knees are turning raw."

"I can see you're not used to rustic ways."

"Rather I'm not used to obsession, darling Bitsy. It must be the Teviotdale air."

"Or my alluring charm," Elizabeth teasingly noted.

"Yes," he admitted, more philosophical in the aftermath of his orgasm. "More likely that. I haven't had raw knees in a decade."

With the lure of a soft bed tempting him and caution recklessly jettisoned, he found some water in a small nearby creek to wash them both, threw on his clothes like a man familiar with speedy leave-taking, and helped Elizabeth dress. He tied the waist bows on her petticoats, laced her corset, buttoned the buttons on her dimity gown; he helped repin her kerchief at her bosom. All with an expertise Elizabeth could have taken issue with if she weren't so bewitched. He even apologized for his lack of a comb.

"Although combs weren't high on my list of priorities when I invited you on this walk."

"Nor mine," Elizabeth agreed, sliding her fingers through her long, pale hair.

"I don't suppose anyone waiting for us expects we were actually walking all this time."

Her lacy brows rose minutely.

"Well, then," Johnnie affably said, "let me tie the bow on your cape, Lady Graham, and we'll do our best to outface that bodyguard of yours."

CHAPTER 14

Walking hand in hand, they approached the carriage and the lounging men; some were playing dice, others resting on the grassy verge of the road. Munro, never without a book, was reading. They all came to attention, and the last hundred yards were a gauntlet of silent scrutiny. "We'll all be going on to Three Kings," Elizabeth said to Redmond when they reached the carriage. "Thank you for . . . waiting," she added, unable to suppress the blush that colored her face.

Redmond diplomatically shifted his glance, but the penetrating look he turned on Johnnie held both warning and caution. A small pause ensued while each took measure of the other—two large, intimidating men capable of making their own rules.

"I was invited," Johnnie quietly said.

"No doubt o' that," Redmond said, guarded but behaving himself.

"It's my decision, Redmond," Elizabeth softly said, touching her captain gently on his arm.

Redmond's hesitation was minute, a notification to

the man at her side that the Redesdale men had a certain
latitude in their decision-making. "Very well, my Lady,"
he said. "Will ye be staying long?" he bluntly asked Johnnie, as a guardian might ask the intentions of a suitor.

"No, he won't, Redmond," Elizabeth quickly interjected. "Parliament is in session. And I don't want any
complications," she added, the emphasis clearly for her
captain, whose scowl continued to wrinkle his brow.
"Ravensby is my guest, coming to Three Kings at my
specific invitation. I don't wish to discuss any of this."
Her voice was low, hurried, with an underlying authority
unmistakable to either man.

"You see . . ." Johnnie murmured with a lazy grin,
understanding Redmond's concern but on his way to
Three Kings with or without his consent, "it's out of my
hands. Lady Graham's in charge."

"Just so long as she stays in charge," Redmond
said.

"We don't have any problem there, do we?" The
look Johnnie cast at Elizabeth was shamelessly impudent.

"Absolutely none." A playful mirth shone from her
laughing eyes.

"It's settled then," Johnnie pleasantly said to
Redmond.

When informed of the change in plans, Munro
readily agreed, pleased at his cousin's interest. It was an
unusual circumstance, he knew, for a man who liked to
limit the duration of his visits with females. And Elizabeth's happiness genuinely gratified him. She deserved
amusement in her young life, although he held reservations about Johnnie's willingness to stay with her. But he
shrugged away the uncertain future in favor of Elizabeth's present buoyant spirits. In addition, he was eager
to see her house. Elizabeth's construction project held a
definite attraction.

So the interrupted journey continued, with Munro
and Johnnie keeping Elizabeth company in her carriage.
They discussed the Graham wedding, the help Munro
could offer the construction crew. They touched briefly
on the business of Parliament and her father, both subjects replete with difficulties. And, as they compared the

qualities of several wines Johnnie had sent to her, she discovered he was a wine connoisseur of some rank.

"But then I'm a wine merchant, darling," Johnnie casually acknowledged. "I transport a good share of Scotland's wine."

"Among other luxury goods . . . and England's wine as well," Munro added. "Although the Privy Council pretends their best wines haven't come over the Scottish border."

"The war's been profitable," Johnnie calmly noted. "Despite Byng's attempt at blockade. He's a timid fool."

"And you've the fastest frigates on the seas."

"The reason I'm still in business."

"And richer."

Johnnie smiled. His profits often exceeded thirty thousand pounds per vessel. "Why be in business otherwise?"

"Do you sail often?" Elizabeth asked, wanting to know more of this man who fascinated her. She was surprised that the rogue and reiving Border Lord operated a thriving merchant empire even in the midst of war.

"I sailed to Rotterdam twice last month; it's a short trip with favorable winds." He didn't say they'd outraced two British ships. "And I saw Dunkirk and Ostend the month before. The French fleet had just come in. Do you like Siamese silks?"

"I'm sure I do." Elizabeth smiled up at Johnnie, who sat beside her, his arm comfortably around her shoulder. She wanted to ask how he'd entered enemy ports in wartime. But she said instead, because he continued suspicious of her Englishness, "I'm afraid that sounded dreadfully greedy, didn't it. I'd be more than happy to *pay* you for the silks."

"Nonsense. I've a warehouse full. Forbes recently returned from Siam. What color do you think, Munro?" the Laird of Ravensby casually inquired.

"Green, of course, with her eyes."

"Perhaps that magenta too," Johnnie suggested, "with the underlay of peach. I'll have some sent to Three Kings when I return to Edinburgh." It pleased him to give her something. He'd include yardage for the walls and windows in her new house, which meant he'd have to listen more attentively when the plans were discussed. Better yet, he'd have Munro draw up a list of rooms and colors.

So the journey passed in companionship and conversation, and Munro noted with astonishment that his cousin even agreed to partake of dinner with neighbors who'd been previously invited to dine.

"I *could* change plans," Elizabeth had said, "but George Baldwin's sister is scheduled to return to London on Thursday, so we'd made arrangements for a small gathering on Wednesday. I'd really hate to disappoint her. She's very pleasant . . . and an excellent harpist. Do you enjoy the harp?"

A man who studiously avoided amateur musical entertainments, Johnnie Carre nevertheless tranquilly replied, "Very much."

Munro's amazement took the form of a sudden coughing fit.

"I hope you haven't taken a chill, Cuz," Johnnie smoothly observed as his cousin attempted to regain his composure.

It was a journey of fascinating revelations—with Johnnie Carre on his very best behavior. Munro considered the three-hour ride to Three Kings the most faultless example of lust-driven prevarication he'd ever had the good fortune to see.

But the lust was mutual, he realized, when they arrived at Three Kings, because Elizabeth was as anxious as Johnnie to disappear into her bedroom. He and Redmond spent the evening together, both careful to avoid the topic of their absent hosts.

"I adore having you in my bed," Elizabeth was saying at that moment, the remains of a barely eaten supper on a table near the balcony door, their clothes scattered pellmell around the room where they'd been discarded in haste, their nude, sweat-sheened bodies lying side by side in abandoned sprawls.

Their hands twined.

Their hearts and minds overcome with pleasure.

"I'm feeling a lively sense of gratitude at being here, Lady Graham," Johnnie murmured, his drawl beguiling, "and once I've sufficiently caught my breath again, I'm thinking about expressing my appreciation"—a smile drifted through his words—"in some shamelessly salacious way. . . ."

"Ummm . . ." Elizabeth purred, Johnnie Carre's talents still very vivid in her memory. "I don't suppose Parliament could do without you for a week or so, while I indulge in sexual excess."

Johnnie thought for a moment of the fascinating possibilities, as eager as she to explore the boundaries of sensation. He found the wild yet curiously innocent Elizabeth Graham endlessly provocative. But Hamilton's dubious evasions, Queensberry's double-dealing, and Goddphin's generosity with English gold threatened the very existence of his country. And much as he wished to stay, he had to be back in Edinburgh by Sunday morning. Which meant leaving on Friday to meet his schedule.

He couldn't tell her that he and Fletcher of Saltoun were planning on introducing an overture to stop the discussion of the army allotment on the first day back. One never knew who were England's paid spies, so he only said, "I wish Parliament could do without me for a month, and we could both expire of carnal license. But I'll do what I can tonight and tomorrow to make you remember me."

She heard rather than saw his smile. "Cheeky rogue," she murmured.

"While you're preeminently bashful and retiring."

"And don't forget virtuous," she playfully interjected, "while you're cataloging."

He laughed, his deep voice velvety in the candlelit chamber. "And celibate. I think I like that most about you."

He tugged on her hand at the sudden vivid reminder of her personal celibacy. "Do we have to see those people tomorrow?" He wanted to lock himself away with her and not come out till Michaelmas or, at least Friday morning.

Elizabeth half turned toward him, her lush body like gleaming alabaster in the dim light. "I think it's too late to reach them . . . but certainly you needn't join us."

"How long will they stay?" he grumbled, not wishing to relinquish her company. It was a first for Johnnie Carre, had he bothered to analyze his feelings.

"A few hours."

A low rumble of displeasure.

"I'm sorry. You said you wouldn't mind."

"A statement predicated by lust."

"Isn't everything with you?" she teasingly noted.

"You don't know me." There was none of his habitual irony in his declaration.

"In some ways I do," she archly reminded him.

"Do you ever travel?" he abruptly asked, ignoring her allusion to their intimacies, his voice oddly speculative.

"Very little. Have we changed the subject?"

His gaze on the coffered ceiling, he said, "No." Gruff, almost forbidding, the single word vibrated with relevancy. She felt his hand tighten minutely on hers. "Why don't you come to Edinburgh with me?" Even as he uttered the words, he wished to retract them, their significance terrifying, the actual sound of them shocking to a man who prided himself on freedom.

Good God, he thought, wondering immediately how to diplomatically recant. He didn't want a permanent mistress; he'd never tied himself to one woman. And an English woman who was the daughter of Harold Godfrey—it was unthinkable with his political affiliations. Bringing Godfrey's daughter to town would be like bedding Marlborough's daughter and insisting your principles were still pure and patriotically Scottish. No one would believe it.

He wouldn't blame them.

"I'd love to, but I can't now . . . with the house," Elizabeth replied, rolling closer so she half lay across his chest. "Maybe later . . ."

And he found himself breathing again, saved from his own stupidity.

"But thank you for asking," Elizabeth added, pleased at his offer.

"You'd probably be bored in any event," Johnnie replied with what he hoped was casualness. He could still feel the hammering beat of his heart. "Between Parliament and the heated debates at Patrick Steil's tavern, I'm hardly home long enough to change clothes."

He was reneging already, she thought, less surprised than she'd been by his sudden suggestion. But she knew as well as he that her presence in Edinburgh would bring with it rumors of her or even him spying for England. Her father was notoriously in Queensberry's employ. His name tainted her as well. She'd not be an asset to Johnnie Carre. "Perhaps you could come back to Three Kings instead when the session is adjourned."

"When they break for the harvest," he said with relief, the danger averted. His heartbeat had almost returned to normal.

"Yes," she agreed, thinking him the politest of men.

But his impulsive invitation was a terrifying lesson learned, and caution curbed any further spontaneous expressions of affection. In no way, however, did it affect his seductive charm, or his performance.

Very late that night, Elizabeth murmured, "No ... I can't ..." Her palms pressed against his chest. "Not again ... not right now ... I'm too sore." But she wanted him still, even as she refused him. And she wondered how one could so lose command of one's senses.

"I can fix that," Johnnie soothed, easing away, his voice confident. "Just relax. . . ." he murmured, positioning himself lower on the bed, gently touching her swollen slit. "It's so small. . . ." Looking, feeling, inserting the tip of his finger, he examined the site of her discomfort. "You're not used to unbridled excess, Lady Graham," he whispered. "Or a large man . . ." he added, spreading her legs apart with the gentlest of pressure, settling between them leisurely, his head resting on her inner thigh, his hair like silk on her skin, his breath warm on her throbbing bottom.

And his tongue touched her swollen flesh a moment later, lightly slid over its distended surface, then slipped inside the pouting entrance.

She stirred restlessly, a lush heat licking at her senses, her fingers twining through his thick hair, the weight of his head on her thigh tantalizing as though she were yielding already, prisoner to that pressure, that strength and power.

She could feel the sweet liquid of desire drench her swollen tissue; she could feel herself open to him as his tongue slid deeper, as his fingers gently spread her labia.

Her eyes shut as the familiar heat spread upward through her body, the throbbing between her legs echoed in her blood, the sensation of cool air as her skin grew hot, the small whimpers fluttering up the back of her throat. Nothing hurt anymore—only the exquisite ache of wanting, only the sweet affliction of carnal need.

And short moments later he moved into position between her legs, his erection stiff against her pulsing flesh, the taste of her on his mouth when he kissed her. "You see how easy it is," he whispered, "to make the hurt go away. . . ."

And she hated him for a flashing moment, for his proficiency acquired with too many women in too many heated encounters. But she wanted him more than she resented his fluent finesse. She could no more stop herself from yielding to him than she could hold back the march of Marlborough's army. And she rose into his hard length and felt the merciless rapture of his entry. She was liquid, slick, panting for him, twined and clinging and hot with need, and he found the added tightness only intensified his arousal.

Exhausted, replete, they slept at last toward dawn.

•   •   •

The maid woke them at eleven when she knocked to remind them of the arrival of their guests.

Wrapped in his arms, still half-asleep and drowsy,
Elizabeth felt luxuriously alive, as if the beauty of the
world were laid out before her, delectable and within
reach.

An overwhelming contentment rang through Johnnie's languorous senses, all the wrangling critical issues
of politics momentarily forgotten, all the sharp-set danger
of Scotland's future disregarded on a warm summer
morning with Elizabeth Graham in his arms. She could
almost make him forget his hatred of English rule.

Almost.

CHAPTER 15

The guests had all assembled in the drawing room before Johnnie and Elizabeth had readied themselves. Munro found himself in the difficult position of playing temporary host to people he'd never met before. Conversation was desultory, although the two Gerard sisters, attuned to local gossip, had already heard the identity of Elizabeth's absent guest. *Their* questions were more pointed.

Munro's replies were politely evasive. He didn't know what dissembling story Johnnie would prefer. And he quite literally exhaled a sigh of relief when Elizabeth and Johnnie walked into the room.

Introductions were repeated for Johnnie's benefit. George Baldwin and his sister, Anne, both fair and slender, greeted their hostess and her guest with identical smiles, polite, tactfully bland. They prided themselves on their Christian charity and overlooked the Earl of Graden's scandalous reputation for Elizabeth's sake. Although George Baldwin was hard-pressed to graciously disregard Ravensby's unnerving handsomeness.

Lord Ayton and his rotund wife, Elizabeth's most

immediate neighbors, talked immediately of the new construction project.

"Looks as though you're right on schedule, Lady Graham," the bluff, heavyset country squire remarked. "If your crew needs any help, I could send some of my men over."

"Thank you, perhaps later," Elizabeth said, politely declining. Avery had nothing to do between hunt seasons, and she preferred not having him overseeing her project.

"Have you selected your drapery and room colors yet, my dear?" Lady Ayton breathlessly inquired, her portliness contributing to her shortness of breath. "I've found the dearest little mercer in Newcastle who would *love* to advise you."

"It's so early yet, Lady Ayton, to be considering the interiors, but I'll have his name from you for future use." Charlotte meant well, imbued with a genuine kindness, Elizabeth knew. "He must have advised you on your new rose sitting room," she graciously added.

"Isn't it a dear little room? So cozy. . . ." Lady Ayton glanced quickly at her husband, whose attention had wandered at talk of decorating. "Although Avery says he can't abide so much satin," she quietly added. "But then," she went on with a bright smile, "he has his estate office to sit in with his muddy boots. You'll quite adore Monsieur Hugeau, Elizabeth. Although we mustn't talk of the French now, must we, with this dreadful war going on."

"Marlborough's damned war has brought the price of my brandy too damned high," Lord Ayton exclaimed, apparently heeding the conversation with a censoring ear, his high-Tory attitude typical of most small landed gentry. "And I can't get fine riding gloves either. Bloody inconvenient!"

"Marlborough's deep into Austria now," Johnnie casually remarked, his access to news on the Continent often superior to the government's with the speed of his ships, his factors posted throughout the trading cities of Europe.

"There's rumor of a decisive battle," George Baldwin noted. "Have you heard as much?" His news came from a cousin in Whitehall, an undersecretary in the Treasury.

Johnnie nodded. "As soon as Tallard and Marlborough decide on an arena."

"Have you ever *killed* a man?" Lucy Gerard addressed Johnnie with a kind of breathless awe.

And a sudden silence fell as the discordant, extremely personal query constrained the flow of conversation.

"I'm sorry," Elizabeth said, speaking first, "you haven't been introduced yet. Lucy and Jane Gerard, the Earl of Graden."

And the Gerard sisters made their curtsies to the notorious Laird of Ravensby, well known on both sides of the Borders. Jane's greeting was distinctly flirtatious. Lucy, the younger of the sisters, her blond curls bobbing, rushed on to explain, "I just meant you seem to know so much about the war and all. . . ."

"I've never served in England's Army," Johnnie said, not mentioning he'd served in the French Army under his uncle's command.

"How fascinating it must have been to be an actual *hostage*," Jane precipitously declared, her mind on its own strategic track, her forwardness not a surprise to Munro, who'd been parrying her questions about his cousin for some time. And while her statement was directed at Elizabeth, her inviting gaze still dwelt on Johnnie.

"Not an unusual pattern on the Borders, Miss Gerard," Johnnie replied to save Elizabeth embarrassment, although even his normally unruffled poise had been briefly shocked by Jane's bluntness. "It's all quite routine."

"How long were you *there*?" Jane went on, her voice breathy with excitement, her glance unwaveringly *not* on the object of her query.

"Really, Jane," Anne Baldwin interrupted, coming to Elizabeth's support. "I'm sure Elizabeth has grown tired of repeating the story of her exchange for Lord Graden's brother."

The story was well known in the area of Three

Kings; only the presence of the disreputable, comely Border Lord had produced renewed, titillating interest in the minds of the inquisitive Gerard sisters.

"Why don't you show us the current progress on your home, Elizabeth," George Baldwin suggested into the uncomfortable pause. "I understand you've actually begun the foundations."

"Would you mind, Munro?" Elizabeth queried, grateful to the Baldwins for their kindness. "He knows so much more than I," she added as she smiled at her neighbors.

And the party proceeded out the glass-paned doors facing the gardens. The estate Elizabeth had purchased with her inheritance included a redbrick Tudor structure with a superb formal garden. The well-maintained grounds rose in terraced parterres to the top of the hill that had once held a small Romanesque folly—now much in ruins. On that picturesque elevation with a magnificent view of the countryside, Elizabeth had chosen to situate her new home.

"It's going to be a long afternoon," Johnnie sardonically murmured, his hand intimately at the small of her back as he and Elizabeth took up the rear of the procession through the neat, trimmed gardens, his gaze intent on the group ahead should he have to distant himself discreetly from his hostess. "No doubt the Gerard sisters will wish to know what he did last night in detail?"

"I'm sure they'd love to know anything at all about *you*, darling," Elizabeth teasingly replied, turning toward him in a swinging half-step, her full-skirted apple-green gown swirling around her ankles, her expression playful. "And if it were proper to pant in public, they surely would."

"Spare me," he grumbled, female busybodies decidedly outside his purview.

"Don't you find Lucy pretty?" she sweetly inquired, touching his fingertips lightly.

"No, I do not."

"Perhaps Jane is more your style." Her grin was cheerful.

"You're enjoying this, aren't you?" he said with a

sudden smile. "And no, Jane is not my style; I dislike simpering blondes."

"She hasn't simpered yet."

"She will, trust me."

"So sure, Ravensby," she teased. "Does it come from vast experience?"

"Damned right it does, Bitsy, my sweet, and if you don't stop aggravating me with talk of those simpleton gossips, I'll embarrass you right now before every one of your neighbors."

"Are you threatening me?" She didn't look alarmed.

"Absolutely."

She cast him a sportive sidelong glance. "Well, maybe I'll just embarrass you back."

"Impossible, darling." He gazed over at her from under the dark drift of his lashes. "Belive me, you're years too late."

"Arrogant man."

"No, just honest. I've been out in the world more than you. And I've also met more Gerard sisters than you could imagine."

He was right; he was also right about the Gerard sisters' avid curiosity. "How *do* I respond to Lucy and Jane?" Elizabeth said with a small sigh, her teasing smile fading, genuine concern motivating her as they approached the party at the crest of the hill.

"You don't," Johnnie succinctly declared. "They have no right to inquire into your personal life."

"We in the country are less blasé. Personal lives are the subject of much comment."

He shrugged. "As they are everywhere, darling. But if you allow people to go beyond certain boundaries, they'll eat you alive."

"Should I fall suddenly ill?" Elizabeth facetiously suggested, each step drawing them nearer to the group at the construction site. The possibility of restraining the Gerard sisters for an entire afternoon was suddenly daunting.

"Perhaps later." A faint smile curved his mouth. "If I can't think of something more plausible."

"I wish now I'd sent a messenger last night to cancel the invitation—even if it was midnight."

"Amen to that," he murmured, an effortless social smile appearing on his face as they came within speaking distance of the party. "Well, Munro, have you sufficiently explained the need for such sizable masonry in the foundations?" His smile held an open, natural charm. "I find it particularly fascinating how Munro can calculate the exact weight-bearing load of the walls and roof beforehand. Tell them how you learned that in Rome."

And with consummate skill he quite literally controlled the conversation throughout the tour of the building site, on the walk back to the house, with cultivated ease over luncheon. He entertained them with stories of the Court in London—a world removed from the environs of Northumbria; he talked of the China seas and the trading depots in the Orient; he described the Sun King's magnificent Versailles, not currently accessible to English subjects. He promised to send the ladies some distinguished French wines, very dear and difficult to obtain in England since the war; to the men he offered some aged brandies impossible to buy for love or money.

And they talked some more of the war on the Continent, and later, more pertinently, of possible war between Scotland and England.

"Hope it don't come to that, by God," Lord Ayton muttered. "London don't always know what's best." Coming from an ancient Roman Catholic family, Lord Ayton had reservations about the Succession. "Don't care for the Hanovers," he bluntly said. What was left unsaid was his strongly Jacobite preference.

"Everyone knows the Scottish Parliament has concerns about the Succession too," Johnnie said.

"Are the Scots going to march?" Ayton demanded. Like so many of the country barons, he was a plainspeaking man without artifice.

"It's a moot question at the moment," Johnnie neutrally replied, disinclined to offer details to any Englishman, no matter his Border affiliation.

"My Scottish cousin tells me the counties are raising levies," Ayton said. "Damned if that don't smell of war. And a regiment of horse came up from Doncaster last week. We're going to be caught in the damned middle again." The boundary between England and Scotland was an arbitrary line on the map; extended families living on both sides of that artificial border often overlooked national interests in favor of familial ones.

"There's some talk of union," George Baldwin said. "Would that allay these overtures to war?"

"The union commission was disbanded in February," Johnnie replied. "Through lack of interest. Have you heard of renewed purpose in Westminster?" It was a polite question only. No one in Scotland wanted union except those magnates who owned property in England and seats on the board of the East India Company and might lose them if war broke out. And the business interests in London and Bristol that controlled Parliament were adamantly opposed to Scotland entering their trade territories. As for the Court, if the English could secure Scottish approval for the Succession, they could continue to control Scotland completely. A union was of no interest to either country, for the moment.

"Thurlow, who represents our riding, tells me the Tories bring up the subject on occasion as though to test the waters."

"Or to gauge their enemies," Johnnie said.

"You go back to the sessions soon then?" George asked.

"Almost immediately," Johnnie answered with deliberate vagueness, having decided on a means of escape for himself and Elizabeth. "It was a short adjournment. You must all call on me," he cordially went on, "if you're ever in Edinburgh or Ravensby."

All in all, he managed to ingratiate himself nicely with the local gentry. He also effectively restrained the Gerard sisters from asking any impertinent questions. And when he said after dessert, "I promised Lady Graham to survey her wine cellar before I leave with regards to setting in a new supply. I'm sorry time is so limited. Would you excuse us, please?" everyone obligingly waved them off.

After a generous measure of wine for lunch, even

Munro didn't mind being left behind to see the neighbors off. After an hour or two of Johnnie's best wines, he found even simpering blondes had taken on an added allure.

Johnnie and Elizabeth retired to their private hermitage, relieved to have gotten away so easily.

"Thank you enormously," Elizabeth whispered, throwing herself into his arms before he'd completely entered her bedroom.

"It was a purely selfish impulse, darling," he murmured, his arms closing around her as he kicked the door shut behind him. "I was literally counting hours," he said, "and I didn't want to waste any more with strangers."

"Umm . . . I love the feel of you." Her hands ran up the back of his beige linen coat. "I kept wanting to touch you this afternoon, but I couldn't."

"I almost dragged you out of the dining room a dozen times, thinking to hell with them all."

"The Gerard sisters could have dined on that for a lifetime."

"My principal deterrent." His grin was beautiful again, personal, for her alone.

"We've a whole day and a half left," she murmured, her answering smile redolent with happiness.

"Two-and-a-half days."

She leaned back in his arms to gain a better view of him. "You said you had to leave by six Friday morning."

He squeezed her, a delicate nuance of movement, as delicate as the slow upcurving of his smile. "I decided to make it Saturday morning."

Her green eyes shone with delight. "Because you adore me so," she cheerfully supplied.

"Because I adore you so. . . ." he repeated.

Their days together were the stuff of dreams, lazy, indolent hours in bed, late breakfasts, leisurely walks in the shady forest or along the slow-moving stream, the water sluggish in the heat of summer; they rode once, although Elizabeth murmured no the next morning when he suggested it as they leaned against the cool stone of the pasture fence—"My bottom's too tender. . . ." And sweeping her into his arms, he carried her into the house from the pasture beyond the stables: "To save you . . . for later. . . ." he said with a lush smile. They ate private dinners with Munro, and he marveled at the attachment shown by his cousin, a man not prone to public displays of affection. Johnnie called Elizabeth "my darling" and "sweetheart" and sat close beside her and fed her. Or she him. It was a side of Johnnie Carre Munro had never seen. And he'd known Johnnie a lifetime.

Their last night together was more tender than rapacious, as if the end of their time together tempered the greedy compulsions of the days past.

It was as if both understood the final limit of their passionate holiday was mere hours away.

Their kisses were sweet and slow and languid, so the memory of them was etched more powerfully in their minds. Their lovemaking grew measured and gentle; the flash and violence and flagrant fever was replaced by a sensitivity, an intensity of emotion.

Elizabeth didn't dare call it love, the word incongruous with the Laird of Ravensby's dissolute life, but she felt a kind of indelible passion that would suffer the precious loss of him.

Johnnie experienced a sense of latent deprivation, obscure and perplexing. He wouldn't recognize love if it knocked at his door dressed in cloth of gold, carrying a placard. But he knew already he'd miss her.

And to that feeling his new tenderness spoke.

Into this blissful night of sweet desire, Elizabeth found herself thinking how wonderful it would be to have a child by this wild, beautiful man. An absurdity she immediately understood as completely irrational.

But the thought lingered with all the buried feelings from her past. She'd always wanted a child in the loneliness of her life with Hotchane. And each of her monthly courses that appeared like clockwork in the years of her marriage had brought with it a feeling of hopelessness and sorrow. It had been easier to blame her aged husband than face the dread possibility her own womb might be barren, but she couldn't know. And as the years went by, her yearning for a child increased; she found herself watching babies and young children with a keen, aching hunger, coveting their soft plumpness and happy smiles, wanting to wipe away their tears, wondering if she would ever be called—lovingly—Mother.

She'd forgotten that dream in the months since Hotchane had died, too concerned with her struggle for survival as an independent widow. She'd not had time between fighting off her father's scheme for her remarriage, selecting and purchasing her land, drawing up the necessary plans, and arranging for a construction crew. But the thought of babies surfaced instinctively as she lay against the heated strength of the quintessentially male Johnnie Carre.

"Do you have children?" she asked into the dimness of the candlelit room.

Shocked from a brief daydreaming doze, he murmured, "Ummm?" hoping he'd misunderstood her question.

"I was wondering if you had children?"

"Why?" he said, automatically evasive.

"I just wanted to know." Ungenerous envy stole into her mind at his cautious response; some fortunate women must have his children.

"I'm not sure." Masculine equivocation.

"Tell me," she said.

He sighed, realizing from her tone it wasn't going to be possible to avoid this conversation. "A few," he reluctantly disclosed.

"That's suitably vague."

"I'm not being vague. There are simply no absolutes, since I never sleep with virgins. A certain difficulty blurs the results. And acknowledging possible children isn't always feasible, even if I were certain."

"Are you saying the women are married?"

He sighed again. "Generally, yes. Why are we on this subject?"

"I was simply thinking how pleasant it would be to have your child."

"Oh, Lord . . ." Even as his groan wafted upward, his brain went on full alert.

"Don't be alarmed. I'd never be coercive."

"It's a little late to be discussing this," Johnnie said, not alarmed at female coercion with his finely honed instincts of avoidance, but distinctly wary. His voice had taken on an edge, and unfolding his arm from around her, he rolled onto his side, braced his head on his hand, and settled an exacting look on her. "Are you suggesting I should have thought of the possible consequences?" he gruffly said, wondering if this conversation was moving toward either of two unwelcome topics in bed—marriage or money.

"Neither of us were thinking much," Elizabeth calmly replied. "And you needn't worry. I'm not positioning myself for advantage."

"Rumor has it you're barren," he softly said, thinking at least one topic of discussion was eliminated. As for money, he was generous to all his lovers. He just didn't care to count guineas in bed.

"You see, you're safe then," she briskly replied. But her eyes grew bright with unshed tears, and her bottom lip began to quiver. She'd never reconciled herself to her deprivation; she'd always hoped.

"Oh, Lord . . . I'm sorry," he murmured, reaching for her, gathering her in his arms. He gently stroked her hair. "I didn't mean to be unfeeling."

"How could . . . you know . . . it mattered—" she replied in a tiny voice, fighting back her tears, his comfort and concern only deepening her melancholy.

"Don't cry, darling. Please . . ." he whispered, the coolness of her tears sliding down his chest. "Maybe you'll *have* a child someday," he said, his words so exceptional in the context of his amorous pleasure, he questioned his sanity for a moment. But he was oddly touched by her distress; she seemed suddenly so vulnerable, so exposed.

"It's not your problem," she replied in a wisp of a breath, bravely trying to stifle her sorrow, aware the subject of babies made Johnnie uneasy. All her old feelings of emptiness were causing her discomfort as well. "Consider the topic closed."

"Gladly," Johnnie said with the haste of a profligate rake. No different from any male of his class, he enjoyed a self-indulgent life in terms of entertainments. There were few rules for wealthy peers. It was a time of carnal license for aristocratic men, for men of wealth, for men of any station who could charm. And the law required only the poor and middling sort to marry the mothers of their children. "I think you need some cheering up," he softly said, lifting her onto his chest so her toes brushed the rough hair on his calves, the warmth of his body solid, strong, a lush inducement to happiness. "I could sing for you." A roguish smile accompanied his offer.

Gazing down into his handsome face, the candlelight modeling its fine bone structure in graceful shadow and plane, his sky-blue eyes under his heavy dark lashes lazily offering her anything she wanted, the elegant curve of his mouth suggestive of options other than song, Elizabeth basked in his seductive charm. Her answering smile, delicious and winsomely amused, radiated a palatable heat. "Now, Ravensby, consider . . . . why would I want you to sing," she huskily whispered like any modish coquette bent on seduction, "when that glorious cock of yours is nudging my stomach?"

"You have something else in mind then," he said, his grin creeping into the sky blue of his eyes.

"I have a few hours more to take advantage of you."

"And I to amuse you." His voice was hushed.

"How fortunate we agree." She reached up to trace the perfect dark curve of his brow.

"But don't we always, Bitsy, my pet?" he whispered, moving her hand down from his brow, easing one of her fingers into his mouth, softly nibbling on the tender pad.

Morning came too early, too swiftly. As the sun rose over the rim of the Redesdale horizon in a glorious flux of gold and dazzling peony, the two lovers witnessed the melting away of shadow in their private universe, the soft glow of sunshine drifting in. And both knew the ride to Edinburgh could no longer be delayed.

Replete, full of love and longing, cradled against Johnnie's powerful body, Elizabeth said, "Remember to come and visit me sometime when the business of state allows. I'll have some new walls for you to see."

"I will," Johnnie promised, warmed by the heated afterglow of passion, his fingertips tracing the silken curve of her spine. "The first chance I get."

A kind of love or affection or fondness had grown between them, indescribable and nameless, a strangely blissful enchantment. And their good-bye kiss was sweet with tenderness.

Their public farewells took place on the graveled drive before Munro, Redmond, servants and bodyguards. He politely bowed, she graciously smiled, and they exchanged all the expected social phrases of leave-taking. Then he kissed her hand lightly, already reverting to the polite courtier, and, mounting his horse, joined Munro, who'd been waiting patiently for some time.

"Good-bye, Johnnie," Elizabeth said, lifting her hand in a last salute.

Leaning over to check his stirrup leather, he seemed not to have heard until Munro nudged him. Looking over, he said, "Good-bye, Elizabeth," with a small distance in his voice, as if his mind had shifted away in those few short moments.

She tried to ward off that urbane coolness—or rather, she told herself to be realistic. Johnnie Carre was a busy man, hours late to meet his obligations in Parliament, with a trading fleet to manage and estates to oversee. His life couldn't possibly revolve around her wishes. But her heart wouldn't so easily respond to the rationale of logic, and an incipient small sorrow insinuated itself into the extraordinary happiness he'd given her.

The men rode at a hard, steady gallop, both aware of the distance to Edinburgh. Johnnie knew he shouldn't have stayed so long. Munro didn't think they'd reach the capital in time for the meeting in the morning. There was no opportunity for conversation on the swift ride north unless they cared to shout at each other over the sound of the wind and pounding hoofbeats.

Just as well, Johnnie thought, knowing Munro was going to take issue with the nature of his sojourn at Three Kings. He had a right to. But it was as if a page had turned or a chapter had closed in Johnnie's mind; his thoughts were focused on the session ahead—so pressing was the decision on the Act of Security. If London agreed to approve it, nothing so monumental had occurred in Scottish history since the two countries had merged. If London continued to resist . . . they would have to see that support continued strong against the Court party. If the Queen's money had found some additional necessitous Lords during the short adjournment, London might have gathered enough votes to pass a limited act of supply. And his mind began the documenting of names, the certain votes, those against, the wavering—a methodical looping litany through his brain so familiar now after two years it had taken on an intimate cadence.

When the two men stopped briefly to rest their horses and eat, Johnnie braced himself for the expected discussion or, if Munro's expression was any indication, he reflected, handing his reins over to the ostler, perhaps "interrogation" would be the more appropriate word.

Their conversation began politely enough over ale while they were waiting for their food. They spoke of the unique beauty of Elizabeth's building site, of the neighborhood gentry they'd met, of the Gerard sisters, of Redmond's exceptional skill with a knife.

"You didn't see all of his exhibition, did you?" Munro said.

"Lord Ayton dragged me off to the stables for a short time to see his hunter after five or six throws by Redmond, but I was impressed—no doubt. The man could cut the wings off a fly at fifty paces."

"Elizabeth is fortunate to have him as her captain."

"And he her," Johnnie said with a smile. "I imagine she's an improvement over Hotchane as master."

"She's genuinely kind, not a quality often found in beautiful women. And she's wonderfully accomplished. Didn't you think her plans for the facade were well done?"

"They were remarkable; *she's* a remarkable woman," Johnnie agreed, responding to Munro's observation as the serving lass put the fowl and fresh-baked bread before them. "I wish she were more available."

Munro's glance swiveled up, the knife he held poised above the roast chicken on his plate arrested in midair. "You sound as though she isn't available."

"She isn't to me. You know I've no intention of marrying anytime soon, and Elizabeth isn't the quality of woman you can take as mistress."

"You mean she's too wellborn? What of Roxane?" He'd laid his knife aside.

"She's not my acknowledged mistress, as you well know, nor is Janet Lindsay or any of the others," Johnnie added, anticipating Munro's challenge to the issue of nobility. "Perhaps I simply hate Harold Godfrey more deeply than I despise any other man on the face of the earth."

"She's estranged from her father."

Johnnie looked over the chicken leg he was about to take a bite from. "Is this a debate?"

"I don't want you to cause her unhappiness. You know that."

"I haven't. I won't." Johnnie put his food aside, his eyes steady on his cousin. His voice when he spoke was carefully modulated. "Elizabeth and I both understood the parameters of our . . . tryst."

"Elizabeth sounded as though she was expecting a future visit from you when we left."

Johnnie had the grace to look uncomfortable. "I may have said something like that to her."

Munro leaned forward the merest distance. "But you won't be going back."

Johnnie hesitated: Munro's posture, his tone of voice, were stamped with temper. "No," he said after a short moment. "Regardless of how you feel," he softly added. "She's the daughter of my most hated enemy, of the Carres' traditional adversary; England at the moment qualifies as a mortal foe with swords locked as we are in the Parliaments, with the Border garrisons being strengthened. But at base, politics aside . . . very selfishly, *I don't wish to marry.*"

Munro leaned back in his chair, his vehemence abruptly muted. "Which you'd have to do with Elizabeth Graham," he quietly declared.

"Yes. I'm sorry." Johnnie knew the affection Munro had for Elizabeth. He, too, was briefly sorry, Elizabeth Graham wouldn't be easy to forget.

"She'll survive, I'm sure," Munro said with surprising calm, as if he'd reached some emotional accord with Johnnie's decision. "After eight deplorable years with Hotchane Graham," he said with the bluntness of long friendship, "her disappointment over you should be negligible."

"Exactly." Johnnie smiled disarmingly, gratified to recognize the Munro of old; his cousin as gallant knight was a more recent aberration. "Elizabeth often speaks of the new freedoms gained in widowhood. She won't pine away for lack of my company."

"Not with the foundation beginning next week and a building schedule to oversee for the next two years."

"Not with George Baldwin constantly underfoot," Johnnie facetiously added, although he experienced a swift twinge of discontent at the thought—as quickly brushed aside. "Now do you care to wager on who's been bribed over to Tweedale's party while we were gone?" he went on as if a change of subject were suddenly necessary. "I'd say Belhaven and Montrose, perhaps Selkirk."

"I'll only give you odds on the amount it took to buy their votes," Munro replied, applying himself to his food once again. "All three have sold Scotland away."

Johnnie paused for a moment before responding as the rancor clutched at his stomach. "It's a dirty game England's playing," he bitterly murmured, "and the poverty of Scotland is making it easy."

"The Court may not win."

"Over time I'm not so sure." A weariness infused the Laird of Ravensby's voice.

"We've kept them at bay for almost two years now."

Johnnie smiled. "Perhaps you're right. Who knows . . . our David might succeed after all against their Goliath. If the war on the Continent serves us."

"And if the Act of Security's approved by London."

"Yes, if . . ."

And the serious state of Scotland's affairs superseded further discussion of Elizabeth Graham's future.

CHAPTER 16

They rode into the outskirts of Edinburgh the next morning, their horses lathered and worn, both men aching with weariness. Arriving at Ravensby House a short time later, Johnnie had barely time to bathe, eat, and dress before leaving for his prearranged meeting with Roxburgh and Fletcher. The Country party planned to discuss strategy that day, prior to the session on Monday.

"You look like hell," Roxburgh exclaimed as Johnnie dropped into a chair at their table in Steil's tavern.

"And I look better than I feel." Running his palms over his still-damp hair, Johnnie slid lower in his chair. "I haven't slept much lately," he said in a voice rough with fatigue. "Tell me what I missed."

"You missed Roxie's sailing party, for one thing," Roxburgh quipped.

"Oh, Lord," Johnnie groaned. He'd forgotten to send his regrets.

"But your brother manfully stepped into the breech," Roxburgh roguishly went on. "In case you care."

"Thank God." The crease in Johnnie's brow disappeared.

"No desperate concern?" Roxburgh knew better; he'd been friends with Johnnie for years.

"Did I miss anything of a *political* nature?" Johnnie pointedly returned, not about to discuss the extent of his attachment to his lovers.

"The messengers to and from London put a tidy sum into the pockets of the proprietors of the post-stations," Fletcher sardonically noted, looking up from his breakfast. "Tweedale's been pressing Godolphin to agree to the Act of Security gossip reports."

"Have you heard how London intends to respond?" The world of Scottish politics was small.

"Rumor has it Godolphin will capitulate."

No immediate surge of triumph invaded Johnnie's soul; he knew England too well. His voice was guarded. "Do you think it's true?"

Fletcher shrugged, breaking a crusty piece of bread in two to dip into his chocolate. "We'll know soon enough."

But it took two more days of debate and behind-the-scenes bargaining, the government still desperately trying to salvage its program, loath to admit defeat.

Until Tweedale finally realized the session of 1704, like that of the previous year, would withhold the vote on supply, would refuse to agree on the Succession. His orders from Lord Treasurer Godolphin, Queen Anne's chief minister, had been clear. With the current military uncertainties in Europe causing the English markets and bankers to tremble, any further provocation of Scotland *at this time*, he had written, was unrealistic. If all else failed, if negotiations broke down, Tweedale, as High Commissioner of Scotland, had Godolphin's consent to "touch the scepter" to the Act of Security, making it law.

This he did on August 5.

The House exploded into uproarious, clamorous revelry. The Scottish Parliament, standing firm for over two years on its policy of transferring power to itself from the monarch of England, had won a *notable* victory.

But the Scottish Parliament's constitutional ideas and its frank intention to increase its power at the expense of the monarchy were regarded in England as something that might be dangerously contagious.

On August 28, before debate could begin on arming Scotland, on orders from London Tweedale quickly adjourned the session. Until October 7, the members were told.

But London had no intention of recalling the Scottish Parliament until Queen Anne's Court had regained its position of power. Marlborough had won a momentous victory against France at Blenheim on August 13—the news reaching London on the twenty-first. Now Scotland's defiance could be dealt with at leisure.

And while the noteworthy business of Scotland's bid for independence consumed Johnnie's time, Elizabeth, too, had been occupied with momentous events—albeit of a decidedly personal nature.

For the first time in her life, her monthly courses had been late.

Initially, she'd dared not consider the possibility she was with child; she'd been disheartened too many times in the past when her hopes had been dashed. It would be a precarious tempting of fate to think about so glorious a dream as having Johnnie Carre's child. And she attempted to dismiss the romantic conceit, an impossible exercise, she discovered. Despite her staunchest efforts, her mind recklessly contemplated nothing else. She found herself totally absorbed with an overwhelming excitement that possessed her heart and mind and soul. She counted the days a hundred times on her fingers and in writing, too, as if the passage of time was more authentic in black ink.

Five days passed, and then a week. . . .

Was it *possible* when she'd waited so long, wished so earnestly?

Ten more days were gone in August, and then two weeks. . . .

She was dizzy with dreams, light-headed with hope.

She lost track of her building project, which had been her entire life until then. Although she appeared at the site each day, overseeing and authorizing, giving suggestions, answering questions, she was oddly detached, heedless to all but the astonishing drama unfolding within her body.

Could it be she *wasn't* barren?

Would she *at last* have a child of her own to love?

Had all her tearful prayers been answered by a curious twist of fate in Robbie Carre's capture?

She didn't entertain fantasies of Johnnie Carre in her enchanting vignettes of plump pink babies. He'd expressed his opinion on babies succinctly enough the night before he left. And she hadn't heard from him in the month since, although he'd sent the silks as promised—an extravagant wagonful—or more probably Munro had sent them; she hadn't been sure the enclosed note was in Johnnie's hand. The brief phrases had nothing in them even remotely personal; he'd only wished her pleasant use of the silks and good wishes on her building. And he'd signed himself simply "Ravensby," as if he'd been writing to his lawyer.

She'd expected no more with the manner of his leave-taking. She wasn't surprised or prostrate with grief. Her life had been too long one of compromise and half-measures to expect sudden undiluted happiness. But she allowed herself a small crowing jubilation on the first day of September. Her courses were now more than two weeks late.

George Baldwin remarked on her special cheer that afternoon when he rode over to bring her a new book he'd received from London and view the progress on her new home.

Over tea he said, "You positively glow, Elizabeth. Have you been out in the sun too long?" he teasingly added, careful not to make too personal a remark.

Elizabeth smiled, thinking how different he was from Johnnie Carre, who dared anything. Who took what he wanted. "Perhaps it *was* the sun, George, or the warm tea," she answered with a smile. "But I admit, my spirits are high. The building is going well," she finished, dissembling with ease, her jubilant mood beyond the scruples of absolute honesty.

"I marvel at your unique abilities, Elizabeth. Most women content themselves with household duties."

Most women didn't have Harold Godfrey for a father, she wished to say, nor were they married to Hotchane Graham. One quickly learned to cultivate competence, a recognizable trait of defense against ruthless men. "This is merely a different aspect of running a household," she pleasantly contradicted. "And as a widow, I must learn to do things for myself," she added with a conventional politesse George would understand.

"There's no need for you to remain a widow, Elizabeth. You need only say yes to me, and I'd gladly take over all your burdens." He'd set his cup aside, and his expression, familiar after numerous proposals, offered her genuine affection.

"Thank you, George. You know how I appreciate your friendship, but you know, too, how I value my freedom. Hotchane was a difficult man." She shamelessly engaged in a dash of theatrics, lowering her eyes briefly in what she hoped was a portrayal of tragic memory.

"He was an appalling man," George heatedly countered. "You deserve better from life. But all men aren't Hotchane," he added, understanding any reluctance she might have for marriage after her first experience. "And while I'd never presume on your good nature, if at any time my affection will bring you comfort, I'd be honored to offer you my heart."

George Baldwin was an enigma to her, a man too benevolent to be believed, too moral for authenticity in a world that honored neither trait. She never quite knew how to respond to him, for he invoked in her no feelings at all other than perplexity and a mild friendship. "You're very kind, George, but, please, let's talk of other things. I'm not interested in marriage. Really. Hotchane was generous to me at least in his will; I'm quite self-sufficient."

"You may get lonely, Elizabeth."

She was already, she thought—for a wild, rash young man who would probably not remember her. But years of prudent caution answered in place of her heart. "I don't have time for loneliness. You see how busy I am."

"I intend to be persistent," George said with a smile.

"Then we'll be persistent together," Elizabeth lightly answered. "But I do enjoy your visits, George. And thank you again for the book."

"I can at least fill your library. But I thought Mr. Falsey much too prudent in his castigation of the Western Rising. Personally, I would have seen the rebels all thrown in the Tower."

"But then that depends on your political persuasion. Others would have seen them go free or take the throne."

"A dramatic womanly solution."

"A realistic one if you were for Monmouth."

A week later two of Hotchane's sons called on her. Their sudden appearance wasn't for social reasons, nor was their visit sociable, and she was ultimately sorry she'd been pleasant enough to let them through Redmond's gimlet-eyed gauntlet.

Matthew and Lawson Graham were obliged to leave their weapons at the door, but a chill of fear struck her as she stood across from them in her drawing room. Large, hulking men, they were younger versions of her husband, although older than she in age; Matthew, Hotchane's eldest, was fifty now, his brother forty-six. And they stared at her with their father's cool detachment.

"I'd offer you refreshments," she said, keeping her voice deliberately distant, "but I assume you've come on pressing business." Their armed retainers filled her drive.

"We've decided you should remarry," Matthew unceremoniously said from the sun-filled threshold. "Your year of mourning will soon be over." He could have been giving her the weather report, so prosaic was his delivery.

"Thank you for your concern," Elizabeth sarcastically replied, her voice icy, furious at their arrogance. "But I don't *wish* to remarry," she emphatically declared, forcefully clenching her fists to contain the trembling rage exploding inside her. She'd been out in the garden when they appeared, and her summer dress was streaked with dirt, her young-girl image incongruous with the chill authority in her voice. "And your father left me sufficient money," she briskly added, "to allow me that option."

"Father left you that money because you bewitched him," Matthew countered, staring at her with a disquieting derision.

"Your father was too passionless to bewitch," she challenged, brazenly outfacing Hotchane's sons with a grit and mettle bred into her by long experience with treachery.

"I told you she wouldn't listen," Lawson murmured, restlessly shifting his stance like a fighter in anticipation.

His older brother's hand came out to constrain him. "It doesn't matter," he quietly said to his sibling. His gaze hadn't left Elizabeth. "We thought you could marry Luke. His wife died last year." Emotionless, his voice reminded her of his father's.

And that familiar tone of voice pricked her temper, not that her flaring resentment needed augmenting. Hotchane's youngest son had already buried two wives; she had no intention of becoming the third. "Let me make this clear to you, Matthew." Indignation snapped in her voice. "I dislike you and all your brothers. Redmond dislikes you even more intensely. So I suggest you leave while all your body parts are still intact." She drew in a deep, steadying breath. "And you can take a message to your family," she added with deadly quiet. "The money your father left me is mine. You *cannot* have it."

"You're a bold piece, Elizabeth," Hotchane's eldest casually said. "No doubt that's what appealed to Da. But we didn't come alone, as you may have noticed. Our escort's outside and well armed." He hadn't moved, assurance in his posture and tone.

"Be my guest then, Matthew. You can fight your way clear. Because Redmond's ready for you, and I won't take your orders."

"We can have the courts declare you a witch." He seemed not to have heard her words.

Elizabeth remembered Hotchane Graham reacting with that identical detachment, and felt unsettled. But then she braced her nerves; she'd learned long ago that tyrants only preyed on easy victims. "I'm not your timid wife or daughters, Matthew. Your threats don't frighten me." She stiffened her back against his cold gaze. "You can *try* to take your case to court, but you'll never find my money if you do. I lived eight years with your father, and next to him Lucifer would tremble; you boys are rank amateurs." She stopped to take a breath because she found herself beginning to shake with indignation ... and she refused to show any weakness. "I suggest you consider this a wasted trip," she went on, having calmed her voice. "And be grateful your father didn't leave *all* his money to me. If I'd truly bewitched him, I wouldn't have settled for a mere sixty thousand."

"You challenge like a man, Elizabeth," Matthew Graham quietly declared, "but you're only a woman, after all—alone and unmarried." He was the leader of the Grahams, not only because he was the eldest, but because he was the most imaginative. "Some courts would consider you *unable* to manage your affairs." His voice was very soft, his stance motionless. "Some judges might think you *need* a husband."

"And some might think your brother Luke needs a *keeper*, not a wife, Matthew, so kindly leave me and my money out of your family plans. Go rob someone else. You must leave now," she said in as soft a voice as his, "or I'll let Redmond at you."

"We'll be back, Elizabeth. With the lawyers."

"Don't waste your time."

"For sixty thousand I can afford to waste some time," he replied with a smile so cold, it seemed as if the temperature had dropped in the room. "Come, Lawson," he said to his brother, as one would call a favorite pet.

And Hotchane's two burly sons walked out, leaving the menace of their presence behind.

As the door closed, Elizabeth abruptly sat down on the nearest chair before her legs crumpled beneath her, sheer willpower having kept her upright. And she shivered uncontrollably while the sun shone brightly outside the windows. It wasn't as though the appearance of Hotchane's sons had been unexpected. She'd always known they'd attempt to appropriate her money on one pretext or another; she had bodyguards against that eventuality. But she hadn't realized how alone she'd feel. How utterly terrified.

Unlike her father, who could be threatened or purchased for a price, Hotchane's family still lived under an ancient code that disregarded the progress of civilization—a barbaric way of life that pitted force of arms against their enemies. And the Redesdale Forest had always protected them from civilization and pursuit.

Two weeks ago she would have been more audacious; two weeks ago she would have been less daunted. But if ... and she hadn't allowed herself to give way completely to the possibility of motherhood. But if indeed Johnnie's baby grew inside her, she had to protect herself. Not with sanguine tactics that might bring harm to her child, but with clearheaded judgment. Vigilant, prepared, expedient judgment.

Which meant, she suddenly realized, a needful reconsideration of George Baldwin's marriage proposal.

Calling in Redmond, she told him of her conversation with Matthew Graham.

"How many men can he muster?" she asked, wanting first to know the extent of her danger. Only recently the heiress Margot Talmadge had been abducted by the Matchmonts and forcibly married to their son. While the courts had eventually ruled in favor of the Talmadges, she'd been held against her will by the Matchmonts for several months. And brutalized.

Cases like Margot Talmadge's weren't exceptional

when large sums of money were at stake.[8] Mercenary or needy families simply mounted their men and forced the marriage. And whether the courts recognized or opposed their actions didn't change the treatment endured by the women. Elizabeth knew some cases continued in court for years.

"Two hundred men, slightly more if he can bring in the Dunstable Grahams."

"Which will cost him."

"But it's money well spent, he'll feel, considering the potential profit."

"We'll need more men then. I might as well spend my money on myself rather than hand it over to the Grahams. How soon can you increase the number of retainers?"

"No more than a week or ten days to bring our ranks even. But you have another choice," he offered, his fingers toying with the bone handle of his dagger, his voice infused with a cold malevolence. "We could go into Redesdale Forest after them." Many years ago Redmond had lost a woman he loved to Matthew Graham's brutal lust, and only his loyalty to Elizabeth had kept him from throwing away his life then on a mission of revenge.

"Catherine Blair wouldn't care to see you die so needlessly . . . nor would I."

Redmond flushed beneath his tan at mention of his new young fiancée. "It's a fact, though," he said in a voice devoid of emotion, "that the world would be a sweeter place without Hotchane's sons. They need killing."

"Even though I wholeheartedly agree," Elizabeth said, "I don't care to be responsible for their deaths except in extremity. Actually, I'd prefer never seeing or hearing of them again." She sighed. "Not a possibility, apparently, with Matthew's greed." Leaning back against the upholstered settee, she cast him a rueful smile. "So in lieu of a perfect world . . . we'll hire more trained fighting men."

"You knew they wouldn't allow you Hotchane's money for long," he quietly reminded her, his gentle voice in contrast to his powerful body.

She gazed for a moment at the man who'd been her bodyguard since she'd first married Hotchane Graham. Redmond's initial assignment, she suspected, had been not only to keep her from flying away, but to protect her from her husband's family. He lounged across from her in a carved armchair, his sword hilt and scabbard, the pistols tucked into his belt glinting in the sunlight, his tawny hair short for convenience, rough-cut, unlike another powerful man she knew, whose sleek hair bespoke the elegant aristocrat. And she wondered suddenly how life could so precipitously change. Only short weeks ago she'd lived in a rapturous paradise, and now her very existence was in peril. "I thought," she said with a touch of bitterness, "they might be content with their share. My sixty thousand is a minor part of Hotchane's wealth."

"It's so simple, though, to take it from you. How could they resist such easy prey?"

"There'd be pleasure, wouldn't there, in killing them," she caustically murmured, "although I have more important issues at stake." A new gravity shaded her eyes; her voice suddenly altered. "Something more critical than Matthew's avarice, more important than the damned money."

"The baby," Redmond quietly submitted.

Her throat closed on the words she was about to utter as she stared wide-eyed. And after a hushed moment she whispered, "How could you know?"

"Catherine told me. . . ." He hesitated at the intimacy involved. It wasn't a man's subject—monthly courses missed or late. "Of the possibility you were with child," he added, a ruddy heat rising in his face at his feelings of awkwardness.

"Molly must have told Catherine." Her personal maid was taking reading lessons from Redmond's fiancée, who taught at the village school. "So everyone in the household is counting days." She grinned suddenly.

His faint smile was one of affirmation. "You seem happy; everyone is pleased for you. And wishing you great joy."

"I'm not sure yet, although you're absolutely right, Redmond, I'm ecstatic. Or I was until Matthew Graham appeared. The thought of witchcraft charges causes some apprehension after the burning of that woman at Lanehead last spring. Everyone understands the Grahams own the judges in Redesdale. And Matthew's voice—when he said I should be married, that a woman alone couldn't manage an inheritance—seemed too confident. He may have spoken to a judge already. I'm wondering if I'd be safer married."

"Ravensby's certainly more influential than the Grahams. Surely, he could protect you."

"But he won't, of course."

"Why wouldn't he protect you?"

"No, marry me."

"Have you told him of the child?"

"It's too early yet. And, if I should be pregnant, I don't wish to tell him anyway."

"He might *wish* to know."

"I'm sure he wouldn't, Redmond. I'm *very* sure. So," she went on as if they were discussing the men's monthly stipends instead of the critical issue of her future, "I'm seriously thinking about accepting George Baldwin's marriage proposal. His is a prominent family in this area, his uncle sits on the Assize Court in Hexham, the Baldwins have been sheriffs of Tynedale for centuries. He could offer the protection I need against the Graham barristers and judges. And you could handle the Graham moss-troopers. I think it's a sensible solution."

"Wouldn't you rather have Ravensby?" It was a gentle question.

"Please, Redmond, don't ask me. . . ." She shut her eyes briefly against the sudden intense longing. But when she gazed again at her captain a second later, her expression had reverted to a bland mask, the longing shut away. "There are countless reasons why Johnnie Carre isn't interested in my predicament," she quietly said. "Foremost, his strong disinclination to marry anyone at all. He *has* other children already, Redmond, and he's not married. Something to keep in mind. So I prefer a more *practical* approach, something within the realm of possibility." A kind of resolute briskness modified her tone. "George Baldwin, sweet man that he is, offers that workable solution. And most women don't marry for love anyway, Redmond. You know that as well as I. My marriage to George Baldwin would be no different from the vast majority. And I'm not asking for your approval," she gently added, her fingers unconsciously twisting the linen of her skirt. "Just your opinion on whether we can stop the Grahams from harming this"—she smiled—"*possible* child."

"Rest assured, we'll stop them," he simply said, wishing her all the happiness within his power. "Between George Baldwin's authority in Northumberland and my troopers, your child will be safe."

"Thank you," Elizabeth said, comforted by his certainty. "I owe you much, Redmond."

"I wish I could give you Ravensby."

"There are times," she said with a winsome smile, "when I wish you could too. But I'm content here, Redmond, I truly am. And if this child is real . . ." She beamed then like a young girl without cares. "I couldn't ask for more."

"George Baldwin may want more," he cautioned. "Most men would want to own you like the old chief."

She shook her head, a small movement but emphatic. "Never again, Redmond, I vow. Not even for love. If George decides to marry me, it'll be on *my* terms. Even for his protection I'll not relinquish my freedom; I'll find some other means of defending myself against Matthew Graham's plans."

"Oh, Baldwin will agree to your terms," Redmond said. "The man wants you. But will he hold to his bargain?"

"This marriage settlement will be ironclad, I assure you." Her mouth tightened in a faint grimace. "With *every* eventuality considered."

"What of the child? If it's a boy, George won't likely want another man's child to inherit his barony."

"Nor would I expect him to."

"I see, Lady Graham," he said with an easy smile, "you've thought of everything then. So all I have to do is find you retainers who dislike the Grahams enough to kill them."

"Will that be difficult?" Elizabeth inquired with a teasing impudence, content with her plan, as aware as Redmond of the Grahams' systematic incursions on Northumberland cattle.

He laughed. "I'll have to turn them away."

Elizabeth postponed talking to George Baldwin for two weeks more, wanting added assurance she was pregnant before bartering away a measure of her freedom to a man she viewed with so little emotion. But during that interval she lived in continual apprehension—watching the drive for unwelcome riders, listening to the guards making their rounds at night, taking lessons from Redmond on the fundamentals of shooting ... wondering what Matthew Graham was planning.

In that short time Redmond had augmented his troop by a hundred well-trained men, and Three Kings now resembled more an armed camp than a country estate.

Which condition George Baldwin remarked on when he entered Elizabeth's drawing room one warm autumn day in mid-September. Trim and neat in brown wool and a plain linen shirt, he dressed simply despite his extensive holdings.

"Apparently, you intend to defend yourself without England's aid if war comes with Scotland," he jibed, pulling his riding gloves off. "That's a rough-looking crew out there."

"Just a precaution," Elizabeth ambiguously answered. She wasn't yet ready to discuss the startling truth.

"Against the war?" His brows rose inquiringly.

"Against the future," she evasively answered. Before further interrogation, she quickly added, "Would you like tea or a brandy?"

And when he chose brandy, she thankfully poured him a substantial measure, thinking he'd have need of fortification before her proposal. They spoke of the weather then in the sunny room overlooking the

garden—the doors open to the unseasonable warmth—
agreeing on the idyllic autumn weather, moving on to the
state of the harvests. They briefly discussed the health of
the Queen, who'd suffered another painful attack of her
gout, which led to conversation on the progress of the
war, during which time Elizabeth considered at least a
dozen introductory remarks, none of them adequate to
her highly irregular situation, when George unknowingly
initiated an opening. "The fall weather must agree with
you, Elizabeth. You look absolutely radiant," he asserted
in his usual complimentary way. "Anne always worried
about your slenderness and lack of appetite. Not that I
agreed with her," he quickly interjected, "for you always
look perfect to me. But the change is one of noticeable
bloom. And very becoming."

She found herself blushing under his admiration,
mainly from guilt, she reflected—knowing, as he did
not, why her appearance was so glowing. "Thank you,
George," she replied. "I do feel well." And she smiled
across the small tea table at him, thinking for a brief
moment his light hair was the wrong color, and he was
much too small. The man she should be making this admission to had dark hair like midnight, and his presence filled a room. . . . "Actually, a matter of health was
one of the reasons I invited you over," she quickly said
before she lost her nerve, before she gave way to irrational dreams.

"Good God, you *are* well, aren't you?" The small
tremor in her voice alarmed him.

"Yes, absolutely." She raised her palms in avowal,
in charge of her feelings once again, the unrealistic
dreams having been relegated to their rightful place. "I
do, however, have a rather delicate matter to broach."

"I'm completely at your disposal," he instantly replied, gracious as usual. "And nothing is too delicate between friends. Although as you well know," he softly
went on, "I wish we were more than friends."

"Well . . . that is . . . apropos our relationship," Elizabeth hesitantly began, struggling to find the appropriate
words, "I have an unusual proposition to suggest. . . ."

"Yes?" He'd set his brandy glass down at the curious import of her words, and his steady brown eyes gazed at her with a penetrating regard.

Taking a small breath, she swiftly blurted out before she lost her nerve, "I'd like to propose a *mariage de convenance* between us."

"My answer is yes," he immediately replied, with a faint smile.

"There's more."

"I rather thought there would be," he quietly said. "After Ravensby was here."

Her shock showed. "There are no secrets apparently—"

"I've heard no gossip, Elizabeth, if that's your concern, but I'm not an unworldly man. So you need a husband now."

She found herself nervously wringing her hands at the subtle degrees of courtesy required in explaining that she needed a husband only because of the Graham menace. How did one tell a man who professed love for you that if your child's life were not in danger, you would never consider marrying him? "I'm not proposing an alliance because of that," she began, and with as much diplomacy as possible, she explained Matthew Graham's threats and her need not only for armed protection but legal protection.

He listened politely, although he needed no added reasons to marry Elizabeth Graham, and when she'd finished the recital of events, he said, "I'd be honored to defend your interests in court. And the notion of witchcraft is utterly preposterous. Except perhaps in the haunted environs of Redesdale Forest. Actually, we could have the Grahams arrested the moment they set foot in Tynedale. Or summarily hanged, more likely, for their damnable cattle stealing." He smiled at her and picked up his brandy again. "Consider the Grahams checked."

He spoke with an authority as self-assured as Matthew Graham's, and Elizabeth felt as though an enormous burden were lifted from her. "Thank you, George, so very much," she whispered, tears of relief welling in her eyes. "You're very kind." And she found herself suddenly crying uncontrollably, her emotions the last weeks unstable and erratic.

Immediately, George went to her and, sitting down beside her, drew her into his arms. "They can't harm you. I won't let them harm you," he soothed, holding her close. "And I love you enough for both of us, Elizabeth. . . . Please don't cry. . . ."

His gentle words only caused more tears to fall as she felt an immense guilt flooding her mind. How could she so take advantage of his affection when she felt nothing in his embrace, not a single spark of feeling? Was she overreacting to her fear and putting herself in a more untenable position? Was she making a terrible mistake to save her child from risk? "Maybe I'm being too hasty," she murmured, drawing slightly away, wiping the tears from her cheeks with her fingers, desperately indecisive, a wave of inexplicable melancholy inundating her senses. "I'm asking too much of you . . ." she whispered, "with an audacity you must think ill-mannered . . . perhaps—"

"I *won't* let you retract your offer, darling," he said with a smile. "Do you know how long I've waited for this day? Since I met you almost a year ago, when you first came here looking for an estate. And at thirty-eight I don't care to wait when I've found the woman I love. So dry your tears, my sweet," he said, handing her his handkerchief, "and we'll begin planning our wedding. How soon would you like the ceremony?"

"Soon," she answered before she bolted from the room, her practical voice of reason repressing her urgent impulse to flee, feeling at that precarious instant not like an independent woman who'd determined the direction of her life, but like a small child deserted by everyone who loved her.

So she dutifully dried her eyes, because there was more yet to explain. Because she wasn't truly that small child except for rare, transient moments of despair, because she must see that her child's future was settled to advantage.

Elizabeth decided on a wedding date three weeks hence; it would take that long to have the lawyers draw up the marriage papers. And the banns had to be posted and the license taken out.

"We can dispense with the formalities if you wish," George declared. "My cousin is a justice of the peace and would be more than happy to handle the legalities if you'd prefer. We could be married immediately, if you wish. If you're concerned with gossip."

No, it's too soon, she thought, wishing in her heart only for delay, although practicality required a speedy consummation. So she said, "Why don't we compromise on two weeks? How does October first sound to you? The weather should still be pleasant."

"Fine." She could have said now, and he would have concurred. "Where do you wish to be married?"

"I don't care." Her kitchen, a closet . . . it mattered little to her.

"In that case I'll indulge my numerous relatives who populate this county," George pleasantly said, "and choose Hexham Cathedral."

She offered him ten thousand as a marriage dower. "But the rest I need to leave to this child, since I hardly expect you to endow him or her from your estates."

"Keep your ten thousand, Elizabeth. I don't need your money. And I'd be pleased to support any child of yours; even my title and entailed property is available, should you wish this child to inherit my baronetcy. No one need know it's not mine."

"Thank you, but you needn't be so generous. Your own bloodlines should inherit. I can't ask that of you." He was the most unselfish of men, she thought.

He was also the most selfish of men, and he would have her on any terms. "Nonsense," he retorted, waving away her remonstrances, "I've no great affection for long-dead ancestors." He shrugged. "Nor for those beyond my personal family, and I've plenty of property—enough for a dozen children and chief seats in Yorkshire, Buckinghamshire, Kent, Middlesex, and Lincolnshire, if any of them should prefer the countryside outside Northumbria." He was lounging next to her, his brandy in hand, his spirits buoyant, the woman he thought beyond attainment suddenly his.

The phrase "a dozen children" overwhelmed Elizabeth's reasonable facade, and for a crushing moment she wanted to hysterically cry out, "No! I only want *this* child ... not yours, not ours ... only his!" And she wondered for a devastating moment whether she could actually go through with this marriage. But she knew at base she could never put this fiercely wanted child in danger. Too, she understood, a child without a father could not expect a normal life. Regardless of her wealth or remoteness from society, regardless of her own feelings, this child needed George Baldwin's protection from the Graham threat, and it needed a name.

"Whatever you wish, George." She heard her polite response as if from a distance and wondered in some equally distant part of her brain whether she could maintain this well-bred facade for a lifetime.

She even allowed him to kiss her when he left— how could she refuse? And she managed to smile as he bid her adieu. She would, she ruefully decided, become a consummate actress in the months ahead.

But her child was safe.

She was satisfied.

CHAPTER 17

On August 29, the day after the session had been adjourned, privy to reliable information that Godolphin had no intention of reconvening the Parliament, Johnnie had sailed for Rotterdam. He was interested in news of the war, and the allied forces were headquartered at The Hague. The continuing progress of the allied offensive against France would have direct bearing on Scotland's future.

Additionally, he had two ships in port, one recently in from Canton, and some of the goods were being off-loaded into his warehouses for sale in Holland. He spent a week in Rotterdam and The Hague with Robbie, who'd been in residence there for most of the month. They saw to the brokering and warehouses and entertained at night, information on the campaign more easily obtained over dinner and cards. The following week saw Johnnie across the lines in the Low Countries tracking down his uncle's regiment. And on the warm autumn day Elizabeth was offering to marry George Baldwin, he was sharing a camp mess with his uncle, the Maréchal de Turenne.

Unaware he was about to become a father.

Highly disturbed by the news he was hearing.

The French general staff was in disarray after the disaster at Blenheim, while the King only relied on advice from his current favorite, the Duc de Chevreuse, or his very religious mistress, Madame de Maintenon, both of whom had no official position.

"You have to reach the King's ear through a damned Mass; Madame won't even let anyone in to see the King unless they share her religiosity," his uncle muttered. "Tallard, who lost us Blenheim, is done as is Marsin; young Berwick, James's bastard, on the other hand, has been winning gloriously, but Chamillart, Louis's crony at billiards, wants his friend's brother, the Comte de Gace, to advance to maréchal. *Merde!* It's going to be damned hard to win this war with the aristos scrapping over the maréchal batons. While Marlborough simply overlooks his allies and does what he pleases. Which would be a pleasant conceit here, if one dared risk his head at Court." He frowned, swearing in an impressive number of languages until his frustration had been momentarily appeased. "To hell with them," he said then with a sigh. "I've my pension, my château, and there'll be other wars. . . ." He smiled at his nephew. "How long can you stay?" The fruitless discussion of the fate of nations was dismissed for more pleasant conversation.

"A day or two. I'm on my way to Ostend to gather news from my factor there."

"So tell me of Scotland's new independence," his uncle said with a grin. "It might bring me home again, if the filthy English can be driven out."

"Keep your French estates, from the sounds of it. If Marlborough wins all, there's no more reason to placate Scotland. London will have time then to turn its full attention on bringing us to heel. With Marlborough's victorious returning army as its bludgeon."

"It's a fearful thing to be so small in the world of nations."

"It's damned depressing at times."

"But you manage to make yourself rich at England's expense, I hear."

"Moderately so," Johnnie replied with a faint smile. "I look on it as my own small measure of retribution. My frigates can outrun any English ship on the seas."

"Watch your back, Johnnie. The politicos will be out to get you for your show of independence in Parliament—or more likely for your flouting of the Navigation Acts. The tradesmen run Westminster, and they dislike those who take money out of their pockets. Although you're always welcome with me in France." His uncle knew whereof he spoke, for he'd been outlawed as a young man for unwelcome political views, and he'd emigrated to France like so many Scotsmen over the centuries, making his fortune in a more hospitable land.

"My ships carry a large portion of Scotland's trade." Johnnie gazed at his uncle over his wineglass. "It'll be a consideration in chastising me. My warehouses abroad hold stock for many of the traders in Scotland." He smiled. "And more pertinently, I handle most of their bills of exchange. But I'll keep your invitation in mind, should it come to that. Now tell me how Aunt Giselle does, and your daughters."

Two days later Johnnie was in Ostend, and six days after that he sailed into the roads at Leith. He spent a restless evening with Roxie, apologizing profusely when he climbed out of her bed in the middle of the night, making unsatisfactory excuses as he hurriedly dressed and left. Surly and ill-tempered, he stopped at several taverns on his way back to Ravensby House, but even the liquor tasted sour in his mouth, like his life of late, he petulantly decided. And leaving his last drink untouched, he walked through the dark streets to return to his solitary bed at Ravensby house.

His busy weeks away from Scotland had allowed him fitful respite from the recurring images of Elizabeth that filled his brain, interrupted his daily activities, permanently tempered his peace of mind. But once he returned to Scotland, she seemed too close, too accessible, and he found himself craving her with a covetous, foolhardy indiscretion.

Although he had no intention of acting out his desires. A strong-willed man, he knew how to master impulse, how to curb susceptible feeling. But society in Edinburgh had paled, it seemed, Ravensby House had become too quiet; he found the modish world of Edinburgh banal. If he stayed, some reasonable explanation of his unorthodox behavior would have to be given to Roxie—and at the moment he couldn't muster one. Toward morning, as the birds began waking in his apple trees, he decided to go down to Goldiehouse. Although too many memories of Elizabeth faced him at Goldiehouse as well, he discovered in his journey south. So he deliberately delayed his passage home, stopping at numerous country estates of his friends, putting off confrontation with the past. Avoiding the overwhelming memories of Elizabeth waiting for him there.

But he finally rode through the gates five days later. It was the afternoon of September 30.

And when the staff came out to greet him, Dankeil Willie said, "Welcome home, Johnnie. You've been away a long time."

"Business and Parliament kept me away," Johnnie dissembled, already feeling Elizabeth's presence on his own grounds. "Where's everyone?" he quickly asked, handing his reins over to a young groom, wanting to deflect the unnerving phantoms.

"Most of the men are down at the stables. The new foals are half-grown already. Adam and Kinmont went into Kelso this morning. Munro's at the new wing, as usual. Will ye be wantin' to see Red Rowan?"

"Later . . . I've been on the road for days. I think I'll have a drink first." And turning to Mrs. Reid, who stood beside Willie glaring at him, he said with a hesitant politeness, "Hello."

"What are ye doin here?" she indignantly replied, looking daggers at him.

"I'm home for a visit," he warily said.

"Humpf. Men!"

He debated asking for an explanation, not sure he actually wanted one, but she'd practically raised him after his mother died when he was twelve, so he gently said, "There's some problem?"

"You might say so if ye have a conscience at all."

He cast a glance at the score of servants drawn up on the drive, looked again at Mrs. Reid's offended expression, and said, "Why don't you join me in the library for a moment?"

"I suppose ye don't wish yer vices exposed to all the world," she huffily retorted. "Just like a graceless man!"

He immediately knew he didn't—at least not in her current frame of mind. "Dismiss the staff," he quietly said to Willie, taking Mrs. Reid's arm, which she indignantly took exception to, dashing his hand away. And as she stamped off in a huff, Johnnie turned back to Willie, his brows raised in query. "Do you know the reason for that?"

Willie's fair skin turned red to the roots of his carrot-colored hair. "Ye best ask her, sair."

"And everyone knows about this but me?"

"Yes, sair, I'm afraid so."

"Should I get back on my horse and ride away, Willie?" he mockingly asked, not sure of the extent of his iniquity.

"I couldn't say, sair. Ye'd best decide yerself."

Which was not a comforting answer.

And when he opened the library door a few minutes later, not certain Mrs. Reid would actually be inside after the style of her departure, he found her sitting bolt upright in one of the tapestry chairs.

"She's gettin' married, you know," Mrs. Reid instantly declared, the harsh syllables of her words booming in the silence of the high-ceilinged room.

It wasn't necessary to ask the identity of her subject. "She has a right to marry, does she not?" he said, entering the room, closing the door behind him, not moving beyond the threshold, as if he could use the distance between them as impediment to the coming conversation.

"Do ye find it strange then, that she dinna choose to tell any of us?"

"Yet you know?"

"Only because I sent over some fruit from the orchard, and the drivers returned yesterday with the news. She hadna even told Munro. De ye find that strange, Johnnie, me boy?"

"She has her own life."

"And ye don't care about it?"

"Do I deserve this dressing-down?" He couldn't understand the outrage, the bristling umbrage. After all these years she understood the pattern of his friendships with women.

"Do ye care that she's two months gone with child? Or dinna ye care about those matters either?"

"How do you know?" His voice had changed.

"Because it's not a secret at Three Kings, ye see, and the drivers brought back the glad tidings. They say Lady Graham's moonglow happy about the coming bairn."

"Who's she marrying?" Curt, pointed, the flattering civility was gone.

"Sir George Baldwin."

Nothing moved in his large body for a flashing moment, not breath or heartbeat, not blood or spark of life. And then he found his breath again and felt the presence of the world return. "Thank you, Mrs. Reid, for the information," he said, responding with a practiced sangfroid. "We should send a gift to the newlyweds. I'll leave it up to you."

"Ye're a coldhearted bastard."

He had his hand on the door latch already, and he half turned at the sound of her words. "I know that already," he quietly said.

•   •   •

Johnnie was unresponsive at dinner that night, and later, when the covers were cleared and the brandy came out, he became even more sullen and moody.

None of his men brought up the subject of Elizabeth's imminent marriage, although all were aware of the event and the reasons for it. Munro was as surly as his cousin, more so perhaps in the depths of his moral outrage; Kinmont was careful to keep the conversation on business matters alone. Adam and several of the younger men had taken bets on the outcome of the evening and watched the Laird of Ravensby closely as he tested his capacity for brandy.

At one minute before two in the morning, Johnnie said in a soft drawl, "How many riders can we raise in an hour?"

Kinmont, half-asleep in his chair, instantly came awake at the lazy inquiry.

While Munro said with heated sarcasm, "It's about time."

Flashing a smile at his compatriots because he'd won the bet by a timely minute, Adam said with the authority of foresight, "Just under three hundred."

Rising from his chair with an energy that belied the number of bottles he'd consumed, Johnny surveyed his lieutenants with a remarkably clear-eyed gaze. "Be ready then in an hour, fully armed. Bring a lady's mount. We ride for Three Kings."

The alarm was raised with hunting horn and beacon fire, and within the hour the Carres were assembled en masse, ready to ride. The moonless night was dangerous for fast riding but helpful in concealing the passage of a large troop. Strung out for miles along the narrow backroads, they made for the border. Lights came on in the villages they galloped through, and occasionally a voice shouted out, "Godspeed, Johnnie!" The Roxburgh villagers knew the sound of night raiders traveling fast into England, and their good wishes followed the Carres like fluttering pennants in the wind.

The small army crossed into England at Carter Bar just as the dark began to fade, Johnnie in the lead on his fast barb, Munro keeping pace, Kinmont and Adam a length behind, all the men whipping their mounts to keep pace.

Johnnie surveyed the glimmer of grey on the horizon with a practiced eye, estimating the time, knowing he had two hours yet till Three Kings. Seven o'clock should find him there; and no one married at seven. He should reach her in time.

Edgy and moody after two hard-riding hours in the saddle, his head aching from the brandy, he wasn't thinking with lucid clarity. Or perhaps he wasn't thinking at all. Perhaps he was riding to Three Kings on instinct alone. Perhaps primitive feeling compelled him, or fatal necessity. He was beyond introspection or rational argument or understanding; he knew only that he didn't wish Elizabeth Graham to marry. He didn't know whether it mattered more that she was carrying his child or that she was giving herself to George Baldwin.

He knew only that he had to stop her.

But it was too quiet when they rode into Three Kings, the bright morning sunlight glinting off the new structure under construction on the hill. Even that site of activity was ominously deserted. And Munro, as snappish and testy as his cousin after the long ride and the longer night of drinking and his resentment over Johnnie's cavalier treatment of Elizabeth, growled, "You're too bloody late."

"Fuck you, Munro," Johnnie curtly retorted, leaping from his mount before the barb had come to a complete halt. "No one marries at seven in the morning. I've just got to find her," he shouted, already sprinting for the house. And while his men milled around on the gravel drive, Johnnie raced to the front door of the redbrick house and, finding it locked against him, pounded on the ancient oak with such force, the hinges squealed.

In short order a retainer timidly opened the portal,

the sight of a multitude of armed men enough to test anyone's courage.

"Where's Lady Graham?" Johnnie tersely inquired, the absence of Redmond and his men evidence of Elizabeth's departure.

The servant recognized Johnnie. "In Hexham, Your Grace," he quickly replied; no one at Three Kings had questioned the paternity of Elizabeth's child. "At the cathedral."

"What time's the wedding?"

The retainer's gaze traveled beyond Johnnie to the mass of armed riders, even the most simpleminded capable of interpreting the reason for their sudden appearance. "At eleven, sir, but Redmond's there," he added, the warning too late for the Laird of Ravensby, who was running full-out toward his mount.

"Hexham," Johnnie shouted to those close enough to hear as he vaulted into the saddle. "By eleven," he cried, already wheeling his horse. And he spurred his tired barb.

Another troop of horse were on their way to Hexham, intent like Johnnie Carre on stopping the wedding of Elizabeth Graham. The Grahams had heard earlier that week of her marriage, and their plans were more prepared than Johnnie's ad hoc gallop south. They rode out of Redesdale Forest that morning two hundred strong, with the object of abducting the bride for a nuptial ceremony of their own.

All five of Hotchane's sons were in good humor. No one would anticipate a raid in the bishop's town, and timing would give them the advantage if their numbers weren't advantageous enough.

They intended to reach the cathedral shortly before the ceremony, when everyone was already seated inside. Daytime raids were rare—almost unheard of. The element of surprise should be complete. They traveled slowly, a festive air to their cavalcade, the bridegroom, Luke, dressed beneath his breastplate in his wedding doublet, ribbons tied to his lance in honor of the occasion. He was looking forward to bedding his former stepmama, while Matthew cheerfully contemplated the return of his father's money.

More violent and uncurbed emotion drove Johnnie Carre to Hexham, nothing as leisured or callous as the Grahams' casual lust and greed. He had more significant personal reasons for reaching Hexham before the wedding ceremony, although in his present black mood, he'd take Elizabeth Graham married or not. And he touched the basket hilt of his sword in assurance. A gauntlet remained between himself and Elizabeth. Redmond, his troop, George Baldwin. It could be a bloody wedding day.

Munro pointed. On the skyline the shape of Hexham came into view, the church crowning the swell of higher ground. Johnnie whipped his horse.

And the Carres reached the crest of the rise bordering the River Tyne at Hexham just as the Grahams advanced from their concealed position northwest of the town.

It was ten minutes before the hour, high morning, and the bucolic river valley lay sleepy under the autumn sun.

The sudden appearance of massed cavalry strung out along the low hills, fronting the river in close-line formation, astonished the Grahams, who'd not expected combatants other than Elizabeth's bodyguard. And the Graham brothers drew together on horseback to assess their foe.

"How many do you think?" Matthew asked his brother Andrew, who held a glass up to his eye.

"Three score, maybe four . . ." Andrew murmured, swinging the glass along the green hills where a line of horsemen were ranged on the skyline, their accoutrements winking and flashing under the sun.

"We'll stand at the bridge then. Let them come to

us. Or they might decide the odds aren't in their favor. Can you tell who they are?"

"No one I recognize, but they've ridden a distance. Their mounts are lathered."

"To our advantage," Matthew remarked, already deploying his younger brothers into position with simple gestures, confident with his overwhelming numbers.

"Is that Redmond?" Munro was saying as he and Johnnie sat their horses on the crest of the hill, scrutinizing the opposition moving into position at the entrance to the bridge leading into Hexham.

"It doesn't matter," Johnnie tersely said, swinging his head around briefly to see that his men had all assembled on the terrain behind him. "We need you at left, Adam at right, I'll take the center. I don't want them to have time to outflank us. We move out as soon as you're in place. Keep your men out of sight behind the hill until we charge. Go!" And he signaled for Adam to come up.

In five frantic minutes of wheeling horses and close-order drill, the Carres were dispersed. Johnnie rode along the lines giving instructions, a nervous energy beneath his casual drawl. Satisfied everyone understood the orders, he rode to the head of his men and raised his gloved hand. His long hair stirred in the breeze as he sat motionless for an abridged moment.

Then his arm came slashing down, his black barb leaped forward, his bloodcurdling scream rent the morning air, and a few men shy of three hundred Carres, their ferocious voices raised to the sky, surged after Johnnie Carre in a headlong charge. There was no time for a detailed battle plan, but they'd fight by eye and ear and tactical sense in a cut-and-thrust brawl that they'd honed to a fine art in years of border raids.

Whipping his horse, Johnnie raced down the hill, the thunder of hoofbeats behind him. Those men below were going to have to move out of his way or fall before him, he grimly thought, his black hair streaming behind him, his eyes half-shut against the rushing wind, his fingers loosely curled around his pistol grip . . . because he was coming through. Because he had powerful reasons to get to the other side of the river. The stocky squared bulk of the provincial cathedral dominated the high ground on the distant bank, drawing the eye from any direction. And she was inside.

Pounding along the flat at the river valley, drawing closer to the defended position, he sighted in on a rider and, bellowing the Carre battle cry, rode headlong at the bridgehead.

Before the Grahams' horrified gaze, those few horsemen on the hill had grown in terrifying numbers, unending waves of riders streaming over the ridge of the hill, galloping toward them packed knee-to-knee like a vast flail sweeping down the grassy slope. The Grahams waited uneasily at the halt, realizing that not four score men had ridden to Hexham from the north, but more like ten times that number. As they sat their horses waiting, the earth under them reverberated with the pounding of hooves, carrying the wild charge toward them with ever-greater momentum.

A horde riding straight out of hell advanced on them, their battle cry a shrieking fearsome harbinger of death, their pistols spurting flame.

The defenders recoiled as the first volley struck them, and Matthew Graham's nerve cracked before such an unflinching, blood-thirsty host, launching at them now with drawn swords. Wheeling his horse, he broke for the west, his men tumbling after him in disordered retreat, their scattered flight dissolving in a panic-stricken swarm across the flats and riverbanks and rolling hills.

Johnnie smiled, his teeth flashing white against his dust-smeared countenance as he galloped toward the stone-arched bridge. Like a fist through a rotten plank, he thought, smiling for the first time since mounting at Goldiehouse long hours ago.

God's mark of favor, he mockingly thought, against whomever those cowards were. Now, if he could rout Redmond's bodyguards as easily. . . .

Inside the cathedral the choir had just finished singing when the piercing Carre battle cry shattered the sanctified silence, echoing like ricocheting warning shots across the peaceful sunlight interior of the medieval church.

"Stay with her!" Redmond shouted to George Baldwin, lunging up from his seat in the front row of the assembled guests, racing down the carpeted aisle toward the entrance, his sword in his hand, his men following him in a pell-mell rush.

And within minutes his troops had surrounded the cathedral in a solid armed wall, so when Johnnie Carre and his men came careening up the cobbled streets to the church at the summit of the hill, they found a strong defense in place.

The market square north of the church facade barely contained Johnnie's mounted men, an agitated melee of horses and riders jostling for space in the area between the storefronts and council chambers, redeploying after the initial confusion into battle array around the smaller circuit of Redmond's men.

Slowly riding to the low stone wall separating the street from the churchyard, Johnnie dismounted, and with a bold courage Redmond couldn't help but admire, he walked up to Elizabeth's captain standing guard at the door.

"Were those friends of yours at the bridge?" Johnnie casually said, slapping the dust from his breeches.

"If you drove them off, I'd say no. Were they a motley crew with their leaders on grey chargers?"

"The same," Johnnie said with a smile. "Did I do you a favor then?"

"A temporary one, no doubt. Those were Hotchane's sons."

"Here to wish the bride good fortune?" Johnnie's smile this time didn't reach his eyes.

"Not likely. They wish her to marry one of them."

"Ah, and return the money to the family. Lady Graham prefers someone else, I hear." His insolence was lightly pronounced.

"Perhaps."

Johnnie's gaze altered from the insouciant courtier to an instant deadly calm. "Meaning?"

"Meaning I'm not sure who to protect her from, Ravensby. You or her bridegroom."

"Let me talk to her." His voice, his eyes, his expression, were unflinchingly grave.

A moment passed, and then two, while the arrogant Laird of Ravensby waited as abject petitioner, his habitual insolence banished.

Then Redmond nodded his head once.

And Johnnie Carre broke into a wide grin.

"Thank you, Redmond, for your inestimable faith."

When Johnnie Carre strode into the nave, disheveled and dust-covered, all heads turned as the heavy tread of his boots echoed in the hushed silence, the metallic clang of his sword and jangle of his spurs keeping rhythm with his long-legged stride. His dark hair framed his face in wild disarray, the plate of his jack flashed, the ivory-handled pistols tucked into his belt attracted an ominous scrutiny, and each guest drew in an unconscious inhalation of fear.

He looked to neither side, his gaze intent on the brilliantly gowned bride before the altar, and when he reached her at last, he said to her, as though the man beside her didn't exist, "Don't you think you should have told me about the child?"

"You needn't answer, Elizabeth," George interjected.

For the first time Johnnie seemed to take notice of Elizabeth's companion. "If you don't mind, Baldwin, I'd like to speak to her alone."

"But I do mind."

As Johnnie impetuously reached for his sword, Elizabeth furiously said, "Don't you dare!" And while Johnnie hesitated, she quickly turned to George. "Just for a moment ..." she placated. "I'll be right back."

"How did Redmond let you through?" she snapped a second later as Johnnie led her away to the side aisle, his fingers biting into her arm.

"He likes me," he curtly said, not looking at her,

marching down the crossing without regard for the churchful of guests staring at them in dazed silence. "Or he doesn't like George Baldwin. I'm not sure." And he stopped her abruptly as they reached the wall, his restraining hand viselike. "Now explain why I wasn't told."

"No."

The vehemence of her answer gave him pause for a moment. But his frustration hadn't improved after seven hours in the saddle, and he said, low and heated, "You'd marry him with my child inside you?"

"I didn't think it mattered," she scornfully replied, as heated as he, as resentful. "Isn't this simply another one of many for you?"

Thin-skinned and hot with temper, he wished to slap the mocking smugness from her face. He opened his mouth to speak, his nostrils flared in anger, then forced himself to curb his rage and said a second later with enormous self-control. "No, it isn't. You should have told me."

"To what purpose, pray tell? Will you marry me now that I carry your child—but not otherwise?"

"Would you have another man raise my child?" he snapped back.

"Don't several already?"

"Talk to me about this child, damn you," he raged. There was no question of dubious paternity here. This child was his. And it mattered.

"You've been drinking," she spat, the smell of brandy cloying at close range. "Tomorrow you'll wonder why you rode so far south on a whim."

"I haven't drunk in the last seven hours," he said between clenched teeth. "I'm miserably sober. And I intend to have an answer to my question." He pushed her back against the stone wall. "Now, madam," he said in a harsh whisper, "don't you think you should have told me?"

"Maybe it's not your child?"

"Try again, Bitsy. My *drivers* even know it's my child; your servants know, my servants know. Everyone knows apparently but me."

"I don't want you to want me simply because your

child is in my belly. Is that simple enough for you?" Raging insult firmed her mouth into a thin line.

"If we're dealing with simplicities," Johnnie hotly replied, "I don't want you to marry George Baldwin."

"Would you have cared if I weren't having your child?"

And she hated him when he couldn't answer. "There," she said very, very softly. "I'm sorry you rode so far for no reason."

"Then you misunderstand my purpose," he replied as softly. "We're going home to Goldiehouse."

"Redmond won't allow it."

He noticed with satisfaction, she didn't mention George Baldwin. "Why don't we ask him?" he smoothly offered, pulling her along the shadowed side aisle to the monks' door under the stairs.

And moments later they stood outside in the bright sunshine, an incongruous melange of armed riders, two commanders carefully taking each other's measure, and one breathless, confounded bride.

"I'm taking her back to Goldiehouse," Johnnie said to Redmond. "Do you have any objections that can't be settled between"—he glanced briefly at the assembled troops—"say, four or five hundred men?"

"I *don't* wish to go!" Elizabeth exclaimed.

Redmond glanced quickly at Johnnie, his brows raised in inquiry. "Did you lose your silver tongue, Ravensby?"

Johnnie shrugged, as resentful and angry as the bride, as uncertain of his feelings as she.

"I'll give you two weeks, Ravensby," Redmond offered, "to state your case. After that I'll come for her."

Elizabeth's heated gaze locked with her captain's. "Judas. What is this? Some masculine game with myself as pawn?"

"It's a trial, Ravensby," Redmond carefully pointed out, his expression grave as he looked at Johnnie. "You needn't stay beyond the two weeks, Elizabeth," he explained, his glance swinging back to her. "You can come back and marry George Baldwin later; I'll tell him."

"Have I no say in this?"

"In two weeks you decide."

"Damn you, Redmond, when did you become my guardian!"

When I saw you crying this morning before you left for the church, he wanted to say, but he wished to give Ravensby no added advantage, so he only apologized for his actions. "You may discharge me in a fortnight, my Lady, if you choose," he quietly said, bowing to her. And then he lifted her onto the pillioned small mare that had been brought up.

And the three hundred Carres and one lady began the long journey home.

Once into Scotland, the majority of the riders pressed on, while a small escort remained behind to see Elizabeth to Goldiehouse. They traveled at a walk for the sake of her health and stopped often at local inns for rest and refreshments.

Johnnie never went inside, his feelings still too heated, too much in disarray, to politely converse with Elizabeth. What he had to say to her wouldn't bear public scrutiny, so he let Munro and Adam and Kinmont entertain her while he remained outside.

It was after ten when they approached Goldiehouse, every window brilliant with lights, the drive lined with torches to illuminate their way, messengers having been sent ahead from Jedburgh.

And if she hadn't been carried back without her consent, Elizabeth thought, like so much baggage, she would have felt joy at returning. If Johnnie Carre had come for her because he loved her, she would have felt inexpressible happiness. But he had come because he wouldn't allow another man to have his child. And for that arrogant authority, she damned him.

She'd fought too hard to build a life for herself outside the perimeters of masculine control; she'd even given herself to Johnnie Carre in open celebration, free to choose for the first time in her life. And he hadn't noticed the delineations of her independence—or cared.

She could be Hotchane's property again or her father's. Only now Johnnie Carre had appropriated her.

And rancor filled her heart and mind.

But all Johnnie's servants greeted her with open arms, Mrs. Reid hugging her like a lost daughter, all smiles and cheerful words of welcome home. Dankeil Willie bowed deeply, his wide smile indication of his pleasure. He spoke for the staff when he said, "It's a pleasure to have ye back at Goldiehouse, yer ladyship."

She was escorted up the familiar ranks of stairways to the tower room by a host of servants and found Helen there to greet her. "Don't ye do nothin now, my Lady," the young maid immediately said, her smile lighting up her rosy-cheeked face, "but lie yourself down after yer long ride, and I'll see to everything." And with a bobbing curtsy she showed Elizabeth to her bed, already turned down for her arrival.

Genuinely grateful for Helen's solicitude after a very long day and as sleepless a previous night as Johnnie Carre's, Elizabeth let herself be helped into bed and undressed. She fell asleep before Helen finished buttoning the pearl buttons of the neckline of the nightgown.

"The poor lady . . ." Helen murmured, waving the other servants out of the room.

"Ye send for food the minute she wakes now," Mrs. Reid ordered, standing at the foot of the bed, her affectionate gaze on Elizabeth's peaceful form. "And the mantua-maker will be here in the morning to see to my lady's new clothes. He dinna want to see that wedding dress again, himself says. He sent a rider into Kelso to summon Madame Lamieur for the morn."

"She'll need robes right soon, with the wee bairn on the way," Helen cheerfully noted.

"And a new wedding dress, himself says," Mrs. Reid said with satisfaction.

The two women smiled at each other.

No one, of course, had consulted Elizabeth Graham.

•   •   •

The next morning Johnnie entered the room as the servants were clearing Elizabeth's breakfast dishes away. As if previously ordered, Helen followed them out of the room. At the doorway she turned to say, "Be careful of the bairn, me Lord. . . ."

"What did you tell her?" he asked when the door closed behind Helen. "That I'd ravish you like some pillaging reiver?" His brows rose in gentle remonstrance. "I have no intention of using you violently." He sat down like an elegant courtier, casual and leisured and smelling of cologne, in control of his emotions after a good night's sleep.

She moved away to the window because her heart had inexplicably begun beating a tattoo against her ribs when he'd entered the room.

"Did you sleep well?" he pleasantly inquired, watching her walk away, his temper gone now that he had Elizabeth Graham where he wanted her.

"Are we going to discuss the weather, too, as though nothing happened yesterday, as though you didn't abduct me from my wedding?"

"Marry me instead," he offered in succinct answer to her heated inquiry.

"I don't care to marry a man who didn't so much as send me a note in the weeks since he left Three Kings. I don't care to marry a man who now feels some unfathomable obligation because of the child I carry. I don't want to marry a man who has no compunction about taking me against my will. Is it some masculine feeling of ownership? If it is—I don't care to be owned again."

"I'm sorry about not writing . . . and about the manner of my reappearance in your life. I don't understand the ownership. And it's not obligation, Elizabeth."

"What is it then? How much do you love me? Honestly tell me you would have ridden after me if not for this child."

For a man who'd perfected facile rejoinder to a fine art, he found himself nonplussed by her bluntness.

"You see?"

"You can't separate one from the other. The child

exists, I know it exists, and I want you to marry me. I don't want you to marry George Baldwin or anyone else."

"A heartfelt declaration of love if I ever heard one."

He sighed, trying to empathize with her feelings, trying perhaps to express his own as well. "Look, I'm not very experienced with confessions of love, but I wish us to marry. As soon as possible."

"Maybe this child isn't yours?"

He shut his eyes for a moment, and when he opened them again, a flicker of anger shimmered in their blueness. "Jesus, Elizabeth, you're making this difficult."

"Pardon me, Ravensby. I forget you're only used to obeisance. Men like you who command what—two or three thousand men—only give orders, never take them. But you won't know for certain, will you, Johnnie, that this child is yours? And then maybe this marriage you want will be entirely wasted."

"You *can* be a bitch," he said very softly, his fingers clenched white over the chair arms. He was making the most significant concession in his life; he was offering his name, his family, his wealth, in marriage, when he'd had no intention of marrying for another decade at least. And all he was getting in return was sarcasm. "Well, let's just say I'll take my chances . . . on the paternity of this child."

"A familiar circumstance for you in any event," she sweetly retorted, incensed that he didn't understand a speck of her anger. His apology was supposed to be enough to wipe clean the slate on his weeks of indifference, on his shocking abduction of her from the church at Hexham—although Redmond was no better in allowing it. Men, she fumed in righteous anger. Damn them all to hell. Reason had been relegated to the farther reaches of her mind at the moment, outrage full stage center in the footlights. And she wouldn't marry Johnnie Carre if he were the last man on the face of the earth.

Which she told him in icy accents.

He wondered for a moment if he was making an enormous mistake, child or not. But he trusted his instincts; he'd survived on more than one occasion because of them. And he'd had plenty of time on the ride to

Three Kings to change his mind about marrying her. "Madame Lamieur will be here at half-past ten for a dress fitting," he mildly replied, restraining the hot-tempered reply that came to mind. "Be ready to pick out the fabric for your wedding gown."

"And if I won't?"

"Then I'll pick it out for you."

And he was there shortly after the dressmaker arrived, strolling into the room as if it were his lordly prerogative, seating himself comfortably in an advantageous viewing position, smiling at everyone—the servants, Madame Lamieur, Helen, and especially the dragooned Elizabeth, who stood resentfully in the center of the group of women, attired in only her ribbon-trimmed corset and chemise.

"Lady Graham will need a complete wardrobe," he said, lounging back in one of the apostle chairs, incongruously framed by ascetic saints. "Something adaptable to her pregnancy."

As Elizabeth blushed a furious red and the dressmaker swallowed her shock, he added, "Perhaps we should select the wedding gown first. Do you have a preference, dear?" His blue eyes regarded Elizabeth with amusement.

"Something black," she said through clenched teeth.

"I prefer cream brocade," Johnnie said, as though Elizabeth hadn't spoken. "We'll need it immediately. Can you manage that?" he inquired of the dressmaker with infinite politeness.

Not quite meeting the eyes of the most powerful man on the Borders, Madame Lamieur stammered her assent. Even Ravensby had outdone himself this time, she reflected ... bringing home his future wife with a three-hundred-man escort—everyone in the county had the story this morning. And a reluctant wife from the look of it—pregnant too. But he paid extremely well, so who was she to question the bizarre conduct of the noble class? "Perhaps something like this, my lord," she obligingly suggested, offering him several watercolor sketches of gowns.

"Come and look, Elizabeth," Johnnie softly ordered, his command seeming to hover palpably in the hushed silence, everyone's expectant gaze on Elizabeth.

"I can see from here."

"Don't be a child."

Her choices were limited short of throwing a temper tantrum and completely embarrassing herself before the servants and local dressmaker. So, after a contemplative moment, she walked over to the table spread with sketches.

Johnnie's smile was benevolent, hers rigidly fixed, and the selection of suitable gowns was conducted as quickly as possible. When a sufficient number had been agreed on, everyone heard the distinct sharp inhalation of Elizabeth's breath as Johnnie gripped her hand, drew her around the curve of the table, and pulled her down on his lap. "Now show us your fabrics, Madame Lamieur. Some warm cashmeres and woolens for the coming winter."

He could feel her tremble on his lap, and unconscionably he felt an excitement streak through his senses. A primitive kind of possession seized him, captivated his imagination, and he restrained himself from summarily ordering everyone from the room. Her soft bottom warm on his thighs aroused him, access to that sweetness impeded by no more than flimsy silk aroused him, simply her presence in his home aroused him beyond reason. And he wondered for a moment whether she exuded some rare scent of undefiled virtue that made a man want to possess her.

She could feel his arousal swell against her, the heat from his body, his power and strength, tantalizing, aphrodisiac. And she steeled herself against the kindling heat inside her, spiking hotter than she remembered, more intense. She sat up straighter to distance herself from contact with his powerful chest and arms, only to find the movement exerted added pressure downward. And she shivered as his erection hardened.

In self-defense, knowing she had to escape, she rapidly decided on a score of different swatches, saying simply, "I'll take that and that and those," pointing at endless swatches, the colors a blur until Madame Lamieur caught a signal from the Laird of Ravensby's blue eyes and said, "I think we have enough to begin, Lady Graham."

"Am I finished then?" Elizabeth said, tense, taut with the old familiar feelings heating her blood, afraid of her susceptibility when she could feel him hard against her, when her body so easily responded to Johnnie Carre.

"A few more measurements, my Lady, if it's amenable to you, my lord," the village modiste cautiously added, looking for her directives from the Carre chieftain.

"Certainly," Johnnie replied with well-bred civility.

The obvious deference Madame Lamieur demonstrated not to her but to the Lord of the manor further ignited the flame of Elizabeth's temper, mitigating for a transient second the intensity of her arousal. Sharply jabbing her elbow into his chest, she rose from his lap and flounced with a distinct dramatic flair to the table ladened with measuring tapes and pins. "Hopefully, this shouldn't take much longer," Elizabeth coolly declared. "I find myself feeling hungry again."

"If you'd like to eat, Elizabeth"—he glanced significantly at the case clock in the corner with his impudent smile shining from his eyes—"so soon again, Madame Lamieur could come back later." Crossing his legs to conceal his arousal, he gently rubbed his chest where she jabbed him, recalling with pleasure her capacity for fierceness in bed. "Madame will be staying at Goldiehouse until your wardrobe is finished, so she can return at your convenience."

Suddenly afraid he'd send everyone away and she'd be left alone with him, Elizabeth quickly replied, "That won't be necessary. Actually, I'm not *that* hungry. Do let's finish the fitting now." She couldn't trust herself; her body flushed with desire.

"I feel we should take a few more measurements

without your corset, my Lady, so—er—well . . . we can better anticipate for the coming weeks the . . . ah . . . waist size."

Elizabeth found herself blushing again before the mantuamaker's obvious discomfort. Or perhaps because she found herself uncomfortable discussing her pregnancy so publicly before an unknown tradeswoman and the servants.

"That is, my Lord," Madame Lamieur went on addressing Johnnie, "if that meets with your approval . . . I mean . . . about the corset, of course, oh dear . . ." And the poor lady stammered to a close before the amused gaze of the most reckless of Border chieftains.

"There's no need for delicacy, Madame Lamieur," Johnnie graciously said. "Everyone is intensely pleased Lady Graham is breeding. Come here, Elizabeth, I'll unlace you."

"I can perfectly well unlace myself, Ravensby," Elizabeth hotly retorted, frustrated at being talked about as though she didn't exist, as though every movement of chalk and measuring tape and fabric sample had to have prior approval from the great Lord seated like some potentate in that damnable apostle chair that only reminded her of how much more devil he was than saint.

"But I wish to," he declared. Although he spoke scarcely above a whisper, every person in the room heard the softly pronounced words and distinguished the touch of impatience beneath the quiet utterance. And the authority.

His command was like a lightly placed lash, and she flinched for a flashing moment as though he'd struck her. And she stood for an abrasive moment more while all eyes contemplated a pale-haired beauty, barefoot, in half-undress, waging a war of wills with one of the most powerful men in Scotland. "Are you playing lady's maid now, Ravensby?" she sweetly inquired, her sarcasm rich with anger.

"I am with pleasure. Now come," he said, unhampered by her derision, the role of sovereign Lord deeply inbred. And beneath the quiet of his words was a steely hardness.

"Certainly, my Lord Graden," she formally replied with a studied coolness. "If it *pleases* you," she snidely finished, having the last word at least in this uneven contest.

"It pleases me *immensely*, Lady Graham," he replied, his lazy smile playful. "It's your turn, I believe," he murmured as she reached him, "for the final riposte."

"My turn will come, Ravensby, when Redmond arrives to get me."

"He's not coming. Now move closer so I can reach the ribbons."

"What do you mean, he's not coming?" she said, shocked and standing utterly motionless before him.

"I mean I sent him a wedding announcement. I expect felicitations from him any day soon. Move or I'll embarrass you."

"More than you have already?"

"Infinitely more," he dryly replied, his blue eyes raised to hers. "Here now," he quietly indicated, pointing to the space between his sprawled legs.

And she went because she knew how shameless his audacity.

She shut her eyes when he pulled the blue silk bow over her stomach loose and wondered as she felt the ribbon slip through the lacings if she could resist the touch of his hands.

"Your breasts are much larger," he whispered, his voice very close, the scent of him pungent in her nostrils. "Do they feel different?" And he brushed a light caress over their swelling abundance. The sound of his voice was intimate, lush, suggestive of all the heated passion in their past.

"Please don't do this to me, Johnnie," she pleaded, her eyes shut tight against the pulsing heat beginning deep within her. "Not in front of all these people."

"But I can any time I want, my sweet," he gently murmured, his fingers warm through the sheer batiste of her chemise. "Remember that," he whispered. And he touched her nipples lightly before he lifted her corset free.

The piercing sensation flashed downward from her

distended nipples, instant, tremulous, melting into hidden recesses of desire. And she swayed forward infinitesimally, as if asking for surcease.

He steadied her. "Not yet, puss," he softly said, his hands on her hips holding her back, more in control after a decade of calculated *amours*. "Now open your eyes, darling," he gently teased, "because all these people in this room are becoming breathless. . . ."

"I hate you so," she hissed, although her green eyes beneath the lacy fringe of her lashes still held a smoldering heat.

"I know how you feel because I hate you, too . . . but in a different way." His smile as he leaned back in his chair held a grim mockery. "And yet I still want to fuck you every minute." His brows rose in a mild irony. "If I were a religious man, I might think I were being punished for my sins. But I'm not, of course . . . so it's only a personal dilemma, soon to be resolved."

"Without my consent, no doubt."

"That's up to you, my dear." He rose abruptly, his derisive smile still in place until his gaze shifted beyond her. "Thank you, Madame Lamieur, for your indulgence," he politely declared to the modiste across the room, as if he and Elizabeth had indeed been discussing fashion plates. "Lady Graham will give you whatever further orders are required. Good day to you all." He bowed gracefully to the room at large. "And I'll see you later," he said to Elizabeth with an insolent wink. "I look forward to taking your new gowns off."

But he stayed away the rest of that day, and she didn't see him again until the following morning, when he strode into her tower room without invitation in his usual way.

"Have you decided on a wedding date?" he asked, dropping into a chair and motioning the servants out with a casual gesture.

"Tell me how long this ludicrous game is going to continue," she snappishly replied. Looking across the table where she'd been seated reading, she laced her hands together and firmly said, "I'll not be ruled by your authority *or* your polite civility that sees this marriage as nothing more than a negotiated business arrangement. Thank you, but I already had a marriage like that."

"Do you want me to fall on my knees in supplication? Is that it? I thought I've been more or less doing that—at least figuratively—since Hexham."

"Everything's just an amusing diversion for you, isn't it? Even this marriage. How do you keep your feelings so easily in check?"

"While you don't? Come, Elizabeth, you're no less restrained than I." He grinned. "Except, of course, for your sensuality, which is damnably easy to arouse."

"Or yours."

His grin widened. "An asset, I've always thought."

"I just don't know if lust is reason enough to marry."

"Better than no reason at all, as in your planned marriage to George Baldwin."

"I needed him against the Grahams. Is that so terrible? You don't *know* the Grahams, so kindly acquit me of your blame. The future of this child matters fiercely to me."

"As it does to me."

"A sore point, as you already know."

"Look," he said with a frustrated sigh, "I don't know exactly what the word 'love' implies, although I know the definition is a point of contention between us. But if love is missing you and wanting you when I know I shouldn't, when I'd prefer not caring for an Englishwoman who happens to be the daughter of bloody Harold Godfrey, then this damnable misery is love."

"Which charming explanation only strengthens my resolve to refuse your kind offer of marriage. How will we live together with that hatred between us?" And she wished to ask him, too, how to deal with her jealousy of all the women in his life, but she'd not humiliate herself with that admission.

"You can't always deduce the proper answers, Elizabeth, with logic and practicality." And he knew better than most, this man who lived on the edge.

"And you can't always have your way, Johnnie."

He stood abruptly as though she'd shot him, and gazing at her for a piercing moment, he turned away from her to gaze out the windows. "Maybe I'll just bring in my own clergyman and be done with it," he heatedly said, not familiar with such continuing resistance, pressed to previously unknown limits of forbearance. This was an era of sovereignty for men; women's wishes counted for less. "Why am I being so polite?" he said, half to himself.

But she heard him in the quiet room and answered with a small heat of her own. "Because I might disgrace you by screaming my dissent in the middle of the ceremony."

She didn't understand, he realized, that his politeness had nothing to do with himself; what efforts at compromise he exerted were for her sake alone. Whether she screamed to the heavens before his clergyman, whose living depended exclusively on his suffrage, was incidental to him. Whether she cried her objection to the entire town mattered not. What mattered to him were her feelings, her sensibilities, and he decided in a moment of revelation that he'd been approaching the situation entirely wrong: he'd been polite and rational.

But theirs had never been a rational relationship. What had drawn them together and brought them pleasure and had kept her heated memory vividly alive for him had nothing to do with reason. They had a unique, extravagant physical bond so intense, he often wondered if he'd be killing himself by marrying her. And while he'd never attempted to gauge the more subtle, sensitive nuances between passion and love, he did know that what he felt for Elizabeth Graham was different from what he felt for all the other women in his life.

Spinning around from the window, he casually said, "I'll be back tonight," as though the words weren't charged with explosive significance.

"Meaning?" Her moods since her pregnancy were

intensely erratic, she'd found, and while her query was sharply put, in contrast, a flutter of anticipation streaked down her spine.

"Meaning, wear something I'll like." He grinned. "You'll want to be nice to me."

CHAPTER 18

She hadn't known what to do with herself that day, so agitated were her senses. She'd tried reading; she'd gone for a walk with Helen. She'd spent the afternoon in the kitchen with Mrs. Reid listening to stories of Johnnie's childhood, which only increased her disquietude. She was finding it increasingly difficult to maintain any coolness of judgment when just living in Johnnie Carre's home seemed to bring sensation to a fever pitch.

Helen seemed to take special care dressing her that evening, seeing that the folds of her skirt fell properly, adjusting the lace at her décolletage to the precise nuance, offering her a rose-scented perfume she'd brought in that evening, tying her hair back with gold ribbons to match the lace on her newly finished embroidered silk gown.

And when Elizabeth complained with a nervous testiness to such exactitude, Helen's smile was indulgent. "The bairn do put one in a nervous way," she kindly said. "But I'm almost finished, my Lady, and ye want to look pairfect for himself tonight."

"Why would I want to do that?" Elizabeth said with a small huffiness. "I can't imagine why tonight is any different from any other night."

Her maidservant glanced away.

"You know something," Elizabeth accused, feeling her stomach suddenly pitch, uncomfortably aware her new gown and carefully superintended toilette had some relevance.

"No, my Lady, I dinna know anything at all. . . ." But anxiety trembled in her voice, and her gaze wouldn't meet Elizabeth's.

There was no point in plaguing the poor girl when she was obviously unable to reveal what she knew, but it gave Elizabeth added warning. Not that she wasn't always cautious when Johnnie Carre had plans.

But she hardly ate her dinner, which Helen had set so beautifully before her with hothouse roses to complement her table. When the recognizable staccato knock came at the door, she actually jumped in her chair.

Johnnie walked in a second later, not waiting for permission to enter her room, and said, "Thank you, Helen," in his dismissive way as he pulled a chair up to Elizabeth's table. In a few brief moments Elizabeth found herself alone at night with Johnnie Carre.

It seemed recklessly different with the candlelight golden on his face instead of the fresh morning sun. *He* seemed different, as though he were no longer a petitioner, as though he were more familiarly in command.

He wore a black velvet jacket, slashed on the arms and across the chest to show off the beauty of his fine white shirt. The lace at his cuffs and throat fell in fluid splendor; a spectacular diamond twinkled from the crushed folds of his jabot. His trews were muted shades of black and grey, and the embroidered red moroccan leather of his shoes matched the red silk garters at his knees. A peacock-blue ribbon tied his long hair back in a queue, the final embellishment to his rich attire.

"My compliments to Madame Lamieur," he said with a dazzling smile, his cheekbones more prominent in the glow of candlelight. "Your gown's magnificent." Silk embroidery picked out the yellow iris on a background of green and deepest purple, while gold lace bunched in a froth of colored ribbons decorated the neckline, elbows, and open sleeves.

"I should thank you, I suppose, for spending so lavishly." Elizabeth knew how costly the hand-embroidered ribbon silk must be. "But I don't need this splendor."

"Indulge me, sweet." He shrugged one velvet-clad shoulder. "And it keeps a dozen seamstresses busy in the village." He grinned with a small boy's sort of dissembling charm.

"Well, thank you then, for the village charity." But she smiled a little at the last; his good spirits were contagious.

"I brought you something," he said, leaning across the crisp white linen, handing her a small velvet box. "For fun," he added with a smile.

Opening the blue velvet lid, she discovered an intaglio ring in lavender jade, the incised design depicting the facade of her new house at Three Kings. "It's beautiful."

"I thought you might enjoy using your architectural design as a seal."

"Am I going back to Three Kings?" But a lightness insinuated itself into her words.

He grinned. "Eventually. I just want to marry you. I don't want to own you."

"Really."

"Really, Elizabeth. This is such a useless argument. You can go where you please once we're married. You're not my ward."

"And you can do as you please as well?"

Her voice had taken on a faint edge, and he wasn't sure how to answer. "Is this a trick question?" he said with a smile.

"Answer me."

"What do you want me to say?" He felt as though he were running a gauntlet blindfolded.

"Whatever you want to say."

"Come downstairs then. I've something to show you." A man of action, he was weary of debate, and polite behavior, and three days of waiting.

•   •   •

He held her hand while they walked down the narrow hallway and descended two flights of stairs, then traversed the wide corridor on the main floor to an elaborate portal through which he took her, ushering her into a large chamber with a muraled ceiling, paneled walls in honey-colored local pine, Turkey rugs on the floor, and dozens of China vases and urns filled with peach-colored roses.

"This is your bedchamber!" Elizabeth exclaimed, not expecting so unsubtle a ploy.

A large tester bed, magnificently hung in forest-green brocade, took up an entire wall, the heavily carved posts soaring a dozen feet toward the gamboling gods and goddess on the ceiling above.

"Do you like it?" he innocently said, as though the room itself were their point of discussion, and finding the range of emotion passing across her face fascinating.

"I'm leaving!"

"I don't think so."

"Would you keep me here against my will?" She'd never considered that he would handle her so roughly.

"Yes," he quietly said, "I would. I intend to bed you and then marry you, Elizabeth Graham, before witnesses." The necessary requirements for a legal marriage that couldn't be severed by court action were a license, a clergyman, the vows repeated by both parties, with two witnesses to the ceremony and to the bedding.

"Just like that," she whispered in shock. "Like a barbarian?"

"Like a barbarian." His voice was soft, his decision made hours, days before.

"And I've nothing to say in the matter?"

"No."

"This is too irregular; it'll never stand up in court. You can't get witnesses to condone this, or a clergyman," she heatedly argued.

He smiled at her naïveté. "It's all quite legal, darling. And I don't know whether they condone it or not, but they're all next door. Waiting."

"They're next door?" Her voice dropped to a murmur.

"You may not want to scream with your usual carnal abandon," he said with a smile.

"You don't actually mean to go through with this?"

"We'll be more formally married in the chapel tomorrow."

"You've thought of everything, apparently."

"I think so." A faint smile touched his mouth.

If he hadn't looked so damnably smug, she wouldn't have hit him with such force, but a frustrated, vengeful fury overwhelmed any normal degree of prudence or control.

And if she hadn't hit him so hard, he wouldn't have responded in so unusual a manner.

He actually stood arrested for a moment, his palm to his stinging cheek, tasting the blood inside his mouth, tamping down his violent urge to hit her back. His voice when he spoke a moment later gave indication of enormous self-control.

"You require a lesson in manners," he said with exquisite restraint.

"And you're the man to teach me?" The moment she uttered the words, she regretted her insolence, for a sudden grim tyranny gleamed from his eyes.

"The ideal man," he said in almost a whisper. With an unnatural courtesy he'd submitted himself to her principled disdain since Hexham, and he'd reached the limits of acquired manners. Without waiting or caring whether she responded, he walked away from her, went to the door, locked it, and tossed the key on the bureau top without breaking stride. "Now we'll see to your instruction," he quietly said, walking back toward her, using the royal "we" with ease, stripping his elegant velvet jacket from his shoulders and dropping it to the floor without notice. He stepped out of his red-heeled shoes, moving nearer like a great cat on silk-stockinged feet. "Don't be frightened, Lady Graham," he murmured as he approached her where she stood in the center of his bed-chamber, "I don't intend to hurt you."

"What do you intend to do?" She stood bravely facing him, refusing to show fear.

He smiled at her courage. "I thought we'd begin with a lesson on wifely conduct."

"No!"

"I promise you no pain, my Lady."

"Don't touch me."

"I'm afraid I'll have to." And while his voice was obliging, he was not. His hands captured her shoulders, his long, graceful fingers firm on the silk of her gown, and as he drew her close, he said, "You must learn to say, 'Yes, my Lord.'"

"I won't. I'll scream, and your damnable clergyman will run away home. And we shan't be married after all."

"Don't delude yourself, darling. They'll stay until I give them leave to go. Now let's see, I think you should kiss me first." And he dipped his head, holding her securely in his hands. His mouth brushed hers gently; his tongue touched the full curve of her bottom lip, glided upward slowly, slid delicately into her mouth. . . .

And she kicked him with all her strength.

He grunted in pain, his fingers tightening on her shoulders until a second later one of his hands swept downward to cup her bottom and jerk her tightly against his lower body as he ground his mouth into hers so brutally, her back arched against the powerful pressure. She couldn't breathe; the taste of his blood invaded her mouth; she felt his erection hard against her stomach as she struggled to free herself from his bruising hold.

Her agitated exertions only increased the friction of her full breasts and soft thighs against Johnnie's hard body, each movement provocative, arousing. She felt it first in her nipples, more sensitive since her pregnancy; she felt a streaking heat race downward from their hardening peaks. And she tried in the flashing moment of heated perception to deny the sensation, discipline it, or chastise it away. But perception and memory had instantly merged as her body began to betray her; her senses recognized the intimate, forceful pressure. She found herself remembering the precise, intoxicating feel of that rigid hardness inside her, and disastrously she felt her body respond further to that memory. In flashing recall that ignored all efforts at suppression, all the indelible sensations revived—how exactly he felt when he was deep inside her, how long he could keep her shuddering on the brink, how his hands touched her intimately—*everywhere*; it almost seemed she could hear again from those days at Three Kings, her keening cries of pleasure. . . .

And all the defenses of reason and logic she'd erected against Johnnie Carre the weeks past fell ignominiously before the inexplicable searing rush of her own desire.

Johnnie felt the sudden change as though a curtain had fallen on the first act of a play, for she ceased struggling; her mouth opened beneath his with a remembered sweetness. And he felt her soft thighs drift lightly against his arousal.

The pressure of his mouth altered subtly, and he seduced her then with the skill acquired in countless scented boudoirs, with the patient application of a nun at her prayers, with infinite variety—until he heard the first breathy whimpers, until Elizabeth arched her eager body against his, until she clung to him like a flagrant invitation to pleasure.

Then he said, very softly, "And now your education begins. . . ."

She shook her head, her platinum curls brushing against his hands that held her close. "No, not now . . . I don't want to play games. . . ." Lying back in his arms, she smiled up at him, her gaze half-lidded with passion. "I want to feel you. . . . Take off your clothes . . . or at least some of them," she whispered, her hands slipping around from his back, reaching for the closures on his trews.

"Later," he quietly replied, catching her hands in his, balancing her for a moment against his thighs, his blue eyes drifting suggestively down her sumptuous body. "Let's take off yours first."

"I might be persuaded," she playfully murmured, swaying in tantalizing promise.

"I thought you might," he murmured, his mouth quirked in a smile. "Could I interest you in my bed?" He tipped his head slightly toward the lavish piece of furniture he'd had made for him in Macao.

"If you come along with it."

"Consider it my pleasure," he promised, taking a step toward the bed.

And she followed him in a sensuous walk as he led her, her hand warm in his, a half-smile of expectation curving her lips.

He stopped at the foot of the bed, beside one of the corner posts, and gently pulled her forward. "One small detour, darling," he said, sliding her arms behind her.

"A swift one, I hope," she murmured, stretching up to kiss him on his chin, her purr vibrating along his jawline.

"You *sound* ready," he whispered, guiding her back one step against the carved bedpost, placing her arms behind it. "This won't take long," he added in a soft breath, looping the braided silk bed-curtain cord loosely around her wrists, binding her to the post.

"What are you doing?" A sudden apprehension appeared in her eyes, a tiny chill frisson raced through her heated body as she recalled the last time she'd been tied and abducted by this man who made his own laws.

"Entertaining you . . ." His voice was a negligent murmur, his eyes lazily assessing her. "Appeasing myself."

"I'm not entertained." She struggled against her bonds, the tumult of her emotions disordered, uncertain, her fevered senses at odds with her temper . . . with her unease.

"I haven't started yet," he said with a faint smile. Reaching out, he touched her nipples through the silk of her gown, lightly, delicately, the pads of his fingers stroking with practiced skill.

"Untie me," she pleaded, but her words were a whisper now, desire trembling under her breath.

He heard it, and felt her nipples like hard jewels under his fingers. His smile was assured. "Eventually I will ... but first we have to take your clothes off. Now ask me nicely, with suitable wifely devotion," he softly prompted, moving back a half-step. "Come now, ask me to unclothe you like a dutiful wife."

"You can't make me," she said, her glance wary under the overt passion glittering in her eyes, "if I don't want to."

"I can *make* you do anything," he gently assured her.

"Only now, when I'm like this," she murmured, her chin slightly raised so she could look into his eyes, the heat of desire spreading languidly through her senses, the throbbing between her legs powerful, echoing a rhythm of urgency in her mind.

"But then I know how to keep you like this," Johnnie said. "So you'll always want more. So ask me sweetly now, puss, and if you do, I'll undress you, and we'll move on to more pleasant things." He touched the white swell of her breasts visible above the sheer lace of her kerchief, his fingertips gliding lightly over their mounded fullness. "Do you like that? Can you feel the tremors slide downward between your legs? Would you like to feel *me* between your legs? Tell me what I want to hear, and I'll satisfy you."

Her eyes flew open at the sudden harshness in his tone.

"You must do this for me."

He was serious, she could see. "You've reached your limits of grace?"

"Yes. I don't understand it, but then, I've never had a wife."

"And if I don't?"

He took a deep breath because he'd never experienced such uncompromising feelings. "I don't know what I'll do. I'm sorry." Perhaps he was making her pay for George Baldwin, for the fact that she'd almost given his child away. Maybe he was punishing her for his own terrible need and his submission to her the days past. Or was he unworldly enough to want recompense for the years she'd offered herself to her husband before him? A curious sense of rage trembled within him, and without reason he required her to humble herself to him.

She looked at him for a moment, her own thoughts racing to keep pace with her emotions, with the glowing heat pulsing through her body, understanding perhaps better than he how each was subject to the other. How she needed him, too, with an unspeakable longing. Her answer reflected both her wild need and remembrance of all her years of unwanted subjection. "I do this of my own free will," she clearly said.

His smile was wry. "One would think this was mortal."

"It could be," she said with a lightly suggestive smile, content with her decision, gracious in her understanding of his own struggle. And rising on tiptoe against the pressure of her bonds, she reached up to touch his lips with hers.

"I will this once," she said in a hushed whisper. "Only this once."

"Because you want me inside you?"

"Yes."

"Yes . . . what?"

She looked at him, a vagrant flash of emotion in her emerald eyes, and then she said, "Yes, my Lord."

"How charming to have a docile wife." His words were a velvety murmur, his blue eyes lenient now. "And for that obedient response, I'll accommodate you." Taking one corner of her lace handkerchief delicately between his fingers, he slid the fabric free of her décolletage.

She felt the fine lace slip over her skin, the slow, languorous withdrawal a whisper on her flesh as if he were promising her more if she conceded more. "My dress, now," she whispered, pliant and tractable, sensible of the pleasurable rewards in her submission. "Unhook my dress." She rubbed her back against the bedpost like a cat in heat, her large, pale breasts spilling over the low neckline of the gown. With the modesty of the lace kerchief removed, her breasts were almost fully exposed, jutting forward like quivering ripe fruit. Tugging against the silk cord, she softly pleaded, "Now, Johnnie, please, my dress." Her garments seemed oppressive, stifling against her heated skin; she wished the liberation, the sensual intoxication of her skin against his.

"But you didn't ask me properly," Johnnie chastised, tapping his fingertip lightly on her pouty bottom lip.

"Please, my Lord," she prudently rephrased, her green eyes on his, restless, tantalized, "please take off my dress."

"So respectful. How can I refuse?" And bending down, he kissed her gently on the soft pink flesh of her neck.

Arching against him, she offered herself to him, wanting to feel his touch, his mouth, everywhere. "Please, Johnnie, I can't wait. . . ."

Drawing away from her, he ran his palms over the luscious plumpness of her breasts, the heat of her body warming the heavy silk of her gown. "Of course you can," he countered, exacting the price of his entangled discontent. "You have to."

And she shut her eyes as peaking sensation made her tremble under his touch. "I can't," she whispered.

"You must." So had the prerogatives of power shifted, and the woman who had rebuffed and taunted him since Hexham was pleading now for his touch. "Now stand perfectly still," he said.

She did, because his voice held the sharp distinct threat of withdrawal, and she needed him above all things.

As she stood motionless, he slipped each dress hook free with a casualness that belied his own intense arousal. Only the delicate sound of fingers sliding over silk, muted recurring clicks, and Elizabeth's agitated breathing resonated in the hush of the large chamber until the last covered hook opened, and the heavy fabric fell away from her body.

"I have another request," Johnnie said.

A small hesitation while she looked at him. "Anything," she whispered.

He smiled at her generosity. "I'm going to untie

you so I can remove your dress, but then you must return your arms behind your back."

"Yes, yes . . . anything."

Brief seconds later the magnificent gown lay in disarray at their feet. He gently placed her hands behind the massive bedpost but didn't tie them. "And now you're restrained only by urgent passion and your need of me."

"Or need of one part of you," Elizabeth murmured on a suffocated breath.

"Which you'll enjoy in due course," he replied with a shameless arrogance. "Should you be wearing this?" he queried the next moment, running a finger over the boning of her lace corset. "Isn't it crushing my son?"

"Or daughter."

He smiled. "I must consider that, mustn't I? Does that mean I should send back the targe and sword?"

"Let me use it on you instead," she whispered, "in the interests of speed. And now, damn you, my *sovereign* Lord," she went on in a heated whisper, "take off the rest of my clothes if you wish, and those of yours that will do me the most good, and kindly do your duty to *me*."

He almost complied out of kindness, until he recalled her mocking obstinacy at his offer of marriage just short minutes ago, and he changed his mind, making her wait while he stripped her chemise and corset from her.

He stood for a moment afterward gazing at her, struck suddenly by the reality of her pregnancy, seeing her former slenderness altered by a subtle new voluptuousness. "You breasts have changed with the child," he said, thinking how rare the phenomenon of pregnancy in his life. How extraordinary.

"They feel tender, more sensitive," she whispered, his eyes on her as sensual as his touch.

"Always?" A hushed query, tentative, venturesome, provocative with suggestion.

"Always," she said, appeal in her voice.

He moved closer, his stocking feet on the carpet noiseless. "Would you like me to touch them?"

She nodded, unable to find sufficient air at that moment to speak.

And he gently took her nipples between his thumbs and forefingers, exerted a mild pressure, watched how they instantly swelled, handled them lightly for exquisite moments more, stroking them while he marveled at their transformation. "Look how long they've become," he murmured.

But Elizabeth stood trembling with desire, her eyes nearly closed.

"Look," he softly repeated, stroking the rigid, elongated pink crests, kissing her eyelids, forcing her to look. "Will you share your milk with me," he murmured, "when these are gorged and full?"

"Yes . . . yes . . . whatever you want . . ." Her voice drifted away, all her senses focused at the hot, pulsing core of her body.

He looked at her, a faint smile touching his mouth. "I want you to scream with pleasure," he whispered. And bending his head, he took the hard, rigid jewel of a nipple in his mouth and sucked, gently at first and then with a forceful pressure, until she cried out in ecstasy.

"You're cruel," she breathed, holding him at her breast, half-mad from the rapture, stifling the pleasure sounds in her throat so those in the adjacent room wouldn't hear her again.

His head came up so suddenly, her hands were dashed aside, and she stood braced against the bedpost, frightened he'd leave her, searching his face, wanting to know his thoughts so she could please him. So he would give her pleasure.

"You're wrong," he said, standing utterly motionless, his eyes different, like a stranger's. "I've changed all my world for you."

She'd never seen his face stripped bare—his charm and playful pretense gone. Even his formidable authority was shut away.

"I'm sorry," she whispered, understanding suddenly how wrong she'd been to so selfishly discount his feelings.

A moment later his capricious mood had passed, and his familiar smile returned. "Don't take advantage of me," he said in his characteristically impudent way.

"I never would, I owe you too much," she answered, artless to his mockery. "You don't know how much I wanted this baby ... from the very first," she softly said, wanting to offer him something in recognition of his openhearted admission, wanting to give him part of her joy, wanting to share this life inside her.

"Then you must be grateful to me," he said with a small smile. Uncomfortable with the depth of his feelings, unfamiliar with sincere attachment, he spoke with a deliberate lightness. But an overwhelming need to hold her moved him—beyond carnal urges, more essential, as if she'd become precious to him. And slipping his arm under her knees, he swung her up into his arms.

"I will always be ... grateful," she whispered, kissing him tenderly, lacing her arms around his neck. "You haven't just changed your world, you've changed mine. I'm having a baby," she exclaimed with joy. "*We're* having a baby."

He smiled at her happiness, wondering if her delight were infectious. And he kissed her tenderly as he carried her to the bed. Laying her on the green silk, he joined her there and, lying propped on his elbow at her side, still dressed as though he hadn't decided yet what to do with her, he traced a delicate finger from her collarbone down to her belly. "This is very ... different," he said, his voice low, his hand warm on her belly. "I'm not familiar ... with pregnant ladies."

"Wives ..." she acceded, "if you'll still have me."

"I would have had you, sweet Bitsy," he declared with a quiet gravity, "if it meant keeping you tied to my bed for a lifetime."

"I didn't last quite that long," Elizabeth teased. "You have a very persuasive way...."

"How *persuasive* can I be?" he asked, insinuation rich in his voice. His palm glided over her stomach, tentative, inquisitive. "I don't know about babies."

"I know nothing as well." Less in doubt than he, she gloried in her condition. "We'll learn together."

A small frown appeared over his eyes. "Should I call in a midwife? Maybe we should talk to someone."

"Now?" she said, feeling so full of lust, she couldn't imagine it was unhealthy.

"We *could* wait," he said with tremendous restraint, not sure he was actually capable of such devotion.

"We certainly couldn't," Elizabeth emphatically replied. "And since we're concerned with lessons of duty tonight, there's one I don't wish you to forget."

He laughed. "Not likely with you naked beside me and so hot, I can see the roses wilting in their vases."

The look she cast at him was unabashedly bold. "Since pregnancy seems to make one—well . . . insatiable, I'll expect you at stud service except when you're sleeping." Shameless and saucy, she lazily winked at him. "And even then I may wake you."

He grinned at her, all impudence and laughing eyes. "I must have died," he softly said, "and gone to heaven."

But he was infinitely careful at first, until she purred, "If you don't ride me, my Lord, I'll have to ride you . . . or find someone else to satisfy me."

He looked down at her, his eyes narrowed in heated contemplation. "You wouldn't live long should you ever look."

"Then you must satisfy me, my Lord," she said, sweet and luscious and twined around him.

He laughed then, this man whose reputation for pleasing women was legend. "Will I be rewarded if I do?"

"I think you might consider it a reward, my Lord." And he did.

After a lengthy interval of prenuptial consummation in which both came to understand the new measure of "insatiable," Johnnie gasped, lying above her, breathless after his second orgasm, "If . . . you . . . would allow . . . a short . . . break in your . . . stud service . . . I think I hear someone rapping . . . at the door." He'd ignored the sound the first time, glanced up the second, and, reliably sure it wasn't going away now this third time, realized some response was necessary. "How well–mannered . . . do you feel?"

Stretching like a sultry feline, she gazed up at him and whispered provocatively, "You have something new in mind?"

"The next seven months should be interesting," he murmured, his blue eyes amused, "and no—not just yet, my darling bride. Listen."

The knocking echoed in the room.

"Someone wants you?"

"Us."

"Why?" Only luscious sensation strummed through her consciousness.

"For our wedding."

"Oh dear." She glanced at the clock on the mantel.

"We should let them in. It's Mrs. Reid, I expect." He grinned. "She has no respect for my consequence."

"Now?" It was ten o'clock. "Like this?"

"If you don't mind?"

"Without clothes?"

"I'm too hot for clothes, and since we have to go through the ritual bedding before witnesses anyway . . . why get dressed only to get undressed again? You can pull the covers up."

Her eyes flew open, aghast, so he rose from the bed and rummaged through his bureau drawers to find her one of his nightshirts. He dressed her in it and brushed her hair and tied it back with his peacock-blue ribbon that he found after much searching under the sheets. "Now there," he said patting the bow in place like a proud father, "the perfect bride."

"There's one other small thing," Elizabeth mentioned, standing before him with his nightshirt in folds over her feet and the sleeves rolled up a dozen times and her green eyes uncertain.

"How small?" he asked, towering over her, unselfconsciously nude, his dark hair in soft waves on his shoulders, the width of his shoulders impressive from her viewpoint.

"Medium small."

His brows rose at her puzzling ambiguity. "Is this a riddle that has to do with elephants and boxes?"

"I'm serious, Johnnie."

"I'm listening," he replied, his smile wiped away.

"It has to do with our vows ... and well—you know—"

"Just say it, darling. You can have anything."

"All right then. If I must promise to love, honor, and obey," she answered in a rush, "so must you promise to obey."

He thought for a moment, this man of authority, a child of fortune who bowed to no one. "Perhaps we could delete obey," he quietly said, too long his own man to relinquish his sovereignty even to ritual.

She smiled. "Agreed."

His answering smile was benevolent. He wished to give her the world on a string. "Is that all now?"

She nodded, content, the specters from her past banished.

Brushing back an errant curl on her forehead, he said, "Into bed with you then, love, and I'll call in all the restless and avidly curious."

After unlocking the door, he casually returned to the bed. Elizabeth expected his chaplain to walk in any minute and discover Johnnie naked. He'd settled back against the pillows and pulled the coverlet modestly up to his waist, however, before those outside seemed aware the door had been unlocked. Gazing fondly at his bride-to-be, who was blushing pink to her hair roots in anticipation of her public embarrassment, he said, "Relax, darling, everyone will be obliging, and this ceremonial drama is mainly for the benefit of all those who might take issue with our marriage."[9]

"Like my father," she said, sighing.

"Or the Grahams, perhaps."

She grinned. "Or your numerous disgruntled lovers."

None of those he knew would be deterred for a second by his marriage, but he didn't want to disturb Elizabeth's good cheer, so he only nodded. "George Baldwin might consider breach of promise, too," he added, "so I want no question of our marriage's consummation . . . particularly with the child arriving early. Smile now," he said with a teasing grin as the door finally opened tentatively, and Helen peeked her head around. "Everyone is very pleased you've agreed to be my wife, and Mrs. Reid in particular feels I've at last done my duty to her satisfaction."

When the crowd pressed into the room like a flood breaking through a dike, Elizabeth was stunned at the numbers. Although generally two witnesses were sufficient for legal purposes, Johnnie had taken the precaution of including several members of the village outside his employ. In the event the marriage was disputed, witnesses beyond his personal retinue would be more valid as unbiased observers. He'd taken the precaution, too, to include a bishop of the Anglican Church in addition to his Church of Scotland domestic chaplain. All eventualities had been considered; he understood the extent of their enemies.

After instructing the clergymen about the minor modification in the vows, he rested back against the lace-trimmed pillows, his bare chest the ardent focus of many female eyes in the crowd of witnesses. Taking Elizabeth's hand in his, as though nude Earls and tousled Ladies in nightshirts were normal wedding partners, he said, "We're ready."

The Reverend and Bishop, both keeping their eyes averted with polite restraint, read from their marriage services, and Elizabeth and Johnnie answered with the appropriate responses—twice; rings were exchanged; the license was signed by the participants and the witnesses; the marriage duly noted in both parish ledgers. The marriage of the Earl and Countess Graden was concluded.

"Could I have something to eat now?" Elizabeth whispered, leaning close to her new husband's ear as the witnesses buzzed around them and the two clergymen saw to the final seals and notations.

"Does this mean your passion for me has been replaced by a veal cutlet now that we're married?" Johnnie teased.

"It's just that . . . I didn't eat dinner tonight because

I was so nervous about—well ..." She grinned. "And now I know I wouldn't have had to be anxious ... but anyway ... I'm always hungry," she finished in apology. "Since the baby."

Johnnie had already gestured for Mrs. Reid before Elizabeth concluded her halting explanation. "We need a small wedding feast up here," Johnnie said to Mrs. Reid, who was beaming uncontrollably like a matchmaker extraordinaire. "Everything else is arranged downstairs?" he inquired.

"The tables are full, the musicians are ready. Everything's in place, my Lord."

"Since Lady Carre is feeling a bit indisposed, we won't be joining the festivities," Johnnie dissembled with ease, not inclined to share his wife's company that night. "Please make our excuses ...

As if his word "indisposed" had been a cannon shot, Mrs. Reid immediately cleared the room with loud clucking noises of disapproval, shooing out the miscellany of locals who were looking forward to the wedding festivities. "And now for you," she said, giving Johnnie a look of censure on her return bedside, "if Lady Elizabeth is feeling poorly, ye make certain ye don't be a brute to her. The poor wee thing is having a bairn and needs to be coddled," she ordered. "If you know what I mean," she ominously added.

After having just spent a physically demanding hour or so in bed with his new wife, Johnnie had serious doubts concerning Mrs. Reid's perception of Elizabeth's delicacy, but in the interests of harmony he said with a smile, "Rest assured, Mrs. Reid, I shall coddle—most earnestly. My word on it."

"Humpf." Her snort was one of suspicion. "And I'll see to it if ye don't," she warned with a raised finger and the authority of a despot.

"Actually, I *do* feel a little weak," Elizabeth faintly interposed, like a bad actress from the provinces, and falling back against her pillows in a melodramatic swoon, she cast Johnnie a reproachful look.

"You see," Mrs. Reid grumbled, glaring at her master, who was trying desperately to stifle his laughter.

"She's not like those tarts of yourn in Edinbura, Johnnie, ready to take on any man jack in town. My lady needs to be treated with a right gentle hand. Now what do ye wish to eat, my Lady?" Mrs. Reid cooed, leaning over Elizabeth, tucking the covers under her chin.

"Maybe a little broth," Elizabeth murmured, smiling weakly, "and an apple tart." She sighed with a credible feebleness. "Perhaps a bite or two of that meat pie you sent up for dinner too—if it's not too much trouble."

"The chef can cook all night for you, my Lady, if you have a mind. You want that bairn of yourn to be strong."

As it turned out, the chef did yeoman's duty in the kitchen that night, adjusting his staff to Elizabeth's changeable tastes and appetite. And much later, when the candles were burning low and the scent of roses was heavy in the air, when the new bride and groom lay amid the debris of a feast scattered across the bed, Johnnie said in amazement:

"How can you eat any more?"

Elizabeth smiled at him across the rumpled sheets and crumbs and half-eaten food. "I'm still hungry. Pass me another of those crème cakes, will you? You didn't eat much."

He'd eaten with his usual good appetite, demolishing a meat pie and a bottle of claret along with a plateful of tarts. But he only smiled at his lush bride, pink-cheeked and sticky from crème cakes, her long, pale hair in tangled disarray, her contented smile reason alone for living. "I wasn't very hungry," he lied. "Would you like some more kidney pie? I should think it would be healthy for the baby."

And that night a variation on Eden took shape on the Borders of Scotland in a baronial mansion, in a sumptuous bedchamber, in an elaborate bed of state with green brocade curtains that shut out the world. It was sweet, lavish delight, heaven on an earthly realm; it was love found after months of disarray. And if it wasn't paradise under the canopy of elegant Italian brocade, it was divinely within shouting distance.

No one saw the newlywed Lord and Lady Carre for

two more days except for the servants who brought in food and carried it away, who saw to bathwater, clean linens, flowers, and fires in the hearth. And even they rarely caught sight of them, for the Laird and his Lady were generally busy behind the billowing green bedcurtains.

But they appeared outside the bedchamber on the morning of the third day for a dress fitting Johnnie had ordered with Madame Lamieur—for Elizabeth's wedding gown. The formal ceremony had finally been scheduled for the following day.

"Oh, dear," Elizabeth said, a short time later, standing in the midst of sewing assistants as Madame Lamieur tried to bring the closing at her waist together.

"My Lady has put on some weight," the dressmaker grunted, tugging at the fabric that wouldn't meet.

As Elizabeth caught Johnnie's gaze over the modiste's head, she broke into giggles. "Come here, darling," Johnnie interposed, waving her over. "Let's see how impossible Madame Lamieur's task is going to be."

It was immediately apparent as Elizabeth walked over to her husband, her hips swaying seductively, that a reconciliation had taken place since last she'd seen them, Madame Lamieur realized. She watched with fascination as Elizabeth seduced her husband as if no one else were in the room.

Moving between his legs, she stood very close to him as he sat in his chair, bending over to whisper in his ear, sliding her fingertip over his mouth, kissing him before she stood upright again.

And he held her casually, imprisoned between his legs, his hands gliding down her waist, then lower over her hips, his mouth moving in conversation meant only for her ears. With a lazy upward drift of his hands, his fingers slipped inside her gown where it gaped at the waist, and Madame Lamieur almost gasped aloud.

Johnnie and Elizabeth both laughed a moment later over some private comment, and she fell into his lap, with the languid propensity of a courtesan out to entice, rubbing against him like a kitten who wanted petting. Her head lay back on his shoulder; he held her close, wrapped in his arms. "Since Lady Carre will no longer be wearing corsets," he quietly said to his rapt audience while his wife nibbled at his neck, "adjustments will be necessary in all the gowns. I hope it won't be inconvenient to you, Madame Lamieur."

"Of course not, my Lord," the dressmaker replied, wondering how rapidly she could arrange for new fabric, wondering, too, how to talk to the Earl without actually looking at him, because his wife had begun unbuttoning his waistcoat.

"We've decided it's best for the baby," he added, kissing his wife lightly in full view of everyone, an affectionate gesture of great gentleness that would have astonished any of Johnnie's old friends. "You'll have to do your best without a fitting for the wedding tomorrow," he went on, curtailing his wife's public undressing of him with a gentle restraining hand over hers. He smiled at everyone. "Now, if you'll excuse us, my Lady is going to rest."

It was clear to everyone the nature of his Lady's rest, and when Helen went down to the kitchen to fill in Mrs. Reid on the shocking proceedings of the abbreviated dress-fitting, she finished in breathless animation, "They're doin' it right this minute on that fine silk sofa in the morning room. Himself locked the door."

"Well, I'd best get the chef to cheffing then, for my lady will be hungry in a wee bit." Mrs. Reid's pleased smile creased her round face. "I expect my Lady will keep the Laird busy enough so we won't be seeing the likes of Lady Lindsay any time soon. And more's the pleasure in that."

"From the looks of it, I think my Lady will keep him at Goldiehouse permanent like."

"And that's no bad a thing," Mrs. Reid said with satisfaction. "Goldiehouse will be a right fine place to raise their bairns."

CHAPTER 19

While bliss reigned supreme at Goldiehouse, Harold Godfrey was in London moving to curtail the newfound happiness of the Laird and Lady Ravensby.

"The papers can be drawn up here in London," Godfrey was saying to his employer, the Duke of Queensberry, a thin, dark man of middle age. They were strolling in St. James's Park so their conversation couldn't be overheard by servants or retainers; it was always difficult to know who was loyal.

"Rape will be much easier to prove in court," Queensberry declared, "although we'll pursue the treason charge as well."

"She's with child already," the Earl bitterly muttered. "And even if he marries her, we'll contend it was a forced marriage."

"It's easy enough to buy witnesses," Queensberry murmured.

"Or see to the disappearance of troublesome ones."

"Yes, of course." The Duke smiled. "Now tell me again the extent of Ravensby's property. And what you foresee in terms of necessary documentation." Queensberry's affable manner was part art and part nature; he was the complete courtier. And while to outward appearances and in ordinary conversation he was of gentle disposition, nothing stood in the way of his own interests. He was covetous and at the same time lavish with his money, squandering much of it, gossip reported. Johnnie Carre's estates, which would be forfeit when he was convicted of rape, would be a welcome addition to the Duke's possessions.

"If you could get a special warrant from the Queen, we could begin court proceedings. Whether he appears or not is incidental to the verdict."

"But you'd prefer he be brought in." Queensberry knew the enmity that existed between the two men.

"He owes me a second debt now. Or perhaps a third, if I wish repayment for my daughter's first abduction. It would give me pleasure to have him in chains."

"He *is* a rash young man. Difficult to control. Although certainly, you better than most understand his reckless effrontery." Rumor had it, Harold Godfrey had had a hand in the death of the previous Earl of Graden. When Johnnie Carre, only seventeen, had come home from France to assume his title, he'd ridden immediately into Harbottle, up to the gates of the castle, and challenged Harold Godfrey to defend himself.

A highly skilled swordsman, Harold Godfrey had willingly taken on the young man and almost killed him. But they'd fought for an hour, and in the end sheer physical strength prevailed. Harold Godfrey could never quite effect the coup de grace, although he had the advantage of experience. And when Johnnie Carre held him under his sword point at last, the Earl of Brusisson had vehemently denied any involvement in Johnnie's father's death. High-principled at seventeen, the young Earl of Graden had found it difficult to kill a man loudly professing his innocence. And he'd walked away.

"He's been a scourge in my life," Elizabeth's father said, his voice cold as ice, "as his father was before him. It would give me great pleasure to relieve him of his wealth."

"How many estates does he have?" Queensberry softly inquired. "And his ships . . . how many of those?"

"A dozen or so properties scattered through the Lowlands. And fourteen ships . . . although he's having two new ones built in Holland."

"You've done your research," the Duke quietly murmured. "I wonder if some of the property might be better left undocumented." He looked at his companion with a lightly raised brow. "For the moment . . ."

"To avoid sharing as much . . ."

Queensberry smiled. "Hopefully to avoid sharing at all," he said. "Which brings to mind the current convulsive rage against Scotland. Haversham in the Lords has requested a full attendance of Peers to listen to a statement on the threat of Scotland's Act of Security. We certainly can use those flaring passions and retaliatory mood to our advantage. The Laird of Ravensby has connections in France—family and factors at several Low Country and French ports. I should think it would be entirely possible he has intercourse as well with the Court of Saint-Germain. We need letters—one or two with suitable signatures. Can you manage that?"

"It might take some time. After Simon Fraser last year, one knows better than to use amateurs for scribes."

"I could put you in touch with someone on the Continent who might help. In the meantime we could begin with the rape charges. At least there's no doubt he's taken your daughter. As for the Jacobite connection, we'll continue to marshal our arguments at more leisure. He has many friends in the Scottish Parliament; I'm not sure we can indict him as readily for treason."

"Even his friends can't defend him on rape. The man's a whoremonger."

"How convenient he developed a *tendre* for your daughter."

"Nothing so romantical," Godfrey snapped. "The man simply takes his pleasure where he wills."

"What of your daughter then? Will she sign the complaint?"

Harold Godfrey paused for a moment, considering

the impediment of his daughter's independent spirit. "I'll see that she does," he firmly said.

In November the Lords and Commons met at Westminster in a angry mood, determined to demand retribution for Scotland's passage of the Act of Security. England resented the Act as a threat and an insult, while the equipment of the Scottish militia was accepted as evidence of hostile intention.

And when the Peers finally assembled on November 20, the anxiety excited by the Act of Security could be gauged from the fact that a crowded audience filled the House of Lords to hear Haversham's speech. His theme was the alarming attitude of the rebellious Scots.

On the seventh of December the Lords went into committee to discuss the measures best fitted to bring Scotland to heel. Retaliation, they decided, would hasten the settlement of the Succession—the overwhelming problem to England's security with the Pretender in France. They agreed to the resolution of Lord Halifax, that all Scotsmen, except those settled in England, Ireland, or the colonies, or those employed in the army and navy, should be declared aliens, until the establishment of a union, or the settlement of the Succession. They empowered the Commissioners of the Admiralty to fit out cruisers to seize all Scottish ships trading with England's enemies; they urged the Queen to take immediate steps to put the Border in a state of defense.

In short, the English Parliament set out to crush Scotland's bid for independence.

And when the news reached north of the border, the temper of the Scots was one of fierce defiance against England's tyranny.

In the meantime, apart from the fulminations at Westminster, unaware of Harold Godfrey's plans, the Grahams of Redesdale were bent on their own scheme to regain

Elizabeth's inheritance. They had called in their judges in the days after their return from Hexham and had already begun the legal maneuvering necessary to charge Elizabeth with witchcraft in the death of their father. Witnesses of course had to be schooled in their reports, their petition placed on the docket of the local magistrate who would examine the accused, and all the documents sent through the required channels for when the case would be heard before a jury. It took time to set the scene, to pay for the players, to see that everyone understood their roles.

The newlyweds spent the days after their wedding dividing their time between Three Kings and Ravensby, busy with their building projects, absorbed in each other, discovering a new depth to their love. Messengers kept Johnnie abreast of the business at Westminster but he'd not expected Parliament to be sympathetic to Scotland's grievances.

One forenoon at the end of October, while walking back to the house, they saw a coach in the drive. Johnnie and Elizabeth had spent the morning with Munro at the site where a new lake was being dredged in order to connect a string of ponds into one large body of water. The fall day was sunny and warm, the autumn leaves brilliant in the parkland.

"Our first company," Elizabeth said. "Do you recognize the coach?"

"I'm not sure," Johnny equivocated, although he knew exactly whose carriage it was. "But I expect our neighbors feel enough time has passed since our wedding to begin making calls."

He noted with relief as they met Dankeil Willie in the entrance hall that the Earl of Lothian had accompanied his wife. His fishing rods were propped against the wall.

"They're in the Jupiter Salon, my lord," Willie formally said to Johnnie, "waiting on ye and the Countess."

"Who is?" Elizabeth asked.

She saw Willie's swift darting glance toward his master and waited with curiosity for the answer.

"Culross and Janet Lindsay are here," Johnnie said, his face a bland mask.

"For fishing?" The splendid long rods were impossible to miss, although she couldn't imagine the sultry Janet Lindsay mucking about in the river shallows.

"To meet you, also, I imagine." He spoke in a neutral voice—without inflection—and began moving through the entrance hall toward the south enfilade, Elizabeth's hand in his.

For the briefest moment she considered digging in her heels, the memory of her last encounter with the Countess an unhappy one. Then, with a touch of sarcasm she asked, "How polite do I have to be to your—"

"I wasn't married then."

"But she was," Elizabeth softly pointed out. "How do you and her husband get along?"

"Culross and I are old friends."

"You must be," she replied, "for him to so graciously overlook being cuckolded."

"He didn't marry her for love."

"Nor she him apparently."

"A not uncommon arrangement in the aristocracy, as you well know."

"Will they stay long?"

"I hope not." He sighed, slowing his stride, pulling her to a halt before the Van Dyck portrait of his grandmother. "I'm sorry, darling," he quietly said, his blue eyes troubled. "If I could keep her away I would, but everyone in Roxburgh calls with great frequency, I'm afraid, and that includes the Earl and Countess of Lothian."

Elizabeth smiled, sympathetic to his discomfort, and pleased by his apology. "Don't worry, I won't tear her hair out," she said, "or rake her painted face with my nails. As long as I have you and she doesn't," she added with a lift of her downy brows, "I can be smugly good-tempered."

He grinned, relieved. "Stay by me, though, for protection," he warned her. "I can't guarantee *her* good temper."

"Are you serious?"

"She's unpredictable," he replied, his expression shuttered.

It annoyed her that he knew the woman so well, knew her with the ultimate intimacy. Elizabeth couldn't help saying with sweet retaliatory spite, "Janet Lindsay's probably less dangerous than Hotchane in temper."

"I wasn't married to her," he repeated.

"Nor was I, by choice. Don't tell me you were coerced into her arms."

He had no answer. That style of coercion had never played a role in his amorous amusements. Inhaling in frustration, he released his breath a second later in an extended sigh. "Maybe they'll leave before dinner," he said

They didn't, of course, as Elizabeth could have told him at the time. She knew the Janet Lindsays of the world would no more retire gracefully from the field than they'd consider appearing in public without their eye kohl and rouge.

The afternoon had been pleasant enough for Elizabeth, for she'd accompanied the men fishing; Janet preferred staying inside where the sun wouldn't touch her delicate complexion. Taking along a picnic basket supplied by Mrs. Reid, the small fishing party had walked down the gently sloping south lawn to the river where Ravensby land marched along the meandering banks of the Tweed for a dozen miles. As the men strolled back and forth along the slowly flowing river casting with their long supple poles, Elizabeth sat on the shore sketching the bucolic landscape.

Even dinner began innocuously enough. Elizabeth was actually considering congratulating herself on handling the awkward situation so well.

The first course had been removed with only two remaining and conversation had been prosaic: country matters of crops and harvests; the state of the economy now that the famine years had been replaced by two years of record harvests; and the issues before Parliament at Westminster.

Lulled into a false sense of security, Elizabeth was struck with numbing force by Janet Lindsay's remark.

"How tedious it must be to be breeding," the dark-haired woman said, gazing at Elizabeth over her wine glass. "Soon you'll be fat and clumsy. And you must be throwing up constantly at this stage."

Elizabeth set down her fork, thinking how she'd nearly survived the evening without mishap. Then, gathering her offended sensibilities into a conciliatory mask, she forced herself to smile. "Actually I've never felt better . . . or healthier."

"I didn't think you were interested in children," Janet said, directing her words to Johnnie. She spoke in an intimate tone that maddened Elizabeth.

Johnnie reached over to Elizabeth and covered her hand with his. "We're both very much looking forward to this child," he said. And then he gazed at Elizabeth with one of the heated looks Madame Lamieur had been describing in Kelso for the past fortnight.

"I've waited a very long time to have a child," Elizabeth added, her glance returning to Janet's peevish face.

"And now this one will be born premature," the Countess of Lothian snidely cooed.

"That's enough, Janet," her husband curtly ordered. "You've had too much wine."

For a moment the Countess seemed to debate how to respond to her husband; her fine dark brows drew together, her red mouth tightened into a hard straight line. But the Earl of Lothian, a distinguished figure despite his years, exuded a forceful command beneath his dignity.

His wife slowly leaned back in her chair and theatrically lifted her glass to him in mock deference.

She didn't participate in the conversation after that, although she drank heavily through the remaining courses, and Johnnie anticipated further trouble before the evening was over. Janet Lindsay in her cups was a volatile explosion waiting to detonate.

After a minimum interval in the drawing room after dinner, Johnnie excused himself and Elizabeth, citing her pregnancy as excuse for retiring early. The Lindsays were staying the night as neighbors often did, distances between homes being considerable and rough roads making travel difficult after dark. But they'd stayed before; the servants would see them to their suite.

"I hope we don't have to entertain too many of your old lovers," Elizabeth said lightly as she and Johnnie entered their bedroom. "They become so sullen after their *tenth* glass of wine."

It was a comment intended to provoke, and Johnnie discarded several replies while contriving to find a non-combustible answer. The alarming truth was, there were several ladies in the neighborhood falling into that category who probably *would* be calling with their husbands in the near future. "I'm sorry," he finally said with utter simplicity. "It's damned awkward."

"How can I compete like this?" Elizabeth said, the annoyance suppressed all evening now simmering in her voice. "She's right, you know, the drunken bitch. I *will* be fat and clumsy soon and forced to watch every flirtatious hussy in Roxburgh over tea or dinner insinuate how *close* you and she have been."

Standing before the cheval glass, she grimaced at her reflection in the mirror. Well-cut burgundy velvet and ivory lace aside, her waist was beginning to thicken, the increased fullness of her breasts adding a new plumpness to her body.

Coming up behind her, Johnnie quietly said, "You're more beautiful than any of them. I love you very much—and I like you pregnant."

"You're just saying that." Even as she uttered the petulant remark, she knew she sounded like a sullen child. But after several exasperating hours contemplating Janet Lindsay's porcelain beauty and voluptuous form she felt surly. "And she's a blatant tart," she moodily added.

Which had been her attraction, Johnnie reflected, although his interest in Janet Lindsay was in the past tense now. "I'll see that they leave in the morning." He touched her arm lightly, wary of his welcome after the difficult visit.

Spinning around like a tautly wound top, Elizabeth scowled at him. "I don't think the Countess *wants* to leave."

He'd learned long ago never to respond to pettishness in a woman's voice. "Why don't I talk to Culross tonight?" he suggested, his voice soothing, "Just to be certain."

"You're going to see *her* again!"

"No. Lord, no. I wish they'd never come." He glanced at the clock. "Anyway, Culross will be playing billiards with the men by now."

"And what will *she* be doing," Elizabeth heatedly queried, "or what did she *normally* do while Culross played billiards? Wait for you in her room?"

Her intuition was remarkable, Johnnie ruefully reflected, feeling strangely guilty for a man who'd never questioned his notorious conduct in the past. "It was all a long time ago," he said quietly. "Look, send Helen down with me as chaperon; she can be my watchdog. I swear, I just want to talk to Culross. He'll understand."

"About your wife's jealous tantrum, you mean."

"No, about my wanting them to come next time with other people."

"Or not at all," Elizabeth tersely declared.

"I can't do that to Culross." His voice was composed but firm. "He was a friend of my father."

"Maybe he'll divorce her." Emotion had overcome logic by now.

"That's possible." His words were infinitely guarded.

"But then the men whose wives you've slept with can't all divorce their wives now can they?"

Now would they care to, Johnnie wished to say. Masculine privilege was a fact of life; he wasn't the only one who'd slept with married women. "I didn't know you then; it won't happen now," he said, uncomplicated and plain. "Do you want Helen to go with me?"

"Yes. No. Yes, dammit . . . I'm going to be a jealous wife."

"Then call her." He understood jealousy; he was even resentful of her dead husband.

He found Culross in the billiard room as he'd expected, playing with Adam and Kinmont. Munro had left for Edinburgh that afternoon in search of an engineer to fix the lock between the ponds and the river. And Janet, as Johnnie had known, was in her room. She disliked watching the men play.

The two men sat down in wing chairs near the fire with a new cognac just in from La Rochelle. Helen stood at a discreet distance, not exactly certain she was capable of chaperoning the ungovernable Laird. But Lady Elizabeth had given her orders and the Laird had quietly listened as his wife spoke, so she gravely kept her eyes on him. The men spoke for a few minutes about the merits of the brandy and their favorite vineyards; then Culross gently said, "Janet is an old man's vanity."

"I understand," Johnnie replied. "I'd do the same thing." He wouldn't, though. *Never.* He didn't have the temperament to watch his wife with other men. "It's just that Elizabeth is more emotional now with the pregnancy," he explained. "As you see, I have a duenna tonight."

Culross lifted one brow. "You indulge your wife. It must be love, although it's clear to see—even if Roxburgh wasn't awash with dramatic stories of your unorthodox courtship. And I know how *enceinte* women respond," he added. "My Jonetta was high strung the entire nine months." Culross smiled in remembrance of his long deceased first wife, who'd borne him six children all grown now with children of their own.

"I don't want Elizabeth to be unhappy," Johnnie said, turning his brandy glass in his hands.

"Did you think it would ever happen, my boy, when you were tasting the surfeit of the world—that love would strike?" The Earl of Lothian surveyed his young neighbor with a clear gaze.

Johnnie flushed beneath his bronzed skin at the

keen observation. "One doesn't know it exists at the time—or care—"

"*Until* it steals away your capacity for vice."

"Yes," Johnnie noted with faint smile. He looked at the brandy in his hands for a moment and then at Culross. "But strangely," he added, "there's no regrets."

"I'll take Janet home in the morning so your wife can sleep well tonight," the earl kindly said.

"I'd appreciate that. Please forgive Elizabeth if she doesn't see you off. She sleeps late."

"Of course. No need for her to rise early on our account," Culross politely replied to the obvious falsehood. "Janet may be difficult for a time," he calmly went on. "She's a woman who dislikes rejection and she doesn't understand the concept of love. Your marriage won't be a deterrent to her."

"Thanks for the warning." Johnnie said. And that was the closest the two men came to openly acknowledging they'd shared the same woman's favors.

As the men were savoring their second drink, Elizabeth answered a sharp rapping at her bedroom door and found herself face to face with Janet Lindsay.

"I want to talk to Johnnie," the Countess of Lothian brusquely said, a glass of wine in her hand as she stood impressively splendid in white satin, framed by the carved garlands bordering the portal.

"He's not here." Elizabeth couldn't keep the faint shock from her tone.

"Where is he?"

"He's not *here*," Elizabeth repeated, about to push the door shut.

"You're lying," Janet retorted, sailing across the wide threshold and walking straight across the large chamber to the dressing room door with a familiarity that bespoke former residence. Opening the door, she peered inside, then moved to the entrance of the adjacent sitting room which she also surveyed. Swinging around, she taunted, "Does he often leave you alone at night?"

"I don't see that it's any of your business." Elizabeth hadn't moved far from the doorway, her temper barely in check with Johnnie's rude ex-lover standing in her bedroom.

"He'll never be faithful," she warned with a sneer.

"I don't expect he ever was to you." Elizabeth felt a profane pleasure in being equally rude.

"Don't be naive, darling. He won't be to you either."

"My husband's fidelity isn't your concern."

Janet Lindsay laughed, a triumphant sound. "Johnnie Carre's fidelity. That's a rich phrase . . . like England's charity, or the Pope's children. You sweet child," she murmured, "I'll give you a month more. Your figure isn't completely gone yet. He's never wanted children, you know."

"Perhaps he never wanted your children." But Elizabeth's stomach had lurched at the Countess' confident tone.

"On that we agree. Can you see him with a squalling brat? He's never even touched a baby."

"How would you know?" And immediately after she'd uttered the words, she wished she could have retracted them.

"Because I've known him, my darling girl, since before he became Laird. *I* know him and you don't."

"A shame, then, he didn't marry you."

Janet Lindsay's anger suddenly showed, the smooth bright malice replaced by a fiery indignation. Her white skin turned an ugly red. "You pale-haired bitch," she hissed, "I'll have him back in a fortnight."

"Have you lost your way, Janet?" Johnnie's voice, bland and cool, came from the darkened hallway.

Both women turned to see his tall form materialize out of the shadows. He stood framed in the ornate doorway, the light from the room casting a sheen on the terracotta velvet of his jacket. His faint smile had no warmth. "I spoke to Culross about you," he said softly. "He's very understanding. He once had a wife he loved." His voice turned rough-edged. "Now get out."

Without waiting for an answer, he moved from the

threshold and walked the short distance to where Elizabeth stood. "I'm sorry again," he quietly murmured, not certain he dared touch her, unsure of her response.

"Damn you to hell!" the Countess of Lothian cried, flinging her glass of wine at him. "What do you know about love!"

With lightning speed, he pulled Elizabeth out of the way of the flying missile, shifting a second later to intercept Janet's headlong charge.

She'd drunk too much to be docile—not that she ever was—and Johnnie caught her by her flailing arms. "Don't think you can turn me out! You damned—" She struggled against his hold but he firmly shoved her out the door. Swiftly slamming it shut, he turned the key in the lock.

"It's your turn now," he said with a sigh, leaning back against the door. "Scream, attack me, any wife would after a visit like that; there's no suitable apology for Janet's gall. But you needn't ever see her again. I'll visit Culross somewhere else."

"Not on your life," Elizabeth sharply said.

His brows winged up in surprise.

"She'll be there too, knowing her. I'm possessive as hell. He can come here. Alone."

One dark brow arched provocatively. "You're my warder?"

"Damn right I am. Perhaps you should warn all your other ex-lovers in the neighborhood that they come here at their own risk."

He laughed. "My leash is to be short, then."

"A choke collar, I'd say."

His smile was amused. "It sounds wickedly indecent. Should we try it tonight?"

Elizabeth grinned. "Don't think you can distract me. I'm serious. You're mine, Johnnie Carre, I don't mean to share you."

"How nice," he whispered, pushing away from the door and strolling toward her. "I look forward to this proprietary faithfulness. It conjures up a certain—closeness." He stood only inches away from her now, very large and dark and beautiful. "I love you more each day," he said, his previous irony displaced by a scrupulous candor, his words utterly plain. "And I regret the years I've wasted without you. You may possess me and gladly."

"I know that," she said with her own straightforward simplicity, her temper dissipated, the Janet Lindsays in her husband's past relegated to their proper insignificance. After years bereft of love, Elizabeth divined the blissful wonder of it with more clarity than most.

"So sure?" he teased.

"Absolutely."

"Who knows?" he said with a smile, bending so his mouth was very close to hers, his kiss only a breath away. "We may set a new fashion . . . in faithfulness."

Shipping quieted on the North Sea after November, the winter gales restricting merchant activity to a minimum. And Johnnie and Elizabeth settled in at Goldiehouse for Christmas, welcoming Robbie home from a last trip to Rotterdam just before the holidays. The festivities were extravagant despite the Kirk's admonitions against the pagan and popish celebration; the Carres had always observed Christmas from the days before the monasteries.

Johnnie gave his new wife a gift of jewelry on each of the twelve nights, although she protested as early as the third evening that he was spoiling her.

"This is too extravagant, darling," she murmured, lifting the enormous pearl ear-drops from their box. It was hushed in their bedchamber, although the noise of the revelers drifted up the staircase from the great hall below. The scent of pine boughs and holly perfumed the room. She smiled at him as he lay beside her. "These are so costly—"

"They're Scottish pearls," he noted, "and I can buy my wife jewelry if I wish." His grin was angelic. "Put them on now, so I can see you undressed in pearls."

"Libertine," she whispered.

"I know." One dark brow rose the merest fraction. "Isn't it nice we get along so well?"

She giggled. "You do indulge me."

A special warmth shone from his eyes. "My husbandly duty, if I recall."

"Am I too demanding?"

He laughed. "Don't worry, darling. I think I can keep up."

One cold frosty afternoon Elizabeth had stayed at Goldiehouse to nap when Johnnie had ridden into Kelso with his men for the races. Two of his barbs were running in the holiday meets.

The sun was gone when she woke, and she lay amidst the down comforters and pillows, drowsily contemplating the winter twilight outside her windows. She missed Johnnie; his absences were rare since their marriage.

Snuggling deeper into the warmth of the bed, she wished him home beside her or, actually, inside her, she thought with a dreamy, luxurious self-indulgence. Her senses, her body, her skin, and her nerves seemed on constant sensual alert, and she wondered if other pregnant women were as single-mindedly focused on passion. There was no one she dared ask—certainly not Helen or Mrs Reid. And Johnnie only took delight in her sexual appetite.

She stretched languidly, infinitely aware of the smooth warm linen rubbing against her nude body. Glancing at the clock on the mantel, she saw the delicate gold hands balanced at half past four. It was almost dark. The racing should be over soon. She stirred restlessly.

For five minutes more she lay abed watching the minute hand move sluggishly across the painted and filigreed face of the clock. Should she ring for Helen to light the candles, or call for food, or have her help her dress? Did Johnnie have plans for the evening, were guests coming? She couldn't recall in the frenzied bustle of the Christmas schedule what had been planned. She wasn't hungry or thirsty or inclined to Helen's company at the moment so she fretted, fidgety, agitated.

She wanted Johnnie.

Then she smiled to herself in the depths of the enormous bed because a flash of an idea had come to her. Something to pass the time while she waited for his return. Something to please her husband and ultimately please herself.

Inspired, she threw off the covers and climbed from the bed. She lit a few candles herself so she needn't call Helen and added coal to the grate because she wanted the room warm.

Because she didn't want to be cold—later.

Then she gathered the gifts of jewelry Johnnie had given her over the past days and walked into the dressing room.

With a taper from the fire burning in the small swedish tile stove set in the corner, she lit the two candles on the brackets of the cheval glass and smiled at herself in the Venetian mirror. Her skin was still rosy from sleep, her tousled hair in need of a brushing. *Later*, she lazily thought, moving to the ornate candlelabra on the dressing table. The five candles set in the silver holder added considerable light to the interior as did the candles in the crystal sconces on both sides of the doorway.

Easing the dressing room door almost shut, but leaving it open a fraction so she could hear when Johnnie came back, she tossed the taper into the green porcelain stove and began implementing her idea. Shifting the mirror so her reflection was visible from the dressing table, she reached for her pearl earrings in the jumble of jewelry piled on the table top.

But the earrings didn't show, she decided, with her hair falling on her shoulders, so she brushed her wayward curls and pinned them up with the new green jade hairpins Johnnie had given her last night. The precious ornaments, owned long ago by a T'ang princess, were smooth as satin, lush to the touch, intricately carved with floral motifs.

There ... she decided with satisfaction. Now the

Scottish pearls were visible—huge tear-drops dangling from diamond rosettes. She turned her head from side to side so they moved and gleamed in the candlelight.

Next she clasped around her neck a small enamelled gold locket—Johnnie's first gift for Christmas—one side set with diamonds, the other decorated with a crowned heart between the letters J and E, the edge engraved *Fidel Iusq A La Mort*—Faithful Unto Death. She stroked the letters for a moment, touched by his tender promise, and then let the elegant locket slip between her bare breasts.

She added two rings to her fingers, a rare gold diamond and rarer Siamese ruby, so deep crimson only kings had been allowed to own it in the country of its origin, Johnnie had said.

Lifting a Baltic amber belt of exquisite canary yellow from the array of gems on the dressing table, she rubbed the magnetic beads over her skin, feeling the small sparkles of energy emitted by the friction, and wondering what other women might have worn this resplendent ornament. The gold and turquoise buckle was Egyptian in design, the stylized palmetto motif sinuous, refined.

After admiring the rich antiquity of the translucent belt, she draped it over her hips, then slid a bracelet onto each wrist, one of enamel and gold, the other of violet sapphires. Another bracelet of heavy gold links that fastened with a heart-shaped padlock she placed on her ankle. When she moved her foot, the chain gleamed in the mirror, the weight of the solid links heavy on her slender ankle, and a little tongue of fire stirred inside her at the barbaric implication.

Extracting from the glossy tangle one of the ropes of pearls Johnnie had given her on the eighth night of Christmas, she draped it around her neck, the rest of the large, lustrous South Sea pearl necklaces following one by one until she was richly adorned in cascades of pearls. Adjusting the long garlands into double loops, she slipped the numerous strands around and under her breasts so they lifted the mounded fullness high, the heavy weight of her breasts pushed upward, suspended by a dramatic halter of pearls.

Swaying slightly, the jewels embellishing her body twinkled and glittered. What a decorative Christmas present, she reflected, gazing at herself in the mirror, her pink-tipped breasts offered up in sumptuous thrusting splendor, the heated amber twined around her waist a primitive, mystical gem. And Johnnie's promise of faithfulness lay nestled in the deep valley between her breasts, his golden chain weighty on her ankle.

She could feel a glowing heat kindling inside her, pronounced and insistent, her restless impulses focused now and hot-blooded; she was turning to check the time when she heard the bedroom door open.

A moment later she stood in the opened doorway of the dressing room. "Merry Christmas, my Lord."

Looking up, Johnnie stopped pulling off his glove, the black leather half-rolled over the back of his hand.

His gaze swept over the spectacle of his wife's ripe body in resplendent undress and his smile slowly spread until his eyes shone with appreciation. "Had I known your plans, sweetheart," he said, "my horses could have run without me this afternoon."

"You're home just in time," she murmured. "You haven't missed anything yet." She was posed like a young Cleopatra, her eyes exuding a mischievous sensuality.

He grinned and resumed stripping off his fringed gloves. "How fortunate. You've been waiting for me then."

"I've been spoiled," she said, leaving the dressing room portal and gracefully walking toward him, her breasts bobbing and swaying like the pearls swinging from her ears. "I prefer you to substitutes."

His fingers were moving quickly on the buttons of his great coat. "I'm at your service," he said with a roguish smile, shrugging out of his coat, and tossing it aside. "Although give me a minute to warm my hands or you'll suffer."

"Touch me with your cold hands," she begged in a delicate whisper.

Her breathy words triggered a flaring lust and he

waited for her, enchanted by her florid sexuality, aware of the surging rise of his erection. As she neared, he saw her eyes raised to him, warm with wanting and when she was close, he leaned over and touched her, his left hand sliding between her warm thighs, his right slipping under her from behind, his fingers meeting, clamping hard over her hot cleft.

She gasped, stunned for a moment, the stark chill of his winter cold hands stinging and thrilling simultaneously, her nipples hardening as if touched by ice. Then a flame exploded deep in her belly, and a fierce wanting swirled through her body, leaving her breathless. Her forehead dropped against his shoulder as she absorbed the shattering sensation; a low, almost indistinguishable moan vibrated in her throat. His fingers were slowly opening her, seeking entrance, finding it. Johnnie's long cool fingers sank in up to his palm.

Her low rapturous cry thrilled him. He could feel her weight settle on his cupped hands as her knees gave way. Lifting her slightly, he put pressure on her pulsing core and she felt every compressed throb more profoundly, felt his fingers more acutely as they stretched her wider. She whimpered as her flesh yielded to his penetration, as the delirious palpitations ravished her senses.

"Put your arms around me," he whispered, scooping her off her feet. Eagerly she complied, flinging her arms around his neck, clinging to him.

Carrying her to a nearby chaise, he gently placed her against the cushioned back and kissed her waiting lips, tasted the sweetness of her mouth as he smoothly freed his hands. Tipping her chin up with a light fingertip, he gazed into her pleasure-hazed eyes. "This is the best Christmas present I've ever had."

Her scent on his fingers drifted into her nostrils . . . stirring a primitive arousal. "Kiss me again," she breathed, reaching up for him, wanting to feel his power.

His lips brushed over hers, his mouth unhurried, gentle. He was always less impatient than she, always more restrained, as if he knew how much better it was with delay. "Would you like your present," he murmured, kissing her rosy cheek, "for the eleventh day of Christmas?"

"If it's you." Her fingers slid through his silky hair.

He chuckled, his breath warm on her skin. "You're easy to please."

"Maybe you just know how to please me."

Sitting upright, he drew away and holding her hands in his, contemplated her jeweled splendor with roguish amusement. "Since you've been pregnant, darling, pleasing you has been uncomplicated. Now let me get your present." He smiled as she took his hand and guided his fingers inside her. "I've another ornament for you."

"To add to my wanton glitter . . ." A small breathy sigh registered appreciation of his masterly touch.

He paused infinitesimally. "Yes, that too," he said.

"You feel strong," she purred, lazily moving against Johnnie's powerful hand.

"You feel eager," he replied, his blue eyes teasing.

"So?" The breathy word was a light command.

"So I'll be right back," he whispered, sliding his fingers out, and rising from the chaise.

She watched him walk to a large marquetry wardrobe and pull open one of the bottom drawers. Dressed simply like a country gentleman he wore a plum coat with his dark breeches and boots, his hair untied and loose. She thought him the most beautiful creature, powerful and tall, graceful, so handsome she always found her eyes dwelling on his finely wrought features no matter that she knew them from memory.

Swiftly rummaging through a drawer of neckcloths, Johnnie came up with a small flat box of royal blue velvet. Forgetting to close the drawer—not a tidy man after being raised with an army of servants—he walked back and handed the box to Elizabeth with a warm smile. "Merry eleventh day, darling."

Sitting down at the foot of the chaise, he began pulling off his boots.

Noting the Valois crest embossed in gold on the box lid, Elizabeth opened it with fascinated interest. At her first glimpse of the dazzling jewel her eyes flared wide. A spectacular pendant rested on crushed white satin: oval in shape, it was a magnificent ruby etched with a passionate depiction of Leda and the swan, and bordered by two rows of gems—first, one of brilliant diamonds, then an outside rim of perfect matched pearls. And suspended from the bottom were three exquisite baroque pearls.

"It's breathtaking," she exclaimed, touching the shimmering dark ruby, her fingers tracing the ardent mythical scene.

"A gift from Charles VII to Agnes Sorel originally. Robbie found it for me in Amsterdam," Johnnie said, shifting around to face her, his boots discarded. "Something for you to wear with your pearl earrings."

"It's gorgeous," she whispered, picturing it in her mind with her earrings—". . . and Agnes Sorel. How romantic . . ."

"Given in love," Johnnie gently said, "then and now." Lifting the pendant from the box, he took the case from her hand and set it on the floor. "Depending on how you want to wear this," he said, holding the jewel in his palm, "we need a gold chain . . ." His voice dropped in volume. "Or—"

"Or?" His insinuation tantalized her.

Setting the pendant down on the upholstered seat, he appeared not to have heard her, his gaze on her breasts. "One of your necklaces has slipped," he murmured, reaching toward her. Cupping her right breast in his palm, he elevated it slightly, adjusting the string of pearls under and around the extravagant fullness so all the strands were back in place. Then, lifting her left breast, he stroked the pale outside flare admiringly before easing the lush weight back into the luxurious halter. "Such magnificent breasts," he said, his fingers tracing a circle around the jutting nipples.

The pink crests responded to his touch, the large tips hardened, and Elizabeth arched her back in languourous ecstasy as a heated warmth rushed downward.

"I like the flagrant display," Johnnie whispered, the pads of his fingers lazily smoothing over the prominent mounded curves held high by the pearls, her voluptuous breasts fuller now with her pregnancy.

"I was hoping you would," she breathed, her smile lush, the pressure of his fingers sending a spiraling heat into the glowing center of her body. "For purely selfish reasons . . ."

Lying against the colorful needlework cushions of the chaise, her skin exquisitely white in the dissolving light, tinseled and bangled with glittering jewels, she looked like an exotic scheherazade made for love.

Johnnie gently eased her legs apart as he shrugged out of his coat, the hot eager feel of her intensely provocative. He shifted his position to ease the tightness of his breeches, then reached for the ruby pendant which lay almost invisible against the intricate colored silks of the needlepoint fabric. "There's a story with this jewel," he quietly said, delicately arranging her legs, spreading her thighs wider, bending her knees slightly so her hot cleft was beautifully exposed. Lightly caressing her inner thighs, his fingers moved up to glide over her rosy distended vulva.

Her eyes half-closed under the flowing passage of his fingers; any thought of reply was made impossible by the intoxicating sensations.

"The king had Agnes Sorel wear the ruby to a ball one night . . . This might feel cool now," he gently said, his fingers parting her pouty folds, opening her, massaging the pliant flesh wider to accommodate the large jewel. He slipped the bottom in first and then, stretching her soft tissue, he forced the rest of the large oval ruby into place until it was tightly confined in her sleek, taut flesh. The tantalizing jewel fit snugly as it was meant to, wedged firmly inside her, the rim of large pearls causing palpable friction against her succulent tissue, the diamonds twinkling festively.

Lounging at the foot of the chaise, observing the luscious view, Johnnie reached up to lightly flick the three swinging pearl drops with his fingertips. "The king periodically verified that the pearls were swinging free," Johnnie murmured. "Do you feel them?" It was a rhetorical question. Her skin was flushed with passion, her breathing erratic, her eyes focused on some internal image.

The tiny tantalizing vibration strummed through Elizabeth's heated senses, moving from the imbedded jewel upward in sensuous waves. Her body was already on fire, and the swinging pearls only added to her feverish desire.

"Bets were taken by his courtiers on how long the lady would last. *You* touch it," Johnnie gently suggested, taking her hand, guiding it between her legs. "Lightly now," he warned, "so you don't force it in too far." And he directed her fingers over the sleek ruby, his other hand tracing her tightly stretched skin where it merged with the pearl border, exerting pressure, the tactile contact quickening her heated sensations, stimulating the distended flesh. Her fingers slid over the wet ruby, the crimson surface fluid with her own pearly liquid, her body lubricated, ready, pulsing in anticipation.

"She was like you," he murmured, gently closing her legs on her hand and on the Renaissance jewel, forcing her thighs together.

She whimpered as the maneuver imbedded the jewel more deeply.

He looked up briefly to gauge the sound and, satisfied it wasn't one of pain, he placed his hands—fingers splayed—on the outer curve of her thighs and rocked her lightly from side to side. The delirium heightened, ravenous need overwhelmed her, obliterating all thought but that of carnal release.

"She didn't last more than one dance," he softly added.

"How could she ..." Elizabeth breathed, barely able to speak, the heated pendant sending wild frissons of rapture coursing through her body, all her senses concentrated on its riveting presence under her hand.

Johnnie's faint smile was knowing. "She couldn't, because the king did this ..." Sliding his hand between her legs, he moved her fingers upward on the slippery gem to the rim of pearls. Covering her fingers with his, he pressed delicately on the top of the pendant so the purposely constructed convex mount on the back plunged into the trembling flesh of Elizabeth's clitoris and then he moved her fingers in a slow circular motion.

A low moan signaled the first glorious spasm, each sublime peaking explosion that followed curling through her with such savage intensity she screamed at the end— the unguarded cry almost immediately engulfed by the shadowed silence of the room.

Afterward she lay softly panting, her body glistening in the firelit room, her breathing the only audible sound in the hushed chamber. "Merry Christmas," Johnnie whispered, leaning forward to kiss her flushed cheek.

Her lashes slowly drifted upward at his touch. "I need you all the time," she whispered with a kind of wonder.

"I'm a lucky man," he said, brushing her jaw lightly with the back of his fingers, charmed by her winsome bewilderment.

Raising her arms above her head in a luxurious indolent stretch, her movement exerting an intoxicating friction on the jeweled pendant resting inside her, she smiled up at her husband with sated contentment. "How are *you* doing," she lazily murmured, "now that I'm selfishly satisfied?"

"I'm fine," he replied with unruffled calm.

"But what will you do with this now?" Elizabeth asked, reaching out to rub her fingers over the obvious prominence of his erection, the fine wool of his breeches stretched in taut ripples over the bulge.

"Actually," he said, with a small half-smile, covering her hand with his so she could feel him more acutely, "I was thinking about replacing Agnes Sorel's jewel with it."

"And if I'm no longer interested?" But her eyes had already begun to change as he swelled against her palm.

His grin was easy. "Then I thought I'd wait five minutes until you were."

Which proved in reality to be longer than necessary.

The jewel was slowly removed, a procedure that powerfully incited her desire. Johnnie stripped off his shirt and breeches, then lifted her on his lap, sliding her onto his arousal with an effortless strength. As the hanging ropes of pearls undulated in great swinging loops between them they moved in a glorious untrammeled rhythm—eager, unrestrained, reckless at times—until they climaxed together in cries of pleasure.

Afterward, when Elizabeth playfully rolled Johnnie off the chaise onto the carpet so she could hold him and rub against him, kiss him and feel every inch of his finely muscled body with a rambunctious giddy urgency, the necklaces caught and snapped, sending hundreds of ivory pearls streaming across the silk pile.

With an anxious cry Elizabeth began to collect them, moving on her hands and knees to follow their scattered paths, gathering them up in a small vase she'd taken from a table near the chaise. Lying in a lithe sprawl before the fire, Johnnie watched his wife with fascinated attention, her nude body in motion a delectable attraction. Her breasts gently bounced and trembled as she crawled across the carpet, their full swollen abundance a sensual feast to the eye, the bountiful curve of her bottom lush and blooming, her position on her hands and knees provocative, as if she were tempting him to mount her.

When she drew within range in pursuit of some pearls that had rolled under the chaise, he leisurely reached out and brushed his fingers over the rivulets running down her inner thighs, tracing a teasing fingertip across her glistening wet vulva, up the sleek crevice of her bottom, around the pale sphere of her buttocks in a tantalizing act of primitive possession, putting his mark on her.

"Leave them for the maid to pick up," he said, enticed by the ripeness of her breasts and satiny bottom, the wanton display of jewels on her nude flesh, the erotic evidence of their lovemaking on her thighs.

She'd gone motionless at his touch, her heart beginning to race, fevered tremors quivering through her senses at the light pressure of Johnnie's fingers. After weeks of extravagant pleasuring, her body was ripe, in constant readiness like a sensuous vessel, devoted to her husband's touch, his voice, his moods . . .

"Leave them," he said more emphatically so she

turned her head and gazed at him through the veil of her pale hair.

"Come here."

His penis slowly surged, rose, grew hard before her eyes and she trembled a little at the enormity of his arousal. A molten heat began to wash over her. Utterly sensitized, susceptible to the sight of him, she felt herself open, felt the sweet liquid of desire dissolve inside her.

"Come here *now*," her husband restlessly repeated, his erection straining upward. Rolling over a half turn he grasped her ankle shackled with the gold padlocked chain and pulled her back. When she was close again, he released his hold on her ankle, turned over on his back and, steadying her with one hand, eased himself under her.

Her heavy breasts were provocative inches above his mouth, her large nipples so near his warm breath caressed a quivering tip as he spoke. "I can't reach you," he said and his tongue flicked upward, barely grazing a tantalizing pink crest.

Shuddering at the infinitesimal touch, she immediately responded to his soft order, and dropped lower so he could reach her. His mouth closed over a taut point and then his lips slid up her nipple as exquisite desire rushed through her body. With lingering deliberation, his mouth surrounded her aureole, enlarged and sensitized by pregnancy; his lips brushed back and forth over the receptive bud, as a baby would searching for sustenance. After a delicate survey, his mouth drew powerfully on her nipple and she shivered at the bewitching rush of pleasure.

He handled and played with the full globes as he suckled, squeezing them gently, his fingers drawing the plump flesh downward in long stroking movements so her nipple slid farther into his mouth, milking the soft swollen roundness, his dark fingers sinking into her yielding flesh.

Needing him with a greedy desperation that had become habit, the throbbing heat between her legs an insistent drumbeat in her brain, she reached for his erection. Her fingers closed so forcefully around his pulsing shaft, he grunted in shock. But then her hand swept downward in a swift sure pressure and sensational feeling overwhelmed him. She watched the dark red crest pulse, stretched taut, glistening and a moment later her fingers slid upward so she brushed over the swelling sensitive rim. And she felt Johnnie's mouth momentarily release the pressure on her nipple as he groaned.

"I need to feel you," she pleaded, her body on fire. She tried to shift her lower body the small distance required to move over him, to straddle his hips. But his teeth lightly clamped down again on her nipple, while his fingers, half-buried in her soft breasts, held them captive.

Tormented, ravenous, she whispered, "Johnnie . . .", swinging her hips over a minute distance, trying to reach him.

His fingers tightened and pain just short of pleasure stopped her.

A moment later, he kissed each nipple lightly as if in recompense for the hurt. "Slowly, darling," he murmured, his finger gliding up her deep cleavage. Then he pulled her on top of him and held her, and smiled into her green stormy eyes.

"Maybe I don't want to go slowly." Hot, moody, frustrated, she glared at him.

He grinned. "One of us has to have his way."

"*I* want to."

One corner of his mouth twitched upward. "You always do."

"You're a businessman; I'll bribe you." Her voice had changed, turned seductive. "I've give you my jewelry and bring you breakfast in bed for a week."

"I don't want your jewelry," he said, a playful gleam in his eyes, "and how can you bring me breakfast in bed when I'm up hours before you?"

Her mouth settled into a pout.

"I want something else."

Her gaze flashed upward and their eyes met.

"We've two hours before our dinner guests arrive," he softly began.

"Dinner guests?" A small startled squeal.

"Mrs. Reid's competent," Johnnie went on, his composure unruffled. "So I'll offer you a proposition," he said, his eyes surveying her with a familiar brazen sensuality.

The startling prospect of imminent dinner guests abruptly forgotten at such bold carnal promise, she smiled—an opulent smile of enticing womanly wiles. "I'm getting my way," she said, moving her lips against his arousal.

"And then I'm getting mine," he said with an answering smile. Opening his arms wide, he grinned at her. "I'm available for your impatient purposes. Or, actually, my cock is available. Where and how would you like it?"

"Hmmm," she said thoughtfully, sliding off Johnny to playfully appraise his sprawled form. "I think first—"

His brows rose.

"You didn't set a limit," she teasingly said, sitting crosslegged and delectable beside him.

"I'll be skin and bones before this baby is born," he theatrically lamented. He wouldn't of course; he was powerful as a young stallion, all toned muscle and restless energy.

"You don't look as though you'll fall into a decline in the next five minutes," Elizabeth said with one mocking eyebrow raised, "so I think I'll sit on you first. . . ."

"Your servant, Ma'am," he murmured insolently, gesturing downward.

He didn't move as she lowered herself onto his rigid penis with exquisite lingering slowness. He watched her from under his dark lashes with a faint smile. And when she was at last completely impaled, his hands moved to her hips and he brought her up to climax so fast she gasped in wonder.

Rolling her under him almost instantly after her orgasm had shuddered to a close, he sent her over the edge again seconds later with an astonishing viruosity. He obliged her eagerness for consummation twice more in rapid, mind-shattering succession, restraining his own orgasm, and then he kissed her breathless mouth and left her sprawled on the floor in a sensual daze while he made himself comfortable on the chaise.

Her eyes opened after a few moments, and in a few moments more she searched for him. Locating him on the chaise, she smiled up at his lounging form. "Thank you, thank you, thank you," she languidly purred. "You're perfection, Johnnie."

"And waiting . . ."

"Ummm . . ." She stretched. "Maybe later. I'm not feeling sexy anymore."

"You're sure?" His tone was pleasant.

She nodded and rolled over on her side so she faced him. "Do you mind?"

He shook his head and smiled, his fingers moving lightly up and down his rigid penis. Then up again, then down . . . the rhythm unhurried. He handled himself easily, naturally, without constraint.

"You can't do that," she said in a heated whisper.

He stopped momentarily to glance over at her, his brows raised in speculation.

"It's mine," she said.

He smiled. "But you're not feeling sexy, so it's not yours right now."

"But I will be later."

"Then you'll have it later." His manipulation had brought him rock hard.

"Johnnie . . ." She sat up quickly, her movement as agitated as her voice.

"I didn't climax those last four times, darling," he gently reminded her. "I was playing the gentleman. But you can't have everything."

"Why not?" she asked imperiously.

"Because"—he grinned—"I'm not that much of a gentleman."

"Let me do that."

"Don't bother. You're tired . . . it won't take long."

"But I want to," she insisted, her voice high-strung, full of yearning.

The motion of his hand stopped and he gazed at her with a lazy, half-lidded look. "How much do you want it?" he asked, running his fingers down the splendidly formed erection, a casual authority drifting through his soft speech.

"I want it more than you." In her breathy whisper was temper and necessity and the tireless passion that had overtaken her placid life when she'd met Johnnie Carre.

"Then come and take it," he whispered back. Sliding in a lithe movement to the foot of the chaise, he casually spread his legs so that the object of her need and desire awaited her.

She crossed the small distance on her hands and knees, then sat back on her heels so her arms brushed against Johnnie's opened legs. "I'm feeling very possessive," she said quietly.

"I know. So am I." His hand came up and slid behind her head, resting at the nape of her neck. With deliberate slowness he drew her head forward. "I want to feel your tongue," he said, his voice low.

Tentatively, her lips touched the satiny smooth crest and then her tongue began to circle its perimeter.

"No . . . just the tip," he commanded softly. "Hold me in your hands . . ." He guided her fingers into place. "There . . . now take the tip in your mouth. That's good." His eyes closed for a moment.

His orders sparked a curious carnal heat as Elizabeth knelt before him, the swollen end of his erection resting in her mouth.

"Now take it all," he murmured, and moved until his penis filled her mouth. He held himself motionless for a moment, letting the exquisite sensations flood his senses. When he could breathe again, he ran his fingers over her cheeks, feeling his hardness submerged in her mouth, tracing a gentle pattern across her brow so she looked up at him. He smiled at her as his hands closed around her head and he began slowly moving in and out, the sensuous friction of her soft lips and tongue exquisite, the small jarring pressure as his erection struck the back of her throat riveting.

"Look," he murmured, catching a glimpse of the scene in the cheval glass near the bed. "You can see

yourself." They were in profile in the mirror, Elizabeth's
kneeling form all curves and rounded pale flesh, her long
light hair drifting over her back, over his legs.

He tucked some tendrils behind her ears so her
face showed clearly in the reflection, so every slow,
plunging movement of his body was visible as his penis
disappeared into her mouth.

Her gaze drifted over in a sidelong glance, the
glowing heat in her body flaring at the sight of her lips
on his enormous arousal.

"It's as if someone is watching us," he softly said.
He stroked her silky cheeks, his eyes on Elizabeth's loving mouth. "What if someone were watching you?" he
murmured, withdrawing again with lingering slowness.
"Waiting his turn? You're very good at this. . . ." He ran
a fingertip lightly over the curve of her top lip, the half
circle of her mouth spread taut to wrap around him.
"Would you want to taste another man?"

She shook her head, her eyes widening for a moment, shamed at the wild heat that streaked through her
at his hushed words, at the sudden intensified throbbing
between her legs.

"Are you sure?" he whispered. He'd seen the carnal
blush infuse her face, her small squirming response. "You
might like it. . . ."

When she shook her head a second time in answer
to his intemperate question, the dizzying friction caused
him to shut his eyes for a shuddering moment.

His hands tightened reflexively on her head and
when his lashes drifted upward, his gaze holding hers
had gone cold. He'd suddenly thought how willing she
was, how ardent, how needful. And he'd recognized with
the cynical eye of a practiced rake how she'd responded
to his suggestion. "I'd kill you if you ever lay with another man," he harshly said, forcing himself back into her
mouth. "No, I'd kill him," he brusquely modified, "and
lock you away." He was buried deep in her mouth again,
his hands clamped on her head, a scowl drawing his dark
brows together. "I won't have you be like the women at
the races," he gruffly said. He'd forgotten in the months

since his marriage how they were, how they crowded around him, offered themselves.

The expression in Elizabeth's eyes instantly altered and her head jerked back. Then, recoiling, she bit him. "What women?" she snapped, resting back on her heels, her green eyes dark with anger.

"That hurt," he growled.

"Good. What women?" she tartly repeated, her hands pugnaciously on her hips.

"There are no women," Johnnie dissembled. "It was a stupid remark. And if you ever bite me again like that—"

"You didn't tell me you were going to renew all your *old* friendships at the races. I suppose that's why I wasn't invited along." She could see him now, damn his blatant sexuality, flirting and lord knew what else. "Did you have sex, then, along with the races?"

"Elizabeth. I went to the races. *Period.* And how the hell would I have any energy left when I fuck you a dozen times a day?" He was still surly at being bitten. His penis throbbed, her teeth marks red indentations on the distended tip. And since he'd turned away all the importuning females today in a shocking reversal of his pre-marital behavior, he resented her accusations.

"If it's a burden to make love to me, consider yourself relieved of the onerous duty." Furious and insulted, she glowered at him.

"If I don't want to, Elizabeth, believe me, I don't need your permission to stop."

"Because there will always be all those women waiting for you—at the races or at the hunts or hawking or across my damned dinner table," she exploded, her jealousy a shocking beast inside her.

"Yes, they're always there," he answered her, his own frustration peaking. "But since I only want *your* ripe body," he declared, moody and grim, "it doesn't matter." Reaching out, he ran a rough ungentlemanly hand over her heaving breasts.

She slapped his hand away. "Don't you dare touch me after flirting all afternoon."

He didn't move for a single black-tempered moment. "What do you mean, don't dare touch me?" His voice was a low growl.

"Just what I said." Her rebuff was swift, flippant and rude.

"Because of some damnable unjustifiable jealousy?" His voice had gone very soft.

She bristled at his tone, at his challenge. "I don't find your explanation adequate."

"And I don't like your question. I'll touch you, Elizabeth, if I wish."

She started to move but he moved faster and a flashing second later she was pushed face down over the foot end of the chaise, her bottom arched up provocatively, her husband surveying her from behind.

"Now then," he lazily murmured, feeling hostile and perverse, "let's see about touching you." And he guided his rigid penis forward until it lightly brushed her exposed sex. Rubbing it back and forth over her pouting lips, he teased her sensitive flesh as if she was a mare being readied for mounting, until she quivered with need. And then he entered her, slowly, a small restrained distance, and paused to let her desire escalate to desperation.

She tried not to move or respond as waves of torrid heat swept over her and her flesh contracted around him. She tried to remember her anger, to nurture her resentment, but he slid in another half inch and her body unconsciously reacted, sliding backwards, searching for the elusive pleasure. He deliberately enticed her, advancing with exaggerated slowness, forcing her to recognize her need, withdrawing once when she tried to set the pace, only entering her again when she'd calmed under his hands. And long moments later, when he was sunk deep inside her, when she was stretched and filled with him, when his stirring presence had refocused her resentment, her senses, her world, he slid his fingers through the amber belt on her hips, grasped it firmly and, holding her tightly pinioned, pushed deeper.

Elizabeth screamed in pure sensual ecstasy.

Only then Johnnie began the sweet ebb and flow, swinging in and out in the agonizing motion of enticement, his lean body driving in a powerful rhythm, her honeyed sweetness lubricating each deliberate languid invasion. And when her breathing became erratic and his mind was no longer capable of dispassionate command, he savagely drove into her with such hot-blooded intensity both groaned with fierce pleasure.

She met him in a restless tumultuous fervor, her soft sighs breathy as each thrusting stroke reached home, his throaty growl adjunct to the powerful rhythm of his lower body. Her need was as excruciating as his. And they exploded hot, steamy, breathless—in a scorching, cataclysmic release.

"There now," he breathlessly declared, stroking her bottom lightly, his smugness plain. "You didn't seem to mind me touching you. . . ." He was beginning to withdraw when she caught him off balance; he was halfway off his knees rolling back on his heels when she twisted around and rose up in a maddened swirling movement, her arms swinging out like a windmill, catching him in the throat, her hip driving him backwards.

He'd hardly hit the floor when she fell on top of him and brutally grabbed his testicles in her fingers. "Now then," she said in a whisper, her wrathful gaze only inches from his, "tell me about the women at the races."

He could backhand her across the room with one blow despite her bruising grip. But he understood her anger because he suffered from the same ungovernable urges. And he was contrite now that he'd forced his own manner of revenge on her. "Accept my apology," he said. "I was boorish and rude."

"Tell me about the women," she hotly retorted. She wasn't contrite yet nor appeased as he was after exacting his sexual vengeance. She was furious for having succumbed to his expertise, raging that he'd consistently avoided her questions about the women. "No more evasion, Johnnie. I want a plain simple answer. I want to know about the women at the races this afternoon, the ones you were alluding to when you said you'd kill me if I was like them." Her fingers tightened on him and he winced.

"I'm letting you do that, you know," he said in a suppressed growl, his blue eyes full of warning.

"How chivalrous," Elizabeth murmured sarcastically, still in hot-tempered dudgeon. "I'm waiting."

His hand moved to free himself from her grip. "Ease up. It's hard to think when I'm about to be crushed."

"You haven't told me anything yet."

He sighed. "All right then ... it's like this. Everyone knows everyone," he began with a grimace. "Everyone drinks deep, including the women. The mood is festive, particularly now during the holidays, and I was approached. That's all," he finished giving a brief, highly edited version of the numerous female overtures. "I was honestly surprised. I'd forgotten how convivial the company."

"Convivial!" She snorted. "A tame word for what they wanted."

"Everyone knows I'm in love with you. They're harmless."

"Maybe they don't *care* whether you love me or not."

"But *I* do, and they *know* that now." His voice was quiet, low, his blue eyes free of subterfuge like a child's. "Please forgive my remark about killing you, although I couldn't deal with it if you were ever like them. I don't love you sweetly," he said with a great heaving sigh. "I love you with my gut and then my heart and then my head."

Her grip had loosened as he spoke; her eyes were bright with unshed tears.

"I don't know how this happened to me," he softly went on, "but it has, and I can't live without you. Everyone's still at Wat Harden's. I was the only one to leave—amidst much vulgar mockery and ridicule, I might add, about the chains of matrimony. But you needed me," he whispered, gently brushing a ringlet behind her ear, "so I came home to you. ..." Drawing her close, he kissed the tears from her eyes.

"I'm violently jealous," Elizabeth confessed, clinging to him. "I want you always close to me, inside me and around me and over me and near me," she whispered, her emotions still feverish, obsessed.

"I know," he soothed, "I'm beset with the same urge. I'm here." His arms tightened around her as they lay in the glow of the fire, her body dwarfed in the shelter of his, the sanctuary and fulfillment she sought willingly given. "You're my precious wife," he murmured against her warm smooth temple. "I'll always be here."

And in the days that followed, as had been the pattern since their marriage, nothing of the outside world impinged on the insulated, sequestered sweetness of their life and love. He indulged her in all things, protected her from any unhappiness, arranged his schedule to conform to hers. They became no more than a country squire and his wife, concerned with the small affairs of their estates, unfashionably in each other's company, content alone together.

They needed no one but themselves.

They rarely wished for company in their retirement from the world.

Their love for each other was enough. It was everything.

And in the days after Christmas the baby began to show, the swell of Elizabeth's belly obvious now, and they made roseate plans for their child's future. For a man who'd never considered babies or children, the full measure of his happiness was beyond explanation. He wondered sometimes whether he'd stumbled into a lavish fantasy land, so alien was his present life from that of his past.

Elizabeth only gloried in the bounty of life's goodness. Pagan enough to feel she deserved such happiness after the previous wasteland of her life, she didn't question her exaltation.

"I feel so healthy ... like I was made to have children," Elizabeth cheerfully said, stretching luxuriously as they lay in bed one morning. "Thanks to you," she murmured, rolling over to drape herself across her husband's warm body, her voice fragrant with indolent sensuality.

"The pleasure was mine," Johnnie lazily whispered, adjusting her comfortably in his arms. "Any time you want more," he said with a teasing grin, "let me know. . . ."

"I'd like lots and lots . . . I've never even been sick a day . . . and I adore this wanting you all the time . . . and just think when we can actually hold the baby in our arms. Oh, Johnnie . . ." she whispered, her eyes welling with unshed tears, "I love you so much, it frightens me. . . ."

"Hush now," he murmured, tightening his embrace. "I'm here. Always . . ." He kissed the softness of her cheek. "We'll be together . . . always. Don't be frightened."

"Tell me you'll never leave me." The fear in her eyes had a childlike innocence, the demons from her past never completely obliterated.

"I'll never leave you," he simply said.

She smiled then, a tentative, shaky smile, and whispered, "I'm sorry. I know . . . men hate . . . demanding women."

"Don't talk to me of other men," he gruffly murmured, his jealousy of her first husband a palpable thing that lingered despite all logic. "I can't bear to think of any man touching you."

She glanced out the window quickly, as if to gauge what sudden gloom had overtaken her spirits. "Talk to me of other things, Johnnie," she whispered. "I feel as though some sinister fiend is outside the door."

"Tell me where the baby kicks you now, my darling Bitsy. And leave all the demons of hell to me. Show me now. Is it here? Or here?"

And he began to do what he did best, this man who knew precisely how to take a woman's mind off anything at all but her pleasure. And Elizabeth's demons were scattered into oblivion that morning in January.

•   •   •

Two days later the local Magistrate from Kelso rode to Goldiehouse and a footman came to Munro's office to give Johnnie the message.

"I'll just be a short time, darling," Johnnie said to Elizabeth as they sat side by side leafing through drawings. "It probably has to do with Crawford's nephew. At the Commissioner's meeting last week there was controversy over the position of revenue collector. As soon as he's gone, I'll be back, and you and Munro can tell me what I missed."

The three of them had spent the morning going over the interior details. With the shell of the new addition finished shortly before Christmas, the workmen had begun the long process of completing the interior.

"Maybe he has news from Edinburgh too," Munro said. "Ask him if he knows how the Commons vote goes."

"Is there any question?" Johnnie sardonically inquired, rising.

Munro sighed. "Hope springs eternal."

"And that's why you're an architect instead of a politician," Johnnie said with a blunt amiability. "England is going to bludgeon us into submission with the menace of commercial ruin and conquest. The question isn't whether we can win against them, but whether we can save our Parliament."

"Ever practical."

"Just realistic," Johnnie said, "with the current mood of Westminster. I wouldn't be surprised if they send troops for us to quarter in our homes. Apparently, Nottingham and Rochester are fanning the flames of English anger with great success."

"Will it come to war, do you think?" Elizabeth quietly asked, the past week's news from London uncompromisingly against Scottish independence.

"Of course not," Johnnie quickly said, determined to protect Elizabeth from the worst of his concerns. "It's just so much campaign rhetoric. Now I'll be back directly I can take care of Drummond's business."

And minutes later he greeted Jack Drummond, who was waiting in his study with a warm smile. "What can I do for you?" he said, waving the young judge he'd appointed back into his chair. "It is Crawford still agitating for his nephew's custom's job?"

"I wish it were, my Lord," the youthful barrister said, his expression grave. "I'm afraid I bring shocking news."

"Out with it. With the state of the nation one expects bad news daily."

"It's about Lady Graden, my Lord."

"Yes?" Johnnie had been about to seat himself behind his desk, but he remained standing, utterly still, his eyes trained on the man across from him.

"As sheriff of Ravensby, I received a summons from Rochester yesterday, my Lord." Jack Drummond swallowed, wiped away the sweat that had suddenly beaded on his brow and softly said, "Lady Graden is ordered to appear before the Magistrate there to be examined and answer charges of witchcraft brought by the Grahams of Redesdale. They're implicating her in the death of her first husband."

"I'll kill them," Johnnie whispered.

The young barrister hesitated, not certain how to respond. "The date is set for Wednesday next," he nervously went on. "Which doesn't leave much time, my Lord, for a defense, but please accept my assistance if I can be of any help." Jack Drummond owed his livelihood to the Laird of Ravensby, but loyalty alone didn't explain his offer. Johnnie had taken a personal interest in his family, seeing that his two younger brothers had the means for university; Jack Drummond looked on Johnnie Carre with great affection. "I wouldn't have served the summons had there been any way to avoid it, my Lord," he murmured in apology. "But if you'd not been informed . . ."

"I understand, Jack." The Laird of Ravensby's voice seemed distant, as though his thoughts were elsewhere. "How much time do we have?" he asked then, his tone normal once again.

"Ten days, sir."

"That should be enough time."

"You must go up to Edinburgh immediately, my Lord, to gather the legal defense, or might I suggest Holt

in London; he's gained acquittal in several witchcraft
cases."

"Legal defense? Oh, yes. Of course." And Johnnie
turned away, his back to his guest while he stared out the
window at his frost-covered parkland. The room was
quiet for a lengthy interval, the Laird of Ravensby motionless, Jack Drummond uneasy. Then Johnnie Carre
strolled away from the window, walked over to a cabinet,
took a key from his waistcoat pocket, and opened the lac-
querwork doors. He pulled open two large drawers,
withdrew several large leather pouches, and, bringing
the bags over to his desk, set them softly before Jack
Drummond.

"If you'd be kind enough to deliver these to the
presiding judge at the Court of Justiciary in Edinburgh
and ask him to see to a fortnight's delay in answering the
summons, I'd be grateful. I'll send along a guard with
you. If it's Comyn, he'll do the job without the *gift*,"
Johnnie softly added. "He owes me a dozen favors."

"Of course, my Lord," Jack Drummond said, rising,
his patron's tone one of dismissal. "Could I be of any legal help, sir?"

"I don't think it will come to that, Jack," Johnnie
said with a grim smile, "once I speak to the Grahams."

Late that night, after Elizabeth fell asleep, he left for the
weapons room, where his lieutenants waited. And he detailed his plans to march on the Grahams.

"I want a thousand men to meet me at Carter Bar
two nights hence," Johnnie began, standing under the
English pennant taken at Bannockburn by one of his ancestors. "Travel there in small groups; we'll rendezvous
in the evening. We'll need ladders and grappling hooks."
His voice was without expression, his directions given
matter-of-factly, not as if they were prelude to a bloody
battle. "There's to be no discussion of this with anyone.
I don't want word of our raid to reach the Grahams, nor
do I wish my wife to know. We'll attack in overwhelming

numbers; I want the Graham brothers killed. Are there any questions?"

"Do you know they're in Redesdale Forest?"

"I'll know by the morning of the attack."

"Might they be inside their castle?"

"They might. If we have to go in after them, we'll need all the extra men."

They discussed the logistics of surreptitiously moving a thousand men across thirty miles without causing comment, of the best way to transport the scaling ladders, heavy crowbars, and axes they required for the assault. They'd need food for themselves and their mounts, weapons and ammunition. Everyone added his suggestions to the plans for the raid.

"We'll send scouts out tomorrow," Johnnie said, "to determine the strength of their defenses. But we're going in," he ruthlessly said, "regardless. I won't have Elizabeth brought to trial."

"They're cowards, Johnnie, to strike at a woman."

"And we're out to teach them their manners," the Laird of Ravensby softly said.

He told Elizabeth he had to spend a few days in Jedburgh handling estate matters for his cousin, and when he took his leave of her, he held her at arms' length for a quiet moment, fixing her image in his mind.

She wore a loose flowing gown of deep crimson, her heavy, pale hair coiled at her neck, an embroidered shawl pinned across her shoulders against the January chill.

"This is the first time you've left me since our marriage. I'm going to miss you dreadfully. . . ." Her eyes lifted to his were shiny with tears. "Why can't I come with you?"

"You know you shouldn't ride, darling . . . with the baby. Something could happen."

"Why couldn't I follow in the carriage? I'd have the driver go ever so slow. . . ."

Johnnie took her hands in his. "The roads are so

badly frozen into ruts, you'd be shaken apart regardless of how slowly you traveled. And I'll be back in two days. Three at the very most. I'll send you a letter every day."

"I'm sorry," she apologized with a small sigh, "for being so clinging." She smiled up at him. "It's the baby, I think, making me so emotional ... but I find myself so fearful of late. You'll be careful?"

"It's not that far," he evasively answered. "There's no danger in Jedburgh." He gently squeezed her fingers. "Now give me a kiss, then go back inside; you'll catch a chill standing out here."

A dozen mounted men silently waited for him on the drive, fully armed, ostensibly his guard to Jedburgh.

"Hold me," Elizabeth whispered, blind appeal in her liquid eyes.

And he pulled her into his arms, her body small against his large frame, the silk tapestry of her shawl, the fine wool of her gown, soft under his gloved hands, her downcast spirits making him heartsick. "You're my life," he murmured, the scent of her perfume, heady in his nostrils, reminding him of rose petals, her soft skin, their nights in each other's arms.

"Take me with you then," she implored, clinging to him, the green of her eyes shadowed with distress.

"I can't."

She recognized the undiluted finality in his voice and, searching his face, asked for reassurance, "Just two days?"

He nodded.

"Promise?"

"Promise," he softly said, adjusting his schedule.

"I won't be able to sleep without you."

"Nor I," he murmured, this man who had never shared his heart before.

"You won't get hurt now?" Her voice quivered.

He shook his head, then, bending, kissed her tear-stained cheeks. "I'll count the hours," he whispered, hugging her close for a moment before he released her. "Take care of our child," he said very low, and then he walked away.

He waved to her from the saddle as he nudged his

horse into a trot. And later he stopped at the end of the long drive to take one last look at the small figure of his wife still standing where he'd left her. She was dwarfed by the enormous mass of Goldiehouse.

"God willing I'll be back," he murmured, raising his hand in salute to his wife, his unborn child, to the centuries-old home of the Carres.

The troop of Carres assembled at Carter Bar that evening, and he wrote to Elizabeth as he'd promised. Already in the saddle, with hours of hard riding ahead and an uncertain outcome facing him, he scribbled with a pencil on a scrap of paper.

> *I haven't time to say more but that I love you above all things and wait to hold you in my arms again. You're in my heart as I write this; you'll always be in my heart.*
>
> *Your loving husband,*
> *Johnnie*

After sending a messenger back with his note to Elizabeth, Johnnie and the Carres rode through the night to reach Redesdale Forest. Reaching the Graham castle two hours before dawn, the men were deployed around the fortress, the scaling ladders set against the rough stone directly below the watch making the rounds atop the walls; the sentinels were unaware of the massed men below them in the dark. A company of horsemen had been left to guard the road between the castle and their route home to assure their retreat after the battle. All was hushed and still in the pre-dawn mist when Johnnie Carre set his booted foot on the first rung of a ladder. And at his hand signal a thousand men began to move.

The Laird of Ravensby led the ascent, the dark shadows of his men spreading up the walls like a soundless coursing tide, swords muffled, dirks in hand, the Lady of Ravensby's life at stake.

The guards were silenced first, their throats noiselessly slit, and all was at peace inside the fortified castle of the Grahams deep in Redesdale Forest. The dogs in the courtyard below moved restlessly for a few moments, the scent of blood striking their noses, but they were tossed some freshly butchered beef brought along to quiet them and they fell to their meal.

When the Carre clansmen set the iron bar to the main door, the alarm was sounded and the drums began beating inside the castle, calling the Grahams to arms. Johnnie led the way through the shattered door, followed by his men, singly at first, until the portal could be breached for wider passage. They fought their way up the main staircase to the first floor, hacking and slashing, their superiority in numbers of no advantage in the contained space, the defenders familiar with each passageway and corridor and hiding place. But Johnnie fought like a man who had had something stolen from him, as if he wanted to slice through every head in his way, and he kept coming and coming, not satisfied until he had the Graham brothers under his sword. Like so many Border castles, the Grahams' home had been built for defense, and the Carres had to break down a dozen doors before they reached the inner wards where they expected to find the Grahams making their stand. Instead, only the women and children were huddled together, terror-stricken, in the huge hall.

The Graham brothers and their main force had bolted through the hidden passage to their escape routes into the bogs and marshes north of the castle. The Quene Moss, accessible only to them, had been their noted place of refuge for centuries. The morass was so deep that, legend had it, two spears tied together wouldn't reach the bottom. In this retreat the Grahams feared no force or power of England or Scotland.

Leaving guards surrounding the Graham women and children, Johnnie walked over the fallen bodies in the first-floor corridors, followed by Kinmont, the men retracing their bloody ascent through the hallways and great rooms of the castle, all guarded now by Carres—to the small doors in the north wall of the castle where his men had lain in ambush should the Grahams flee into their marshes.

And outside in the waning light of morning under the shadows of dark pine and the naked limbs of winter hawthorne and beech, a group of Graham prisoners and dead and wounded gave evidence of their flight from the castle.

"Four brothers dead," Adam quietly said to Johnnie's nod at the bodies on the ground.

"What of the fifth?" he quickly asked.

"We missed Matthew. He's in Carlisle, according to the captain of their guard."

"Bloody hell," Johnnie swore in disgust.

"This should make him reconsider his lawsuit."

"I'd prefer more surety," Johnnie grimly said, relentless in his quest to protect his wife. In a time when nobles were tortured, hanged, beheaded, drawn and quartered, for supporting the wrong monarch or political cause, when the lives of the poor had little value beyond their physical labor, when loyalty could be openly bought and sold, when protection of one's lands and possessions depended on personal strength and force, Johnnie Carre would have preferred that all the Graham brothers been dispatched to hell. "We'll have to go and find him."

"Now?"

He shook his head, his gaze surveying the carnage, his expression unreadable. "I promised Elizabeth I'd be back in two days. We'll return to Goldiehouse first. Although a small troop should make for Carlisle immediately. When Matthew Graham receives reports of this, he'll bear watching. I expect he'll ask for protection. At least there's only one left," Johnnie softly said, the faintest smile curving his mouth.

Within a short time the Carres were mounted, their wounded tended to; miraculously, none of the Carres had been killed. Although the Grahams weren't noted for taking a stand, their defense had been less vigorous with their leaders in flight.

The large group separated again at Carter Bar, taking different routes back to Ravensby with Johnnie reaching

Goldiehouse shortly after dark. Quietly approaching the house from the service drive, he washed in the stables, leaving his jack and sword behind to be cleaned of blood-stains. And when he walked into the house, to be greeted by Munro, who'd received word of his coming from Kinmont, Johnnie cautioned his cousin to silence with a raised hand. "Have Mrs. Reid send up some dinner to my suite in an hour," he said to Dankeil Willie, "and I'll announce my return to Lady Elizabeth myself."

Motioning Munro to follow him into his study, Johnnie shut the door behind his cousin. "I'll give you the details tomorrow; Elizabeth is waiting, but I wanted to thank you for staying behind and taking care of her. How is she?"

"She'll be fine now that you're back. In almost one piece," he added with a smile. "You should bind that arm."

Johnnie glanced at his sliced shirt and the gash in his right arm. "It's nothing. The Grahams didn't fight to the end once the brothers bolted. Not that I expected them to. But you heard, Matthew lives. A bloody shame."

"Kinmont tells me he's in Carlisle."

"Perhaps, or on his way back to Redesdale Forest. I think he'll stay in Carlisle, since it's one of the English garrison forts. A troop's on its way to find him. I'd promised Elizabeth to return in two days, so I'm briefly back."

"You can't let him live, of course."

"No." Johnnie flexed his fingers, restless against his urgent need to destroy Matthew Graham.

"Must *you* do it? Send someone else."

Johnnie gazed at his cousin from under half-lowered lashes and then smiled, a grim, swift flexing of his lips. "He's mine."

"Don't risk your life for him."

"I don't intend to." Johnnie smiled again, this time a smile of notable warmth. "But thanks for the concern."

"When will you leave again?"

"When I hear from Adam. Probably in three or four days."

"Don't let me keep you now," Munro generously

offered, gesturing toward the door. "Elizabeth will be pleased you're home."

"I'd travel across the wastelands of the world to come back to her," Johnnie murmured.

"You'll have to tell her that," Munro said. "She's been crying a lot."

"It's the baby ... her moods are skittish now."

"Or perhaps psychic. You could have been killed."

"Then I'd have had to come back from the netherworld to be with her."

Munro gazed at Johnnie for a brief moment, reflecting on the profound changes he'd witnessed in his cousin's capacity for love. "And if anyone could cross that black passage," he quietly said, "it would be you."

"Damn right," Johnnie said with a grin. "Now let's not be morbid. I'm back more or less undamaged, and the most beautiful woman in the world is upstairs waiting for me. I have to change quickly, so adieu." One brow lifted roguishly. "I'll see you about noon tomorrow."

Elizabeth was seated by the fire when he entered the room, wrapped in the folds of a midnight-blue cut-velvet robe, her hair gold in the firelight. She rose with a cry of delight when he stepped through the door and ran to him, the heavy velvet flaring out in wings behind her.

And he moved forward in great long strides, so gladdened at the sight of her, he wondered how he'd ever lived before he'd met her. She flung herself into his open arms, and he caught her, swinging her around in a transport of joy. She squealed with pleasure, and he laughed, lighthearted as a young boy.

"You were gone too long in Jedburgh," she complained as he gently placed her on her feet, but her smile was dazzling.

"I'll make it up to you," he promised, his own smile impudent, his arms lacing around her waist.

"Do you think I can be so easily appeased?" she teasingly inquired.

"I *know* you can be so easily appeased," he seductively replied, drawing her closer so their thighs brushed and then their lower bodies. So she could feel him.

"I've turned wanton since I've met you," she whispered, her body's response intense, immediate.

"A charming quality in a wife," Johnnie murmured, his hands drifting downward over the luxurious velvet of her robe. "Show me. . . ."

Reaching up, Elizabeth placed her small hands on his face and, pulling him downward, kissed him with slow, lingering intensity. Then she whispered against the warmth of his mouth, "I haven't had sex in two days. . . ."

The implication of her deprivation added length to his arousal. "Could I be of some help?" he asked, his fingers tangled in the pale silk of her hair.

"Let me see," she quietly replied, as if some vetting might be necessary, drawing back a small distance, her hands drifting down his chest, past his belt buckle, then lower to the obvious bulge under the soft chamois of his breeches. "Ummm . . . this is marvelous. . . ."

"I'm glad you approve," he said with a grin. "Will you require some . . . measurement?"

"It seems quite acceptable," she said with an arch look, her fingers tracing its length, exerting pressure so it swelled against her touch.

"I stand relieved," he dryly murmured, his smile sunshine bright. And then he sucked in his breath as she squeezed the very tip with knowing subtlety.

Several tremulous moments later, when his respiration was restored, when his eyes opened again, and reality intruded into his consciousness, he swept her up into his arms, carried her over to the bed in swift strides, and lowered her gently onto the silk coverlet. "I didn't give you leave," she softly said, her green eyes like emerald fires, her white nightgown and dark blue velvet robe swathed around her in a flourish of ripples and heaps.

"Really," he replied, unbuckling his belt. "Do you think that should stop me?"

"I thought it might. . . ." Her words were coquettish.

"But then I don't have manners," he bluntly declared, pulling his belt loose, dropping it on the floor, beginning to untie his neckcloth.

"So you expect only compliance in a wife?" Her eyes followed his hands as he opened the neckline of his shirt.

"I *expect* a hot, wet welcome," he said with a lazy smile, pulling his shirt over his head. "Can you accommodate me?"

Her hips moved slightly as if in response to his words, and her fingers closed on handfuls of velvet and silk, crushing the luxurious materials, sliding her robe and nightgown upward so her calves came into view, then the white satin of her thighs. As Johnnie Carre sat down on the bed to tug off his boots, he viewed the slow unveiling of the golden down between her legs.

Leaning over, he placed his large hand over her silken curls, a proprietary gesture as natural to him as breathing. "Don't go away," he softly said, "I'll be right with you."

"You're hurt," she softly cried, half-rising, the wound on his upper arm visible when he turned.

"A scratch from a tavern brawl, that's all. You can sew it up later." And he exerted pressure on her mons to keep her down.

"You're sure? . . ." The heel of his hand moved in slow circles, pressing downward, and puzzling questions slipped away, muted by irrepressible passion. "Will I ever have enough of you?" Elizabeth whispered, intemperate desire coursing through her body, her gaze traveling over his muscled torso, down his powerful arm to his strong, long-fingered hand holding her captive.

"No," he said, plain, unhesitating. "Never."

And a moment later his boots were tossed aside, his chamois breeches disposed of, and he was lifting her into a sitting position on the bed so he could undress her.

"Kiss me," she said like a *jeune fille*, all lush, coaxing innocence, her face lifted.

And he kissed her gently as he reached for the closures on her robe.

"More," she murmured, hushed and low, seated in a tumble of dark velvet.

"Soon . . ." he whispered.

Swiftly unclasping the braided frogs on her robe while she tried to kiss him, he pushed the heavy fabric from her shoulders, slid it down her arms, gracefully dodged her hands as she attempted to pull him close. Her nightgown came off as rapidly, and then he stopped eluding her, his mouth available once again, yielding to her feverish pressure, letting her taste him, letting her lean into his hard body, her wafting sigh of pleasure sliding down his throat.

Selfishly, she wanted to possess his raw strength, the memories of his absence still crowding her thoughts. She wanted to absorb him, engulf him; she wanted to concentrate on sheer physical sensation to drive away two days of apprehension and fear. "Touch me everywhere," she whispered as she came up for breath.

"So you'll know I'm back. . . ." he murmured against the sweetness of her parted lips.

"So I can keep you with me. . . ." Allure as old as Eve resonated in her breathy voice.

And he gave her what she wanted, understanding himself how urgent his own need to ground himself in her. His hands drifted over her breasts, heavy and swollen with pregnancy, glided around their rounded abundance, paused to delicately stroke the distended nipples, moved upward between her cleavage, spread the weighted globes apart so she felt their heaviness in her brain and in her throbbing core, in the tips of her fingers and toes.

Then he released his hold, and they sprang back like ripe fruit on a trembling limb. He let them vibrate and quiver as his warm palms slipped over her rounded belly, traced the curve of her hips, moved downward to rest for a moment on her soft thighs before his fingers slipped over her pubescent curls and disappeared inside her throbbing labia.

"Can you feel me now?" he whispered, his gaze on her face, knowing the answer to his question from the expression in her eyes.

"I'm glad you're home." Her voice held a rich undertone of passion.

"I can tell." His fingers were drenched. "Now lie

down and spread your legs," he said with a lush smile, "and I'll show you know how pleased I am to be home."

He kissed her for a lazy interval, and she basked in the flagrant glow of undisguised sensation.

"I can smell the scent of paradise . . . it's so close . . . like sweet coconut. . . ." she whispered.

"Ummm," he murmured, tracing a warm path with his tongue over the lush, pouty fullness of her bottom lip. "My paradise tastes more like"—his hand slipped downward, his finger dipped inside her honeyed warmth as if testing its readiness, and a moment later, he touched his finger to his mouth and then briefly to hers—"shrimp. . . ."

"Make love to me," she whispered, her piquant flavor on her lips.

"I am," he said, placing his hands gently on her face and kissing her.

"It's not enough." She touched his erection lying hard against his stomach. "Give me that."

And he did then, turning her on her side, his chest warm against her back, easing himself slowly inside her until she was filled with him. She moved back into the solid wall of his body to feel him penetrate inches more, and sighed then in blissful ecstasy. And he moved away a moment later until she whimpered . . . and he glided back in. Filling his hands with her breasts, he pulled her closer so she felt every nerve attuned to the extravagant feeling. Reaching down between her legs, she touched him as he slowly glided in and out, her fingertips sliding over the swollen veins and velvety skin sheathing his rock-hard erection. He could feel himself lengthen under her massage, and he held himself motionless inside her for a moment as his arousal swelled.

She moaned, a luxurious pleasure sound.

He smiled in contentment, holding her close.

And they explored the rarefied world of sensation, gently at first, and then with unbridled passion.

Because he'd been gone from her, and she'd realized in his absence that she wasn't whole without him.

Because he'd found the only woman in the world he could love—and because, too, killing always had a turbulent arousing aftermath only she could satisfy.

CHAPTER 20

Adam returned in three days. But his unorthodox arrival was a panic-stricken, whipped, and spurred gallop up the long drive. His shouts of alarm carried across the tranquil winter landscape—faintly at first, and as he neared, his yells echoed from the high stone walls, frightening the peacocks on the terrace lawn, and bringing several of the staff racing from their duties on the grounds. Dankeil Willie was roused from the main house so he was waiting at the steps of the entrance when Adam hauled his lathered mount to a skidding stop on the gravel.

"Dragoons! At the tavern in Kelso!" he cried, leaping from his horse. "Come to take the Laird away!" Racing toward the bank of steps leading into the house, he shouted, "Where is he?"

Already sprinting back up the stone staircase, Willie shouted, "Follow me." And as the two men rushed through the double doors held open for them by two footmen, Willie snapped orders to the lackeys in the entrance hall. He needed Mrs. Reid, he shouted as he ran, two grooms, Munro, and Kinmont to meet him in the breakfast room immediately. There was no time for finesse or respectful courtesies; Lady Elizabeth would know soon enough anyway.

"How much time?" Willie tersely queried, dashing headlong down the corridor toward the east wing. He didn't ask why; he knew the Laird of Ravensby had enemies enough in the current embroiled state of the nation.

Keeping pace at Willie's side, breathless after his headlong flight from Kelso, Adam said, panting, "I left Nab ... and Dougie to buy them ... some rounds of French ... brandy. Hopefully ... an hour. Maybe longer ..." The men's boots beat a racing tattoo on the parquet flooring, the richly decorated rooms flashing by in colorful progression as they sped toward the breakfast room: a wink of gilt-edged mirror, the sheen of brocaded wall-covering, crimson, cobalt, verdant green, the mellow glow of polished brass *torchéres*, Ming vases, Dutch porcelain, painted ancestors stiff in Court costume.

And they burst into the sunny morning room like cannon shot.

One look at their faces and Johnnie was out of his chair. In a flashing moment more he'd gestured them out of the room. "I'll be right back," he murmured to Elizabeth, who'd half risen in surprise. Leaning across the small table, he brushed a kiss across her cheek. "Adam was on an errand for me."

"I'm not a child who needs protection." She knew Willie would never have so impetuously intruded without serious reasons.

"I'll tell you when I get back." He smiled. "Five minutes," he murmured, holding his hand up, fingers splayed. And he spun away, already planning how he was going to garrote Matthew Graham with his bare hands.

"The Edinburgh dragoons are in Kelso. Come to get you," Willie brusquely said when Johnnie shut the door behind him.

"I saw them not twenty minutes ago," Adam said, "at Wat Harden's."

"For me?" It wasn't Elizabeth. "Did you hear why?" Politics was always a dangerous business, but enormous sums of money, men's livelihoods, were at stake in the deteriorating relationship with England; which of his enemies had felt him so dangerous to his aims?

"The major said you ... were being delivered up to Edinburgh ... to answer a rape charge," Adam replied, his chest heaving, his face flushed red from his exertions.

"A lie that is!'" Dankiel Willie's eyes snapped affront.

"But it's the only charge not included in the Indemnity Act," Johnnie thoughtfully noted.

"They'll emit letters of fire and sword against you," Adam said, the dread words etched on every man's liver.

"Outlawed." Johnnie's voice had gone very soft. "So when I'm banished or hanged, my estates are forfeit, with no hope of pardon. And Elizabeth will be obliged to testify, so he'll have her back in his hands. He's thought of everything, apparently." It wasn't as though Johnnie hadn't considered retaliation from Harold Godfrey, yet he'd not anticipated such thoroughness. Godfrey was by nature a plunger; the subtle machinations smelled of Queensberry

"And what of Matthew Graham?" Johnnie's tone was so normal once again, Adam wondered whether he misunderstood the degree of his peril. He'd been in effect sentenced to death wherever he could be found.

"You don't have much time, Johnnie," he nervously declared.

"Nor do any of us." The two men's eyes held for a moment. "You'll all have to leave Goldiehouse," Johnnie went on, "or at least those of you they might wish to impress for witnesses. The Tolbooth isn't a healthy place to await a court appearance. But tell me first of Matthew Graham, so I know where else to expect attack."

"He's huddled frightened inside Carlisle Castle now, but when he hears of this, he'll come sniffing round like crows at a carcass."

Johnnie nodded, apparently agreeing. Catching sight of Kinmont and Munro, he waited until they reached him before motioning over the staff Willie had summoned.

"Some of you may have heard already the dragoons

have come from Edinburgh for me," Johnnie said. "I'm being summoned to Criminal Court."

"They're out to hang ye then," Mrs. Reid interjected. "Ye'd best be gone."

"I'm on my way. I've only time to give instructions once, so everyone listen carefully." And then he issued a rapid-fire round of orders: the valuables that could be carried away in an hour were defined and allocated for safe destinations; arrangements were made for housing his staff at homes of his friends and relatives; his stable had to be dispersed so Queensberry and Godfrey wouldn't profit by his prime bloodstock; when it came to his library, he sighed. Reputed to be the greatest library in Britain, it was impossible to move at such short notice. "I need provisions for Lady Elizabeth and myself for a fortnight, Mrs. Reid. Munro, Robbie must be found immediately. As he's my heir, they'll be out to capture him as well. Tell him I'll need a ship off the coast as soon as possible. You know Robbie's haunts in East Lothian. Kinmont, take what records you feel shouldn't fall into England's hands. Adam, clear out the weapons room and give everything to the men to take away. In the meantime," he briskly went on, "Lady Elizabeth and I will await the outcome of my trial in a more salubrious location than the Tolbooth." The outcome was inevitable and, whether he was present or not, he knew the verdict had already been decided.

He took a few minutes then to answer the rush of questions, assuring his staff that he intended to return, and when he did, they'd once again be welcomed back to Goldiehouse. But he didn't linger over his farewells.

"You don't want a guard?" Munro asked when the staff had dispersed to see to their tasks.

"I don't want to attract attention with too large a party. I anticipate a week or so at Dens Cottage to give the hue and cry time to settle, and then we'll make for the coast. That should give Robbie time to bring a ship into Margarth Cove. Stay with the ship; I'll need you with me abroad."

"Will Elizabeth be able to ride that distance?"

"It's my greatest worry," Johnnie replied, his brows

drawn together in a mild scowl. "The rest of us could fight our way across Scotland if need be. But I can't with her. . . ."

"We can see that the way is clear into Margarth, at least," Munro assured him.

Johnnie smiled. "Then we've only twenty miles to manage from the forest's edge to the coast. If there're no patrols on the roads, we'll see you in a fortnight."

The cousins embraced, perhaps for the last time in the home they'd both known from childhood, and then Johnnie returned to the breakfast room.

Elizabeth's face drained of color as he explained what he'd heard, what was required of them. "I'm sorry, Johnnie," she whispered when he'd finished. "It's my father, of course," she added in a small, tortured voice, overwhelmed with self-reproach, horrified at the terrible price he was paying for loving her.

He went to her immediately, kneeling beside her chair, taking her hand in his. "Don't blame yourself," he said very softly, knowing Godfrey's animosity was of long standing, separate from her. "It's Queensberry, too, your father's not acting alone," he added, his dark hair limned by the sunshine pouring in the windows of the gilded breakfast room, an incongruous setting for such appalling events.

They shouldn't be talking about dreadful possibilities, of treachery and persecution, Elizabeth thought, with the day so bright and beautiful. "What if you went to Edinburgh?" she asked in a small, hopeful voice. "I'd testify that you never raped me; I'd tell them how much I love you. How I was more willing than you, more wanton. It wasn't your fault, Johnnie. I could make them believe me. . . ."

He was gently stroking her hand, his long, slender fingers dark against her pale skin. "It takes considerable influence to bring charges against me, sweetheart. The particular type of accusation doesn't concern them; if not rape, they'd have trumped up something else." And he was convicted already, he knew; the trial would be a mere formality. "What we're going to do now," he said, carefully keeping his voice reasonable, "is leave Scotland

for a time. Until I can arrange some settlement ..."
There wasn't time now to go into the complex process
necessary to organize his partisans, to outmaneuver
Queensberry's greed and Godfrey's need for vengeance.
He shifted his position, restless, precious minutes ticking
by. "But we haven't more than an hour right now...." He
came to his feet.

"Sometimes I wish my father were dead," Elizabeth murmured, her voice trembling with emotion, wondering if her father's perfidious blood had been passed
on to her. She felt utterly coldhearted at the moment.

"I should have killed him when I had the chance,"
Johnnie declared. And to the startled query in her eyes,
he said, "You had gone to Hotchane already; you weren't
there." He grimaced at lost opportunity. "And I was naive
enough to be taken in by your father."

"One learns." A chill ruthlessness cooled her words
to ice.

"One learns," he quietly agreed. "And we must fly
now, love, or we'll be spending tomorrow in the Tolbooth."

Taking both her hands in his, he pulled her to her
feet, the baby very large already, her health in the coming days a distinct worry to him.

"We'll ride very slowly," he said, beginning to walk
toward the door, her hand in his, "so the travel shouldn't
be wearing on you. And we'll wait out the search parties
at my gamekeeper's cottage." Only a few of his staff
knew of its location.

"I can ride, Johnnie. You know I've never felt better. There's no need to coddle me."

But he insisted she wait downstairs in the small
drawing room just off the entrance hall while he went
upstairs to supervise the packing. He needed money and
pistols, and ammunition enough to see them to the coast;
he wanted to see that Helen packed warm gowns for
Elizabeth, and he had her send Elizabeth's cape and
boots and shawl down so she was ready when he came to
fetch her. He put a miniature of his mother and father in
his coat pocket, then went to his dressing room to see

that his valet packed the shaving kit his father had given him when he left for Paris.

Elizabeth had put on her fur-lined cape, the seal-skin soft as velvet. Booted and gloved, a lavender plaid draped over the green wool of her cape, she paced, feeling not only the disastrous cause of Johnnie's adversity, but useless at such a harrowing time.

"Let me do something," she pleaded when Mrs. Reid ran into the room for the second time with a question about food.

"Ye just sit still, my Lady, and take care of ye and the bairn," the housekeeper replied, pushing her toward a chair. "I've a houseful o' help. Now tell me whether ye wish sweet wine or claret, for the Laird dinna know."

And the next half hour passed with numerous staff rushing in to query her about her preferences on food, clothing, reading material—even her jewelry.

"Thank God," she said with anxious relief when Johnnie appeared at the doorway, booted, spurred, a dull green plaid wrapped around his shoulders. "I'm going mad with worry just sitting here. No one will let me do anything."

They were only following his orders, but he smiled and said, "You can ride your little bottom off now, my darling Bitsy. The next hours should be more eventful."

"Will they harm Goldiehouse?" she asked, rising with less grace than in the past.

"We'll lose some portraits and family papers. I don't expect Queensberry will want to be reminded of the Carres. But"—he shrugged then, as though he'd reconciled himself to the inevitable—"I'm sure he'll enjoy my home. He shouldn't become too attached though," he added with a modicum of his familiar impudence.

"You can't defend yourself against this?"

"Not at the moment." Moving toward her, he smiled, her beauty always a source of pleasure to him. "But eventually I will," he said, taking her gloved hand in his. "We'll talk about this later." He had to see that she was safe away.

When he lifted her onto the padded pillion, he indicated a holstered flintlock pistol hanging from the saddle pommel. "It's small enough for a lady to use," he said. "Redmond tells me you're his best pupil."

Swallowing a twinge of apprehension, she answered with what she hoped was equal equanimity, "Just let me know what you want me to shoot."

"If it comes to that," he quietly said, arranging her cape so it covered her legs. "I'll be very specific."

And within the hour, Johnnie and Elizabeth were away from Goldiehouse with two packhorses and enough silver and supplies to see them safely to the Continent. They traveled at a sedate walk, avoiding the villages, traveling cross-country when they could, keeping to the valleys as much as possible. He would have preferred traveling at night, but the dragoons in Kelso wouldn't wait for that convenience, so they kept off the main tracks, and once they reached the forest of Dens in the early afternoon, he stopped looking over his shoulder.

The dense undergrowth concealed them as did the towering ash, sycamores, and firs planted by his grandfather. And they stopped a short distance inside the tree line, safe from detection. He lifted Elizabeth down from her pillion so she could stretch her legs.

"Does anything hurt?" he solicitously asked, still holding her, his hands firmly at her waist, bending his head so their eyes were level. "We're almost there," he added.

"Good," she said, rosy-cheeked and smiling, "because I'm hungry. And you can stop talking to me like a three-year-old child because I feel fine and I shan't break."

He grimaced, a half-smile of acknowledgment. "Forgive me, but I know so little of what you feel, and my ignorance breeds anxiety. I worry that something might happen to you out here in this isolation. . . ." His voice trailed away before her clear, steady gaze.

"Food then," Elizabeth said, "before the calamities strike." Her grin gave pause to his inchoate apprehensions.

"Food I have," he quickly replied. "Sit down right here," he went on, his words coming in a rush of relief, reassured by her prosaic response. Quickly undraping his plaid from his shoulders, he spread it on the brown pine needles covering the ground. "Mrs. Reid packed a basket for the trip, but I can't start a fire yet," he apologized.

"Cold food will be wonderful. Any food will be heaven." She hadn't dared mention her hunger, knowing their danger.

And he told her of his gamekeeper's cottage as they ate, talking of the days of his youth when he'd spend weeks with his father's gamekeeper, Polwarth, learning to hawk and track and fish. "I'll take you hawking while we're here. There's a small rise to the north that picks up some of the winds from the coast; you can see the peregrines slide along those gusts and then turn over and dive almost in dead fall. There's nothing quite like the sight of a falcon dropping at incredible speed from a lofty pitch. And you learn to recognize your falcon's stoop from a long way off." He grinned suddenly. "You needn't share my enthusiasm; I brought books along for you."

"I'd love to watch." She would have loved to have seen the young boy, too, all coltish eagerness and interest. And she thought with joy of the new child within her who might share his father's love of hawking.

They reached the small cottage set on the fringe of a small clearing, framed by soaring dark pines just as the early winter twilight turned all the world to grey.

Lights shone from the windows of the thatched-roof structure, the golden glow offering warmth and welcome. A dog barked at their approach, a black-and-white border collie whose tail stood straight up for a moment and then began wagging in big, lazy circles. He'd recognized Johnnie.

Polwarth came out on the porch to see who his visitors were, a pipe in his mouth, his eyes narrowed in the dimming light. And then catching sight of Johnnie, he waved.

They were safe.

    •   •   •

Nearly of a size with Johnnie, Polwarth was a big, raw-boned man whose red hair had faded with age to a sandy grey. But he stood straight and tall yet, and when he clasped Johnnie in a hug, his uncovered arms revealed solid muscle.

When Johnnie lifted Elizabeth down from her horse and said, "Polwarth, I'd like you to meet my wife, Elizabeth," she knew from the unceremonious introduction that the two men were close.

"Evening, ma'am," the old man politely said, tipping his head in an awkward courtesy. "So ye're married now," he said to Johnnie with a wide smile. "And you look right happy."

"I am," Johnnie said with an unselfconscious frankness, the young boy yet to his father's man.

"But ye're no on a leisure ride," Polwarth said, his gaze passing over the two packhorses, coming to rest on Johnnie's face. He nodded toward the house. "See your lady inside, lad, while I put this bloodstock of yours in the stable."

"You go and help Johnnie," Elizabeth suggested. "I can certainly walk a few feet into the house."

"Best see her in, Johnnie . . . what with those high steps built for a man. Then come help me if ye please."

"He's very nice," Elizabeth said as they entered the stone cottage. "Now go, I'm perfectly capable of entertaining myself."

"I won't be long." Johnnie glanced around the immaculate room that served as a sitting room and kitchen. "The fire will warm you if you take Polwarth's chair."

She stood for a moment after Johnnie left, surveying the functional room that smelled of pipe tobacco and the crackling fire. The furniture was simple, designed for large men; an oak trestle table, four high-backed chairs, a tall, carved cupboard taking up most of one wall. The fireplace was used for cooking, although the copper oven built into one side of it bespoke a woman's touch. It was the best Swedish copper polished to a fine luster, and the distinct smell of bannocks mingled as an undertone to the tobacco and pinewood. As recognition struck her

brain, she began salivating, and she smiled at the fundamental drives of motherhood.

Two well-worn sofas flanked the fireplace, although
their symmetry was broken by Polwarth's upholstered
chair, which faced the fire. The fabrics indicated their
original provenance had probably been Goldiehouse, for
despite their mild dilapidation, the fine damask still
gleamed richly crimson. Taking Johnnie's advice, Elizabeth dropped into Polwarth's chair and warmed herself
before the small blaze, resting in the depths of the soft
chair, rising occasionally to check the progress of the
bannocks in the oven. Not that she had any expertise in
baking, but she could recognize if they were burning.

Luckily, the men returned before she was required
to remove the round loaves from the oven, because she
wasn't certain how to accomplish that feat.

Polwarth slid the crunchy loaves out with a long-
handled heart-shaped spade that he took down from the
rafters the minute he walked into the room. And Johnnie
said, "Mealie bannocks," with distinct delight.

The following week was one of simple pleasure despite
their narrow escape and the harrowing uncertainty of
their future. In Dens Forest they could forget a dangerous world existed outside the protective wood; in their
happiness they could overlook for a time the price on
Johnnie's head. And if he could have put aside all his re-
sponsibilities as Laird, there were moments during the
week at Polwarth's cottage when Johnnie found himself
wishing he and Elizabeth could stay in this secluded hermitage, disregard the fractious outside world, and raise
their child in peace.

In the mornings after a leisurely breakfast, they
would all go hawking. Elizabeth would sit on a worn Turkey rug on the windy knoll while the men took pleasure
in their sport. Johnnie and Polwarth hunted with wild-
caught hawks instead of eyesses, the nestlings. Rarer,
they were the best, well-taught by their parents in the
wild, natural hunters with a desire for prey. The birds

were beautiful to see let loose from their leashes and cast up. They mounted slowly at first in ever-widening circles, then more rapidly, borne higher and higher by their broad wings on the breeze. Some high flyers climbed to an elevation of a quarter mile so they appeared the size of a swallow. Then, poised for that half second, they'd sight their quarry, turn over and, head first, drop in their glorious downward rush.

Elizabeth came to understand Johnnie's pleasure in the thrilling sport on those cool fresh mornings, and she watched with fascination as the falcons responded like pets would to Johnnie and Polwarth.

When they returned to the cottage, she and Johnnie would help feed the small gamebirds Polwarth was raising; the hens were beginning to ready their nests for their spring broods. She observed an aspect of her husband she's not previously seen as Johnnie labored alongside Polwarth, his transformation from polished courtier and chieftain to gamekeeper another facet of a complex man. He repaired the coops with quick, competent hands, hammering the wooden bars in place with a swift efficiency, as familiar with their construction as any keeper. He handled the nesting birds with a casual ease, putting his hand slowly inside the coops with a quiet confidence, touching the edgy hens with sure, gentle fingers. And the relationship between Johnnie and the older man revealed much to her of Johnnie's boyhood, for he deferred to the gamekeeper in all things, not for courtesy's sake but out of deep affection. Polwarth even sat at the head of the table when they ate, serving out the portions as the master of the household would.

Elizabeth acquired some rudimentary culinary skills during their sojourn at Dens Cottage when Polwarth agreed to show her how to mix the ingredients for his bannocks. When she took her first farls— small triangles cut from the rolled circle of dough—from the griddle—her face smudged with flour and soot from the fire, sweat gleaming on her brow from the heat, a smile of triumph gracing her face, she was given a hearty round of applause by the two men. They ate the hot fresh breads with butter and plum preserves, complimenting the novice cook by devouring them all.

And a staggering sense of accomplishment animated Elizabeth, regardless the feat was no more than what thousands of women did every day in Scotland. But she'd never cooked before; she found pleasure even in small things.

They slept in one of two small rooms tucked under the eaves, in a huge four-poster bed wedged between the wall and the window. A built-in cupboard, oddly shaped to fit under the roof, offered modest accommodations for their clothes, while a small fireplace kept the tiny space warm and cozy.

"See those initials," Johnnie said one morning as they lay under the goose-down quilt, pointing at the rafters above the doorway. "I was eight when I carved them. It took me all day to make them deep enough to see in that petrified oak."

"Tell me what you were like at eight," Elizabeth said, wishing to know the boy she'd never seen.

He shrugged slightly, her head moving as it rested on his arm. "I don't know ... asking a lot of questions, I think. I wanted to learn everything Polwarth knew."

"Did Robbie ever come here?"

"Later he did ... but not for as long as I. Mama died when Robbie was four, and we traveled a good deal after that." He didn't say she'd died in childbirth, she and the child both. "Papa was in trading, too, so it wasn't unusual to spend time on the Continent."

"How did your mother die?"

"I'm not sure," he lied, superstitious about tempting the fates and not wishing to alarm Elizabeth as well. "A fever of some kind." He took her hands in his.

"How old were *you* when you lost your mother?" Johnnie asked Elizabeth. As long as he could remember, Godfrey had been unmarried, preferring his mistresses to a second wife.

"I was two. I don't remember her at all. My nanny took her place." She smiled at more pleasant thoughts. "You abducted me from my old nanny's school that day in Harbottle. I thought you were some heavenly host for a moment when you appeared so suddenly in her parlor in those minister's robes."

"And I thought you so tempting, I had to remind myself why I'd come to Harbottle."

"I knew that."

He lifted his head off the pillow a fraction to look down at her. "No, you didn't. You were faint with fear."

"Later I did. . . ." She stuck her tongue out at him. "When you put me on my own horse at Uswayford."

"Astute woman," he murmured, dropping his head back onto the plump pillow.

"I was flattered."

He grinned. "They all are."

She slammed him in the stomach with her fist. Hard.

"Umpf," he grunted, surprised at her strength. And then, with an angelic smile, murmured, "I'm completely reformed now."

"You'd better be."

"That gimlet-eyed look certainly puts the fear of God in me."

"Forget about God," Elizabeth emphatically declared, "for *I'm* your avenging angel should you ever stray from the path of fidelity."

His brows rose and fell swiftly. "I'm convinced. Totally." And then, without mockery, in a different voice of simple sureness, he said, "I've found the absolute love of my life. Why would I be interested in other women?"

Elizabeth threw her arms around him, her heart in her eyes. "Tell me we'll be happy forever."

"Forever" was a relative term at the moment, Johnnie couldn't help thinking, but his hopes were as wistful. "Forever . . . my darling Bitsy," he said, very, very softly, his eyes naked with emotion. "Always and ever . . ."

But there were still search parties out prowling the countryside for the escaped Laird of Ravensby. Later that morning, when the small party from Dens Cottage let their falcons loose on the windswept hillside, Johnnie noticed the birds' flight patterns had altered. They hovered restlessly in the distance, flying in tight circles, not soaring in great sweeping arcs. "Look," he said to Polwarth.

"A large party must be out."

"Bring the birds in," Johnnie tersely said, already moving to call in his falcon. "They might be followed."

Within minutes the birds were back on their gloved perches, their hoods in place, and their descent down the grassy knoll proceeded with as much speed as Elizabeth's clumsiness would allow.

After securing his bird on its perch in the aviary, Johnnie said, "I'm going back up. They saw something disquieting." Dashing into the house, he grabbed his perspective glass from the table and sprinted back outside, running into the forest behind the cottage, crashing through the underbrush, jumping fallen logs rather than taking the time to go around them, rushing up the hill with compelling speed. Putting the glass to his eye, he scanned the countryside hurriedly until his breathing slowed and the glass settled. Then he carefully dissected individual sectors, swinging the polished-brass glass back and forth across the landscape with measured care, stopping when he detected some movement, bringing the object dead in his sights—a minister walking down the road, a single horseman riding over an unplowed field, a deer, two deer ... then sweeping over another portion. He concentrated on the area where the falcons had hovered, going back twice to screen the ground between himself and the sea.

A flash of light caught his eye briefly and disappeared. He swore under his breath, recognizing the glimmer, telling himself some country gentleman had bought himself a new toy ... it didn't mean anything. But he kept his glass on the open ground behind the trees partially screening his view, his spine rigid, controlling his breathing so his perspective glass didn't move.

A dragoon came riding out from behind the planted hedgerow. Johnnie stopped breathing, counting the number of troopers as they emerged from behind the greenery. Three ... five ... eight, nine, ten, fifteen ... eighteen, with the officer in the lead.

He waited a moment more to see if they veered west. The officer raised his hand to stop his troop, and some discussion occurred. Then the leader pointed at

Dens Forest, directly at him, it seemed to Johnnie, who could see his face through the glass. He instantly dropped the instrument from his eye. If the sun flashed off the lens . . .

His return to the cottage was accomplished with record speed.

"A patrol's heading this way," he said, careful to keep the alarm from his voice. "We'll have to leave."

"I'll go with you," Polwarth declared.

Johnnie shook his head. "Stay here. Detain them if you can, should they find the cottage." He was taking his baldric and sword down from the hooks by the door. "Bring up a flagon of claret from the hogshead in the cellar so it's on the table; I've never seen a soldier yet who won't have a drink." He slipped the sword belt over his head. "An hour, even a half hour, will help."

"You can't go east now."

"We'll attempt it in a few days. We'll make for the shepherd's hut up in the hills behind Letholm. It should be remote enough."

Both men knew Letholm was farther yet from the coast, but neither mentioned the added distance.

"I'll put food in the packs," Elizabeth offered, aware of the unspoken communion between the men. Both were clearly reticent to reveal their feelings, unusual after the days of easy informality she'd witnessed.

"Just load one with food," Johnnie said. "We'll have to leave the packhorses behind. The pasture is limited in the hills."

"I could bring up more supplies tomorrow or even tonight," Polwarth offered as he and Johnnie were saddling the horses.

"No, you might be followed. If the patrol comes this way, they could be searching the woods because they know this is Carre land. In which case I'd prefer you don't change your routine and arouse suspicion. We've enough supplies for a few days, then we'll make for the coast."

"I could go for Munro and Adam and bring back a large enough troop to escort you to Margarth Cove."

"I can't risk battle with Elizabeth. How can I protect her in a melee? There's nowhere she'd be safe."

"And she couldn't travel fast enough to outrun the dragoons from Edinburgh."

Johnnie shook his head. "If she hadn't been with me, I would have made straight for the coast. My barb can outrun any horse in Scotland. But Elizabeth can't ride at a forced pace. The dragoons would have overtaken us by Coldstream. But we'll reach the ship," he said. "The journey will just be in stages."

They reached the shepherd's hut in the foothills of the Cheviots late that afternoon, the snow at the higher altitude making the horses' footing treacherous. And after Johnnie had helped Elizabeth inside the rough stone structure built into the hill, he started a fire. They were both chilled; the temperature had dropped as the trail climbed, the wind frigid and blustery, tossing the light snow on the ground into swirling clouds.

He led the horses in out of the wind also, securing them against the wall away from the hearth. They couldn't afford to lose their mounts to the bitter wind. And while Elizabeth tried to stop shivering, slowly turning before the fire, Johnnie unloaded their few supplies.

"We won't be here long," he said, placing their food pack on a rough table. "A day or two at the most. You may have the chair," he added with a courtly drawl, pulling a small three-legged stool from under the table and bringing it over to the fire.

"How far *is* it to Margarth Cove?" Elizabeth asked, sitting down, thanking him with a smile for his gallantry.

"Probably twenty miles from here," he said, dissembling slightly in the interests of optimism.

"Would it be better to travel at night?"

He nodded, squatting down beside her, warming his hands at the fire. "There's less risk." He stared into the flames for a moment. "If we do meet troops, though, they'll be more suspicious of travelers out so late."

"We could cover twenty miles in five hours even at my snail's pace."

It wasn't twenty but more like twenty-five, Johnnie knew, with the first several miles in the hills desperately slow going. "It's possible," he lied. Then he stood abruptly, his frustration level acute; familiar with a life of reckless incaution, he was restless under the necessary restraints dictated by Elizabeth's pregnancy. "I'm going to find some more wood for the night," he suddenly said. "If you get hungry before I return, there's a meat pie right on top," he added, pushing the table closer to the hearth.

"I feel like a damnable burden." Her sigh curled frosty white in the frigid air. "I'm discovering how useless I am outside a fully staffed household."

"Good God, I don't expect you to know how to chop wood. What woman would?" Reaching over, he tousled her hair so she looked up at him and saw his affectionate smile. "You can, however, say a prayer to whatever deity is in charge of fires that the last occupant left a supply of wood. Otherwise, I'm going to have to go back to that copse a mile down and bring back a few trees."

"In that case," Elizabeth said, attempting to return his smile when she was cold, tired, and hungry, "I shall surely pray for you. It's too cold to be out tonight. Why not burn the table?"

"A resourceful woman," Johnnie said with a chuckle. "But it won't last the night."

And as Elizabeth huddled before the fire, a stream of curses reported Johnnie's irregular progress outside in the dark, followed a short time later by a yelp of pain—more curses, and then a howl that seemed to signify gratification. He returned five minutes later, carrying an armload of neatly split oak. "I think our fortunes are on the upturn," he said with a grin, shaking the snow from his hair and shoulders. "There's enough wood stacked in a hole dug out of the hill to keep us warm."

His good spirits amazed her; he had certain cause for bitterness with a price on his head, his title and estates confiscated, his very life at risk. But his optimism cheered her in the drafty, dirt-floored hut when she was cold, wretched, and plagued with doubts about their chances of reaching the coast. "How do you do it?" she asked.

"Actually, I fell into the hole."

"No, I mean stay so cheerful."

"Look, I found the wood, which means I don't have to walk a mile on this god-awful, miserable night, chop down some green wood, drag it back uphill a mile, and then try to get it to burn." He shook his head again so the melted snow scattered in a flurry of drops. "I'd say that's a damn good reason to smile. And if I could get you to toast some bannocks while I bring in enough wood to last the night, I'll dazzle you with my good cheer."

"Maybe I could warm that cooked grouse on the spit and put some of those ham slices on that grate." His cheer seemed to be infectious.

"I knew there were other reasons to love you madly beside—well ..." His smile flashed white in the shadowed interior. "The obvious ones—your skill at needlework, your mastery of the tea table—"

"My sexual abandon?" she reminded him with a theatrical batting of her lashes.

His smile widened. "I was getting to that."

He could make her forget the cold and her hunger, the oppressive danger; he could make her smile sitting on a rough stool with her back cold as ice and her face burning from the fire. "I love you," she whispered, taking strength from his confidence, hope from his determination.

"We'll reach the ship," he quietly said, placing the wood on the floor and going to her, understanding the extremity of her despair.

"I know," she murmured, when she didn't, when she wondered how they could possibly cross twenty miles of patrolled land undetected.

Sitting on the cold earthen floor, he pulled her into his arms and held her on his lap, warming her with the heat from his body, with his love, rocking her gently as one would a child. "Tomorrow night we'll go east. Most of the route is through property of my friends and neighbors. We'll be fine. Robbie should be at the cove by now. And you've never seen Holland."

He kissed her gently when she smiled. "It's warmer there," he murmured with a faint smile. "You'll like that."

"Tell me about it," Elizabeth said, wanting the images and words and dreams. Wanting to forget the cold and her fear. "Tell me of your house there."

And he spoke then with uncustomary detail and at great length because he understood her need for hope. He told her of his home outside The Hague, set out in the country a short distance from the city, painted pale yellow with an enormous garden surrounding it. "The gardeners planted another five thousand tulips last fall," he said, "and they'll be blooming next month when we're there." He hugged her closer and told her they'd find a midwife she liked in Amsterdam or Rotterdam or The Hague. The ones in France weren't as fastidious as those in Holland, a country where housewives even washed their steps and sidewalks every day. He volunteered to live in any of his homes she preferred, although he admitted that the one in Rotterdam was more hectic, with the warehouses attached.

"We'll reach safety," he repeated at last.

"I wish I weren't a hindrance ... slowing you down."

He went still suddenly and took her face gently between his great large hands, so his eyes held hers, and he said so softly his voice didn't carry beyond the circle of their warmth, "Never say that. Don't even think it." He'd been reared to assume responsibility, to fulfill his duties, to rise to difficult challenges, and now he had two lives in his care that meant more to him than all his worldly possessions. His deep voice was only a whisper now. "We'll see the coast tomorrow night."

Her eyes filled with tears. "And our child will be born in Holland."

He nodded. "My word as Ravensby."

Well fed from the supplies they carried, they slept on a bed of dried ferns covered with a plaid, the stone walls heated from the fire holding warmth, the quiet sounds of the horses munching their grain a peaceful presence on the cold winter night. The solitude brought with it a tranquillity that eased Elizabeth's anxieties; Johnnie's powerful body warm against her back offered security. She slept as though they weren't being hunted, weren't on the run.

They brought the horses outside in the morning, for the sun had come out, and patches of snow were beginning to melt, leaving grass exposed. And later they replenished the woodpile, Elizabeth helping, and feeling more optimistic in the bright sunshine. How long could a twenty-mile ride take? she more cheerfully considered. Surely, two people in the dark of night could elude a few patrols. She doubted soldiers would be conscientiously out all night anyway. And Johnnie had said they'd be traveling through private lands.

As her thoughts turned inward, she didn't properly attend to the difficult terrain, and she slipped, her feet suddenly going out from under her on an icy patch. With an abrupt cry of alarm, she dropped heavily on her back, the wood in her arms tumbling on top of her.

Johnnie was at her side in an instant, tossing the wood aside, kneeling beside her in the snow, checking for broken bones. And when he'd assured himself nothing was broken, he picked her up and carried her back inside the shepherd's hut. Laying her down on the fern bed, he tucked the plaid around her.

"You're not to help anymore," he firmly said. "That's an order."

"Yes, sir," she faintly said, her breath knocked out of her when she fell. And with the troubled look in his eyes, she didn't dare tell him cramping spasms had begun drifting up her stomach. Just a consequence of the abrupt jolt to her body, she told herself, rationalizing away the seriousness.

But the spasms continued, and in another hour she couldn't conceal her suffering as stabbing pains accompanied the seizures. Struck by another convulsion, she winced, worry creasing her brow. And a short time later, when Johnnie returned with a drink for her from the stream outside, she nervously whispered, "I think I'm in labor."

His skin went pale beneath his dark tan. "It's too early. . . ." A baby could never live at seven months, he thought, terror-stricken.

"Maybe the pains will stop." They must, she silently prayed, knowing she'd lose her child if they didn't.

Johnnie only nodded, unable to speak. No matter his strength or will, he was powerless to relieve her. He couldn't even go for help; Elizabeth couldn't be left alone in this crisis.

"See if I'm bleeding . . . I'm not sure."

No, he wanted to reply, because if she was bleeding . . . there was no hope the child would live. But he couldn't refuse, even if he wished to ignore reality, so he slowly lifted the green plaid, gently eased the fine saffron wool of her skirt aside, and looked, his heart thudding in his chest. The irregular light from the fire poorly illuminated the hut. "I don't think so," he said, straining to distinguish detail in the half-shadows, feeling inadequate to the task.

"Take my handkerchief." Elizabeth said, pulling the white linen from her throat. "If there's no blood . . ." Wistful hope infused her voice.

He took the crisp fabric, placed it between her legs, and held it there for a moment. Lifting it free, his breath in abeyance, he looked swiftly as if he wished the bad news over. Then he looked again. And then he smiled, holding the white square of Holland cloth so Elizabeth could see it. "Nothing," he said, a small triumph in his voice.

"At least not yet," she said with an immediate relief, but the strength of her cramps hadn't diminished.

"Now lie perfectly still; I'll fetch and carry for you," Johnnie said. "Order me about," he added with a grin, "if it will make amends for the state I've put you in"—trying to distract her with humor, trying to distract himself, too, he realized, from the impossibility of dealing with this life-threatening condition.

"You *are* to blame . . . coming up to my room that

night at Goldiehouse," Elizabeth replied with a small, reminiscing smile.

"And not letting you say no."

"I never can with you."

His smile wasn't the familiar roguish one, but a rueful faint quirk of his mouth. He'd never thought in the glory of their passion of this possible extinction of life, of her pain. He kneeled beside her, his hands on his thighs, his broad shoulders slumped, feeling wretched, his eyes filled with pity. "I promise you celibacy from this moment on," he quietly said, "to guard you from this again. . . ."

"Don't make me cry, Johnnie," she whispered, touching his cheek with her fingers. "I've no regrets of loving you."

Taking her hand, he held her fingers to his lips, his grip tender, his breath warm in the coolness of the hut. He kissed each finger, a butterfly caress. "It's my fault. This is all because of my selfishness," he murmured, tormented by the pain he'd caused, by the horrendous consequences of that casual seduction so many months ago.

"I wanted this baby, Johnnie, ever so much. You gave me what I wanted. You made me happy, Johnnie."

He shivered, this powerful man who ruled men's lives. Then, placing her hand under the warm plaid, tucking the wool material around her neck, he said, disquieted, restless under conflicting emotions, "I'll be back in a minute. I have to finish carrying in the wood so you won't get cold."

He walked a few feet beyond the small door that required care to navigate for a man his size, past the shadow of the hut, feeling the hypocrite because he'd always been indifferent to the gods of other men, to the need for intercession in his life. Clenching his fists at his sides, he lifted his head, his powerful body etched against the endless blue sky. "You don't know me," he whispered, "but please listen." He stood motionless for a moment more, handicapped by the previous impiety of his life, grappling with the means of communication. Then he slowly dropped to his knees on the snowy ground and bowed his dark head under the sun-

drenched heavens and, clasping his capable strong hands
together, prayed for the lives of his wife and unborn
child.

He beseeched in a swift, wrenching entreaty,
pressed for time with Elizabeth expecting his return. He
pleaded with a directness natural to him, promising
atonement, promising concessions, offering all he had for
their safety. Then he came to his feet with swift grace
and brushed the snow from his knees. And wiped the
wetness from his eyes.

When he returned to the hut with the wood, he
stoked the fire high so the small room lost its chill, and
he sat beside Elizabeth, entertaining her with stories of
his escapades with his cousins at Ravensby, safe adolescent stories without the knotted entanglements of maturity. He poured them both some claret and unearthed a
tin of Mrs. Reid's plum cake for a snack when Elizabeth
complained of hunger, taking it for a good sign that she
still had her healthy appetite. She ate one piece and then
two and then a half more as he found himself counting
bites, cheered at the mounting numbers. After refilling
her wine cup and seeing that the crumbs from the cake
were brushed away from under her chin, he continued
his innocuous tales. His voice was no more than a deep,
low intonation in the silence of the mountain hut, a dis-
traction to possible catastrophe, perhaps—at some primitive level—a means of keeping evil at bay.

When she dozed off, he kept talking, the resonance
of his voice filling the dim interior of the hut. He didn't
move for a lengthy time as he continued his soliloquy, superstitious like some pagan from long ago that the spell
would be broken, not wishing to disturb the tranquillity
of his wife's sleep. But when Elizabeth sighed in a great
relaxing exhalation that soothed the crease between her
light brows and brought a faint smile to her face, he
gently placed a hand on her belly mounded beneath the
green pattern of his plaid and waited to feel the contrac-
tions that she'd had him monitor a short time before.

And he waited, every muscle poised, tense, a man
of logic, too, as well as pagan sensibilities. He counted to
fifty, slowly, a reasonable man attuned to empirical evi-

dence, then to fifty again, not daring yet to give way to elation. And then to a fresh one hundred because his wife and child were too important, too essential to his life, to allow credulous hope.

But at the last uttered number computed under his breath, when no movement had occurred under the light pressure of his palm, not a ripple or shiver or the tiniest quake, he lifted his hand, covered his mouth with it and, falling back on the packed earthen floor, let out a mute whoop of jubilation.

He looked very young at that moment in the rough shepherd's hut despite his mighty body, despite his reputation as a warrior and rogue, despite his titles and honors and acclaim. He was only twenty-five, and the woman he loved in all his mercurial moods, who had brought him love when he'd not thought it possible, his dear and precious wife, was safe.

He blew her a kiss, restless in his jubilation, and came standing in a smooth uncoiling of muscled strength. "Thank you," he whispered heavenward, his sense of obligation profound. She looked so peaceful now on her rough bed, he almost wondered if it'd been some evil dream. Until his gaze fell on the crumpled linen handkerchief, and his stomach tightened. He *had* to bring her safe to the coast; his thoughts raced ahead, planning their flight, assessing all the possibilities when their travel required even more restraint. Elizabeth couldn't be jarred or jostled or forced to ride too long. Where to stop, what tracks best met their needs, how close must he stay to villages should they need a midwife?

She was too fragile and he too uninformed to tolerate this isolation again. He would have been helpless if the baby had come early . . . helpless to save Elizabeth or the child in case of complications. He wouldn't allow that danger again.

They didn't leave that night as planned, although when Elizabeth woke, she insisted she was well again.

"Wait one more day," Johnnie suggested. "We've

still food. Give yourself a chance to recuperate from your fall. Whether we leave tonight or tomorrow won't matter to Robbie."

"Once we start," Elizabeth said, her voice level, her glance steady, "don't stop. No matter how I feel, I can survive four or five hours. Mrs. Reid tells me first babies are slow in coming. She said sometimes it takes one or two days."

Johnnie blanched noticeably even in the flickering firelight. "Two days?" he said in a choked voice. "Good God."

"Promise me, Johnnie. I won't be the cause of our capture. I've done enough to ruin your life."

"You didn't ruin my life. When one opposes England's Privy Council in such a public way, one understands the risks. The possibility of retaliation was always there."

"But the rape charges are related to me, to my father's partisanship with Queensberry. I feel responsible."

"If you're going to discuss responsibility, darling," he gallantly noted, "my seduction began it all. You didn't stand a chance."

Elizabeth sighed. "You're too damned honorable."

He grinned. "Never with seduction. But I shall drive us unmercifully tomorrow night if it pleases you," he went on, capitulating, not wishing to argue uselessly over an issue upon which he had his own strong feelings. "You win."

But he was too cordial to believe entirely, and Elizabeth wished in a small part of her brain, as she had on occasion lately, that she wasn't pregnant at this inopportune time.

CHAPTER 21

They left the small hut in the foothills of the Cheviots when the slim crescent moon had risen midpoint in the winter sky. The descent down the snow-covered slopes was treacherous, a thin glaze of ice from the day's hot sun left on the surface of the snow. When Johnnie's barb went down on its knees on loose stones and ice, it only managed to scramble upright because Johnnie had instantly leaped from the saddle. After that, Johnnie slowly led both horses down the rough track, not wishing to risk a like tumble with Elizabeth's mount.

Once they reached flat country, despite Elizabeth's urgings, Johnnie kept the horses to a walk. They passed Eccles on the outskirts of the village, only two dogs giving warning of their presence, and Johnnie cut cross-country shortly after, moving in the direction of Blackadder, his cousins' property. The bulk of the darkened manse rose on the crest of a rise as they traveled on the fringes of the parkland an hour later, reminding Johnnie of carefree times long gone. Hunted by his enemies now with torture and death the outcome were he captured, the land and old house took on a poignant tranquillity.

Godfrey had done this to him, and Godolphin's puppet, Queensberry, who never had enough money to sate his greed. A burning need for reprisal, for vengeance, burned inside his brain. Once he had Elizabeth safe in Holland, he could unsheath his sword and retaliate against his enemies. He'd never run from a confrontation before, and were it not for Elizabeth and the child, he'd be riding now to kill Godfrey wherever he was.

He glanced up at the moon, ever conscious of the passage of time; the trip down the foothills had caused delay, as he knew it would. He wasn't sure they could reach the cove before daylight.

"What time do you think it is?" Elizabeth asked, aware of his concern.

"Close to midnight. Do you need to stop?"

Elizabeth shook her head.

Leaning over, he touched her hand. "It's a cold night. Everyone's inside."

"Including the patrols, I hope," she said.

"I'd say yes, regardless of your father or Queensberry's orders. The common soldier knows they're both lying in a warm bed tonight."

"A pleasant thought ... a warm bed," Elizabeth said with a smile.

As they made for the coast that night, neither was aware of the critical events transpiring in the days of their flight, events that might impact on their plans for escape.

Westminster had finally passed the Alien Act, and as part of its immediate implementation, British cruisers were now patrolling the coast "to seize all Scottish ships trading with Her Majesty's enemies." In addition, in an incident altogether separate but incendiary in the present climate of hostility, the British East India Company had seized and confiscated a Scottish ship in the Thames, citing breach of its privileges in its hiring of English seamen in an English harbor. Outraged, Scotland had

instantly retaliated by capturing the *Worcester*, in harbor
at Leith, a ship reportedly belonging to the East India
Company. The captain and crew had been swiftly
charged with piracy, robbery, and murder, all charges
punishable by hanging. The British seamen were currently standing trial in Edinburgh. Angry mobs were out
in the streets north and south of the border.

Animosities were high in both England and Scotland. A raging storm of retaliation was brewing . . . a retaliation that would be hazardous to their escape.

They reached Margarth Cove at last, coming to the
grassy verge of the harsh rocky shore when the moon
had begun to fade. Gazing out over the small secluded
cove where Robbie's ship should have been anchored,
they saw only the grey winter sea.

No ship rested there. Only white-capped waves, a
few hardy birds. And emptiness.

Johnnie swore, a long, low steady stream of invective. Elizabeth burst into tears, hating herself even as she
sobbed for being so susceptible to her emotions. The
hours of the past night had been excruciatingly tense,
each sluggish mile passed in a nightmare of apprehension, fear in every sudden sound. And now that they'd
reached their destination, now when they should have
been safe, their vision of freedom evaporated before
them.

Nudging his barb closer to Elizabeth's mount,
Johnnie reached over and wiped her tears away with the
back of his gloved hand, the leather warm from the heat
of his body. "The British patrols must be out. We'll just
wait. Don't cry, darling. Robbie will come."

"What if they've captured him?"

He stared out to sea for a moment, then shook his
head. "They'll come for him later . . . after I've been
found guilty. As he's my present heir, they'll want him,
too, but"—he paused, understanding how laws were often despotically managed—"even if I was convicted *in*

absentia, Robbie would have had sufficient warning from Munro."

"Oh, God," she whispered at the word "conviction." It meant a hunted death, anywhere in the world. Fresh tears slid down her cheeks. "I'm sorry," she apologized, knowing strength and resolution would be more useful to Johnnie now, not a sobbing woman. "All I do is cry . . . I never used to cry. . . . Really," she added in a hiccupy holding back of her tears.

"Lord, sweetheart, you've reason enough," he said, putting a hand on her shoulder. "*I* felt like crying when that damn ship wasn't there. But, look," he went on in a reasonable tone that belied none of his intense frustration, "there's an inn south of Saint Abbs—it's off the main road, local and secluded. It's only another few miles." His voice softened. "Are you tired of riding? Should I carry you?"

She shook her head and smiled at him, licking away a tear that had slid into the corner of her mouth. "Do they have good food?"

He laughed, her appetite a constant now. "Better than yours or my cooking."

"An enormous incentive then," she said with an experimental smile she wasn't sure she could maintain. Sitting up a little straighter, adjusting her reins in her fingers, she said, "Lead on."

Within the hour, before daylight had fully replaced the dawn, Elizabeth was ensconced in a soft feather bed in Traquir's best bedchamber, contemplating her third boiled egg and crumpet with more pleasure than she should feel, considering their danger. Johnnie sat by the window, still dressed, his gaze on the sea beyond the low hedges, a pewter tankard of ale in his hand, the remains of his breakfast on the table beside him. He'd seen two British cruisers patrolling the coast in the past hour, indication of a near blockade. And on their arrival the landlord had heatedly related the recent news of the Alien Act, the capture of the *Annandale,* and the repercussions of both.

"The lobsterbacks are out in force, damn their hides. Came up from Harbottle last week. And they don't always pay, bloody sods. As if we haven't been bled dry already by the damned English."

"Is anyone asking questions?" Johnnie had inquired as they'd waited in the small entrance hall while the maid had readied their room.

"Seems they're looking for a Lord and his Lady, dark like you," the heavyset tavern owner had answered, gazing at Johnnie with a smile. "And the lady has white hair, they say." His bright blue eyes twinkled as he'd looked at Elizabeth seated on a wooden bench against the wall. "Now even if we saw fine folks of that description," the landlord had gone on with a mischievous grin, "dinna seem to me that a Scotsman would tell a bloody lobsterback."

Johnnie smiled, relaxing for the first time in many hours. "If our horses could be stabled away from the inn," he had said with a mild insinuation. Standing caped and booted, he was a large, overpowering image, all in black from the top of his sleek head to his finely made boots. "They'd prefer the quiet. . . ."

"Old George Foulis has space." The innkeeper nodded in the direction of a farmyard across the road. "Out o' the way, 'tis. Secluded."

"How convenient," Johnnie had said, placing a well-filled leather purse on the table in the center of the hall.

And now with Elizabeth comfortable and their horses out of sight, he pondered the serious logistics of getting a message to Robbie, or finding him, or perhaps . . . hiring a vessel to sail them to Holland. While it was possible to linger briefly at Abbs Inn, the longer they stayed, the more visible their presence. And while the innkeeper was a loyal Scots, some of his employees might be poor enough to be tempted by English guineas. When he'd seen so many in Scotland's Parliament selling their votes for modest sums, he had no illusions about an impoverished chambermaid or ostler.

But he kept his reservations to himself because Elizabeth needed a modicum of tranquillity after their days on the run, and he couldn't venture out again until dark anyway. Sighing softly, he slid down lower in the wooden armchair, rested his tankard on his chest, and shut his eyes.

"Are you coming to bed?" Elizabeth asked, her green-eyed gaze traveling down Johnnie's sprawled form, wishing she could offer some comfort. He looked exhausted.

"In a minute," he replied, swiveling his head to send her a smile. "Do you think you'll be able to sleep?" he teased.

"For a week." Every muscle in her body ached.

Tipping the tankard up a moment later, he drained the remains of the ale and, setting the vessel down on the table, he hauled himself to his feet and stretched, his arms flexed high above his head. Then, relaxing again, he moved around the room, checking the lock on the door and windows, placing his pistols on the chair beside the bed, unhooking his dirk from his belt and hanging it on the bedpost above his head.

"None of that inspires restful slumber," Elizabeth said with a faint smile as Johnnie sat on the bed and began pulling off one boot.

He arched a brow at her over his shoulder. "I find loaded flintlocks damned soothing." His boot hit the floor, followed shortly by another, and seconds later he dropped back onto the pillow in a weary sprawl.

"You're not even taking your jack off?"

He grinned. "Not today. In Holland ask me again."

"Where do you think Robbie might be?"

He lifted his brows into perfect dark half-moons and then let them languidly fall over blue eyes that held a reflective speculation. "Staying out of the way of the damn British fleet, from the looks of it. I've never seen such a tight cordon; two ships in less than an hour. They're practically sailing up each other's backsides. Robbie will have to come in at night, or we'll meet him off shore. Which means we have to settle on a rendezvous time and place."

"How?" It seemed impossible with the vast ocean outside and no idea of Robbie's whereabouts.

Johnnie shut his eyes, the pillow soft under his head, the bed blessed comfort. "I'll have to get word to him; I'll go to Berwick tonight." He was half-asleep already, his breathing slowing, his voice faint. "Wake me up . . . if you need anything. . . ."

He fell asleep as he often did, instantly, with utter release. And she was reminded of other beds and other days, happier times when he'd slept exactly that way, as though he didn't have a care in the world. And oddly, she felt less fearful now that they'd arrived at the coast, the sparkling sea outside the windows their means to freedom, the worst of their journey behind them. She felt a curious well-being in this sunny room, the warmth of the sun second only in comfort to the coal fire in the grate. And she gazed at the man she loved with a mysterious blind necessity and thought him even more beautiful in sleep, the perfection of his features in repose classic, patrician, like those knightly effigies detailed to the minutiae of their armament, peacefully asleep on their marble sarcophagi in the cathedrals.

His long hair lay in dark, silken disarray, on his shoulders, framing his face in soft waves, one black lock drifting across his forehead, his heavy brows perfect counterpoint to his deep-set eyes, their lashes thick and long like a child's. His nose was fine-boned and straight with perfect chiseled nostrils, while his mouth vividly reminded her why he was irresistible to women. He had a sensual mouth, his upper lip fluid, graceful curves offset by a full passionate bottom lip with almost a hint of lushness in its curvature. His beautiful mouth was framed by the shadow of a beard, the dark stubble drifting down his strong jaw, evidence of their rough accommodations the days past.

He slept with a curious dignity, his arms at his sides, his long legs almost closed although his tartan knit stockings in shades of yellow and black defied stately grandeur. But the word "grandeur" consummately defined the awesome strength of his hard, honed body. Dressed in the primitive severity of black leather jack and breeches, he took on an indomitable power.

Leaning over, she kissed him lightly on the cheek, and he moved in his sleep, drawing her close, settling her head on his shoulder. A reflex action, she thought, for a man popular with women.

"It's me," she said, a quiet but inescapable independence in her words.

"I know. . . ." he drowsily murmured, giving her shoulder a pat. "You feel good. . . ."

They woke much later to a pounding on the door, and Johnnie was instantly on his feet, both his pistols pointed at the threshold. "Yes?" A quick glance out the window to gauge the time.

"Ye wanted me to tell ye when it was five o'clock."

A great whooshing exhaled breath signaled Johnnie's recognition of the proprietor's voice. "Thank you," he called out. "We'd like supper in half an hour." Swiveling his head toward Elizabeth, he lifted his brows in query.

She nodded, making washing motions with her hands.

"There's water over there," he murmured, tipping his head toward the west wall.

"A bath," she whispered, putting her palms together in entreaty.

"We'll need bathwater too," Johnnie shouted.

And when the proprietor replied, "Yes, my Lord," followed by the sound of receding footsteps, Johnnie set his pistols back on the chair and collapsed on the bed.

"Feel my heart. The man woke me from a dream. Lord," he softly exclaimed, throwing his arms above his head, "that was stimulating."

Placing her hand over the leather above his heart, she felt the frenzied thudding like a soft echo in her palm. "We need a watchdog," she said, smiling down at him.

"We need a bloody ship."

"Maybe you'll discover Robbie's whereabouts tonight."

"I'd better."

"Is it possible . . . he's been captured?" The words half stuck in her throat.

He stared at her for a moment. "I don't know," he said with a small sigh. "The troops and ships are out in force. The timing could have been better on the passage of the Alien Act."

"Could we stay here until you find him?" There was a curious restfulness to the small inn.

"We can't stay anywhere long. Everyone realizes we're not travelers simply passing through when we're five miles off the main road."

"Would Berwick be better? It's larger—we'd be less conspicuous."

His dark head moved in a negative motion. "Too English down there," he muttered. "I'll know more by morning."

Her brows drew together. "I hate having to wait . . . not knowing where you are, what you're doing. . . ."

"I can't take you to Berwick." A quiet authority touched his words.

"I know, I know. . . ." She sighed. "I can't ride, I can't run, I can barely move, I can't help you. It's so damned inconvenient, so aggravating."

"Hush, hush now," he soothed, reaching up to touch her cheek with a gentle hand. "Just a few more days now, darling," he whispered.

"Really?" Her voice held a hopeful poignancy.

They had no choice, he knew. They couldn't afford to wait with the number of troops in the vicinity. "Really," he said.

The bath water and tubs were brought up first. Placed before the fire, the tubs were filled with steaming hot water carried into the room in tall covered copper pails. Sinking gratefully into the heated water after the maids had left, Elizabeth eased her body down. Leaning back against the dented headrest, she exhaled a satisfied sigh. "This is very close to heaven, or at least my current view of heaven after days on the road. Wake me," she said, shutting her eyes, "when the water begins to cool."

"Stay as long as you want," Johnnie replied, stripping of his clothes. "They're going to leave more hot water outside the door. I'll bring it in when you need it."

And while Elizabeth half-dozed in the blissful luxury of a bath after their rough days in the hills, Johnnie stepped into his bath. Rested, energetic, his plans to contact Robbie that evening animating him, he immediately submerged himself, coming up with water streaming down his face, and then briskly scrubbed and washed. Although the copper tubs were large, they weren't comfortable enough for a man his size to lounge in, so a short time later he climbed out, dripped across the floor to the door, and brought in the extra pails.

Using one to rinse, he poured the water over his head as he stood in the tub, the streams sluicing down his lean rangy body. After rubbing himself dry with a large linen towel, he sank into a nearby chair. Generally optimistic about Robbie's imminent appearance, he was determined to find a way tonight to send a message to him. Stretching out his long legs, he relaxed into a comfortable sprawl, his gaze dwelling on his wife's alluring image. With her head tilted back against the headrest, the graceful curve of her throat drew his eye; pale, elegant; it swept into the dip of her collar bones, a small pool of water in the hollow above one. And just breaking the surface of the water were the shiny mounds of her breasts, the sleek tops gleaming white in the darkening room, her gentle breathing sending small ripples over the surface of the water, stirring the floating tendrils of her blonde hair.

He felt oddly at peace, considering troops were scouring the countryside for them and their departure had been delayed. It was enough to be with her, he thought, as if the world outside didn't exist.

He rose to light the candles after a time, when the failing twilight shrouded the room in shadow; their supper arrived as he was going about the small domestic task. Wrapping a towel around his waist, he answered the door, taking the trays from the serving girls, not wishing them to enter the room and disturb Elizabeth. Oblivious to their appreciative glances as well as their flirtatious giggles, he retraced his circuit three times, thanked them in a detached way, and pushed the door shut.

The tittering laughter had brought Elizabeth from her drowsy repose. "You have admirers everywhere," she mildly said after they'd gone, her gaze drifting over his tall, muscled body. The draped towel left little to the imagination.

"I didn't notice; only one admirer interests me," Johnnie said with a lazy smile, "and she's the soaking wet nymph in my bedchamber. Do you want to bathe now before you eat or eat before you bathe?" he asked, still holding the last tray. "Or both?"

"Both, I think, because the water is still luscious and as usual I'm hungry."

"You'd conform well to a harem, then. The eastern houris amuse themselves primarily with eating and bathing. Which languid activities develop the plumpness relished by their masters."

"And how exactly do you know that?" Her words held a wifely tone of censure.

His expression was inscrutable. "One gleans these tidbits of culture in the Levant trade."

"I hope you also gleaned an appreciation for plump females since I can no longer see my toes."

"I definitely have," he courteously said. "The plumper the better. So tell me now, do you want dessert first?"

After five months of marriage, he knew she did and was already pulling the table near her tub.

He fed her as one would a baby, so she didn't have to move her arms from under the warm water. They ate gooseberry pie with cream first, then nibbled on an excellent fresh butter cheese. During a short rest between courses Johnnie poured in an extra bucket of hot water to maintain the temperature of Elizabeth's bath and padded over to the hearth to build up the fire.

He'd discarded the towel he'd put on for the maids. Elizabeth's glance followed him as he went about his tasks, his dark hair still damp on his shoulders, the power of his biceps and pectorals fluid beauty as he lifted and poured the heavy pail of water into her bath. Unconstrained in his nudity, he moved with a natural grace—broad-shouldered, fine-honed, athletic.

As he crouched in front of the fire to add more coal to the grate, the muscle and sinew of his back and buttocks rippled as he moved, and his testicles swung when his weight shifted from one foot to the other, their undulating outline limned by the glow of the fire.

"I need a kiss," Elizabeth murmured, the splendid sight of him stirring her senses, enticing her, his conspicuous virility irresistible.

He glanced at her over his shoulder and smiled. "I'm almost finished." After shoveling in two more measures of coal, he rose and walked over to her. Placing his hands on both sides of the tub he leaned over to kiss her.

And stopped midway in his descent when her wet palm cupped him and her fingers gently squeezed. "Let's not start that," he softly said a moment later after he'd fought back the leaping flame of response. "It's only been a few days since your fall." Easing her fingers loose, he stepped back beyond her reach.

"I feel perfectly fine. I feel *extremely* fine. You look—wonderful," she added in an appreciative murmur, her eyes on his rising erection.

He was helpless against his body's instant response but resolute in his decision, the memory of Elizabeth's crisis in the shepherd's hut still too fresh.

"Bathe me," she whispered.

"Only if you behave." His voice was rough, hoarse with a self-imposed discipline.

"I'll try." But she had the look of a breathless young siren.

His stern glance impaled her.

"I'll really try," she promised.

He exhaled, discomfited, his spirit at odds with his body. "As you can see," he softly said, "I'm more than willing to—"

"Come in here with me. . . ."

"Or come in you anywhere," he said, emitting another frustrated sigh. "But I'm worried about the child. . . ."

"I don't feel sick though, I feel rested and warm and amorous and you look—" Her eyes rested on his arousal and he saw the familiar tempting eagerness.

"No," he said with soft emphasis. "I won't."

His refusal was flat, unequivocal. "I understand," she said to the forbidding words. "I'll be good."

After rummaging through his pack to find the bar of soap Mrs. Reid had sent along, he began with her hair, working up a lustrous lather so the fragrance of clover filled the room. He kept his distance though, maintaining a kind of detachment, not leaning in too close, not making intimate eye contact. And after he'd scooped out the suds from her tub and rinsed her hair with fresh water, he said, "There," with the inflection of a man who'd wrestled a bear to the ground.

"It feels wonderful to have clean hair again," Elizabeth said with satisfaction, raising her arms to run her fingers over her damp tresses. Her gesture lifted her breasts partially out of the water so they floated like luscious half-moons, the nipples peeking out, water running in trickles over their slippery whiteness.

"You can't do that," Johnnie said on a suffocated breath.

"Do what?"

He saw the sly, secret enticement in her eyes and it took enormous self-restraint to resist in the warm heated room with their journey almost over, with the wife he adored posing for him like a courtesan. "You better wash yourself," he gruffly said, holding out the soap.

Her arms drifted downward and sank under the water. "I'm too tired. . . ."

"This is going to be very fast then," he muttered, moving toward her with a glowering look. And he soaped her breasts while silently reciting the constellations in the southern sky in alphabetical order, but even then his erection grew. It didn't help that Elizabeth's nipples hardened as if by magic the second he touched them or that she felt so soft and inviting when he washed her bottom.

He abruptly pulled her to her feet after that, bringing her bath to an end. His control fast eroding, he quickly and with a deliberate neutrality rinsed her off. Wordlessly he lifted her from the tub, placed a towel around her shoulders, and stalked away.

Unfamiliar with abstinence in the presence of his nude, amorously disposed wife, pressed to almost unbearable limits, Johnnie stood at the far side of the small room, gazing out into the night, his hands clenched at his sides.

He heard her come up behind him a few moments later but he wasn't in command yet of his body and he didn't stir.

When she touched him lightly on his hip, he shuddered faintly, steeling himself against the hunger twisting in the pit of his stomach, forcing his attention instead on the darkness outside.

"Could we make an exchange?" she inquired softly.

"If it's as tempestuous and charged as the one that brought us together," he said, his voice grating and sharp, "no."

"It's easier."

"Nothing's very easy right now," he brusquely replied. He'd never kept himself from a woman before. But he wouldn't make love to her and risk harming the baby, no matter what she said.

"You don't have to make love to me."

He digested the words, warily assessing them if he were circling a trap, then slowly turned around. "I'm listening," he said with caution.

"I could do something with this," she said, touching the swollen crest of his rigid arousal, the veins on the velvety skin visibly pulsing.

"So could I," he said, removing her hand.

"*I'd* like to, though."

"As you can tell, I'm resisting. I worry about you."

"When I fell up in the hills, that was different, Johnnie. I fell really hard and the wood tumbled on top of me and . . ." Her words came to a whispery end. She took a deep breath to steady her trembling body. "That was different than this. I'm burning for you, I need you to touch me."

He hesitated; he had the strength to resist. Within him was a hard, nerveless core. But he wished to please her too. "It's not that I don't want to. You understand that, don't you?"

She nodded, a small barely perceptible movement.

He expelled a deep tormented sigh. "Maybe I could . . . help you some other way," he softly suggested.

Her smile reminded him of the artless woman he'd made love to that first night at Goldiehouse—unsure but ardent.

"I'd be very grateful." Her whisper held the temptation of the ages in its innocence.

"I'm being very careful," he warned, standing apart from her, his urges held tautly in check.

"I know," she said, standing perfectly still before him, only her fingers trembling slightly.

And when he took her hand in his to lead her to the bed he seriously wondered if he was capable of this benevolence. He lifted her onto the curtained bed in the heated room, their young bodies clean and smelling of soap, their hair cool and damp, their lust a palpable spirit between them.

And he piled pillows behind her so she reclined on the stark white linen, lush and fertile, her skin flushed from the warm bath and from the desire burning inside her, her eyes half-shut against the urgency of her need.

He began very gently, not quite sure himself how far he could proceed, how fully he could respond to her eagerness. Sitting beside her, he lightly touched her nipple with a brushing fingertip. Suddenly a drop of fluid appeared on the pink crest. Intrigued, he bent his head to taste it.

Elizabeth sighed as the light contact trembled through her swollen breasts, coiled in heated rivers down between her legs.

And two more drops of pearly liquid appeared.

Johnnie lifted her large breasts in his hands and watched the little droplets form, kissing away the wetness as it emerged. Elizabeth would whimper at each delicate suckling contact of his lips on her tingling nipples, at the intoxicating river of sensation that flowed downward.

"Look . . ." Johnnie murmured, gently squeezing her breasts. "You have milk . . ."

When her eyes lazily opened in response to the fascination in his voice, he smiled at her, then bent his head and took her moist nipple in his mouth. As he sucked, she felt the bewitching tremors and the flash and heat and sparking conflagration clear down to her toes. Her eyes drifted shut again, her hands came up to hold his head to her breast, the new, startling rapture captive under her palms. "Do it again . . ." she whispered.

Johnnie smiled around the nipple in his mouth. And his voice when he spoke was muffled by her soft breast. "Like this?"

"Ummm . . ." Her sigh was low, throaty, her fingers tangled in his hair, her mind slipping away.

He accommodated her wish for more until she began to need him frantically . . . and then he lay between her legs, softly opened her with exquisite care, and captured the swollen bud of her clitoris with his fingertips. He rubbed it gently, sliding the pad of his finger in slow circles around the pliant nub.

She was glowing hot against his hand, impatient after a few moments, arching up to tempt him. And he was as eager as she to be drawn in.

But his fingers slipped inside instead, cautiously, gauging the distance, a steely determination keeping temptation at bay. He swept his fingers gently over all her lush surfaces, stroked, massaged, brought her teetering to the feverish brink.

She wanted *him*, though, not the alternative, no matter how lush the seduction. With ravenous desire stoking her nerves and brain and pulsing senses she tried to touch his erection but he held her firmly against the pillows, pushing her hands aside, calling on every shred of will he possessed to say, "No, don't, or I'll stop."

She fell back with a smothered sob, and he kissed the silky skin of her thigh as sweet recompense, his tongue tracing a slow luscious path upward until his mouth grazed her heated pouty flesh. Parting the sleek folds of her labia with his fingers, he licked the melting wet tissue. His tongue slid inside her, plunged, submerged, penetrated her throbbing sweetness.

As Elizabeth writhed under his mouth and hands he bit her gently, tasted her scented flesh, felt the answering spasm with his tongue as it rippled up her slick interior, heard her heated whimper. Nibbling on her succulent sweetness again, he slid in three fingers past his mouth and her high wild cry began. . . .

"Are you feeling better now?" he asked long moments later when she'd returned to a cooler reality.

"I think I'll keep you," Elizabeth purred with the sultry half-smile of a sated woman. "You've passed all the tests."

"Thank you, my lady," Johnnie murmured as he lay beside her, his grin brazen impudence. "I try."

"And with sublime results," she murmured. "I can't move, I'm too weak."

"Weak with love. Languid, shaken, drowsy with love . . ." He traced a lingering path from her shoulder over the curve of her breast and pregnant belly, ending in the blonde curls between her legs. "I'm available," he promised, stroking her pale crisp hair, "whenever the mood strikes you."

"You look available now," she said with a grin, her gaze on his arousal.

Johnnie glanced down briefly. "We're on holiday until after the baby's born."

"You're a compassionate man," she whispered.

His eyebrows rose in surprise. "Maybe I am for you," he softly said, this border lord who'd lived most of his young life by the sword, "and for our baby . . ."

She opened her arms to him, the tears always so close to the surface now springing to her eyes. "I love you, Johnnie Carre, so much it makes me cry."

He gathered her in his arms, tucking the blankets around her, cradling her body against his, kissing her nose and eyebrows, nibbling at her earlobes, telling her how much he loved her too in a dozen different languages. They giggled when she tried the strange languages he'd learned at school and in all his travels and then they kissed some more because bliss enveloped them, dissolved around them, filled their noses and tickled their toes.

They existed in a delicious, isolated contentment, the sound of the sea that would take them away lashing against the shore outside their windows.

They finished eating much later when they finally left the comfort of the bed. They ate fresh salmon, hotch-potch soup, and potatoes, taking inordinate pleasure in the simple meal and in each other's company.

And when Johnnie left shortly before eight, neither spoke of the uncertainty of his return. He hugged her and said, "I'll be back by morning. You know where the money is."

"Don't say that," she whispered, refusing to consider the possibility he might not come home to her.

"Then I'll just say au revoir. . . ." He kissed her, a tender, warm kiss. Then he unwrapped her arms from around his waist. "Go to sleep," he whispered. "It won't seem so long. Lock the door behind me."

Staying off the main road to Berwick-on-Tweed, he arrived on the outskirts of the city before ten and went directly to a tavern by the sea where Carres had sold French wine and brandy to Charlie Fox for years, where his father before him had considered Charlie a friend.

Dressed plainly in a blue coat and dark breeches with no jack, no obvious weapons other than his sword, he entered the low doorway and sat down on a bench against the wall, surveying the smoky, low-ceilinged room, alert for the presence of British soldiers on this side of the border, or possibly for some of Harley's men, who wouldn't have been as easy to distinguish. No soldiers, at least, met his gaze. He relaxed his grip on the pistol in his coat pocket. When the young serving girl Meg came up to him in her circuit of the tables some minutes later, he distinguished from her startled glance that official inquiries had already been made concerning him.

"Surprised to see me?" he queried with a wicked smile.

"They're lookin' for ye, Johnnie, from Wick to London," she fearfully murmured, leaning close to his ear so her words wouldn't travel. "Get yerself to Holland."

"I'm trying to. Have you heard where Robbie might be?"

"Aye, the sweet boy was in here three days ago, askin' for you. He's waitin', but the cruisers are making the coast right hot. He talked to Charlie. I'll tell the old man ye're waitin' outside. Now git where it's darker."

And moments later, when Charlie Fox walked outside, Johnnie moved out of the shadows and greeted him with a tap on the shoulder.

"Christ's blood," the stout man exclaimed, startled. Spinning around, his eyes lighted on Johnnie, and his expression became stern. "Get the hell back in the dark," he warned, pushing Johnnie around the corner of the building into a small alleyway. "They've emptied Harbottle Castle looking for you," he growled. "The price on your head is enough to tempt even an honest man."

"Godfrey's anxious for my property."

"Ye should have killed him after your pa died."

"A youthful indiscretion," Johnnie drawled. "Which I plan to resolve one day, but now I have to get a message to Robbie or else hire a vessel to take me to Holland."

"The government agents talked to all the captains hereabouts; I wouldna trust any of 'em. Robbie's movin' along the coast, stayin' out o' the way of the cruisers, waitin' for you. He couldna anchor in the cove with the blockade so tight."

"When next he comes, tell him I'll be at the cove

we spoke of every night. When he can, he should come for us."

"Aye. Now go, for the agents are everywhere, and one canna always tell their ilk. Come back for a drink," he added with a smile, taking Johnnie's hand in his, "in safer times."

"When Godfrey's gone," Johnnie said to the man he'd known since childhood.

"Aye. When the world's a better place, my Lord."

CHAPTER 22

The days of waiting began, and the nights as well spent at Margarth Cove until each new morning brought fresh frustration. They moved lodgings often so they might appear as travelers and attract less notice, but with each change the risk of recognition increased. They lived with the fear that one day on entering a village in the confined environs of the cove, someone might identify them from their description being circulated up and down the coast. The price on Johnnie's head inspired treachery.

Several days later their lodgings for the night were near enough to Margarth Cove that Johnnie suggested Elizabeth stay in their room while he waited on the shore. If Robbie appeared, he could be back within minutes to fetch her. If the ship didn't arrive, she wouldn't have to spend another night out in the bitter cold.

"I'd rather be with you," she replied, more frightened alone. She'd begun having nightmares of Johnnie being torn from her arms; the delay in their rescue was wearing on her.

"You're losing sleep every night," he softly said, solicitude in his voice. Her health was more fragile than his. "You could rest and be warm here inside; it might be several days yet before Robbie can get through the blockade. I can be back here in five minutes."

Logically, she understood the reasonableness of his suggestion, and she struggled with her emotions. Reacting to dreams and uneasy feelings was not her normal, sensible way, so she agreed, although reluctantly. "I'll wait here. But," she added with a sudden smile, "I'm sleeping in my cloak."

But when Johnnie began preparing to leave, taking up his weapons, putting on his heavy cape, she found it impossible to present a brave front. The strain of the past fortnight defeated her resolute attempt at fortitude, and she cried.

Her unhappiness tore at his heart, but he was equally concerned with her declining energies. "Just stay inside tonight, sweetheart," he whispered, holding her in his arms, "and if Robbie doesn't come, you can spend tomorrow night with me outside. Compromise?" It would at least give her one night's respite from the cold, bone-chilling winds off the ocean.

"I hate being this way," she sniffled, her tear-stained face lifted to his. "All weepy and clinging." Taking a deep breath, she forced a smile, her lips quivering with the effort. "Just go now, and I'll wait here by the fire."

Their kiss was tender and sweet in the rough room so far from Goldiehouse, so distant from their former privileged lives. And they lingered in the warmth of each other's embrace, his chin resting lightly on her head, their arms holding each other tight, reluctant to be separated, avoiding the last good-bye. Until Johnnie finally whispered, "I have to go. . . ."

He turned back at the door, to blow her a kiss. "And one for baby," he said, sending another kiss across the dimly lit room. For a small moment he paused, his gloved hand on the latch as if he wanted to say more, then he smiled instead and opened the door.

After Johnnie left, Elizabeth paced, debating whether she could follow him, restless and agitated with the awful uncertainty of another night's vigil, not knowing whether she was capable of waiting here alone beset by solitary fears. She walked to the window and rubbed away the moisture on the glass, peering through the small aperture, seeing only solid darkness. There was no moon tonight, clouds having scudded in from the sea that afternoon, bringing squally weather ashore. She shivered, her fingers chilled on the cold pane, acknowledging the merit in Johnnie's suggestion; she was glad she hadn't gone out. The threat of snow hung in the air, errant flakes striking the window at intervals, as if in warning of a storm.

Moving to the fireplace, she sat down on a simple chair pulled up to the small grate, hands clasped in her lap, her feet tapping. Then, restless after a short time, she walked back to the window—as if she could see something in the dense blackness. As if her wishing would bring Johnnie back. She tried reading for a brief period, but the flickering tallow candles offered poor illumination; she abandoned the book in exasperation. And so the evening went in an uneasy fidgeting from chair to window and back again, her legs and back aching after hours on her feet, the baby persistently kicking in reaction to her agitated movement.

When the sudden knock on the door disturbed the silence, she went very still.

It was too late for anyone to be up. And Johnnie wouldn't knock, she thought, feeling a shiver of fear race down her spine—he'd call out so she'd know his identity. Fainthearted, shaky, she didn't answer, wishing like a child did with unreasonable simplicity that the sound was an ordinary mistake—a guest who had lost his way, perhaps. Although in these modest lodgings, with only three bedchambers, it would be difficult to get lost.

Standing rigid in the center of the room, she listened. A moment passed, and then several more. All was quiet; she began to relax.

And then the sudden clash and clang of metal hammering metal ruptured the quiet, the lock on the door quivering under the impact. A scream rose in her throat, instantly muted, an unconscious self-defense, and she raced for her cape she'd thrown on the bed. Perhaps the attackers didn't know she was inside; she might yet have time to escape through the window if the door held. Darting a glance toward the old wooden portal, she nervously focused on the hinges pulling away from the frame.

If it only lasted a few minutes more, she desperately hoped.

No longer concerned with subterfuge, men raised their voices in exhortations and harangues against the ancient wood and iron. For a stark moment a familiar voice struck her ears, extinguished in the next flashing moment by a burst of invective, the besiegers bickering over the means of entry. Against the shouting, clash, and banging and rending of wood, Elizabeth struggled with the lock on the small paned window, the old rusty mechanism stubbornly resistant to her strength. Her heart beating frantically, she wrenched the handle again with a vigorous effort, and a small piece of rust fell to the floor. Tears of frustration sprang to her eyes at her weakness, and she jerked on the latch again with desperation and fury. A small crack in the corroded metal appeared; she threw her weight into another powerful tug, and the ancient clasp broke free. With a savage thrust of her hand she shoved against the moldy iron frame, and the window moved a few reluctant inches on its rusty hinges. Gritting her teeth against the pain in her hand, she gave the window another violent push ... then another, until the creaky window spread open enough to allow her egress.

Now if the door would just resist a few seconds more, she fervently prayed, dragging a chair up to the opened casement.

Just as she was balancing her ungainly weight to step up on the chair, the door crashed open, swinging away lopsidedly on its single remaining hinge, banging then dangling against the wall. Soldiers burst into the room, the first still armed with the iron bars they'd used to force the door.

She lunged up onto the chair, intent on throwing herself out the window, preferring the unknown, however perilous, to her rough attackers. But the room was scarcely a dozen feet wide, and before she could maneuver her bulk complete with dragging skirts and voluminous cape through the window, a rough hand was dragging her back. She struggled against his grip, but the heavyset soldier shoved her into the chair she used as a ladder, held her there with his elbow at her throat and, reaching around her, pulled the window shut.

The small room filled with soldiers as she slumped in the chair, feeling slightly faint after her strenuous physical exertions, trying to concentrate on her breathing so she didn't lose consciousness. And intent on subduing her dizziness, she didn't notice the gradual suppression of conversation until the room had become totally silent. She looked up as the sudden hush struck her to see the throng of men slowly part in two.

Her father stood on the destroyed threshold.

"Where is he?" he said, harsh and chill, his eyes like ice.

"I don't know," she replied in a tone only audible because of the utter quiet. Then she straightened her back almost in reflex reaction to the presence of her father, drew air into her lungs so her voice was stronger and lifted her chin. "And if I did know, I wouldn't tell you," she said, her uncertainty of the black unknown vanished, her personal fear evaporated before this familiar adversary. When she added, "He left three days ago," her eyes were as cold as his.

"Amusing," her father curtly snapped. "Your landlord of course doesn't agree." Surveying the crowded room with all the curious faces trained on him, he said to his men with an imperious gesture, "Check the room for weapons and then wait below."

"Maybe you didn't pay the landlord enough for the truth," Elizabeth mockingly replied, unconcerned with public disclosure of his deceit. "You'd understand that particular subtlety better than most, I expect." Her expression matched his for imperiousness.

"He left you like that then." His eyes swept her swollen form.

"It's his habit, I believe."

"And you're dwelling in this hovel for ... ?" The room had emptied now so his gaze could take in the full measure of the meager furnishings, the limited dimensions.

"For what I'd hoped would be deliverance from you. You generally prefer a more refined milieu."

"He's made you love him, it seems, for you to so blatantly protect him. We'll have to see you're properly schooled before the trial. A reluctant wife is more to our advantage."

"You mean the verdict isn't decided yet?" she said. "I find such nicety of principle out of character for you. It must be Queensberry's discriminating political acumen that insists on a trial. You'll understand," she added, "if I don't wish you luck in finding him."

"We've four squadrons out. We won't need luck. Is that Ravensby's shirt, or have you taken on new habits?" Harold Godfrey's gaze rested on Johnnie's wool shirt hanging on the bedpost.

"He left it for me. It's warm."

"How chivalrous. Although I suppose his resources are more limited these days. He was formerly conspicuous for his largess to his lovers."

"He was formerly a wealthy man."

"Yes, well . . . such are the vagaries of fortune." Her father's faint smile was unpleasant. "Now if you'll excuse me for a moment, I must see to our planned welcome. In case," he said with delicate emphasis, "my Lord Carre is still in the vicinity."

But he left two soldiers at the door to guard her, and when he returned some time later, he had the hinges hastily renailed so the door was back in place. Then, drawing up a chair by the small fireplace, he sat down, stretched out his legs, crossed them at the ankle, and gave every indication he intended to stay.

He didn't invite his daughter to join him at the fire, nor would she have if asked. In the shadowed silence of the room she racked her brain for some means of warning Johnnie. Would he spy the troopers or recognize a discrepancy in the door despite the unlighted passageway? Would Robbie have come and Johnnie not be alone when he returned? Could she stand by the window and hope he'd question her presence there? But the few tallow candles guttered low in their holders. The only light soon would be from the grate, not conducive to a clearly visible image through the wet panes. And as if her father had been reading her thoughts, he curtly said. "Move away from the window."

She didn't.

Glancing over to her, he leisurely recrossed his legs. "You won't be able to warn him, my foolish girl," he quietly said into the fire, "because he'll come for you regardless of the danger. The fool should have left you at Goldiehouse and run for the coast. He might have saved himself. But he wouldn't leave you then, and he won't leave you now. So you can stand there if you wish, or scream warnings when you hear his footfall, or do anything you think might help, but he'll come for you. You're our bait."

"Take all my money," she quickly said, urgency in her tone. "I'll sign it over to you immediately if you let him go."

There was the minutest pause before he said, "I don't need your money now." His voice in contrast to hers was mild, almost engaging. "I'll have some rather large estates gifted to me once the trial is over," he softly added.

"What if he can defend himself?" Elizabeth swiftly proposed. "What if you lose? You could have my money *now* . . . without the uncertainty of a trial."

Her father looked over at her briefly. "The jury has already been selected." He laughed, a pleasant sound if one didn't know his history. "Save your money for the lawyers."

At least Johnnie would be alive, she thought, taking heart. He would remain alive tonight and tomorrow and all the days of the trial.

But she preferred him to escape. Later, when she heard his familiar tread in the passageway, she screamed in a pealing cry so the shrill words tore at her throat, "Get out, Johnnie! Run! Run! They're here!"

His footsteps paused for a moment and then continued, and she saw him through a blur of tears seconds later as he pushed open the door and walked into the room. His cape swirled around his ankles as he came to a sudden halt, his height distinctive in the low-ceilinged room his dark head almost brushing the rafters.

"Let her go," he said, his heated gaze on Harold Godfrey who had risen from his chair, a pistol in his hand, pointed not at Johnnie but at Elizabeth. "You don't need her."

"But I do, of course, at least temporarily, as you well know. She's a necessary witness at your trial."

"Then you won't shoot her," Johnnie brusquely said, moving a step toward him.

"I won't kill her."

He stopped.

Godfrey smiled. "We understand each other then."

"I don't want her harmed."

"What you want matters very little to me, Ravensby. But if you don't cooperate, Elizabeth may rue your stubbornness. Not to mention your child, who from all appearances is due to enter this world soon." His voice altered from its mannered calm to a cutting authority. "Now kindly hand over your weapons. Captain," he ordered, calling in his dragoons. In a few moments the room swarmed with soldiers.

There was no opportunity for communication, as Johnnie was immediately surrounded by a cluster of soldiers and bound securely. He looked at her over the heads of the red-coated dragoons as they dragged him away, his gaze holding Elizabeth's for a brief moment. "Don't despair," he told her.

More powerful than despair at the moment, overwhelming even that potent emotion, was her violent anger. Elizabeth wanted to kill her father and, had she a weapon available, she would have without thought. For the first time in her life she understood murderous rage. "I'll see you dead for this," she said to him, her voice trembling with hatred.

Her father only glanced up from his search of Johnnie's belongings. "Somehow I'm not alarmed."

But she was left with a guard in the room after everyone had gone to ready himself for the journey to Edinburgh. Turning her back on the soldier standing by the door, she plotted revenge on her father, knowing she could rely on Redmond and her men at Three Kings to help her if she could get a message to them, knowing, too, her time was limited, and Johnnie's life at stake. She also needed to find a means of reaching Robbie or Munro. Surely, in Edinburgh there would be more opportunity to communicate with the Carres or their friends. And she looked forward impatiently to leaving.

She was surprised to see a coach waiting at the door when she was escorted from the tavern several hours later. Carriages were still a luxury in the country. And surprised as well to see her father standing at the door of the vehicle. He wasn't solicitous by nature.

"This conveyance was arranged for you, compliments of your husband," her father smoothly said, gesturing with a negligent hand in the direction of the stables. "In his devotion to you," he murmured with mockery, "my Lord Carre was willing to pay the price."

Elizabeth's startled gaze followed her father's idle sweeping movement, his insolent jeer so full of foreboding warning signals began drumming in her mind.

The warning came too late. She was unprepared for the sight and her piercing scream disturbed the birds in distant Margarth Cove.

In the middle of the stable yard her husband was tied to the large wheel of a munitions cart, unconscious. His powerful body hung limp, dangling like a broken puppet from the bloody ropes securing his wrists to the wheel. His legs trailed in the dirt and snow, his breeches and boots spattered with blood.

Stripped to the waist, his lacerated back oozed blood, streams and rivulets and slowly ebbing drops tracing scarlet paths, splashing onto the white snow in horrific puddles.

Not a piece of flesh from his neck to his waist had any remnant of normal color. Torn and shredded ribbons of skin hung in flayed strips, lash marks sharply defined in brilliant crimson. Some whip strokes had cut deeply to white bone and cartilage, the heavy muscles and tendons looped across his shoulders, visible in places as though he were a medical specimen recently dissected.

His graceful head drooped at an awkward angle against his left arm, his hair splattered with bits of flesh; drops of blood slid down the silky dark tendrils, pooling when they struck the ground in tiny round circles like pink pearls, like liquid death.

"He didn't cry out so you wouldn't be disturbed," her father casually said, watching her pale with dispassionate eyes, his disclosure a knife thrust to her heart. "Allow me to help you in."

Sickened, Elizabeth felt her stomach lurch. A ringing vibrated in her ears at the horror; dancing white spots exploded before her eyes. Dizzy, light-headed at the harrowing agony of Johnnie's martyrdom, she trembled as her legs collapsed under her, her brain shut down, and she crumpled slowly to the ground.

Harold Godfrey snapped his fingers with no more sentiment than when calling for his carriage after the theater. "Put her inside," he curtly said to the two men who came running up. "We leave for Edinburgh directly. And see that the prisoner is cut down now."

CHAPTER 23

When Elizabeth woke, she found herself on the floor of the carriage. She lay there for a time, nauseated afresh by the shocking image etched on her brain, tortured by guilt at the torment Johnnie had undergone so she and their child would come to no harm, afflicted with self-reproach and blame for her father's viciousness, at a momentary loss of initiative and hope, of energy and will.

Their flight had been physically and emotionally draining; her father's capacity for evil was at the moment beyond the powers of her exhausted vitality. And she despaired, heart-stricken, of her husband's life.

She lay lurching slightly from side to side as the coach passed over the frozen ruts on the winter road, inundated by misery and self-pity until her indomitable spirit that had enabled her to survive in the past gave her fresh courage, reminded her with a chastising censure that she at least didn't have the flesh flayed from her back. And if she wanted Johnnie to live and if she wanted vengeance—an impulse that heated her blood and inspired action—she'd better pick herself up from the floor and deal with her father.

She felt better already, convinced that her father had only temporary power over their lives. Also, she thought with a rush of renewed vigor, she still had most of her fortune locked away at Three Kings under Redmond's guard. And regardless of her father's plans for taking over some of Johnnie's wealth, she'd noticed his momentary hesitation at the inn when she'd offered him her fortune for Johnnie's freedom.

So she gathered herself up from the floor, seated herself on the front cushions of the coach, brushed the dirt off her cape, and ran her fingers through her hair as if the state of her disordered tresses mattered. And taking off her heeled boot, she commenced a vigorous banging of the studded heel on the forward ceiling of the carriage, directly under the driver's seat.

She heard the coachman nervously call for her father, and she waited for his reaction, feeling more hopeful, recognizing she might have the means of mitigating Johnnie's immediate pain.

When her father rode alongside, she pulled down the window. "I have a proposition for you," she said, the chill wind rushing against her face.

"He's not going free."

"I'm only asking for a doctor, not his freedom. And I'll pay you well for the favor. If you'd join me, we could discuss your terms." She could almost see the calculations spinning inside his head. "I'm prepared to be generous," she added. "Extremely so."

He looked at her for a penetrating moment.

"You realize Queensberry is going to take more than his share. Knowing him, you can't be sure how you'll profit," she reminded him, her breath curling into the icy air. "You might as well compensate yourself with some of my money."

His large gloved hand resting on his thigh flexed during his deliberation. Her words were unpleasantly astute. "Very well. I'll listen," he curtly replied.

And after a brief delay for her father's horse to be exchanged for a seat in the carriage, she found herself opposite him, the confined space intensifying her feelings of hatred, his imposing bulk and cool contempt the same unregenerate force she'd been struggling against all her life.

"If Johnnie doesn't have a doctor," she said, forcing her mind to put forward the options with a cool detachment, knowing she'd be at a disadvantage if her feelings showed, "he might not survive the trip to Edinburgh. You'll find it more difficult to convict a dead man. *I'd* have no incentive to be a cooperative witness if Johnnie were dead. And even if you have your amenable judge and jury and witnesses, my contrary testimony—*considering* my intimacy with the defendant—might at least arouse the public ire. Queensberry's been afraid to show his face in Scotland for over a year. Johnnie Carre, on the other hand, is a popular figure in Edinburgh. I believe he's cheered in the streets during the sessions of Parliament. And as I recall, the mob stoned Boyle and set fire to Seafield's house last summer when the people were angered. Tarbot barely escaped with his life. It's possible you and Queensberry might not survive the trial."

She knew him so well that when he opened his mouth to utter the words, she interrupted. "The baby isn't due for two more months," she declared, dissembling by a few weeks. "So you can't force me to falsify my testimony by threatening the child's life. And my testimony *is* rather essential. If Johnnie dies, and if you wait two months for the baby's birth, by that time Robbie would have assumed the title and would have had great leisure to marshal his influential friends and relatives. All you and Queensberry would have is a dead defendant accused of rape."

"And treason."

"Really. Are you that hopeful? Even more so then, you should prefer my husband alive. The heir to Ravensby is woefully apolitical. There might be enormous public support for an eighteen-year-old about to be pillaged of his inheritance when he has no political enemies...." She smiled coolly. "Besides you, of course."

"How much?" her father bluntly said.

Elated she had struck a nerve, she said, "For a doctor only. We're negotiating for a doctor—in the next hour. If you delay or procrastinate, my price goes down. If my husband dies, you get nothing. If he's well cared for, I'm prepared to pay you handsomely. In gold. You can have a man ride directly to Three Kings from here. Redmond has previous orders to comply if my message is properly delivered. You begin."

"Twenty thousand guineas."

"Five thousand. It's many hours yet to Edinburgh. You can earn more."

"Fifteen."

"Eight."

"Twelve."

"Twelve if the doctor comes along to Edinburgh."

"Done. We'll be in North Berwick in ten minutes."

"Did I mention if Johnnie dies, Redmond will come for you?"

"Redmond won't know."

"A man of Ravensby's stature doesn't die unnoticed, Father. And I've added my personal stipulations to Hotchane's standing order. Redmond starts at the fingers and toes. It's quite a slow death, I'm told." It gave her immense pleasure to see her father blanch beneath his ruddy complexion. "I hope you find an excellent doctor."

Her father required the note be sent off to Redmond before Johnnie was taken from the cart. At a small desk in the doctor's office she wrote a brief few lines requesting the money be given to the messenger, a businesslike note censored by her father's keen survey as she wrote it. By prior arrangement, an agreement of long standing, she signed her note "Lady Elizabeth," a formality Redmond would recognize as a plea for help. Although Redmond would have heard of their flight already, some of the Carre retainers having been sent to Three Kings, he wouldn't know yet that they'd not gotten free of Scotland. With the money requested being delivered to a henchman of her father's, however, Redmond would know her adversary.

Blessedly, Johnnie never regained consciousness as the doctor cleaned the hideous wounds, a grim, slow process of swabbing raw flesh and cutting away dead skin. He'd groan when the pain became intolerable even in his stupor, deep, low animal sounds of pain.

Elizabeth wasn't allowed to talk to him, but she covered one of his clenched fists with her hand, and he responded to her touch in some deep refuge of his mind. . . . His fingers opened, she slipped her hand into his, and his hand closed over hers. She would have cried if she dared at that small recognition, but her position was precarious—totally dependent on her father's whim—so she hid their hands behind a billowing fold of her cape and silently mourned.

Elizabeth refused to let the doctor bleed Johnnie. He was already ashen from loss of blood, and even the doctor had to admit that if bleeding was useful in reviving good health, Johnnie would surely recover. A poultice was gently spread over the gaping slashes and torn flesh, and the rough cart was made as comfortable as possible with fresh hay and quilts. And when the doctor said, "Drink some poppy juice, my Lord," Johnnie seemed to have heard, because he swallowed the medicine.

When the laudanum tempered his breathing, when its effect had diminished his pain, Elizabeth had him transferred to the bed prepared for him in the open cart.

The cold winter day had helped stanch the worst of the bleeding, and in the remaining ten hours to Edinburgh the chill temperatures would further aid in reducing any fever. For an additional six thousand guineas, Elizabeth had bought herself a seat next to her husband in the cart with the stipulation that a guard accompany them. She'd agreed to no conversation beyond the most prosaic; she would have agreed to anything to stay beside him.

He barely stirred on the long journey, for which she was grateful, the laudanum sedating him, allowing his maimed body freedom from pain at least temporarily.

But after they reached Edinburgh late that night, they were immediately separated.

Her prison was more benign than Johnnie's destination—Edinburgh Castle dungeons. Her place of detention was a spare but clean apartment in one of Queensberry's properties off the Canongate. She was to be held incommunicado, she was told by her jailer, Christian Dunbar, Queensberry's niece, until such a time as her testimony was required in court.

Because he was an accused felon in a notoriously political trial, Johnnie's imprisonment was more public, although the dungeons at the castle were by no means accessible. They were deep in the old foundations, well guarded, secure. In any event it was still moot whether he would survive to stand trial.

Very late that night, immediately news of their return reached Queensberry, Harold Godfrey was summoned to Queensberry's apartments, where he was exposed to the vicious blasts of the Duke's wrath for having allowed his personal vendetta against Johnnie Carre to possibly deprive them of the richest estates in Scotland.

"In the future," Queensberry said with barely contained fury, moving about his paneled office in agitation, "flog any number of your expendable soldiery. I don't care how many you kill, nor does anyone else. But kindly use more discretion with prisoners of such importance. If Ravensby dies before he can be properly convicted, and I lose out on the finest property on the Borders, I'll see that you pay dearly for your stupidity. I'm informed, too, your daughter refuses to cooperate if my Lord Carre dies, you damned fool! While we may not need her testimony, I'd rather have it than not." Queensberry was a shrewd and skillful manipulator. He disliked displays of raw savagery. It made diplomacy difficult; people who preferred taking their bribes and quietly staying in the background balked at such notorious brutality.

"No need for hysteria. He'll live," the Earl of Brusisson insisted, sure in his skill at judging that precarious line at which life was extinguished. "I know when to stop a flogging."

"You'd better be right."

"Really, James, consider you wouldn't even have him in the castle dungeons if not for my persistence," Harold Godfrey softly said from his comfortable chair. His pale eyes regarded the Duke of Queensberry's exasperated pacing with mild disparagement. "Allow me my small amusements."

"It won't be so amusing if our defendant dies." Regardless of the purchased judge and jury, Queensberry didn't want the embarrassment of a dead defendant. He preferred not to show such a heavy hand. "I don't want any problems convicting him. I don't want them to say we killed him. I want the properties legally—without grey areas open to further litigation. Ravensby's library alone will bring a fortune."

"You're welcome to it. I've my eye on his racing bloodstock."

Queensberry's head snapped around; he coveted the stable as well. But he smiled instead, not wishing to expose his interest. There remained adequate time to see to a favorable distribution of Ravensby's holdings . . . one satisfactory to him. "We shall have to delay the trial," he briskly said, as though they'd not been discussing outright robbery like two cutpurses, "until the prisoner is an object of less sympathy. Your perverse amusements will cost us a fortnight at least."

"If it gives you pleasure to assign blame," the Earl of Brusisson said in a wearying tone, "entertain yourself with my blessing, but I repeat, Your Grace, *I* brought the man in for you. Not your scheming or your clever manipulation of judges and impoverished nobles, but *my* steadfast pursuit." He stood then, having accorded as much civility as he was willing to give after a long day on the road. "You needn't thank me now, my Lord," he sardonically said, with the merest indication of a bow. "Your gratitude can take the form of land deeds at a later date." And with the faintest of smiles he turned and left the room.

Queensberry was left irritated, sulky, and nettled

over the delay in his plans. Harold Godfrey was always
rankled when he had to deal with courtiers who never
wished to actually soil their hands with the blood of the
men they slaughtered. And both men's designs on the
Ravensby estates continued unabated.

CHAPTER 24

Christian Dunbar greeted Roxane Forrestor, Countess Kilmarnock, with a mild restraint when the Countess was shown into her drawing room on a dull grey afternoon two days later. Gracefully sinking onto the crocus-yellow sofa, Roxane murmured, "Good God, Chrissie, you'd think I was here to steal your prisoner. Now what use would I have for Johnnie's damned wife?"

"How did you know?" the small, dark-haired woman exclaimed, her normally prim mouth open wide in astonishment. The Duke had wanted Elizabeth's location kept secret.

"Darling, what a silly question. The caddies even know who had dinner in Lady Nicky Murray's bedchamber last night," Roxane dissembled. Searching out Elizabeth's jail had been more difficult than she expected. "Actually, I meant to come yesterday, but my dear Jeannie must have me watch her progress with the new Italian dance master, and before I knew it, it was too late to call. So tell me, what is the woman like?"

"The Duke left express instructions," Christian

pointedly said, "she is not to be discussed." As the daughter of Queensberry's sister, a noblewoman who had formed a mésalliance but had returned to the family fold when her scapegrace husband had conveniently died, Christian Dunbar depended on the charity of her uncle, the Duke of Queensberry.

"Ah, well then . . . and I was hoping for some gossip about the woman who stole Johnnie from me. Admit you can understand my vindictive impulses." The lovely Countess smiled. "Now that she's less exalted." Lounging back against the padded cushions, the yellow satin perfect foil for her vibrant red hair and aquamarine gown, she said with a theatrical small sigh, "And I was hoping to gloat over her reverses."

"I just don't dare," the Duke's niece replied, but her uncharitable soul was piqued by the possibility of a juicy scene.

"I understand," Roxane replied with a gracious lenience. "But you know how it is with a rival. One loves the opportunity to be insulting. Tell me instead," she dulcetly went on, "while you're pouring us some of that very good claret your uncle favors, what you think of Katie Malcolm's newest child. To my eye it's definitely not a Malcolm."

And the afternoon settled into a cozy exchange of malice, Roxane taking pains to offer up luscious tidbits of scandal, aware of Chrissie's insatiable appetite for other people's misfortune. Very much like her haughty mother, who considered her youthful indiscretion happily repaired by her husband's death, Christian Dunbar had been raised to be conscious of her superior Douglas bloodlines. Overly proud, she'd not yet found a man who came up to her family's standards; she was in fact a younger version of her mother, dainty, prim, concerned with appearances, and grudging of other's happiness.

And Roxane's hopes that the claret would relax her hostess's restrictions against discussion of her uncle's prisoner proved true as the afternoon progressed.

"Lady Carre's very beautiful," Christian Dunbar admitted after her third glass, a small grimace accompanying her words as if it pained her to utter them. "Even now, when she's big with child. And she's not a bit afraid." She divulged the last in irritation.

"Do you speak to her often?"

"She refuses conversation."

"Arrogance in her position? I'm surprised."

"She even railed at her father when he left her here. I think your lover found himself a shrew for a wife."

"Perhaps her fortune interested him," Roxane snidely said, her lip curved slightly in disdain.

"Not likely sixty thousand pounds will be overlooked by any man." The bitterness in her voice was unsurprising; Christian's own lack of fortune had been a distinct disadvantage in luring eligible men.

"No man had ever left me before Johnnie did," Roxane quietly disclosed.

"I can see then why you're interested in her."

"There's a certain resentment." Roxane's glance had narrowed, her dark eyes shadowed by her lashes. Then she flashed a brittle smile and lifted her wineglass in salute. "To all our rivals wherever they may be . . . Speaking of which . . . I heard the young Earl of Eglinton decided on Callander's youngest daughter. What a shame, when he'd paid such pleasant attention to you last month."

"She has blond ringlets," Chrissie said with scathing sarcasm, "and a grandfather who's given her twenty thousand for a portion. Andrew didn't have to look any farther." Her face had reddened at the affront to her own cherished plans.

"Blondes often find favor in men's eyes," Roxane thoughtfully noted.

"True enough—your Johnnie Carre's wife's hair is flaxen pale," Christian said hotly, as though the mere ownership of such hair were a personal insult.

"Does she have bouncing ringlets like Callander's daughter?" Roxane flippantly inquired, watching the rising flush on her hostess's face—a condition of either the wine or her discontent.

"Nothing so girlish for the proud Lady Carre. Her tresses fall in sleek, gleaming waves."

"She doesn't wear it up?"

Christian peered at her over the rim of her wineglass, her eyes speculative. "Can I trust you?"

"Most assuredly," Roxane smoothly replied.

"Do you want to see her?"

After two hours of banal conversation having prayed for such an offer, Roxane struggled to appear suitably blasé. "Out of curiosity only," Roxane murmured, balancing the bowl of her wineglass between her ringed fingers, "I'd find it interesting . . . to see this woman who lured Johnnie away."

"Not a word to anyone now."

"Of course not." Her smile was indulgent.

"Come then," Christian said, rising somewhat unsteadily from her chair, her diminutive body more susceptible to spirits than Roxane's tall, voluptuous figure.

And leaving her small beaded purse behind on the sofa, Roxane followed her hostess through the door of the drawing room to the narrow stairway curving upward to the stories above.

When they entered the unguarded apartment, secured only with a simple lock opened with a key hung from Christian's chatelaine, Elizabeth looked up from her reading, wondering at the change in her routine. It was too early for dinner.

"I've brought you a visitor," her jailer said.

Elizabeth, immediately recognizing the slightly slurred speech, understood to what she owed this unusual appearance, but when the spectacular redhead behind Christian Dunbar surreptitiously put her finger to her mouth in a swift gesture of caution, she rose from her chair, alert to possibility.

Turning around to Roxane, Christian said with a sneer, "Well, what do you think of your rival?"

"She looks very blond," Roxane said with a grin. "To be sure, we've been struck by a plague of fair hair this year."

"Damned irritating, too," Christian said with pursed lips. "You may gloat now if you wish."

"Thank you, Chrissie, for your understanding." Roxane patted her hostess's arm. Then she strolled across the room until she stood before the small table behind which Elizabeth stood, her back to the light from the window. "I had to see for myself . . . what Johnnie Carre's wife looked like." Her tone was a well-modulated drawl verging on a sneer, but her eyes, incongruously, were friendly.

"You see then," Elizabeth quietly said, taking in the gorgeous redhead, something about the splendid beauty striking her as familiar, and the mixed messages she was receiving cautioning her to temperance.

"He was mine, you know," the fashionable woman said then, her tone sharper.

Roxane, Elizabeth immediately knew it must be. Johnnie's liaisons had been discussed by the servants during her first stay at Goldiehouse. The beautiful redhead, the belle of Edinburgh . . . standing before her now like the Queen of Sheba, exactly as she was described in the servants' hall.

"I'm sorry." It wasn't apology but acknowledgment.

"I hadn't considered your ploy," the redhead coolly said, her gaze traveling down Elizabeth's swollen belly.

"I don't have to talk to you. But you may look if it pleases you," Elizabeth calmly answered.

"I told you she was arrogant," Christian said, moving closer. "Tell her how long Ravensby was your lover."

"Better yet, Chrissie, I'll show her," Roxane decided, turning back to her hostess. "There're some love letters from Johnnie in my bag on the sofa. Would you mind getting them?" She knew Chrissie Dunbar couldn't resist; since they'd been girls in school, she'd been prying and meddlesome.

"I'll have to lock you in with her." Christian's duty to her uncle came first.

"Of course." Roxane smiled. "I promise not to damage her."

Christian giggled. "Maybe I should go and see little Annie Callandar, show her the letters Eglinton wrote to me last month."

"Indeed you should. It would serve her right for being so bouncy and pert. Now run off, because I feel malicious."

"You promise not to hurt her." A note of caution underlay an odd gleam in her eyes.

"I promise, darling." And Roxane pushed her gently toward the door.

When the metallic grate of the key sliding from the lock was followed by the diminishing sound of footsteps retreating down the hall, Roxane turned to Elizabeth and said in a hurried whisper, "Forgive me for the subterfuge; it was the only way I could convince Christian to allow me up to see you. She's an unpleasant woman. I'm Roxane Forrestor, as you may have guessed, and I'm here in behalf of Munro and Robbie."

"How's Johnnie?" Elizabeth appealed, her every thought in the days past of her husband.

"He still lives."

Tears sprang into her eyes, and she suddenly sat down, her legs giving way. "Thank you," Elizabeth whispered.

Moving near, Roxane touched Elizabeth's shoulder gently. "He's been told where you are, and he responded." She drew in a quiet breath, the lawyer's description of Johnnie's condition still too shocking in her memory. "And don't think me unfeeling," she went on a second later in a quick, low voice, "to launch into my message, but I've so little time before Christian returns. I'm here to tell you Robbie and Munro are planning your escape. They must free you before they can attempt a rescue of Johnnie. Otherwise, Queensberry and your father will continue to use you as leverage against your husband. Now that we know where you are, and if Chrissie doesn't speak of my visit to her uncle so he moves you, the plan is to come for you tomorrow night. First you, and then Johnnie, immediately after you're clear of this house."

She abruptly moved away from the table at the sound of a door shutting on the floor below, walked over to the threshold, and listened for a moment. "Now regardless of what I say when Chrissie returns, just remember . . . Johnnie was never mine," she quietly said. "He was never any woman's until he met you." She smiled ruefully, this woman who'd had adoring men at her feet since adolescence. "Do you know, he left my bed one night. Just walked away without explanation. I knew then he'd never be back. He went to you. . . ."

Elizabeth smiled. "He came to take me from my wedding."

"So everyone in Scotland heard," Roxane replied. "I must admit to a touch of jealousy, my Lady Carre," she added with a faint smile, "to be the object of such devotion from Ravensby. He guards his feelings."

"And I admit to envy that you've known him for so long."

"Together perhaps we can help win him his freedom."

Elizabeth wiped her eyes with her fingers and rose from her chair. "Just tell me what to do."

"I'm going to be insulting when Christian returns. The letter isn't real, but it's hurtful. Cry if you can, and shout and strike out at me. Chrissie will find sport in your unhappiness, and perhaps if we entertain her well, I'll be invited back tomorrow for an encore. It would be advantageous to know you hadn't been moved."

"I hear her coming," Elizabeth whispered.

"Then we must put on our actress masks," Roxane said with a wink and a smile. "You hateful thing . . ."

At the time Elizabeth and Roxane were speaking, Redmond was traveling north with ten handpicked men. He didn't know where Elizabeth was or what her danger, but they were following Harold Godfrey's messenger, who was carrying the gold he'd received at Three Kings back to his master. Careful to remain out of sight, they were perhaps twenty minutes behind him; it looked as though his destination was Edinburgh. As they neared the city, two of Redmond's men pulled ahead to keep the Godfrey retainer in sight; unlike Redmond, they'd go unrecognized by the messenger. Keeping pace with him as the roads became crowded with coaches and riders, they looked over their shoulders occasionally to take note of the single rider a hundred yards back. The first of the remaining eight men, strung out at hundred-yard intervals to attract no notice; Elizabeth's bodyguard—men who'd protected her since she was sixteen—entered the city one by one.

In the meantime the only man who'd seen Johnnie since he'd entered prison was sitting across the table from Robbie and Munro Carre in a private room of a tavern near the Lawnmarket shaking his head.

"He doesn't have the strength even to move a hand yet. I'm telling you, it's too early. Let me see if I can get a doctor in to examine him; then at least you'll know his capabilities."

"The longer the ship sits there, the less chance we have of remaining undiscovered. Even with Norwegian flags," Robbie said. "The customs men won't let us anchor there indefinitely."

"We could carry him out if he can't walk," Munro suggested.

"It's going to be tough enough just getting a few men inside without calling down the entire guard. Carrying a man of Ravensby's size up those narrow stairways . . ." Douglas Coutts shrugged at the impracticality.

"If Johnnie stays in there, rather than growing stronger, it's more likely he'll die of prison fever in his weakened condition." Robbie's voice was rough with fatigue. He'd hardly had any sleep since fleeing his property in East Lothian, playing hide-and-seek with British cruisers off the coast. And when the news of Johnnie and Elizabeth's capture had been conveyed to him by Charlie Fox, he'd immediately sailed for Leith. "I'll talk to Roxane when she returns from seeing Christian Dunbar," he said with a sigh. "But if she's seen Elizabeth, my gut tells me to take them both out tomorrow night." He looked to his cousin for his opinion.

"They won't be expecting anyone to try and move a man as near death as Johnnie," Munro said. "I agree. Tomorrow. If Roxane has good information. But timing's essential. Once Elizabeth is freed, the alarm may be

raised. We have to be ready to go into the prison the second she's out of Queensberry's hands."

"In that case, gentlemen," their lawyer said, giving
in gracefully, "I shall be ready with the gold to open
those first doors aboveground." His smile was grim. "The
keys for the rest, I'm afraid, will require a fight."

Early that evening, Roxane, Robbie, and Munro ex
changed information in her private sitting room.

"Elizabeth isn't even guarded," Roxane said. "They
must feel she's well hidden. And considering the usual
state of news in this small city, she is; it took over a day
for my very competent caddies to find her."

"If she's not guarded, her rescue should be rela-
tively simple," Munro noted.

"The key to Elizabeth's room is on Christian's chatelaine, if you prefer not breaking the door down."

"I'd like to be as unobtrusive as possible, since
we're going into the prison almost simultaneously."
Robbie was sprawled on Roxie's sofa, his boots resting on
the curved padded arm. "I think we'll use Christian's key
and then make sure she and her staff are locked away
when we leave."

"If Johnnie can't travel or if you don't dare make for
Leith immediately, you're welcome to come back here."

"Notice how optimistic our hostess is," Munro said
with a faint smile for Robbie.

"Cathcart escaped a year ago without a trace,"
Roxane reminded them. "The price of freedom is negoti-
able apparently even in the castle prison."

"Douglas tells us he can pay to open the doors
aboveground," Robbie said to her, "but Queensberry has
his own men at the final gates."

"Take enough of your Carres then to deal with
them."

"Too many men will raise the alarm."

"I'm tempted to talk to Commander Gordon himself. Perhaps he has a price."

"If he weren't dependent on Queensberry's patronage for his place, I'd say your idea might be feasible. Unfortunately ..." Munro's voice trailed away.

"We'll have Johnnie free, Roxane," Robbie assured her. "One way or another."

"Remember, if you need them, those rooms on the top floor where you're staying will continue to be safe; I've enough influential friends—no one would dare search my home." She was being modest; as the reigning beauty in Edinburgh, some even said in Britain, she had most of the powerful men in the country eager to please her.

"We hope to make for the ship."

Robbie nodded his agreement. "Although it depends on Johnnie's health. Coutts says he's desperately weak."

"Where will Elizabeth be taken?"

"Directly to the *Trondheim*."

"I shall be at a dinner party and ball at the Chancellor's house tomorrow night anxiously awaiting news. I expect the outcry over the prison escape will reach some of the Privy Council before morning. Tonight I go to the Countess Pamure's. I may hear gossip of Queensberry, for he's known to have had a *tendre* for her in the past."

"We ride for the *Trondheim* after dark," Robbie said, "to bring in sufficient arms for tomorrow night. I'll leave one of our men to accompany you to the Countess's should you need to reach us with a message; he can pose as one of your footmen. I don't envy you your evening though," he added with a grin. "The Countess is likely to recite her newest love poems. . . ."

"And you're not romantical?" Roxane teased.

"One in the family is enough," the young Master of Graden ironically noted. "Although none of his acquaintances would have bet a shilling on Johnnie Carre's understanding of love a year ago."

Redmond's men had been on surveillance at Harold Godfrey's lodgings since they'd arrived in the city, changing watch every two hours so their appearance wouldn't be conspicuous, hoping the Earl of Brusisson would lead them to Elizabeth. But he'd not exited his apartments since the messenger had arrived. And according to the occupant of the floor below Godfrey's flat, Harold Godfrey lived alone.

As they continued their watch, an elegant coach drew up to the entrance of the building late in the evening, and moments later Harold Godfrey, dressed modishly in blue velvet and black lace, strolled through the door and stepped into the gleaming carriage.

As the vehicle rolled away, a figure pushed away from the shadows of the wall and, picking his way across the garbage-strewn cobbled street, moved into another shadowed doorway on the opposite side. "He gave Countess Pamure's as his direction," one of Redmond's men said to him.

"I'll send another man to you," Redmond quietly replied, "and I'll find my way to the Countess's; the drivers should have some information. I'll see what I can discover."

So Redmond was curbside with a group of coachmen when Roxane's carriage deposited her at Countess Pamure's town home. While he didn't recognize the copper-haired beauty alighting from her carriage, he knew the woman's footman who was assisting her from her blue-lacquered coach.

As Roxane carefully navigated the short distance to the entrance on her high pattens, her hooped skirts and velvet cloak gripped firmly in her hands, Redmond moved slightly away from the gossiping drivers so he'd be visible to the footman following his mistress toward the torch-lit doorway. Neither man spoke to the other, cautious in a city of strangers, but their eyes met in recognition, and the Carre clansman murmured, "Wait."

A short time later, when the disguised Carre clansman came outside, he and Redmond walked away from the cluster of waiting coachmen and grooms, moving down the street a small distance. Briefly, they exchanged information, and Redmond made arrangements to speak to Robbie later that night at Roxane's. The men parted after only a few minutes, and Redmond returned to his surveillance.

CHAPTER 25

Roxane had never met the Earl of Brusisson, but she knew the Duke of Queensberry as she knew everyone in the limited ranks of the Scottish nobility. And the man standing beside the Duke met Robbie's description of Harold Godfrey. Returning her attention to the young man who was complimenting her on the beauty of her gown while his gaze was focused several inches below her collarbones, she smiled graciously at him until his fulsome flattery came to an end and then said, "I'd be eternally in your debt, dear Buchan, if you'd fetch me a glass of claret. It's dreadfully hot in here." Tapping him lightly on his cheek with her ivory-and-lace fan, she added flirtatiously, "If you don't mind . . ."

After he rushed off to accommodate her, she glanced in the candle-lit mirror on the wall beside her, minutely adjusted the lace at her décolletage, practiced a fleeting winsome smile and, satisfied at her theatrical skills, glided toward the man who was attempting to end Johnnie Carre's life.

Queensberry saw her first as she approached and

half-turned toward her with a welcoming smile, interrupting his conversation so the taller man beside him turned to look as well. Roxane smiled at them both, flipped open her fan with practiced ease and, dipping into a minute curtsy that showed off her fine bosom to advantage, raised her seductive dark eyes. "It's so pleasant to see you back in town, James," she cordially declared. "The city loses a certain sophistication when you're absent."

"You're still beautifying it wonderfully, my dear," the Duke replied with an easy smile. "I find myself suddenly wishing I'd come back sooner."

"You haven't lost your smooth tongue, darling." Lightly brushing the lace edge of her fan under his chin, she winked at him, blatantly coquettish.

Harold Godfrey gently cleared his throat.

Queensberry's glance drifted over to him, and he said as if in afterthought, "Roxane, I'd like you to meet the Earl of Brusisson. He's in Scotland looking over some property. Brusisson, the Countess Kilmarnock."

Raising her eyes to Godfrey's extremely attentive regard, she immediately understood the accomplishment of her mission in approaching the two men was going well. Her smile took on a sultry opulence. "Will you be here long, Brusisson?"

"I haven't entirely decided. Do you stay in the city?"

"Most always . . ." The brutality in his eyes gave her mild pause; he made no effort to conceal it. "My children go to school here," she added, tamping down her squeamishness.

"Does your husband enjoy city life?"

"He did."

"Roxane is the most beautiful widow in Britain," Queensberry graciously interjected. "What do you hear of your brother? Is he still with Argyll?"

"He was in winter camp at The Hague last he wrote." As in so many Scottish families, her politics and her brother's didn't always agree. "He's enamored of the great Marlborough."

"As are a great many of our young cubs. The man can command."

"So Colter tells me with a nineteen-year-old's unequivocal enthusiasm. Will you be in Edinburgh for the sessions this year?"

"Perhaps."

"Then perhaps we'll see each other again. Give my regards to Isobel. There's Buchan now with my claret. It was a pleasure to meet you, Brusisson." And with a nod of her perfectly coiffed head, she left.

"She was Ravensby's lover for years," Queensberry declared as the men watched her gracefully swaying walk.

"She didn't seem stricken."

"She's buried two husbands. It tempers one's sense of commitment, perhaps. But if you call on her, Harold, a small warning. She's a friend of mine."

"I didn't say I was going to call on her."

Queensberry's smile was tolerant. "We both know you will."

But Roxane's very tight schedule wouldn't allow for the leisure of uncertainty, so she made a point of running into Harold Godfrey later that evening when he was standing alone for a moment. As she approached him, he stepped into her path so she was obliged to stop.

"I find Edinburgh much more interesting suddenly," he said, looking down at her from his formidable height.

"Could it be Cecilia's fascinating poetry recital?" she purred in a lush undertone, noting his interest in her décolletage.

"I despise poetry." He said the words very low, so she understood there were other things he saw he didn't despise.

She smiled provocatively, a well-practiced device in her repertoire. "A shame," she murmured, "for I'm having a few people over tomorrow night to listen to Edinburgh's favorite son. I thought you might enjoy his verse."

"When?"

She tipped her head a little to one side and looked up at him from under her lashes. "Come later. . . ." Insinuation was rich in her voice. "When the readings are over . . ."

"When?" No subtlety in his harsh response; his message was explicit.

"Say, half-past nine?"

"I'll be there," he said.

And there was no doubt in her mind he would be.

The group assembled in Roxane's private sitting room very late that night was augmented by Redmond's presence. And every detail had been gone over, for timing was everything in the success of their venture.

"I can keep Godfrey waiting for perhaps an hour and a half," Roxane said. "I'll see that my company doesn't leave as expected. . . ."

"Two of our men could pose as your guests, and after having sampled too much of your brandy could be disinclined to leave your fascinating presence," Robbie suggested, finding himself reluctant to leave her alone with Godfrey.

"I won't be able to put him off indefinitely, though, or he's apt to become suspicious."

"There's absolutely no need to bring him into your bedroom. He could be dangerous." Robbie gazed at her for a potent moment. "I know what you're thinking, but *don't* under any circumstances—"

"He *is* dangerous," Redmond quietly interjected. "If I didn't have to see Elizabeth to safety, I'd stay to help. He's killed many times in particularly brutal ways," he added in a carefully restrained murmur. "He's not normal."

"There," Robbie declared with a stabbing look at Roxane. "Do you understand?"

"I'll be extremely careful."

"All right, let's go over the schedule again," Robbie briskly said. "At nine-thirty Redmond and his men go in for Elizabeth. . . ."

And everyone recited the timetable again and then once more again . . . until each minute was accounted for, until every possible eventuality had been discussed, until every option had been considered in the execution and accomplishment of their plan.

Near dawn, everyone had left except Robbie, who had made himself comfortable on the sofa and was reluctant to remove himself upstairs, and Roxane, who lounged across from him on her favorite chaise. The young Master of Graden spoke in a hushed murmur. "Johnnie didn't appreciate you enough."

"No, he didn't," she said with a faint smile, "but he was lovely in other ways. . . ."

"Did it hurt you when he married?"

She thought for a moment. "In a way I was happy for him, because he'd never believed in love. . . . How could I begrudge him that joy?"

"Have you ever been in love?"

"A long time ago; I was very young."

"What happened?"

"I married him. Jamie Low, my first husband . . . and if he hadn't been killed at Namur, I'd still be in love."

"And what of Kilmarnock?"

"My parents said I was too young when Jamie died to be unmarried."

"Kilmarnock was older."

"Yes."

He didn't pursue his questioning about her second husband after Roxane's brief, terse reply. Apparently, it hadn't been a happy marriage. "And you're contentedly widowed now."

Her smile reappeared. "Very."

"We should be back to Scotland by summer," he said, thinking he'd miss her most of those he left behind, thinking it odd how tumultuous events distilled feelings to raw essentials. He lay there, elegant and lean, his rawboned young body all muscle and sinew beneath his well-cut clothes, one slender hand trailing on the floor, his long legs propped on the rolled arm of her sofa.

"I'm glad. I'll be here."

His head didn't move from its restful ease on an embroidered pillow, but his eyes traveled slowly down her form. "Don't marry again before I return."

"Not likely. I definitely prefer my freedom."

"I'm jealous of your freedom." His voice was only a whisper, his dark eyes half-lidded in lazy appraisal.

"I don't allow that."

He shrugged, one dark brow rising speculatively. "As if you could stop me, darling Roxie."

"You sound like your brother."

"I'm not my brother though. I'd appreciate you."

She gazed at him for a long moment, thinking how different their looks. Robbie's features were more refined, more fluent, than the harsher modeling of his older brother, his auburn hair drifting in unconstrained curls to his shoulders. Robbie's broad-shouldered, rangy body still retained a flaunting air of coltishness. "I'm ten years older than you," she said, the rich flamboyance of his youth a striking reminder of her own age.

"It didn't seem to matter that night last summer."

She sighed, a soft sound of regret. "I shouldn't have stayed."

"But the stars were brilliant that night," he reminded her with a grin.

"Ummm . . ." Her own smile recalled pleasant memories. "And the sea air always makes me amorous."

"I'll have to remember that."

She shook her head. "Darling, you're too young. I told you that the next morning . . . and my sentiments haven't changed. I've five children, my oldest only a few years younger than you." She gazed at him from under half-lowered lashes. "I can't."

"When I come back, I'll change your mind."

"No, you won't."

"We'll see," he said, dropping his booted feet on the carpet and hauling himself upright. "If I had more time tonight, I'd try to convince you." And strolling over to the chaise, he leaned over, placed his hands gently on her shoulders, and kissed her, not a youthful adolescent kiss, but a hot-blooded, dangerous kiss that recalled a wild, sensational night on Johnnie's yacht last summer. "Promise not to get married, now," he murmured when his mouth lifted from hers. "Because I'm coming back . . ."

"You shouldn't," she whispered, but her voice held an intoxicating tremor of passion, and her face lifted to his was enticingly flushed.

"But I am," he softly said, no more likely to take orders than his brother. He glanced quickly at the clock on the mantel. "I suppose your children will be up soon." It was a question, too, but lightly put because there wasn't time to press his suit with the seriousness of their ventures that night.

"Yes . . . very soon," Roxie swiftly answered, moving back the scant margin the bolster behind her would allow, as if mere physical distance would save her from Robbie Carre's temptation.

He smiled, recognizing her response. And then his expression changed, and he said in a serious tone that didn't sound young at all, but like that of a man familiar with command, "If I don't see you again before we leave, thank you for all you've done for Johnnie and Elizabeth. All the Carres are deeply indebted to you." Then his voice took on a curt, flinty edge. "And you're to take no chances tonight with Godfrey. Absolutely none. I won't have you hurt by him. I want your word."

She looked at him for a moment, fascinated by his abrupt transformation, his penetrating stare. And then she quietly said, "My word on it."

His smile reappeared. "I wish you luck then."

"You'll be careful?"

"Of course."

"Send me a note through Coutts when you reach Holland."

"That air of assurance sounds like a blessing."

"It is. I never tempt the deities with the possibility of misfortune."

He preferred less mythical benefactors, good weapons and loyal clansmen his first choice, but he smiled his agreement. "Until next summer then," he said with a small bow. And left.

Roxane found it difficult to sleep after he'd gone, her emotions in turmoil. It was all well and good to repudiate Robbie's advances and declare herself aloof from his youthful charm. But she wasn't, of course, physically at least, and he'd perfectly well understood her response. It was unthinkable though, utterly impossible. The boy was eighteen.

CHAPTER 26

At nine o'clock in Edinburgh that night, Roxane was listening to the renowned poet as she sat in her drawing room, surrounded by her guests. The candlelit room was ablaze with light; footmen circulated among the guests offering wines and spirits as harpsichord music drifted in from the adjoining room, soft background to the poetry. She glanced at the clock, felt the palms of her hands sweating inside her kidskin gloves, and reached for her glass of claret, fortification for her dangerous game with Harold Godfrey.

At the same time, Redmond and his men were in place in a shadowed wynd near Queensberry's Canongate house, waiting for nine-thirty. A timepiece rested in Redmond's palm, tipped slightly toward the meager light shining from a window across the narrow lane, and the gold-chased minute hand was moving slowly toward the six. A carriage waited on the next street, its shades drawn, the driver well armed, alert for the arrival of his passenger.

In a tavern near the castle gate Robbie, Munro,

Adam, and Kinmont sat in a curtained cubicle, its grimy drapery left open enough so the doorway was visible. When the runner from Redmond crossed that portal, it was their signal to leave.

Elizabeth sat at the table in her room, a book open before her, the words an unfocused blur. She'd not heard again from Roxane, but she was alert to any sound—tomorrow night, Roxane had said. Tonight, now. She cast a glance toward the armoire where she'd left her cloak conveniently hanging near the half-opened door, tried to calculate for the hundredth time how many hours had elapsed since her dinner had been brought to her. Without a clock in the room she was desperately unsure and so tense, her clasped hands showed white at her knuckles.

Outside the house Redmond whispered, "Now," jamming the watch into his coat pocket. "Stay out of sight until the servant opens the door," he warned his men. And he walked out of the wynd into the cobbled street that faced on Queensberry's house, the bodyguard from Three Kings like shadows behind him.

But he stood alone at the door when he knocked, dressed like the city guard, his face composed, his hands empty of weapons. When the small peephole slid open and the servant inquired his business so late at night, Redmond said, "The Duke has sent me with a message for Miss Dunbar."

The sound of bolts sliding brought his men melting closer to the entrance from their positions along the masonry wall, and when the studded door opened that first fraction of an inch, Redmond was inside in a flash, his hand over the old porter's mouth. No one spoke, not a sound indicated that ten men had just entered the narrow six-story house. The porter was bound and gagged in seconds and deposited in the entrance closet where he normally slept—with two of Redmond's men to guard him and their exit route.

It was a silent swift sweep of the floors, overpowering the servants in the basement rooms and Christian in her bedchamber, along with her maid. Then, as a man stood guard at each stairway level, Redmond proceeded to the fourth floor, where Roxane had described Elizabeth's room. He spoke for the first time since he'd entered the house.

"It's Redmond, don't be alarmed," he said, very low, his mouth near the door. "I have the key."

A moment later he stood in the narrow doorway, his uniform strange but his face and form blessedly familiar, his smile offering her salvation. "Are you ready?"

Elizabeth nodded and grinned. "You're a long way from home," she said, walking swiftly toward the armoire to gather her cloak.

"So are you."

"Hopefully, I'll be even farther away by morning," she replied, tossing her cloak over her shoulders as she moved toward him. "Roxane said I have to be out first."

"We've five minutes. Give me your hand, the stairs are steep."

They were outside in three minutes after navigating the spiral staircase, the door closed behind them, all peace and utter silence in the Duke of Queensberry's house. Another two minutes to reach the carriage on the adjacent street, and Elizabeth was traveling through the streets of Edinburgh on her way to the ship at Leith, Redmond and his men riding guard.

It was so easy, Elizabeth thought, hanging tightly to the carriage strap as the driver whipped his horses through the narrow streets. Thanks to Roxane, whose caddie had discovered her location. Thanks to Roxane, who'd managed to talk her way upstairs. She didn't know it then, but her husband's rescue would be aided as well by his former lover, Roxane, who was at that precise moment smiling at Harold Godfrey.

"You're very prompt," she was saying as she greeted Elizabeth's father at the gilded archway to her drawing room. "Forgive the hordes of people yet, but he recited a bit longer than I'd planned. Would you like brandy?"

As a man who played the suitor poorly, the Earl's displeasure was obvious; he'd not expected company. "Yes, brandy," he gruffly replied, scanning the room as if counting the number of people he must manhandle out the door.

"It won't take long to see them all on their way," Roxane murmured, putting her hand on his arm to guide him through the guests. "Most are going on to the assembly at Blair Close. Are you in a hurry?" The amorous suggestion in her voice mildly insinuated speed wasn't a particular favorite of hers.

"No, of course not." He wasn't a fool; a woman of her voluptuous beauty was worth waiting for.

"How nice." She leaned into his arm slightly so he felt the swell of her breast. "Now come along, and we'll see you get some excellent French brandy."

And as Roxane was giving orders to a footman, thanks to Coutts's lavish bribery, the most remote outside portal into Edinburgh Castle was sliding open to admit the Carres. Two more barriers gave way to them after a signal knock with the same silent unsealing, as though ghostly hands cleared their passage, and then they were on their own. Through the Portcullis Gate they raced up Hawk Hill to the lower levels of the Great Hall. Two men carried burning torches into the gloomy depths of the vaults beneath it, illuminating the damp channels cut into the earth as they descended deeper underground. The first cavern they came to with cells cut into the walls had two guards, who died where they sat playing dice, their throats cut.

At the next level they rushed the three men and killed them, too, ruthless in their mission, not willing to leave witnesses. And at the last metal door that required unlocking from the inside, Robbie wore a uniform from one of the dead guards to gain admittance. When the door began to swing open, he pushed through and shot the last two guards point-blank, his two pistols blazing fire in the underground gloom. Deep in the bowels of the earth the sharp explosions went unnoticed.

Jamming the smoking flintlocks into his shoulder holsters, he swiftly plucked the keys from the dead man's fingers, and striding to the single door that had been so carefully guarded by three separate barriers, he slid the key into the lock. The man on the rude pallet lay motionless as the grilled door opened, the light from their flickering torches casting a dim light on Johnnie's sprawled form lying facedown, utterly still on the filthy straw.

Even though they'd been warned by Coutts, the sight was shocking.

He was still clad in his bloodstained breeches and boots. Johnnie's savaged back was so hideous—infected, inflamed, oozing pus—that Robbie wondered for a stricken moment whether they'd arrived too late.

Quickly kneeling at his brother's side, he placed his palm on Johnnie's cheek; his skin was hot, burning with fever, but he was breathing. Not sure whether he was conscious, Robbie leaned close, his mouth near his brother's ear. "It's Robbie! Can you hear me? We're here to take you out."

Johnnie's eyes opened slowly, by fractional degrees, as if it took all his strength to achieve that simple feat, the incandescent glitter of fever evident even in the half-shadow. "Elizabeth," he whispered, his voice so faint, Robbie had to strain to hear the words.

"She's safe."

A faint smile appeared, the merest movement of his mouth, and a moment passed before he could gather his strength to speak again. "Help me up," he whispered.

"Swallow this first." Robbie placed a small pellet in his brother's mouth, the opiate a suggestion of Coutts, who'd seen Johnnie's condition. Taking a flask from his pocket, Robbie opened it, gently lifted his brother's head, and tipped a trickle of water into his mouth. The small effort seemed to have exhausted Johnnie's strength, for his eyes closed again. Turning to the others standing above him, Robbie said under his breath, "We'll have to carry him."

"How?" Adam murmured, swallowing hard, the raw flesh on Johnnie's back ghastly.

"There's no choice. He's going to die here if we don't get him out. You and Kinmont on either side of him. Munro and I'll clear the way. Any questions?"

Robbie waited a brief moment for a response, then bent over his brother again. "The morphine will take a few minutes to affect you, but we can't wait." Speaking directly into Johnnie's ear, he pronounced the words slowly and carefully. "We're going to lift you up now. Do you understand?"

Johnnie nodded, bracing himself for the pain.

When they lifted him to his feet, he groaned like a wounded animal, his ravaged body swamped, overwhelmed by a merciless pain that left him drenched in a cold sweat. He swayed unsteadily even supported by Adam and Kinmont, his powerful body sapped by fever and infection, only sheer willpower maintaining him upright. Bracing his booted feet, locking his knees with a conscious dogged determination, he slowly brought his head up. "How much time do we have?" Robbie's head swiveled around at the sound of his brother's voice, restored to near normal with what effort he could only imagine. "Very little," he honestly replied. "A guard makes rounds every half hour."

"I'll try and walk then," Johnnie murmured, the muscles across his jaw clenching with the strain of remaining erect. "Give me a dirk." A ghostly smile flitted across his mouth. "In case I meet Godfrey."

Robbie transferred his dirk to Johnnie's belt, and they began the laborious journey upward, Robbie and Munro in advance as scouts, Kinmont and Adam following more slowly, with Johnnie supported between them.

Johnnie silently counted his steps, as if the words would be conscious impulse to his brain to move his limbs. He tried with what slender control he had over the debilitating pain to set up a barricade, in his mind against the agony racking his body. And he managed by grit and nerve to maintain the shaky equilibrium between locomotion and collapse.

Kinmont and Adam held him firmly by his upper arms, taking great care to avoid touching his back, standing well away from him, letting him set his own pace. They moved upward without incident through two levels, divesting several of the dead guards of their tunics, progressing laboriously up the last steep stairway until they reached the outside door to the vaults.

Drenched with sweat after the grueling climb, Johnnie's fevered body responded to the blessed coolness of the winter air, and he inhaled as if the cold could penetrate his heart and lungs as well.

All was quiet in the shadow of the masonry wall, the city below them invisible beneath the misty fog.

"Another ten minutes," Robbie whispered. "Can you do it?" In the darkness he tried to discern the state of his brother's debility.

"I'd crawl ... through ... hell," Johnnie murmured, his breathing still uneven after the exertion up the steep flight of stairs, "to get ... out."

"The next few hundred yards might be a close approximation," Robbie declared, his voice cautionary.

"I'm ready," Johnnie said. Whatever reserves of strength he still retained would be needed to carry him through the last great distance. The morphine had finally begun to invade the outermost fringes of his mind, and his legs seemed to have the ability to move now without overt directions.

The men dressed in the guards' jackets closed ranks around Johnnie, whose wounds wouldn't allow the weight of a coat, and they began the slow, torturous gauntlet down the curved cobbled road of Hawks Hill to the main gate. It was dangerous to be so exposed, five men against the castle garrison, out in the open with no concealment, but there was only one way out; the next few minutes would test their courage.

No moon shone through the smothering cloud bank spreading over the city from the firth, the shadows inky black beneath the walls bordering the road. And they moved down the damp, slick cobbles toward freedom. Only a single soldier passed them going back up the hill toward the barracks, but he was half-drunk from the look of his straggling walk and paid them no notice.

Three guarded portals remained before the last gate opened; the first two gave way as planned, their guards rich enough for their night's work to retire in the morning. But in the small room commanding the gatehouse, four officers had just entered from the street as the Carres reached the entryway, the men apparently back from a night in the taverns on the High Street from their raucous good spirits. To the Carres' dismay as they waited in the shadows beyond the lighted doorway, the officers sat down to join in the guards' card game.

They waited in the narrow stone-walled corridor, watching through the half-opened door, their time limited before the prison guards would make their scheduled rounds in the vaults.

Johnnie's strength was almost depleted, his force of will barely able to maintain his flagging energy. Kinmont and Adam were bearing most of his weight now.

"Go in and get them," Johnnie murmured, understanding the limits of their time, of his strength, and that freedom lay just beyond that last gate. Liberty was too near to relinquish without a fight.

"Can you stand alone?" Robbie whispered, needing all his men against those in the guardroom.

"If you hurry," Johnnie replied with a touch of his old smile, bracing his hands against the wall.

They attacked immediately, every minute crucial, bursting through the door, swords drawn, and within seconds, they were fully engaged. The previously paid guards slipped out the door when the skirmish began, not wishing to jeopardize their lives with their new wealth already in hand, and the officers defended themselves alone against the fierce assault. As one officer went down, another shouted for help, his cry echoing across the artillery ground toward the Portcullis Gate of the castle.

Immediately increasing the attack, pressing hard against the possibility of reinforcements, the Carres forced the remaining swordsmen to retreat, their blades slashing and parrying, cutting, thrusting, driving their opponents back, a new intensity to their movements, their time disastrously limited, the High Street just beyond the bolted doorway.

Braced against the wall in the darkened passage, near collapse, Johnnie watched horror-stricken as the fallen soldier raised himself from the flagged floor, propped his weight on one elbow, and, drawing his pistol—unnoticed in the fray—carefully aimed at Robbie's back.

Automatically, Johnnie reached for the dirk at his hip, the movement instinctive, the result excruciating. He staggered as the lacerating agony flooded his senses. Wavering, not sure for a flickering moment he could retain consciousness, his mind struggled to overcome the brutal torment. He had to continue to think, to act and quickly. He saw the man's finger tighten on the trigger. In the transient moment when the smothering pain began to recede from its convulsive peak, he reacted, knowing he'd be incapable of movement when the next annihilating spasm savaged his body; he jerked the dagger from its leather sheath and hurled it in a single uninterrupted flowing motion, its trajectory volatile, true, impelled by superhuman necessity.

He saw the double-edged blade sink into the man's neck at the base of his skull just as the next tide of corrosive agony struck him, and he doubled over, writhing from the shock, nauseous, his ears ringing, the pain unbearable. His knees gave way. He caught himself with his hands as he fell, the damp cobblestone cool on his palms, and he struggled to rise. But a heavy blackness engulfed him, and his arms gave way.

His clansmen carried him outside moments later over the slain bodies, and with what speed they could manage under the burden of his weight, the four men traveled through the narrow dark wynds and alleys the few short blocks to Roxane's, secreting themselves in the small stable at the back of her garden.

"Wait here, while I go in and see if Godfrey's left," Robbie murmured, thankful his brother was still unconscious. While they were transporting Johnnie, his back had begun bleeding and, rather than leave a trail in their flight, they'd tied their shirts around his torso. The makeshift bandages were soaked through with blood.

At the conclusion of the poetry reading, Roxane had watched her guests leave with rising apprehension, not sure the two Carre clansmen feigning sleep on her fine chintz sofas would be sufficient to guard her from the forceful Godfrey. But she'd kept watch of the hour, and the allotted time for Johnnie's escape had passed. Now, as her last guest descended the curved stairway, she found herself on the landing with Harold Godfrey beside her, standing much too close for comfort. No servants were in evidence, a fact the Earl of Brusisson had noted as well. Taking advantage of the first opportunity he'd had to have the Countess to himself all evening, he grasped her by her arms and pulled her close.

"Now show me your bedchamber, Countess," he said, his voice brusque. "I've waited all evening for your favors."

"Really, Brusisson," Roxane murmured, attempting a placating smile, "you could observe a modicum more gallantry."

"You tease, madam, as if I were an adolescent." His tone was a low growl. "Acquit me of any further need for gallantry. I've dangled after you through a great number of revolting poems."

"I think, sir, you must have misunderstood your invitation." A touch of sharpness shaded her words. Taking a step backward, she attempted to pull away.

His grip tightened on her arms. "On the contrary, madam, perhaps you misunderstood my intent."

"And if I did, surely you don't intend to threaten me in my own house." Her voice had risen, a warning to the men in her drawing room.

"Why would I threaten, Countess?" he serenely replied, his calm voice counterpoint to the menace in his eyes. "Consider my interest only an intense fascination, impatience for your enticing charms."

"Perhaps when I know you better, Brusisson," Roxane retorted, struggling against his grip. "I find you moving too fast on such short acquaintance. Would you please leave now?" she said, and jerked away.

Only to find herself recaptured a second later. "Not so fast, my puss. I find I don't wish to leave yet."

"You should listen to the lady," a male voice said. The Earl swiveled around to see the two guests no longer sleeping but at attention in the doorway of the drawing room. "And you two can bid the Countess good night," he ordered, "and be on your way."

"The Sassenachs never did have any manners," the dark-haired man drawled, his hand on his sword.

"Unhand her, Brusisson," the other man ordered.

At that inopportune moment Roxane saw Robbie materialize out of the shadows of the corridor behind Harold Godfrey, at the far end of the hall where the servants' staircase lay. Instantly placing her hand on Godfrey's arm, she urged him toward the main staircase, a smile she hoped was sufficiently real considering her panic gracing her mouth. "I have a suggestion, Harold," she cajoled, her voice husky, frantically concentrating his interest on her so he wouldn't look around. "Perhaps you could return some other time when the ah"—her glance flicked toward the two men—"situation would allow us to become better acquainted. Come back tomorrow," she added in a whisper, "when these young cubs are gone. They're both too drunk to reason with. Please . . ."

He looked down at her for a brief moment, weighing her sudden reversal, the sincerity of her offer, against the possible problems arising from two inebriated Scotsmen with their hands on their swords.

"Tomorrow at five," she murmured definitely. "I'll make certain that we can visit . . . privately."

His eyes held hers for a moment more, and then he released her. "Your servant, madam," he curtly said, resentment still prominent in his tone. Not prone to bloody himself for her, he added, "Until tomorrow."

Robbie was striding toward her before Godfrey had disappeared down the stairway. Casting a nervous glance down the carpeted stairs at the receding figure, she rushed to intercept him, pushing him backward, with a whispered warning. "He's going, Robbie. Don't do anything foolish. Think of Johnnie."

His resistance lessened at the logic of her words, although his expression was still mutinous. But he relented enough so she was able to propel him back into the shadows, where he stopped so suddenly, she ran up against him.

He steadied her against his body, his arms sliding down her back, an instinctive impulse. "He touched you," he heatedly whispered. "I'll kill him."

"No, don't say that," she pleaded, covering his mouth with her fingers, her heart pounding against her ribs at the near calamity. "It's over. He's gone. Please . . ."

His gaze seemed to focus again, the violence vanished from his eyes. Whether because of her entreaty or some internal perception, his blind incaution was gone as suddenly as he'd appeared from out of the shadows. His hand came up to capture her fingers at his mouth and he kissed them briefly, a courtier's mannered caress. "Thank you for keeping Godfrey occupied." His voice was calm again. "It was absolutely critical. But we have to get Johnnie inside now." His hand on her back slid away from her body, and he signaled for the two men who waited at the end of the corridor to follow him. "We have him safe," he added, pulling Roxane along toward the back staircase. "But he's unconscious and seriously hurt."

Within the hour Johnnie was washed, medicated, fed, and sleeping peacefully in a clean, soft bed. But Roxane's housekeeper who'd cared for his back had shaken her head in dismay. "It's putrid, my Lady," she'd said, "and I don't rightly know if the poultices will save him."

A message had been sent to the *Trondheim* so Elizabeth would know Johnnie was free. And the rescue party gathered in Johnnie's bedchamber, anxiously keeping vigil, concerned with his condition. The process of cleaning his wounds had been a gut-wrenching experience. Even familiar with battle wounds as all of them were—Roxane had seen her husband Jamie die after Namur—the mutilation and suppuration of Johnnie's flesh, the taint of decay in the open, oozing flesh had alarmed them all. An apothecary who could be trusted had been sent for, an authority to prescribe the proper regimen.

"Do you think Elizabeth will come tonight?" Adam asked.

"Do you think Redmond can stop her?" Robbie quietly replied. "Even though the streets must be swarming with patrols by now."

"*I* wouldn't stay on the ship not knowing my husband's condition," Roxane declared, a disturbing solemnity in her voice.

Robbie gazed at her, the firelight bathing his face in flickering iridescence and shadow, his eyes veiled in shade, their expression obscured. "You went to Jamie at Namur, didn't you?"

"Yes," she said, those long-ago events, the overwhelming sorrow, vividly recalled in this sickroom with a man half-dead as Jamie had been.

Her grief was obvious, and without speaking Robbie rose and went to sit by her on the settee. Taking her hand, he enclosed it gently in his. "I wish I could have been there to help," he murmured, his voice low, grave, inaudible to the others.

She leaned into him, and he put his arm around her, the half-forgotten memories fresh again, graphic, and she needed him for comfort against the sudden aching emptiness.

Munro diplomatically talked of other things then— of the plans for Holland, of the apothecary's return, of Redmond's competence to see Elizabeth safely to Roxane's. He handled the conversation so there was no need in the shrouded firelit room for Roxane to exert herself to be sociable or act as hostess to her guests. She appreciated his kindness; she wasn't capable at the moment of the least politesse.

The apothecary arrived first bringing a satchel of drugs and potions, salves and ointments. He was deeply engaged in his diagnosis, with everyone standing about him, carefully listening to his discourse, when a flurry of sound in the corridor alerted them to Elizabeth's arrival.

She was running, as were her guards, and the door swung open before a servant could reach it; Elizabeth stood framed for a moment on the threshold, her face haunted with fear.

Under the circumstances no one had the inclination for polite salutations, or the heart to acquaint her with the grim truth. And she didn't ask or stop or deflect her gaze from the man on the bed as she crossed the large room in a swift direct course.

She stood by the bed for an affected moment, utterly thankful to see her husband alive; without reservation, grateful. Her eyes blurred with tears. Then she touched Johnnie's hand gently, as if to reassure herself he was real, and her hand moved after a time to his head, careful not to wake him, her fingers light on his dark, ruffled hair. Her face was wet with tears, her heart tormented with anguish; she thought of how terribly he'd suffered, how much pain he'd endured.

No one dared intrude until she turned from the bed. "Thank you all for putting your lives at risk, she said quietly, "and for bringing Johnnie out in time." His wounds weren't bandaged, for any pressure caused new bleeding, so the extent of his injuries was grimly apparent. "He's going to live," Elizabeth softly murmured, a tentative smile transforming her tear-streaked face. "I'm going to see to it."

She moved to hug Robbie first and next Roxane, who stood at his side, and then Munro, Adam, and Kinmont. Even the housekeeper and apothecary were included in her joyous gratitude, although they weren't quite certain how to respond to such democratic behavior. After embracing everyone, her relief tangible, vital, as if nothing were unattainable now that she had her husband back, she turned to the apothecary. "Now tell me what we have to do," she briskly said, this woman who thought nothing of taking on five-year building projects and an abusive father, who had survived eight years in the Graham household. Untying her cloak and tossing it on a chair, she added, "I intend to learn how to nurse a fever. Although," she went on in warning, "I also intend to feed him well and forbid cupping. Just so we all understand each other."

Her voice—its competent tone, its unhesitating

certainty and brisk optimism—must have touched some part of Johnnie's brain because his eyes half opened even in his sedated state and his lips moved. And he whispered, "Bitsy," with a faint smile.

Spinning around at the sound of his voice, she flew to the bed and, placing her face close to his, she looked into his half-lidded gaze. "I'm here," she whispered, fresh tears in her eyes.

His eyelids drifted shut again, in his drugged state the effort to hold them open as arduous as moving mountains. "Don't go," he murmured, his hand moving toward her fractionally.

Her fingers laced through his, she squeezed his hand. "I'm never leaving," she whispered.

His fingers tightened infinitesimally on hers, and he drifted back to sleep.

CHAPTER 27

In the next half hour everyone gradually took their leave as Elizabeth settled into the sickroom with the nursing help and a full complement of servants.

It was almost three in the morning when Robbie walked Roxane down two flights of stairs to her bedchamber. As they stood outside her door, a small silence fell between them, the events of the evening wrenchingly emotional, their feelings sensitized by all the reminders of the fugitive quality of life. "Thank you for your kindness tonight," Roxane softly said. "I'd thought those memories long buried."

Robbie shrugged, a negligent acquittal. "The circumstances were too similar. Of course you'd remember." Then his smile flashed in the dimly lit hallway. "At least Elizabeth's uncompromising in her optimism and prepared to take charge of the sickroom. She and the apothecary were heatedly discussing whether they should wake Johnnie with a new poultice when we left."

"They make a good pair, she and Johnnie," Roxane

noted. "They're both prompt to take action, they have a way of dealing—"

"May I come in?" he softly interrupted, his gaze on her face, his interest at variance with their conversation.

She stopped in midsentence, a half-formed word on her tongue, her breath in temporary suspension. She looked up at him for a trembling moment, her heart in her eyes, and then said, "No," in a breathless rush. The temptation to say yes was powerful in the darkened hallway, with her emotions in disarray, with his lean young body so close, with the unsubstantial specter of Jamie's death haunting her.

Robbie drew in a deep breath of restraint and courtesy, his desire sharp-set. "Good night, then," he murmured, touching her hand lightly with his fingertips. He didn't dare kiss her; there were limits to his self-discipline.

"I'll see you in the morning." Her voice sounded unnatural, constrained.

He nodded, not capable of casual speech. And watched her turn and enter her bedroom, the door softly closing behind her.

Quiet settled on the large house off the Canongate, on a night crowned with success, the Laird of Ravensby and his lady free from their captors, the Carres in safe refuge, secure from the hue and cry raised at their escape.

Candles burned in a small number of rooms in the Countess's house, but their radiance was shrouded from the outside by heavy draperies. Those few occupants still awake, Roxane among them, found sleep elusive.

She was curled up in a soft chair near the fire, contemplating the rich color of the claret in her glass. She'd thought the wine would help her sleep, but she'd hardly drunk it, she realized, turning the glass in her hands, her thoughts too much in tumult, too restless. She set the glass aside and rose from the chair, turning away from the grate.

In midrotation, she stood arrested, her hand on her

mouth, her eyes wide with shock, the firelight shimmering off her yellow silk gown.

"I couldn't stay away," Robbie said, leaning against the door, still dressed as she'd left him or rather half-undressed, as he'd been since returning from his deliverance of Johnnie. His potent virility struck her like a blow. As he'd given up his shirt to bind Johnnie's wounds on the journey from the prison, his upper body was nude, except for his unbuckled leather jack. His muscled arms and broad chest gleamed in the candlelight.

His tall frame seemed taller in the shadowed room, his presence perilous to her shaky resolve. "How long have you been here?" she asked, as if it would help qualify her response.

"Not long. I went upstairs when I left you. I was going to be compliant."

"And you're not going to be now." She found her heart begin to race with a disquieting excitement.

"I don't think so."

"This is my house," she reminded him, standing straight-backed, attempting to intimidate him with a kind of propriety.

"I know." His voice was quiet, without inflection.

"You've picked a poor night."

"I know."

"I should call for a servant to put you out."

"You should," he murmured, pushing away from the door and moving toward her. "You really should."

The opened buckles on his leather jack jingled as he walked, and she found herself drawn to the small ringing sound, her gaze mesmerized by the lean, hard modeling of his chest, the ridged muscles sharply defined as he neared, the sleek length of his torso tantalizing at close range, his bronzed skin disappearing beneath his belt—her glance drifted lower ... inside his chamois breeches.

As if reading her thoughts, he took her hand when he reached her and placed it on his chest, holding it there under his palm. "I'm on fire for you," he whispered. "Feel me."

He was hot, despite his lack of clothes, and her

hand quivered under his. "I'm trying to fight this," she whispered, her eyes lifted to his.

"I am too. I told myself it was unseemly, indecent to intrude on your sorrow. Yet here I am, tactless, selfish, impatient, disinclined to listen to another rebuff."

"Is that a warning?" But she said the words with a quiver in her voice.

He drew in a very slow, deep breath, shut his eyes for a moment, and then exhaled. "Probably not," he said with a faint smile.

"A small equivocation yet?" Her tentative smile tantalized without meaning to.

He swore under his breath; he'd not had occasion before to restrain his desire, and he was finding the effort difficult if not impossible. "Come talk to me," he suggested, curling her hand in his and pulling her toward the chairs arranged near the fire. "But don't tell me you're twenty-eight and have five children," he said, looking down at her with a sidelong glance, "because I don't care."

And when she tried to sit across from him, he drew her onto his lap instead, leaned back, made her comfortable in his arms, smoothed her billowing skirt, and said, "I'm listening."

"You're too nonchalant," she began, a small agitation fluttering up her spine.

He shook his head. "I'm serious."

"I'm too vulnerable tonight." She spoke in almost a whisper.

"I'll hold you."

"I'll hate myself in the morning."

"I'll see that you don't."

"What will the servants say?"

He gazed at her from under his lowered lashes, his expression mildly incredulous. "That's not a good one."

Her grin was conciliatory. "I have a headache."

"I can fix that," he replied with an easy confidence. "Now, if you've run out of excuses .. " His right hand leisurely slipped under her legs.

"Wait—"

Poised to lift her, he paused.

"You know this isn't wise."

At eighteen, not known for his prudence, Robbie smiled at her choice of words. "If that's the best you can do ..." His left arm tightened its hold on her back, and he rose from the chair with an effortless strength. "I'll lock the door," he casually added, "against early risers and," he went on with a grin, "inquisitive servants."

"I'm guilt-ridden," Roxane whispered against his shoulder as he twisted the key in the lock. "Indecisive ... totally unsure ..."

"I know." He held her very close for a moment, then bent his head and kissed the tip of her nose. "You'll feel better in a few minutes."

"Arrogant youngster," she said, but her violet eyes held a strange heat, and her arms held him tightly.

"I'm so hot," Robbie whispered, "I'm burning...." And he strode swiftly toward the bed, not sure he could wait, not sure he could control himself much longer, not sure he could keep from ravishing her. Placing her gently on the bed, he slipped her silk shoes off, tossed them on the floor and began climbing on top of her.

"Your boots ..." she incongruously said like a mother.

"Later," he murmured on a suffocated breath, and covered her body with his so she felt the extravagant extent of his arousal. Covered her mouth with his so she felt a reckless hot invasion as his tongue plunged like a portent of pleasure down her throat. A spiking lust streaked through her senses at his wild urgency; cool air swept over her thighs as he roughly pushed her skirts and petticoats out of his way. She lost the feel of his weight lightly braced above her for a moment while he ripped the buttons open on his breeches, and she wondered with a breathless gasp as he drove into her why she'd denied herself so long.

She'd forgotten how vital he was, how rash and reckless and wild.

She'd forgotten how he teased and tantalized, how he filled her so completely, rapture melted through her pores, sang through her senses.

She'd forgotten how orgasmic he was, how insatiable, how innovative.

"You didn't want to remember," he bluntly said when she told him much later that night, or morning, as it was—when he lay beside her stroking her breast in ever-widening circles as she arched her back and sighed in pleasure. "But I won't let you forget again." His hand slipped down her stomach, then lower, and she lifted her hips to encourage him. "I'll leave an indelible memory tonight," he whispered as his fingers slipped inside her.

And she realized in the morning when she woke to his kiss that against all reason and logic and sensible remonstrance, she was in love again after all these years. And she was terrified.

"You have to go," she whispered, frantic with fear. How could she deal with the overwhelming problems? She couldn't. Her life had resolved itself into a placid existence since Kilmarnock's death. Falling in love would disrupt that hard-won serenity, disorder her children's lives. And the shame of it! Everyone would titter. Ten years' difference. It was too great a divide.

"Do you have chocolate for breakfast?" Robbie's mouth was drifting over her cheek.

"You can't stay. I can't deal with the—"

"Scandal?"

"Yes."

"I'll put my clothes back on. I'll be your gallant at your morning toilette. I'm not going."

"Oh, God . . ."

"I've loved you since that night last summer."

"No, don't say that."

His large hands imprisoned her head, and he held her face firmly between his palms. "Look at me," he ordered. "I'm not going away. My loving you isn't going to stop. I'm here, and I'm staying here, and you can deny and pretend, but I know better. You said you loved me last night."

She tried to shake her head.

His dark eyes drilled into hers. "I remember."

"No!" Distress. Alarm.

He smiled. "Maybe this time you won't send all my presents back, like you did last summer."

"Oh, Robbie . . ." Her eyes suddenly filled with tears. "It won't work. I can't handle the ridicule. You're going too fast. Why don't we just take pleasure in the—"

"Sex?" His voice was curt, his eyes suddenly cool, and a second later he abruptly released his hold on her and rolled away. Lacing his arms beneath his head, he stared at the pleated canopy overhead. "Do you tell all the men that you love them?"

"There aren't 'all the men.' "

His head turned toward her, his eyes chill. "Really." Insolence colored the single word. "There was only Johnnie after Kilmarnock?"

"No, of course not."

"That's right. There was that lapse with me when the sea air made you amorous. And how many others?"

"I don't answer to you."

"Answer this though. Do you tell them you love them?" A murmur, no more, wrought with hotspur temper.

She didn't answer him at first, struggling with the tumult of her feelings, but his heated gaze impaled her where she lay on the stark white linen, and she answered honestly, "No," in a faint breath.

"I didn't hear you," he harshly rebuked.

"No!" she sharply repeated, her own temper kindling at his enroachment, at his aggressive intrusion into her well-balanced life. "Are you satisfied? Are you happy now? I'm in love with you, dammit! And you're going to ruin my life and my children's lives! And I'm going to be miserable and the brunt of every May/December mockery in society! I hope you realize what you've done by walking into my room last night when I asked you not to, and climbing into my bed when I was trying to resist you! I hope you're bloody happy!"

"Do you scream often?" Robbie's grin blandly disregarded her temper.

"All the time," she threatened, her fair skin flushed with anger. "I'd leave now while you have the chance."

He only smiled, his gaze drifting over her face. "I'm a tolerant man."

"You're a boy."

"Not for a long time," he quietly refuted, immune to her baiting, secure, self-possessed. When he'd left for the university at thirteen, the pattern at the time, he was already proficient with weapons, with raiding, with women; Edinburgh, and then subsequently Utrecht and Paris, had further schooled him in the academic disciplines and vice in equal measure. "And I'm unconcerned with your age, if vanity's your problem."

"Easy for you to say now. What about later? What about my having to face all the snide remarks? I don't know if I'm that brave. I would have said I was, but when actually faced with the prospect—I'm not sure."

"Think of it this way . . . the children like Johnnie. They've always treated him like an uncle, and now he will be."

"I can't *marry* you!" She'd been considering a liaison only, and even that would have been difficult enough. Many, however, would understand her amorous interest in his youth. But *marriage*! "It's impossible. Every broadsheet in the nation will detail our love life."

"Lord, Roxie, how can it matter?"

"You don't *know*!"

"Apparently not. Why don't you tell me."

"Do you remember when Lady Keir married her young curate?"

"No."

"Well, she did, and every jest for a year had to do with his youth, her age, and his godhead."

"Now, darling, I don't want to argue over your qualms about age or anything else, for that matter, but in all honesty, I'm bored to death with this issue because I don't give a damn. And I wish you wouldn't either. I'm going to be out of the country till summer anyway, so look—that will give you time to adjust."

"Or *you* time to adjust," she retorted, one dark brow arched speculatively.

"Yes, dear."

"You don't mean that."

"Lord, you're argumentative."

"Maybe you'll find you don't love me after all," she said, moody and sullen.

"You're frustrated." His voice, in contrast, was mild.

"Damn right I am."

"I can help you . . . relax." Suggestion, promise, drifted through his soft drawl.

"Won't you rise to anything, damn you?" she peevishly queried, sitting upright suddenly and glaring at him, her hair a blaze of color on her pale white shoulders.

His extremely long lashes drifted upward until he gazed at her from under their dark fringe. "I'd be happy to."

She laughed and tossed her hands up in the air. "I give up."

He unlaced his hands from behind his head and stretched leisurely. "It's about time." A smile slowly formed on his sensuous mouth. "Now about that frustration . . ."

CHAPTER 28

"I can smell you." A whisper of sound, a familiar deep resonance.

Elizabeth opened her eyes. Resting on Johnnie's bed, she looked across the quilted coverlet to where he lay some distance from her. But his eyes were closed, his breathing moderate, and she dozed off again, short of sleep after a night of vigilance at her husband's bedside.

Johnnie's dark, spiky lashes raised a short time later, and his blue eyes scanned the immediate area, searching for the location of the recognizable fragrance. Where was she? Her scent filled his nostrils. *There.* Joy suffused his soul.

"Bitsy." His voice was stronger.

She jerked awake and saw his eyes on her and squealed with delight.

His hand stirred in her direction.

Scrambling up, she moved closer so their fingers touched, the delicate contact life to life, heart to heart, a reunion of spirits, of love. And leaning over, she very carefully kissed him as he lay on his stomach, her cheek resting on the pillow beside his. "You look wonderful," she whispered, her unutterable joy overlooking the shocking state of his health. His vital spirit shone in his eyes, as if in the core of his being all was well.

"I missed you."

She fought back her tears at the thought of his suffering, of all he'd gone through for her. "I'm never letting you out of my sight again."

"Are we safe?" he asked, as if he, too, were remembering.

"We're at Roxane's."

He smiled. "Good. Then kiss me a few hundred times more."

Which she did, leisurely and with pleasure, until Munro interrupted them, waking early to check on Johnnie. He stood to the side of the bed so Johnnie could see him and filled him in on the details of the previous evening. When he finished, Johnnie asked, "How much longer do you think the *Trondheim* can ride at anchor?"

"It sailed this morning. They're scouring the country for you. The cargo was on board; they couldn't wait."

"Eight days, then, to return from Veere."

"Or a fortnight, depending on the winds and gales this time of year."

"So I don't have to get up this morning," Johnnie said with a grin.

"Wait a day or so," Munro suggested with a pleased smile.

But the next morning Johnnie insisted he be helped into a chair. It took two men to bring him upright on the side of the bed, and he sat braced by his arms until he could unclench his teeth. Pale sweat beading on his brow and upper lip, he walked with assistance the short distance to the chair and eased himself down, using the chair arms for support.

Several minutes passed before the color returned to his face, and a short time more was required before his breathing had subsided to normal. And then his pale blue eyes lifted to the circle of anxious faces surrounding him. "I'm not going to fall over," he said with a faint grin. "At least not for five minutes or so. Does my nursing staff think a glass of wine might be good for my health, because I'd prefer it to the morphine for pain."

Six people moved at once, and shortly Johnnie was drinking a very fine claret.

His recuperation was swift, his youth an asset to the speed of his recovery, Roxane's apothecary skilled in those medicinals and herbs most useful in treating wounds. Often called upon to treat the hotheaded bucks who settled their arguments with duels, he understood how to heal brutally maimed flesh.

Roxane continued her social activities, albeit on a somewhat reduced schedule, so as not to call attention to her household. She managed to put off the Earl of Brusisson on the few occasions she met him in public, apologizing for her cancellation of his planned visit, explaining her children had taken ill and she wasn't accepting callers.

In public she was able to curb his demands to see her, for they were never alone, and politesse sufficed in those group drawing-room conversations. Her children had been surreptitiously sent off to one of her country estates the morning after Johnnie was brought into her home. Although the older children understood the subtleties of politics and the need for silence, the younger ones were incapable of discretion. To the children's friends they were simply indisposed by illness.

But she didn't admit that her decision to send the children away for a fortnight might have been predicated by her irrepressible passion for her young lover.

She and Robbie spent most of their time in her rooms, although they appeared often for luncheon in the Ravensbys' suite. It was obvious to all they were mad for each other, although both maintained a public silence about their feelings. But they seemed often oblivious to others even at times when they were in company, and they touched each other with that special privilege reserved for lovers. As a couple, they were striking, their coloring so similar, they had a conspicuous resemblance, like brother and sister. Even in likeness they bore a corresponding general conformity of classic features, although Roxane's dark eyes were a deep violet and Robbie's a rich, vivid brown, nearly black, and her hair was touched with gleaming flame while Robbie's held darker auburn tones. And gender differences were manifest in their skin tones—hers supremely pale beside his as if she were a hothouse flower and he of rugged, less cultivated stock, bronzed from the sun and sea.

But in terms of ingenuous desire they were equal counterparts. Unaffected and natural, they'd given themselves up to love.

One night when Elizabeth had fallen asleep, when Roxane was out and Robbie was pacing restlessly waiting for her return, Johnnie asked him, "Are you bringing Roxane to Holland?"

"No."

"It's not serious then?" He was surprised. Appearances suggested otherwise.

Robbie stopped for a moment in his perambulations, his gaze on his brother, who lay on a chaise near the fire. "I told her we should be back by summer. Leaving would be too disruptive for her children anyway. But yes, it's serious. And don't mention her age, because I don't want to hear it."

"I wasn't going to." Roxane had been older than he as well, and he had a great affection for her. "We may not be back by summer though. It could take longer to arrange things."

Dropping into a nearby chair, Robbie grimaced at the unwelcome news. "Regardless," he muttered, "I'll return earlier, and we can decide then what to do."

"You're sure now."

"You of all people to ask that, with Harold Godfrey's daughter your wife."

"You're right, of course. Forgive me."

"Lord," Robbie exclaimed, "will it take *that* long to

regain the estates?" Impatient, not wishing to be thwarted in his designs, he'd been more optimistic.

"Queensberry has the court behind him. We, however, hold bills of exchange from every man of wealth in Scotland. We also factor their trade and handle most of their credit in Europe. And with the French privateers out in force, the international price of exchange has gone to extravagant heights ..." Johnnie smiled. "We control their exchange rate too. The potential for ruin becomes more powerful with each passing day."[10]

"Being the Continental banker for most of Scotland has its advantages," Robbie murmured. The Carre commerce and banking contacts stretched from Paris and Bordeaux to London, Edinburgh, Amsterdam, Hamburg, Danzig, and Stockholm.

"Don't forget we're financing some of the Scottish regiments in Marlborough's war as well." Several officers banked with him in Rotterdam. "Coutts has made my position clear to everyone; I expect an urgent petition to be presented to the Privy Council within the month."

Robbie sighed. "But they'll still have to set a date for the trial, and hell, who knows how long that'll take."

"Not necessarily. The Privy Council can simply abandon the process. No trial, no conviction ... and Queensberry can move out of Goldiehouse. And then there's Godfrey." Johnnie's voice went very quiet. "I look forward to killing him."

"What of Elizabeth?"

"I haven't talked to her about it, and I won't. Godfrey's too dangerous to my family, regardless of how she might feel. Think of our child ... what he might do to it."

"Perhaps she won't know."

Johnnie shrugged. "It depends on how public the occasion."

"When you have your estates back, you mean."

"And my title ..."

"As early as next summer perhaps."

Johnnie's smile was dangerous. "Wouldn't that be pleasant?"

• • •

The following days passed serenely at the Countess Kilmarnock's home. Johnnie's health was steadily improving, Elizabeth's pregnancy moving very near term, and the Countess and Robbie exploring the rarefied world of new love.

And then the *Trondheim* sailed into the roads at Leith one sunny March afternoon.

And the guests at Kilmarnock House made ready to leave.

CHAPTER 29

It took some days for the *Trondheim* to clear customs and have her cargo unloaded, time for those at Kilmarnock to ready themselves for the voyage. Food had to be brought on board and arrangements made for a doctor and midwife to accompany them. Although convalescing well, Johnnie was still not completely restored to his former strength, and Elizabeth was so near delivery, the baby might not wait until they reached Rotterdam.

Roxane continued to appear at those social affairs she couldn't politely refuse, and the night before the *Trondheim* was due to sail, she attended a dinner party at Countess of Sutherland's. A friend of long standing, the Countess was hosting an engagement party for her eldest daughter. Roxane intended to stay only for the small dinner party preceding the ball, having begged off from the larger entertainment open to an extended guest list.

She was in fact waiting in the entrance hall for her carriage to be brought up when Harold Godfrey arrived with the Duke of Queensberry.

There was no avoiding them, and she dared not

anyway, should her behavior arouse suspicion. While the initial widespread pursuit after Johnnie's escape had abated, a search was still in progress. So her smile was gracious as they approached her.

"You're just arriving too?" Queensberry said, bowing over her hand.

"Actually, I'm leaving," Roxane replied. "My children are ill, but I'd promised Jean I'd come for dinner."

"A shame," the Duke politely said, his attention suddenly caught by one of his aides waving him over to a group of guests at the foot of the staircase. "We'll miss your lovely company. Excuse me, Countess," he added, "Fenton seems agitated." And sketching a bow, he moved away.

Harold Godfrey didn't follow him but stood large, solid, and glaring directly in front of her. "You've managed to avoid me, Countess, for many days." The heat in his voice matched the blaze-red damask of his lace-trimmed coat.

"I'm not avoiding you, Godfrey. With my children sick, I'm not receiving visitors." She caught her orchid velvet cloak closer in unconscious protection.

"You're out occasionally," he gruffly declared. "You could come to my apartments."

"I'm sorry." She tried to project a courteous blandness to such coarse bluntness. "But my time is very limited at the moment. I attend only those functions that are absolutely necessary. With five children, my Lord, all in various stages of smallpox,[11] my social engagements are much curtailed. Perhaps later."

"Perhaps, madam, you could find the time now." He grasped her upper arm through the velvet of her cape, his grip painful.

"Really, Godfrey, I dislike aggression." Her violet gaze held his steadily. "Kindly unhand me, or I'll call for assistance."

He held her arm for a moment more to indicate his capabilities. "I don't intend to wait much longer, madam." His tone was silky with malice as he released her.

"You'll wait, Godfrey," Roxane softly replied, unable to disguise her rising temper, "upon my convenience."

"We'll see." His grey eyes, framed by his powdered, full-bottomed wig, were utterly cold.

"Indeed we will," she replied, her posture regal, her eyes meeting his boldly. And with the barest inclination of her head, she swept toward the doors, not caring whether her carriage was ready or not, raging at his brutish rudeness. Damned English! And damned Queensberry, too, for all his smooth courtesy. She was sick to death of men with no principles.

The following evening Roxane was writing a note to her children when Johnnie walked into the drawing room. She was surprised to see him on the main floor. Regardless of his miraculous recovery, he was still weak.

She smiled across her small writing desk. "You managed three flights of stairs."

"As you see." He held his arms out briefly. He'd not regained all his weight yet, and he was leaner than he'd been in the past, but his smile was the same.

"You're ready to leave?" He wore an embroidered russet leather coat for travel, and his sword gleamed at his side.

"As soon as everyone returns from last-minute errands. They waited till dusk to go out." Strolling across the candlelit room, he dropped onto a high-backed sofa opposite her. "I wanted to come down and thank you again before I left."

"You're very welcome." Her smiled flashed. "It was a pleasure to thwart Queensberry and Godfrey."

"You don't wish to join us in Holland, Robbie tells me."

She set aside the pen she was holding and folded her hands on the inlaid desktop before she answered. "I can't consider it, with the children—although I shouldn't consider it at all if I were sensible. He's much too young." She gazed across the small distance to where

Johnnie rested, her mouth in a thoughtful moue. "I'm allowing myself to be very foolish about him."

"I probably would have agreed with you a year ago, when I didn't understand there were pleasures beyond those of a casual nature. But if you care about him, it's not foolish. Good God, Roxie, certainly you and I can distinguish the difference between love and *amour*. We've spent enough years practicing one and avoiding the other."

"It's different for a man in our world. A young woman's a delectable prize, as available to him as any *bijoux* he cares to possess."

Johnnie grinned. "Do you wish to possess my young brother?"

She smiled back. "Honestly, yes. Wouldn't that be simple? I could just add him to my collection of fine things and bring him out to admire when it suited me."

"If you didn't love him," Johnnie quietly volunteered.

"Yes—and therein lies the complexity. He wouldn't be docile, would he, like a young mistress?"

Johnnie laughed. "Knowing my brother, you'd he hard-pressed to find that word serviceable."

"It's a damned dilemma." Leaning back in her chair, she sighed.

"It doesn't have to be ... if it's only society that causes you misgivings."

"I wouldn't have considered myself so timid or vain. I'm surprised at myself."

"You're a beautiful woman familiar with adulation," Johnnie softly said, taking in the splendor of her pale skin, rich copper hair, her extravagant womanly body adorned in opulent green Genoa velvet. "Fear of mockery has to be a novel sensation for you. But consider, darling, once we've wrested our estates back from Queensberry, you'll have Robbie and myself to discourage any disparaging remarks."

"The children will surely be exposed to the ridicule as well," she added with a small frown.

"Are you talking about the same children I know? The ones who've tested the patience, endurance, and valor of a dozen tutors and governesses and dancing masters over the past decade? They've never struck me as overly sensitive."

"Are you saying my children are hellions?" Her smile was companionable.

"In the nicest possible way—" He grinned. "Yes. But then that's why the children and I always got along so well."

There was a small silence in which she leaned forward and unnecessarily straightened the writing accessories on the desktop. Her voice when she finally spoke held a guarded apprehension. "Robbie's actually talking of marriage."

"I know." He understood the apprehension, this man who had so recently discovered the unfamiliar universe of love.

"I tried to dissuade him, but he won't have it."

"He's in love with you. He doesn't have a choice. Why not marry him?"

"So you're an advocate now that you find the state so blissful."

"A wholehearted advocate—if you love him. There's nothing better in the world."

"An authority speaks."

"One to another. Confess, darling, all these years after Jamie's death, aren't you truly happy again?"

She looked at him for a lengthy moment, her eyes pools of violet shade in the candlelight, then nodded her head. "I feel guilty because I don't feel *more* guilty about forsaking Jamie's memory. But I'm wildly in love again like I was at sixteen."

"At least you recognize the feeling."

"And you never did, until you met Elizabeth."

"I didn't recognize it even then, until she was about to marry someone else."

"You'd been running from women too long to so abruptly change your habits."

"Did I run from you?"

"No," she declared with an amiable smile, "but then I wasn't chasing you."

"Ah . . ." He cast a discerning glance at the woman

who'd shared his leisure for so long. "That's why we muddled through so well."

"It was a pleasant game, Ravensby."

"Yes, and thank you, too, for that," he softly said. "I enjoyed our friendship as I'll enjoy having you for a sister-in-law. By the way," he added, "you might wish to have your wedding dress ready by summer, because Robbie's intent on not waiting past June."

"And I must subordinate myself to his wishes?"

Johnnie put his palm up in mild defense at the touch of umbrage in her voice. "Leave me out of the conflict, darling. I was just repeating my brother's fond hopes." His eyes shifted toward the windows, the distinct sound of horses and a carriage stopping in the street below. "Are you expecting guests?"

She also turned to listen. "I can't imagine who that could be." She shrugged. "Samuel has orders to refuse all callers. He'll send them away."

And a moment later the muffled echo of a male voice raised in agitation reached them—together with Samuel's more moderate tones.

"One of your disgruntled suitors?" Johnnie inquired with a grin. He was sprawled on her sofa as he had been so often in the past, and for a fleeting moment she had a sense of *déjà vu*—the room quiet and candlelit, Johnnie's long, lean body so familiar.

"I don't think I *have* any disgruntled ones," she replied coquettishly.

"I don't suppose you do," Johnnie noted, his grin widening, his memory excellent.

The voices from the floor below quieted.

"Samuel seems to have taken care of it," Roxane said, relaxing in her chair.

Johnnie didn't mention that the carriage hadn't left yet, his ears alert for the sound. "How are the children doing?" he asked instead.

"They're enjoying the country. I was just writing to tell them I was coming to fetch everyone home." Her gaze swiveled toward the doorway as the measured cadence of striding footsteps reached the drawing room—augmented by Samuel's protests.

"Who ever it was got past Samuel," Johnnie casually said, listening like Roxane to the emphatic tread.

The drawing-room doors crashed open a moment later, and Roxane's hand came up to her cheek in a gesture of horror.

"At last, Countess . . . I find you at home."

"I'm sorry, my Lady," Samuel apologized, one step behind Harold Godfrey, his expression distraught, his face red from his racing progress upstairs. "He wouldn't listen."

"Out, you old fool," Godfrey growled, pushing the majordomo backward and slamming the door in his face. With quicksilver speed he turned the key in the lock, pocketed it, and spun around. "And now, my dear Roxane," he growled, malevolent and surly, "you can entertain me tonight."

"Why don't I entertain you instead?" Johnnie said, rising from the high-backed sofa that had hidden him from view.

If Harold Godfrey was surprised, he masked it well. "Have I interrupted a love nest?" he sardonically drawled. "No wonder the Countess has been so reluctant for company. A willing wench, Ravensby, while your wife is breeding?"

"Just draw your sword, Godfrey," Johnnie said in a controlled voice, flexing the fingers of his left hand, "so I can send you on your way to hell."

Nothing moved in the bulk of Brusisson's large frame but his gaze drifted down Johnnie's rangy body. "You've lost weight, Ravensby," he silkily murmured, anticipation in his voice. "Do you think you're up to it?"

"Come and find out, Godfrey," Johnnie murmured, his quiet voice clear in the utter silence. Without turning toward Roxane, he added in an undertone, "Step back into the window seat and don't move." He was sliding his dirk out as he spoke, the fluted blade dagger held lightly in his right hand, its finely worked handle custom fit to his grip.

"I'll take pleasure in killing you, Ravensby," the Earl of Brusisson casually said, stripping off his citrine satin coat, "and damn Queensberry's trial."

Johnnie had slipped his coat off as well in those brief seconds; aware of the man's treachery, he never took his gaze off Godfrey. "You can try, Godfrey. . . ."

They stood facing each other, Godfrey's sword in his right hand, his dagger in the left, the sheen of silver hilt and chased work gleaming in the candlelight, the wolf mark of Passau on Johnnie's German blade glinting like the evil eye. With the left hand dominant in the Carres, Johnnie met Godfrey not juxtaposed in the normal way so dagger met rapier, but thin-tempered rapier matching rapier, and dagger, dirk. More dangerous . . . making the outer arm and outside line more vulnerable.

Johnnie stood motionless in Roxane's drawing room, tall, slender, calm, only his eyes vivid with anticipation, waiting for his enemy to advance.

Face-to-face, Godfrey's proportions appearing measurably broader since Johnnie had lost weight, the Earl of Brusisson cooly said, "You'll never last, Ravensby. . . ."

"Then I'll have to kill you quickly," Johnnie softly said.

There was an angry growl from Godfrey, and he thrust, traversed, and lunged, his rapier in a straight path for Johnnie's gut.

Johnnie slipped sideways. "You're slower than you used to be, Godfrey." His voice was insolent. Then he ducked as the dagger blade slide by his ear.

After that no one spoke as the blades cracked together, slipped in and out, and the men fought in earnest—sliding, moving, their respiration labored after a short time, the four blades a flashing blur in the candlelight.

Redmond recognized the Earl's blue carriage from the bottom of the street even in the indistinct light from the lanterns outside Kilmarnock House.

"Your father's equipage," he said, pulling Elizabeth around the corner so they could approach the house from the back. "He must be trying to see Roxane again."

As they entered the kitchen, it was immediately apparent a crisis existed. The servants were in a ferment, chaotically massed near the upstairs doorway, their conversation agitated, disordered, everyone speaking at once. Two footmen armed with kitchen knives guarded the stairway. Setting aside the packages they'd received from the apothecary, Redmond and Elizabeth quieted the tumult enough to discover what had transpired. "Stay here," Redmond ordered Elizabeth when the story was disclosed. "I'll go up to help. There's nothing you can do," he added in warning, familiar with the determined look in her eyes. "Don't get in the way," he admonished, already halfway across the kitchen.

With no intention of quietly waiting to see if her husband was killed, Elizabeth followed immediately as Redmond disappeared up the stairs.

The conspicuous, rending sound of splintering wood gave indication to those inside the drawing room that the door would soon be breached, but neither man could chance a glance at the gilded panels.

Roxane, pressed against the wall of the draped embrasure overlooking the street, wanted to scream, "Hurry! Hurry!" Johnnie was exhausted, and looked almost at the end of his endurance. No longer forced to defend himself, Godfrey was attacking now. Fearful of attempting to lend aid if her efforts would compromise Johnnie's concentration, she'd helplessly watched as Johnnie's strength declined.

For a man only recently risen from his deathbed, he'd fought with unusual vigor. But both men were wounded, and Johnnie had fewer reserves to call on, his loss of blood more debilitating to his weakened body.

Although he still defended himself effortlessly, his sword parrying Godfrey's attacks smoothly, precisely, he no longer had the quickness needed to lunge, the strength to thrust, and it was just a matter of time before his ability to parry would flag.

Godfrey had been counting on Johnnie's weakness,

advancing, retreating, forcing him to constantly keep moving, waiting for him to tire and let down his guard.

Johnnie fought by instinct, coordination between hand, eye, and brain automatic after the years under his father's tutelage, after the refinements of his Parisian training, each parry an unconscious response, fluid, sure.

But he needed that vital power to launch an attack, to lunge, to go in for the kill—and he wasn't sure he had it.

Godfrey was attacking with increased intensity, knowing the door would give way soon, moving brutally fast, and Johnnie met him with every trick at his command, his parrying arm taking again and again the jar of the meeting blades.

Godfrey fought with textbook mastery, taking every advantage offered him, protecting himself cautiously, biding his time, practicing classic swordplay.

Johnnie, his shirt soaked with sweat, recoiled continually, again and again thwarting Godfrey's follow-through and thrust, his strong wrists withstanding the constant pressure of Godfrey's aggression, every trained muscle and sinew responding with flawless reflex.

The splintered door finally burst open, and Johnnie caught a glimpse of Elizabeth. The sight of her almost cost him his life, for in that frozen second he dropped his guard infinitesimally, and Godfrey lunged.

He just barely caught Godfrey's blade, desperately jerking his sword arm up in time to protect his chest.

Godfrey's sword point slipped down his blade, vibrating against his sword hilt with bone-jarring impact. And leaping back, Johnnie slid out of range.

The near debacle refocused his concentration, his eyes intent once again on the naked blades threatening him. Parrying again, retreating, knocking over a chair to give him five seconds to catch his breath while Godfrey shoved the barricade aside, he knew he'd have to make his decisive attack soon before his energy was completely depleted.

• • •

With his pistol raised, Redmond tried to sight in on the moving figure of Godfrey, the target difficult with Johnnie so near his mark, the poor lighting troublesome, Roxane's presence an added problem once the men moved toward the south wall.

Standing beside him, fearful and fainthearted yet strangely earnest in her resolve, Elizabeth said, "Let me do it, Redmond."

He debated a split second while she held her hand out for the flintlock weapon—the impediments to a clear shot were numerous, and he was not sure she was capable. Until he saw the murderous look in her eyes.

"Remember it throws to the left," he said, handing her the silver-inlaid pistol.

"I know. Two inches." Her voice was devoid of emotion, her hand perfectly steady. Raising the weapon, she stabilized it with her left hand under the iron barrel mounted on rosewood and followed her father's figure as he attacked and retreated and attacked again, waiting for the opportunity to have him in her sights without jeopardizing Johnnie or Roxane.

Redmond quietly drew his hunting knife from its sheath at his waist and balanced it for a moment in his palm—reinforcement for his mistress should her aim be faulty.

Marshaling his remaining strength before his legs gave way and his hand lost its cunning, Johnnie moved into the attack.

Frantically, Godfrey defended himself against the ferocious assault, Johnnie's blades moving with blinding, astonishing speed. The two men were well matched, both natural swordsmen, and they fought now with a desperate equality. The blades clashed and slithered in *contes, froissées*, beating and binding, the men directing the graceful, elegant, lethal steel, freeing their blades for the ultimate stroke, beating their blades aside, opening the way for a lunge only to be thwarted by the other's adroitness.

Johnnie was stretched to the limit, his breathing raucous, when Godfrey's dagger caught one of the notches on the flat back of his dirk by fleeting accident and, taking advantage of his power, Godfrey stiffened his arm and wrenched it from Johnnie's hand.

Springing back, at a dangerous disadvantage now, Johnnie defended himself against Godfrey's fully unleashed assault.

Fiercely concentrating on her moving target, Elizabeth frantically prayed for a clear shot.

But the men were moving at blurring speed.

Godfrey seemed infused with a resurgence of energy, turning on Johnnie with blades swooping, driving him savagely back, nearly overpowering his single blade, knowing it was just a matter of time before the Laird of Ravensby was dead.

Although visibly tired, Johnnie defended himself like a fiend, holding off the attack, giving ground slowly. But he found himself trapped finally, gasping for air, his back to a solid table, a wall to his right. And he knew there was only one way out—an attack to be used only when everything else has failed. It was risky, dangerous, almost impossible.

He waited, unflinching, for Godfrey's lunge, knowing the closer he let the rapier point come to his body, the stronger his parry would be and the less would be the distance his own point would have to travel.

Confidence and steadiness were required. He couldn't shrink or draw back even a little, and there was a perilous time limit to his riposte. It was a question of timing, speed, and absolutely no hesitation.

"You're . . . dead . . . Ravensby," Godfrey puffed, his eyes glittering as he took a moment to savor his victory, to gather his breath.

And then he lunged.

Johnnie's rapier whipped up to parry as Godfrey's forward momentum drove his sword directly at Johnnie's heart. In a single flashing movement Johnnie's blade ran along Godfrey's right up to the point, and as it parted from it, he swung his blade up and over, turned his wrist, extended his arm, and drove his point toward Godfrey's chest.

A brilliant stroke only sparingly used.

It required steel nerve, incredible speed, and a steady hand.

Holding her breath, Elizabeth squeezed the trigger.

Redmond's arm swept forward over his head, and the stiletto blade sliced through the air.

Harold Godfrey died when the knife blade entered his right eye and brain, although the musket ball that tore away the top of his skull would have killed him, too . . . or the sword blade through his heart. He fell in eerie slow motion, the point of his rapier blade caught in the carpet, balancing his weight for a moment before his fingers lost their grip on the hilt and he tumbled over at Johnnie's feet.

Johnnie stood with his arms hanging loose at his sides, his chest heaving, gazing at the body lying inches from the toes of his polished boots. "Compliments of . . . my father," he panted. Then his long, slender fingers released their hold on the silver-wire-wrapped handle, and his bloody weapon fell to the carpet with a soft thud.

A wound in his left shoulder bled as well as one on his right forearm, the crimson stains creeping down his shirtfront, drops of blood falling from the lace on his cuff. Johnnie raised his head and turned, his blue eyes searching for Elizabeth, and, finding her, he smiled. Almost faint from the strain, his lungs deprived of air, he steadied himself for a moment before stepping over the body. Then, carefully placing one foot before the other—not sure his body was going to respond to his mind's commands—he moved across the floor . . . a trail of blood evidence of his passage.

Standing motionless, Elizabeth still held the pistol in her hand. When he reached her, he lifted it from her grasp and handed it to Redmond.

"You both . . . saved my life." He was breathing quickly.

"Helped," Redmond laconically replied, glancing at the dead man on the floor, recognizing the impressive talent required to execute the fatal thrust. "I'll see that he's not found anywhere near the Countess's house."

The two men's eyes met over Elizabeth's head. Both were familiar with the sight of death, and an understanding passed between them. "Would you go to Roxane?" Johnnie murmured, and at Redmond's nod, he took Elizabeth's arm to lead her from the room.

"You're bleeding," Elizabeth softly cried, as if returning from some distant world.

"Dagger cuts," Johnnie acknowledged. "They're not deep. Let's go upstairs." She was beginning to shake.

He carried her up the three flights, finding the strength because she needed him, because the awful reality of the bloody scene had overcome her, and she was shuddering in his arms.

He sat with her in their bedchamber, holding her on his lap, his arms around her, letting her cry, wishing to comfort her but bereft of consoling words. Harold Godfrey had in all probability murdered Johnnie's father and now had nearly killed him as well. He felt only satisfaction at his death.

"I'm not crying for him," Elizabeth whispered after a time, reaching up to touch the small gold earring in Johnnie's ear, sliding the pad of her finger over the velvety softness of his earlobe, substantiating his closeness. "He deserves to die. I kept thinking he could have killed you."

"I wasn't going to let him." And in that answer was the same decisive courage that had brought him victory at seventeen in his first match with Harold Godfrey.

"I want to leave—right now," she said, urgency in her voice. "I want to be safe with you in Holland. I don't care about your estates or titles. I just want to be as far away as possible from all the treachery. And I don't care if we ever come back."

"We'll leave just as soon as Robbie returns," Johnnie soothed, gently stroking her shoulder. "He should be back shortly from escorting the doctor and midwife to the docks." Johnnie didn't comment on their return to Scotland or the future of his estates. But he didn't intend Queensberry to long enjoy the properties that had been the heritage of his family since ancient times.

"How many days before we actually see Holland and set foot ashore?" A high-mettled disquietude animated her words.

"Two with good winds." He brushed the wetness from her cheeks and smiled at her. "We're almost there."

When Robbie arrived back at the house, they took their farewell. Johnnie's new wounds had been dressed, a familiar process now. After arranging the disposal of the bloody carpet, Roxane had seen that the drawing room was set back to rights in the event of an investigation. Redmond had returned from his mission. Godfrey's driver had been sent away ostensibly to wait for his master at Queensberry's, where his body now lay—thanks to Redmond's stealthy dispatch—in the garden behind the Duke's house.

The good-byes took place in Roxane's sitting room, away from the disturbing scene of violence. And beneath the gravity of the leave-taking was a consoling optimism, for soon the Carres would be safely away.

"I expect you'll be back by fall," Roxane said, kissing Elizabeth and Johnnie.

"Perhaps," Johnnie replied, cautiously aware of Elizabeth's disquiet. "We may stay in the Netherlands."

"Coutts anticipates late fall," Robbie interjected, wondering briefly at his brother's curious answer.

"Our heartfelt thanks, Roxane," Johnnie interposed, not wishing to debate an uncomfortable subject. "And give the children a hug from us."

"You must send me word of *your* child immediately it's born."

"Captain Irvine will bring you the news posthaste."

"And if you'll send word to Three Kings," Elizabeth said to Roxane, "I'd be obliged. Redmond has promised me progress reports on the building in return. And perhaps of his marriage?" she added with a sidelong glance at her bodyguard.

"We'll wait until you come back," Redmond said, a faint pinking of his cheeks visible beneath his tan. "I'll have enough to do keeping Lord Ayton from taking over the construction site."

The clock chimed then to remind them of the hour, and after another round of hugs, Johnnie and Elizabeth exited the Countess's house by the kitchen door and entered a closed carriage waiting for them in the small courtyard.

Robbie lingered after everyone left, saying his own reluctant good-byes.

Holding Roxane in his arms, he stood at the door to her sitting room, unwilling to end their embrace. "Maybe I should stay," Robbie murmured, the scent of the sea still lingering in his hair and clothes.

"No! It's too dangerous!" Roxane's face lifted to his, her eyes wide with fear. "Especially now, with Godfrey dead. Queensberry will call in every spy he has, wondering if he's going to be next. If you don't go, they'd find you and kill you!" A note of hysteria trembled in her voice. "Do you think I want to lose you?" she whispered.

"I can't wait till summer to see you," he bluntly said.

"Robbie, listen to me. You have to wait until *fall*. Coutts said October or November."

"I'll be back next month." His voice was terse, low-pitched.

"You can't!"

He stifled her cry with a wild, violent kiss, frustrated desire at rebellious odds with the unnatural prohi-

bition. Crushing her body into his, he savaged her mouth
as if he could possess her through brute force. And when
he relinquished her bruised mouth at last, he said very,
very softly, "I'll be *back* next month. . . ."

Breathless, she yielded to his impetuous passion,
understanding she could no more curb him than she
could hold back the passage of the sun. "Send me word
through Coutts," she said, "and I'll meet you in the country, away from Queensberry's spies."

"God . . . I'll go insane before a month." His whisper touched her cheek and drifted up her temple; his
arms slid down her spine. "You can't look at another man.
Promise me." He held her away suddenly so his dark
eyes stabbed into hers. "Promise," he gruffly repeated.

"Yes, yes, I won't."

His sudden smile seemed incongruously divorced
from the flinty intensity of a moment before. "I adore
you. . . ." he breathed. "Kiss me quickly now, for everyone waits."

Their kiss was lush and sweet that time, without
the previous ravishment and outrage—dulcet like spring-
time, heated. . . .

And he left her trembling with need.

Immediately Robbie climbed aboard the *Trondheim*, the
anchor was raised, the frigate's sails billowed out, filled
with wind, and short minutes later the vessel made for
the open sea.

"Are you sad to be leaving?" Elizabeth asked sometime later, standing at the stern in the curve of Johnnie's
arms, her back against his chest, both of them watching
the lights of Leith grow smaller in the distance.

"No. I want you and our child safe. I'm content to
be leaving."

"I hear a certain restraint."

He shook his head and pulled her closer, his body
warm against hers. "You heard wrong. We'll stay in Holland as long as you want."

"What if I say forever?"

"That's fine." He loved her; he meant it. Robbie could manage the estates as well as he.

"You're too good to me." And she wondered for a moment at her selfishness for demanding so much.

He turned her around then so he could see her face in the moonlight. "It's you who've been good to me," he gently said. "You've given me a love I never would have known. And soon a child ... and infinite happiness." He smiled slowly as the tenor of his mood shifted to his more familiar playfulness. "And enormous pleasure, I might add ..."

"I *am* pretty wonderful," Elizabeth replied with a lighthearted grin, understanding how rare solemnity was to Johnnie.

He laughed. "The best *I've* ever known."

"Does that imply you've known a great many?" A small heat vibrated in her voice.

"Not at all," he quickly responded. "I lived the life of a virtual hermit before you."

"You're very suave, Ravensby."

"Accommodating as well, my Lady," he said in a deep, lush murmur, "if you recall."

She smiled. "I recall exactly. And we should have considerable leisure in Holland to make use of your obliging talents."

"All the time in the world ..." he murmured, his blue eyes enlivened with roguish amusement. "I'll show you how the Dutch indulge their sense of pleasure."

"Is it different?"

"You'll find out, Bitsy," he murmured, brushing her lips with his, "in due time. ..."

EPILOGUE

Their son was born at The Hague ten days after their arrival in Holland, conveniently waiting until they'd settled into the pale yellow manor house set in the midst of acres of tulips before entering the world.

They named him Thomas Alexander in honor of his paternal grandfather, and as Johnnie had promised that cold winter night at Letholm, they took pleasure in the lush, tulip-filled gardens of Gradenhuis. Tommy became the center of their lives, this plump, dark-haired baby who'd inherited his father's smile and was learning to use it with the same dazzling effect.

He was smiling already with great charm when Robbie set sail for Scotland the following month. The Privy Council had already begun to question the reasonableness of its verdict in outlawing the Earl of Graden, for its members were all facing financial ruin, their bills of exchange impossible to recover from their accounts held by Ravensby's bank in Rotterdam. And with the collapse of the Bank of Scotland in December, many of them were in dire straits. The merchants of the royal burghs had added their petitions testifying to the Earl of Graden's honesty, loyalty, and aversion to any rebellious and treasonous principles. Rumor had it the verdict might be reversed as early as August.

"Are you happy?" Elizabeth said one summer day as their small family basked in the sun under the infinite azure sky.

"Desperately," Johnnie said, leaning over to kiss her as they lounged on the grass.

The remains of their luncheon were scattered over a white linen cloth spread on the ground. Tommy was sleeping in his basket under the dappled shade of a plum tree.

"Do you realize under ordinary circumstances we might never have met?"

"I would have found you some other way." He said it with the same unequivocal authority that tempered his life.

"Or perhaps I would have found you."

Johnnie paused for a moment to consider the potent spirit behind his wife's words and diplomatically said, "Yes, or that."

"Do you believe in fate . . . in destiny?"

No, he thought. He believed in making one's own destiny, but a fragment of pagan impulse existed beneath his pragmatism, and he also knew what would please her.

"Sometimes I do," he said, touching her arm, her skin warm from the sun. Then he felt her suddenly not just with his sense of touch but deep in his heart and soul, as if some mystic impulse had reached inside and marked him. "You're my life," he softly murmured, "the air I breathe, my joy, my pleasure. And maybe it is fate," he said tentatively, "like a part of my father living again in Tommy."

His graceful words reminded her how generous was his love, how benevolent, and the guilt she'd been struggling with the past weeks reached uncomfortable levels. "If you want to return to Scotland when the Privy Council reverses their decision," she said, coming to a sudden decision, "I'd be amenable to going back."

"Would you?" He spoke very softly, as if not quite certain of her meaning.

She nodded. "I know how much it means to you."

"You needn't do it for me." He cast her a searching glance as he lay beside her.

"I know. But I'd like to. And our son should grow up in his own country."

His blue eyes held hers for a lengthy absorbed moment, and then, reaching over, he caught her in his arms and kissed her—a light, joyous kiss. Rolling on his back a second later, he carried her with him so she lay on his chest. His eyes shone with glowing happiness. "Thank you," he quietly said.

And she realized then how oppressive had been his exile.

"You can work on Three Kings again," he declared, undiluted cheer in his voice.

"I'd like that," she declared, genuinely heartened by the thought. "Munro is discontent here as well."

"Everyone is."

Her eyes flared wide at her obtuseness. "How did you manage to keep them all so reticent?"

He wondered she didn't know. They were his men. He shrugged. "There would be an end to it, everyone knew."

"And you've all been waiting for me?"

He smiled. "You and the Privy Council."

"I have enormous command then." The provocative notion pleased her.

"In some things," he cautiously replied.

"Actually, I was thinking about prevailing on you for a small favor right now," she said with a lush enticement, her smile deliberately seductive.

"Were you really?" His voice deepened.

"If I were to demand it, would you comply?"

He glanced over to see that the baby still slept. "Probably," he said with a grin.

"*Probably?*" she sweetly prodded.

"*Probably,*" he firmly replied. She could push him only so far.

Her lashes half lowered over her verdant eyes. "If

I were to *request* it of you instead?" she murmured, her voice fragrant with temptation.

"In that case consider it my pleasure, ma'am." His hands lazily drifted down the gentle curve of her back, smoothing the pale primrose muslin of her gown.

"And mine as well," she whispered, feeling the warmth of his hands, tantalizing, languid, gliding over the curve of her bottom.

"I know . . ." he breathed, his cheeky smile touching her mouth. And then he rolled her under him so quickly she gasped.

"You're fast." Breathless and teasing, she didn't just mean his powerful, swooping roll. His arousal, hard and long, was pressed against her bare stomach, her skirt in crushed folds at her waist, the sun hot on her legs.

His laugh was warm, close, as he lay atop her, the cloth of his breeches silky on her skin. "I'm learning from my wife," he murmured, undoing the buttons at the neckline of her light summer gown. "Besides, Tommy may wake any minute . . ." Slipping his hand inside her bodice, he brushed his palm over the fullness of her breasts. ". . . and want these back." His fingers found a tender, tingling nipple, and stroked it until it peaked.

A precipitous, luscious heat began melting through her; his touch was sensitive, acute. "He can share them with you," she whispered, lost to all but the sensuous, intoxicating pleasure inundating her mind.

His dark head bent low, and his mouth closed over one quivering pink crest with exquisite, compelling pressure. The flavor of love was rich with the sweet taste of Scotland that warm summer afternoon in the manicured garden of the Low Country manor house.

They were going home.

NOTES

1. Tradition has it that the Carres (Car, Kar, Ker, Kerr) were notoriously left-handed. A left-handed person is still called ker-handed, car-handed, or corry-fisted in the Scottish Borderland.

The stairways in the Carre castles and defensive towers built in the centuries of continual border warfare were constructed to accommodate their left-handedness.

The early peel towers, generally three or four stories, were built of stone with massive, thick walls. Built singly or attached to dwelling houses or castles, they were easily defended. The only entrance was through a double door at ground level, the outer door of iron grating, the inner one of oak reinforced with iron. The ground floor was used as a storeroom, and the upper floors were reached by a narrow curving stair called a turnpike. This stairway usually rose in a clockwise spiral so that a defender retreating up the flight had his unguarded left side to the wall and his sword arm to the outside. His attacker, coming up, was at the disadvantage with his sword arm to the wall

In the Carre homes their stairs were built anti-clockwise to accommodate their left sword arms.

2.   Queen Anne convened the Scottish Parliament in 1703 because England needed a vote of money from Scotland to pursue the war with France. The Court hoped that the Scots Parliament would vote supply for the army, and when that was accomplished, everyone could go home. But after Darien and the Massacre at Glencoe, after a century of English foreign policy that ignored Scotland's interests, the Scots were determined to make constitutional changes.

In the summer of 1703 Parliament drafted two important Acts that would effectively transfer power from Queen Anne back to the Scottish Parliament. The most important was the Act of Security, which stipulated that after the death of Queen Anne and heirs of her body (she had none), all offices civil and military, formerly under the control of the Monarch, would in the future be appointed by the Scots Parliament. Since the dispensing of government positions and pensions was the basis of political control, England would no longer have any power in Scottish affairs.

In addition, twelve limitations on the power of the Crown were proposed that would give Scotland authority over its own government. Among them would be: that elections would be held annually; Parliament would choose its own president; royal assent to laws would be automatic; declarations of war and the negotiations of peace treaties would require the approval of the Scottish Parliament.

It was also agreed that the first meeting of the Scottish Parliament after the death of the Queen would have the power of nominating and declaring her Successor, provided that the same person not be the Successor to the Crown of England. The wording of the proposal meant that the Successor chosen by the English would be automatically excluded as Scotland's Monarch unless Scotland's Parliament was assured freedom.

In open defiance of the Court, the Scottish Parliament had strongly asserted the national independence of

Scotland. And it kept its bargaining power intact by refusing to vote supply for the army or agree to the Succession in England.

From the English point of view, it was outright rebellion.

3.   The Wine Act of 1703 authorized the import of all wines and other foreign liquors, repealing an Act of 1700, which had prohibited French wines. The reason Queensberry introduced such a measure in the middle of a war with France was that England was desperate to raise money through import duty, and such an act would also curry favor with members of the Scottish Parliament. Appointments as collectors of import duties would mean lucrative jobs for those members of Parliament selected to fill the posts. And these men would then be beholden to the Court interests to retain their appointments. The Act was additionally tempting to the Peers and Barons of the Shires because they had the privilege of exemption from customs duties.

Most Scots approved the Act in the spirit of challenging the English embargo on trade with the enemy. While smuggling was a reality of life, and French wines had always been available, with legal importation profits would increase. And the Burghs and nobility were the major merchants of Scotland. The costliness of the cargoes in relation to their bulk gave French wine a value to the merchant that was out of all proportion to its significance in overall trade. Some observers believed it to be the main import trade of Scotland.

4.   Most authorities agree that "clan" tartans were not known before the second half of the eighteenth century. Until Stewart of Garth wrote his book on the Highlanders between 1817 and 1822, no definite statement ascribing tartans to clans, septs, and families as something analogous to heraldic insignia has ever been discovered, with the exception of that in the *Vestiarium Scoticum*, a work of more than doubtful authenticity.

The lack of reference to "clan" tartans by the bards at the time of the Jacobite Rising is significant. Nearly all of them mention the romantic appeal of the Highland dress, but not one word defines "clan" tartans.

In a range of Grant portraits at Castle Grant, for example, no tartan repeats, and none has any relationship with the *Tartan Book* patterns. All the pictorial evidence suggests that the Scottish gentleman or lady regarded the use of such patterns in his or her clothing in the same spirit that we select the material of our suiting today; he or she simply fancied a certain color and design. Nevertheless, it is reasonable to accept that certain dyes would prevail in different regions and that traditional types of pattern might be followed in various areas.

If there was any uniformity in dress of the Jacobites at the battle of Culloden, or any "clan" tartans, it would seem that one of the many accounts or descriptions of the battle would mention them. In an account published in 1749, James Ray writes that the only forms of identification were the white cockades of the Rebels and the red or yellow crosses of cloth or ribbon of the Loyalists. A fragment of Macdonald of Kingburgh's tartan and Macdonald of Keppoch's tartan, both worn during the '45, are reproduced in Stewart's *Old and Rare Scottish Tartans*, and neither conforms to the many Macdonald "clan" tartans worn today.

And, as indication of tartan as fashion rather then heraldic device, here is an ad from the *Caledonian Mercury* for October 4, 1745:

"Gairdner and Taylor, in their Warehouse at the Sign of the Golden Key, opposite to Forrester's Wynd, Lawn-Market, Edinburgh, continue to sell, in Wholesale and Retail, at lowest Prices, all sorts of Woollen Narrow and Broad Cloths of the Manufacture of Scotland ... At above Warehouse to be sold at lowest Rates, great Choice of Tartans, *the newest Patterns*, [obemphasis mine] Cotton Checks and Sarges, of which they are also Makers."

5.   If Scotland was to join in the trade with America, Africa, and Asia on an equal footing with other European countries, it needed a company authorized by the government. In 1693 the Scottish Parliament passed an Act

declaring that Scottish merchants could form companies for trading in all parts of the world. This was seen by the English companies as a challenge to their monopolies, but the Act was approved by King William, who was anxious to distract attention from the inquiries concerning his part in the Massacre of Glencoe. Since it was only an enabling Act, the King and his ministers and the English trading companies intended no more would come of it.

But in May 1695, the Scottish Parliament passed an "Act for a Company trading to Africa and the Indies." The reaction of the English trading interests was swift; both the Lords and Commons presented a petition to the King expressing their displeasure. King William proceeded to do all he could to sabotage the Scottish Company. The English subscribers withdrew. English diplomatic pressure prevented subscriptions in Amsterdam and Hamburg. A circular letter was sent to the Governors of the Plantations instructing them to prohibit all assistance to the Scottish Company.

Thrown on their own resources, the Scottish population responded with an outburst of patriotic fervor. The full £400,000 called for was subscribed, although it amounted to half of the total money in circulation in the country. Many people invested their entire fortunes.

With English hostility the original scheme of trade with Asia, Africa, and America became more problematical, and the fatal decision was made to commit the entire venture to the establishment of a trading colony on the Isthmus of Panama at Darien. The Scots were not to know that King William would have his Ambassador virtually encourage Spain to attack the colony.

Within four years, mismanagement, English hostility, tropical disease, and Spanish attack led to the abandonment of the colony and the loss of most of the men and ships. Disaster couldn't have been more complete or humiliating.

Darien exposed the problem of Scotland's disadvantageous relationship with England. Constitutional change was now inescapable.

At the same time Darien impoverished the whole country. It ruined the people who invested in it, and that meant a large proportion of the members of Parliament. These legislators were now much more vulnerable to bribery than ever, and it's significant that one of the clauses of the Treaty of Union of 1707 provided for the compensation of the shareholders in the Scottish Company.

6.   The postal service originally began as the King's post and was gradually made available to the general public. By the end of the seventeenth century the various Masters of the Post had established postal service throughout most of Scotland. In the Post Office Act of 1695 the scale of charges for carrying a letter was set, and the use of personal carriers and express delivery was allowed beyond the services of the state monopoly.

Speed of service was, of course, of importance. Reports of English parliamentary proceedings sent from London on Saturday were said to reach Edinburgh by the following Thursday. In matters of confidentiality the postal service was held in low regard. You could almost be certain your letter would be read, so if they were going to contain any comments of a political or sensitive nature, precautions had to be taken in advance. Someone trustworthy delivered a key letter to the person with whom you corresponded with a code to interpret subsequent letters. Each prominent political figure would in the future appear as some relative or friend whose utterances couldn't be used by authorities as an excuse for taking proceedings against you.

Envelopes were rarely used; the sheets were simply folded, secured with a seal, and addressed on the back. From August 1693 the Bishop mark began to be used by the Edinburgh Letter Office, at least for mail to England. Oval-shaped, it gave the day and the month, but not the year, of posting. On the question of cost, in 1689 correspondence from London to Edinburgh cost five shillings per letter, and from Aberdeen to Edinburgh, three shillings.

7.   In the early eighteenth century the town of Edinburgh, all enclosed within the city walls, consisted prin-

cipally of one long street—Canongate and High Street—that stretched a mile long from Holyrood Palace to the Castle. From this main thoroughfare branched off innumerable side streets and alleys, all bordered by towering houses, some up to ten and twelve stories. With so many inhabitants crowded into so small an area, the disposal of garbage and refuse was a problem.

The method of disposal was systematized if not hygienic. At ten o'clock each night the filth collected in each household was poured from the windows with the warning "Gardy loo" (*Gardez l'eau*), and passersby not fleet enough of foot would receive an ill-scented drenching. At the dreaded hour when the domestic garbage was flung out, the smells (known as the "flowers of Edinburgh") filled the air. Citizens burned sheets of brown paper to neutralize the outside odors that penetrated the interiors of their apartments.

The dirt and ordure lay on the street all night until laborers came at seven o'clock in the morning with wheelbarrows to remove it. Worst of all was Sunday, when strict piety forbade all work, and since street-cleaning was deemed an act of neither necessity nor mercy, the refuse remained till Monday morning.

Edinburgh wasn't unique in its unsatisfactory method of refuse disposal. London streets were equally filthy.

8.   One example of an abduction was the case of the heiress Jean Home.

When the Laird of Ayton died, his daughter, Jean Home, age eleven, was put by the Privy Council in the care of her grandmother, Countess Dowager of Home, and her cousin, Charles.

Another relative, John Home of Prendergast, applied with some others to the Privy Council on December 6, 1677, for the sequestration of the young girl from the influence of her appointed guardians. It was ordered that her grandmother, Charles, and Jean Home should appear before the Council to answer or object to the petition.

Instead of doing so, Charles and five Lairds, all but one of whom represented different branches of the Homes, decided to take the young heiress and her future literally into their own hands. In the Council's words, "they did ride away the said night and seiz upon the persone of the said Jean and caried her away to the English bordours," where they married her off to their seventeen-year-old nephew George.

Court proceedings against the clandestine marriage began almost immediately, and legal wrangling continued for years. The heiress in this case never did regain her freedom from the marriage and died six years later.

9.   In order to be legally binding, English marriages before 1753 did not have to be performed in church by a clergyman of the Church of England, according to the rites laid down in the Book of Common Prayer.

A valid and binding marriage was created by a mere verbal contract, performed by an exchange of vows to this effect between a man and a woman over the age of consent (fourteen and twelve), witnessed by two persons, and expressed in the present tense. A promise in the future tense, however, was binding only if it was followed by consummation.

A marriage performed by a clergyman, however, offered further advantages over a mere contract marriage. The first was the participation of the clergyman, whose presence gave it the appearance of respectability. The second was that the ceremony was recognized by both the canon law and the common law as legally binding and as carrying with it full property rights. The third was that it was easier to prove, since there were witnesses, usually a written entry in a marriage register, and often a written certificate.

In Scotland from 1560–1834, there were two essentials of a regular marriage: the proclamation of the intended marriage in the parish church and the celebration of the ceremony by a minister of the established church. But for the price of a fine, those who preferred home marriages were accommodated and, by several seventeenth century acts, a scale of fines and penalties were imposed on clandestine and irregular marriages.

10.   The idea for this plot element came from a real-life story that illustrates the power of the profit motive over politics.

Andrew Russell, the second son of a well-to-do Stirling merchant, went to the Low Countries in 1668. Settling in Rotterdam with his wife and family, he served as factor for many Scottish traders until shortly before his death in 1697. He became a wealthy man brokering goods for Scottish merchants, and the importance of Russell's factorial business in Scotland's trade was thrown into sharp relief during the dramatic events of 1683.

In 1679 Archbishop Sharp of Saint Andrews, Lord Primate of Scotland, had been assassinated by Covenanting fanatics. On January 11, 1683, the Privy Council ordered a process of treason to be raised against Andrew Russell for complicity in the murder and commanded him to appear before the Lords of Justiciary in Edinburgh. On February 8 his brother-in-law sent him a copy of the libel and warned him that a few days earlier William Blackwood had been sentenced to death for "naked concourse with the rebels," although he had only been seen talking to them. On March 31 another merchant wrote of further arrests, remarking that "your friends are not apprehending to sie [see] you here." In these circumstances it's not surprising that Russell declined to appear.

His decision, though expected, caused a remarkable panic amoung Scottish merchants. On March 21 a group of nine, including three bailies of Edinburgh and men from Stirling, Perth, and Aberdeen, presented an urgent petition to the Privy Council "for themselves and on behalf of the merchants of these burghs." They began by reciting that "the most considerable trade and commerce of the product of this nation consists for the most part with the provinces of the Low Countreyes, and without able and experienced factors there the trade here will certainly perish." They then pointed out that the accused Russell, "who has a considerable business in management from this as only factor there," was at that moment in possession of very considerable quantities of money and goods entrusted to him by the merchants of "most of the trading tounes of this country." Since their exports were sold on account, it would be virtually impossible to recover these debts from him at short notice; they begged, therefore, that his trial and the embargo might be postponed until he could satisfy his employers. Otherwise, "it will not only tend to the discouragement of the trade of his kingdome in generall but to the irreparable ruine of these who have the greatest part if not all their stock in his hand."

The Privy Countil wavered and decided to write to the Conservator of Trade, asking him to confirm whether Andrew Russell was "such a person as the merchants here generallie represent him to be." The Conservator declared Russell to be "a sober loyall persone" and "seeing the said Russell manadges the wholl trade allmost not only of this citty but also of a great part of the natione, and is a great encourager of the trade of the steple port," the process was finally declared abandoned.

11. Although smallpox was a dread disease with a high mortality rate, there was little understanding of contagion. So Roxane's presence at social engagements wouldn't have been considered dangerous to other guests.

Lord Lovat writes to his agent in Edinburgh in the early eighteenth century, "My house has been all the week full of company as well as the last and my child's lying in the small pox makes me unfit to answer such a letter of business as yours." The very survival of the letter shows that the agent worried no more about it than did the company who went on staying in the house. And diaries show that mothers carrying their own children would often visit relatives sick with smallpox, not realizing they were exposing their children to the disease.

On the other hand, some people seemed to understand the possibility of transmission, because when the Duke of Marlborough's only son, Jack, contracted smallpox at Cambridge in 1704, his mother and two sisters immediately set off for Cambridge as fast as horses could pull a heavy coach.

The Duke of Marlborough, who had *not* had the disease, stayed in London, waiting in trepidation for the news. He writes to his wife:

"I hope Dr Haines and Dr Coladon got to you this morning. I am so troubled at the sad condition this poor child seems to be in, that I know not what to do. I pray God to give you some comfort in this great affliction. If you think anything under heaven can be done, pray let me know it; or if you think my coming can be of least use, let me know it. I beg I may hear as often as possible, for I have no thought but what is at Cambridge. Medicines are sent by the doctors. I shall be impatient to the last degree until I hear from you."

But there was no hope. Jack died on February 20, 1704, just as his father, who had been sent for by Sarah, finally arrived from London. He came when his son was dying, despite the possibility of contracting the disease.

Dear Reader,

I hope you enjoyed this story of early eighteenth-century Scotland. It was a pleasure to research the time period, to see all the beautiful countryside of Scotland, and, as always happens, my characters take over my life during the writing process. Johnnie Carre and Elizabeth Graham exist as real people in my mind . . . bring on the therapists!

When I first began researching Scotland, I read some general histories to introduce myself to the era. It wasn't until I was reading more specifically on the events leading up to the Union of 1707 that I became conscious of the distinct differences in viewpoint between English and Scottish authors. From that point I always checked provenance of both author and publisher; it mattered. Doesn't it always, in politics?

A further illustration of that clear division was brought to my attention when I was in Scotland later doing more research. My husband and I were checking into a lovely old hotel in Edinburgh that would be hosting the European Economic Community Conference. Although the conference was still two months off, the police were interviewing all guests. We were questioned by an elegantly dressed young detective with a wonderful Scottish accent, and my husband asked him whether the police were concerned with possible IRA bombings during the conference; we'd just come from London, where there had been several bombings in the last three weeks.

The detective said, "They never bother us. Their argument is with England." I found his contemporary comment fascinating. Even after almost three hundred years of Union, Scotland is perceived as distinctly separate from England.

So in a way Johnnie Carre's aspirations for Scotland were achieved.

Best wishes,

P.S. I enjoy hearing from readers. If you have any questions or comments, I'd be pleased to answer them.

13499-400th Street

North Branch, MN 55056

ABOUT THE AUTHOR

Susan Johnson, award-winning author of nationally bestselling novels, lives in the country near North Branch, Minnesota. A former art historian, she considers the life of a writer the best of all possible worlds.

Researching her novels takes her to past and distant places, and bringing characters to life allows her imagination full rein, while creative process offers occasional fascinating glimpses into complicated machinery of the mind.

But perhaps most important . . . writing stories is fun.

Don't miss any of the sensuous historical romances of

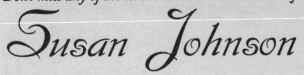

Susan Johnson

___29957-3	*Blaze*	$5.99/$7.99 Canada
___57213-X	*Brazen*	$5.99/$7.99
___29125-4	*Forbidden*	$5.99/$7.99
___56328-9	*Love Storm*	$5.99/$7.99
___29955-7	*Outlaw*	$5.99/$7.99
___29956-5	*Pure Sin*	$5.99/$7.99
___56327-0	*Seized by Love*	$5.99/$7.99
___29959-X	*Silver Flame*	$5.99/$7.99
___29312-5	*Sinful*	$5.99/$7.99
___56329-7	*Sweet Love, Survive*	$5.99/$7.99
___57215-6	*Taboo*	$5.99/$7.99
___57214-8	*Wicked*	$5.99/$7.99
___57865-0	*A Touch of Sin*	$5.99/$8.99

Ask for these books at your local bookstore or use this page to order.

Please send me the books I have checked above. I am enclosing $_____ (add $2.50 to cover postage and handling). Send check or money order, no cash or C.O.D.'s, please.

Name _____

Address _____

City/State/Zip _____

Send order to: Bantam Books, Dept. FN 69, 2451 S. Wolf Rd., Des Plaines, IL 60018
Allow four to six weeks for delivery.
Prices and availability subject to change without notice.   FN 69 1/99

Bestselling Historical Women's Fiction

⚬ᴀᴍᴀɴᴅᴀ Qᴜɪᴄᴋ⚬

____28354-5 SEDUCTION ...$6.99/$9.99 Canada

____28932-2 SCANDAL ....$6.99/$9.99

____28594-7 SURRENDER ....$6.99/$9.99

____29325-7 RENDEZVOUS ......$6.99/$9.99

____29315-X RECKLESS ....$6.99/$9.99

____29316-8 RAVISHED ....$6.99/$9.99

____29317-6 DANGEROUS ....$6.99/$9.99

____56506-0 DECEPTION ....$6.99/$9.99

____56153-7 DESIRE ....$6.99/$9.99

____56940-6 MISTRESS ....$6.99/$9.99

____57159-1 MYSTIQUE ....$6.99/$9.99

____57190-7 MISCHIEF ....$6.50/$8.99

____57407-8 AFFAIR ....$6.99/$8.99

____57409-4 WITH THIS RING .....$6.99/$9.99

⚬Iʀɪs Jᴏʜᴀɴsᴇɴ⚬

____29871-2 LAST BRIDGE HOME ...$5.99/$8.99

____29604-3 THE GOLDEN
               BARBARIAN ....$6.99/$8.99

____29244-7 REAP THE WIND .....$6.99/$9.99

____29032-0 STORM WINDS ....$6.99/$8.99

Ask for these books at your local bookstore or use this page to order.

Please send me the books I have checked above. I am enclosing $____ (add $2.50 to cover postage and handling). Send check or money order, no cash or C.O.D.'s, please.

Name _____

Address _____

City/State/Zip _____

Send order to: Bantam Books, Dept. FN 16, 2451 S. Wolf Rd., Des Plaines, IL 60018
Allow four to six weeks for delivery.

Prices and availability subject to change without notice. FN 16 4/99

Bestselling Historical Women's Fiction

⚡ IRIS JOHANSEN ⚡

____ 28855-5 THE WIND DANCER . . . $6.99/$9.99
____ 29968-9 THE TIGER PRINCE . . . $6.99/$8.99
____ 29944-1 THE MAGNIFICENT
                        ROGUE . . . . $6.99/$8.99
____ 29945-X BELOVED SCOUNDREL . $6.99/$8.99
____ 29946-8 MIDNIGHT WARRIOR . . $6.99/$8.99
____ 29947-6 DARK RIDER . . . . $6.99/$8.99
____ 56990-2 LION'S BRIDE . . . . $6.99/$8.99
____ 56991-0 THE UGLY DUCKLING. . . $6.99/$8.99
____ 57181-8 LONG AFTER MIDNIGHT.$6.99/$8.99
____ 57998-3 AND THEN YOU DIE.... $6.99/$8.99
____ 57802-2 THE FACE OF DECEPTION. .$6.99/$9.99

⚡ TERESA MEDEIROS ⚡

____ 29407-5 HEATHER AND VELVET .$5.99/$7.50
____ 29409-1 ONCE AN ANGEL . . . . . $5.99/$7.99
____ 29408-3 A WHISPER OF ROSES . . $5.99/$7.99
____ 56332-7 THIEF OF HEARTS . . . . $5.99/$7.99
____ 56333-5 FAIREST OF THEM ALL . $5.99/$7.50
____ 56334-3 BREATH OF MAGIC . . . $5.99/$7.99
____ 57623-2 SHADOWS AND LACE . . $5.99/$7.99
____ 57500-7 TOUCH OF ENCHANTMENT. .$5.99/$7.99
____ 57501-5 NOBODY'S DARLING . . .$5.99/$7.99
____ 57502-3 CHARMING THE PRINCE . . $5.99/$8.99

Ask for these books at your local bookstore or use this page to order.

Please send me the books I have checked above. I am enclosing $_____ (add $2.50 to cover postage and handling). Send check or money order, no cash or C.O.D.'s, please.

Name _____

Address _____

City/State/Zip _____

Send order to: Bantam Books, Dept. FN 16, 2451 S. Wolf Rd., Des Plaines, IL 60018
Allow four to six weeks for delivery.
Prices and availability subject to change without notice.

FN 16 4/99